Praise for Helen

'*In the Shadow of the Hill* is a thoroughly excellent thriller which explodes into a finale which I dare any reader to predict. Her style is smooth and sweet.'

Roger Hutchison, Author

'Helen Forbes has hit the ground running. The page-turning climax has more twists and turns than the Road to the Isles, making it impossible to put down.'

Press and Journal

'*Madness Lies* is a murky tale, Forbes twisting her noose ever tighter around some sympathetic characters. Gritty and ominous, Forbes's brand of 'Highland Noir' is shaping up to be a good series.'

Sunday Herald

'The climax is superb, and the ending flows well from all that has gone before. This book definitely comes into the category of difficult to put down. First class crime fiction.'

Anne Stormont, Author

'*Madness Lies* was full of twists, shocks, and heart-rending moments as I got completely caught up in the lives of the characters. Helen Forbes has created a cracker of a read and she is certainly a name that I will be looking out for.'

Sharon Bairden, Author

Also by Helen Forbes

In the Shadow of the Hill

Madness Lies

UNRAVELLING

Helen Forbes

Copyright © 2021 by Scolpaig Press

Printed and bound in Great Britain by Clays Ltd, Elcograf S.p.A

First paperback edition 2021
ISBN (paperback): 978-1-9168883-0-2
ISBN (ebook): 978-1-9168883-1-9

www.helenforbes.co.uk

Book design by Creative Covers

For Margaret, Donald, Ishbel, Archie and Anne with love and fond memories of Sunday afternoons 'up the hill'.

Prologue

THE SWAY OF the noose was mesmerising against the shimmering light that danced between the branches. Tiny bullets of yellow and blue, grey and buff, flitted around the tops of the trees, darting and disappearing, their song too high, too bright. Below, the colours of the forest flowers and ferns taunted him. It was wrong. The day should be grey and bleak, all colour banished.

Heavy footsteps crashed through the forest, as the echoing sound of his name was hurled into the wind. He reached for the noose, and a sudden golden shaft of sunlight illuminated the tree and his last hiding place. He lifted his face to the sun. Through the softness of the shifting leaves, he heard the sigh of another voice. The whispered, half-formed words were compelling. He was making a mistake, it told him. The pain would pass. He just had to breathe into it. Stop resisting. Accept and let go.

But how could it pass? He would carry this ache forever. He'd never close his eyes, but he'd see her body, twisted and broken. Her whispered last words would never leave his head. His guilt would eat away at him, turning him into a pale shadow haunted with regret, mocked by what might have been.

As the crashing and the shouting came closer, the noose in one hand, his other hand steadying himself against the tree trunk, he wavered on the edge of infinity.

And then he made his choice.

Part I

1

Go, A VOICE cried in my head. *Run. Before it's too late.* A little overdramatic? Not really. Who wouldn't run from a seven-hour shift of spooning mushed-up food into gaping, toothless mouths, wiping backsides, and mopping up body fluids? But I didn't have a choice. Not without another job, and I lacked the energy or motivation to find something else. Pushing open the front door, I caught the scent of tangerine and lemon. Mrs Shelby had been at the homemade air fresheners again. It made for a pleasant welcome to the foyer of the care home, but a few essential oils couldn't cover up the natural scents of warm cabbage, bed sores and incontinence. Not that it was a bad care home. A large Victorian villa with high ceilings and big rooms, clean and well-managed, it was one of the better ones. There were just some scents that couldn't be shifted. And some residents.

I heard Smyth before I saw him, his entitled plummy tones and the squeak of his wheelchair grating through me. Scarcely a shift passed that I didn't fantasise about smothering him with a pillow, but that would be far too kind. He needed to be strung up and eviscerated.

'Pole, you come here right now.'

Stefan was at the reception desk. He ignored Smyth and smiled at me. Deep in my belly, something primitive tugged and taunted. It was another good reason for running, but I'd left it far too late.

'Pole!' Flecks of spittle shot from Smyth's mouth. His face was twisted with venom. There were bulging veins on his forehead, a crimson flush creeping up his wrinkled neck. I willed Stefan to pull the old man from his wheelchair and throw him on the floor.

He didn't. Of course, he didn't. He held out his hands. 'Mr Smyth. What may I do for you?'

Smyth's eyes narrowed. 'What is your name?'

'Stefan Nowak.'

'Why are you here? Aren't there care homes in your own country?'

Stefan nodded. 'There are, Mr Smyth. Remember, we talk yesterday and I tell you all about them. The story of my grandmother and the tattoo?'

'Yesterday?' The old man's eyes shifted between us. 'A tattoo? Don't be ridiculous. I've never seen you before in my life. I couldn't believe it when Matron said you came from Poland to work here.'

Stefan's smile didn't falter. 'I did, Mr Smyth, with others.'

'There are others? My God. Matron, get me out of here.'

As Smyth's frantic hands wheeled his chair down the corridor, I apologised to Stefan, and not for the first time. He waved his hand. 'Kate, it is not your fault. There are many head-dicks.'

'Dickheads.'

He laughed. 'Ah, yes. I will learn.'

'What's this about your grandmother and a tattoo?'

'My grandmother is… was… in a care home in Warsaw. My young wild sister – you know, I tell you about her punky hair and purple lips – she take my grandmother out one day and she comes back with a little black cat on her ankle. There is… what do you say? Hell to pay. My father, he doesn't speak to my sister again. Yesterday, Smyth, he almost die laughing when I tell him this.'

'Almost died?' I shook my head. 'Stefan, you have to try harder next time.'

He laughed. 'Today, he remember nothing. His head, it is full of holes.'

'Full of shite.'

'This too.' Stefan smiled. 'Forget him. He is just an old man. Tomorrow he will be my...' He frowned and fished his notebook out of his pocket. He thumbed through the pages of scribbled vocabulary. 'Ah, he will be my beastie.'

I couldn't keep my laughter in. Stefan looked devastated. 'This is not right?'

'Let me see.' I looked at his notebook. 'I think you mean *bestie*, though you're not too far wrong with *beastie*.'

'Whatevers.' His hand rested on my arm. 'You are tired, Kate. How is she?'

I would have told him. I might have cried, and he might have held me, but our conversation was severed by the shrill voice of Mrs Shelby, a cloud of stale perfume, the crackle of starched polyester, and then the woman herself. She looked about to cry. 'Stefan, whatever have you said to Mr Smyth? He's in quite a state. His daughter will be here shortly and we mustn't upset her. She's very generous...'

Stefan shrugged. 'I no know what you ask, Madame Shelby, but you look very... how you say...?'

'Haggard,' I muttered.

Stefan sighed. 'Very beautiful, Madame.'

Mrs Shelby blushed and waved her hand. 'Oh, Stefan. Just be more careful. It's not your fault things get lost in translation. Kate, there's a new resident in room nine. She's a little fragile. Younger than our usual clientele. She's refusing to get out of bed. Says she can't walk, but she had no problems yesterday on arrival. Perhaps you could have a chat, see if you can get her up and dressed, and into the dayroom.'

I nodded. 'I'll try. What's her name?'

'Lucille Leonard. You'll need the key. She wants the door kept locked.'

That was understandable with the likes of Smyth roaming around, interfering with everyone else's business.

'What's wrong with her?'

Mrs Shelby frowned. 'It's tragic. Alcohol-related brain damage. Korsakoff's. Causes early dementia. Her language is rather choice.'

When I knocked on Lucille Leonard's door, I was met with a volley of abuse that told me where to go and how to get there. It called into question my parentage, my hygiene, my intelligence and my integrity. Nothing new there. Some of the most genteel of our demented residents were prone to similar outbursts. Mostly, they were oblivious to the meaning and effect of words they would never have uttered in their lucid past. Occasionally, you'd get someone on the cusp, who still kept a morsel of clarity and was aghast at their own language. That was sad. Much easier when all the filters were gone. It never bothered me. They were just words. I'd read somewhere that swearing was a sign of intelligence. Must be. I was prone to it myself, in certain circumstances, especially where Smyth was involved.

I knocked again. 'Ms Leonard. I'm Kate Sharp. I just want to have a chat. I'm going to open the door now.'

She was still screeching as I eased the door open. The room was dark. There was a musky smell that reminded me of the New Age shop in town. I loved their clothes and bags and wall-hangings, but I could never buy anything, or stay long, the smell of incense and musky perfume giving me a headache. I'd not be staying long in here, either, if I could help it.

'Ms Leonard.'

'It's Mrs, you retard.' The venom in her voice was chilling. The room was dark and cold, the curtains drawn. She was a huddled shape in the single bed to the right of the door, her back to me, long dark hair covering the pillow.

'Sorry, Mrs Leonard. How are you doing?'

'Doing what, exactly?'

Fair enough question. I almost left her to it. She'd only just come in. It'd take a while for her to settle down. Mrs Shelby should be more patient. But she'd be disappointed if I didn't at least try. I waited in the icy silence. She didn't move. I crossed the room and opened the curtains a little. There were things hanging from the ceiling above the bed. Feathered dream-catchers and crystal droplets, mandalas and glass sun-catchers. There was a massive wall-hanging with bright elephants on one wall, a patchwork tapestry on another. There was a framed wedding photo on the dressing table. It looked like it was taken at Belladrum Temple, a small chapel on a private estate near Inverness. The bride was barefoot, in a pale blue dress with a coronet of flowers atop her long dark hair. The groom was shorter than her, plump and balding.

'Don't fucking touch it.'

She was sitting up, watching me.

I smiled. 'You were a beautiful bride. Will I open the curtains more?'

'If you must.'

It was bright outside. She screwed her eyes shut against the light, and she muttered. I sat in the chair at the end of the bed and waited.

'What exactly do you want?' she asked, eyes still closed.

'World peace.'

There was a hint of a smile on her lips. 'Smart arse.'

'Mrs Shelby asked me to have a chat. She usually complains I chat too much to the residents, says I don't get through my work fast enough, so I don't expect she'll encourage this too often. Would you like to chat? Or get up? I could take you to the dayroom.'

'Bugger off. I'm not sitting in there with the living dead.' She rubbed her eyes and opened them.

I almost gasped. She had the strangest eyes I'd ever seen. Huge and emerald green; so green, I could have sworn she was wearing coloured contact lenses. She was in her mid-fifties, maybe, though it was hard to tell. Her long hair was thick and healthy. It made her look younger, but there was no mistaking the ravages of alcohol and time on a face that had once been beautiful. She didn't seem angry now. She was leaning forward, smiling a strange, twisted smile. There was an unnerving gleam in her eyes.

'Princess? Well, fuck me sideways. Never expected to see you here. Thought you were…' She shook her head as if to clear it. She shrugged. 'This bloody head. Never know what's real and what's not. But you're real, Princess.'

She was up and out of the bed like a shot. Nothing wrong with her legs. 'I'll grab a quick shower. You look in the wardrobe, choose a dress for me. Then you can take me to the dayroom.'

***

THERE WERE HALF a dozen men and a couple of women in the dayroom. Some were watching television, others staring into space. I fancied Lucille's arrival, in her flowing yellow Egyptian print dress, her green eyes sparkling and her grin wide, might have the effect of a grenade, shocking them out of their inertia. It didn't. Tom Wright was the only one that took any notice. A former GP, he'd been in the care home longer than anyone else. He was a gentleman, always dressed in tweed plus-fours, diamond-patterned socks and polished brogues. He hated the Tories with a passion. I liked him for that, and his gentle manners. Though he sometimes forgot where he was, and had tried occasionally to leave to do his round of house calls, he was never rude or demanding. Now, he folded his *Guardian* and put it on the table, placing his pen on top of it. His eyes travelled from her head to her bare feet. She'd refused to wear the sandals I'd found at the bottom of her wardrobe. I didn't think Mrs Shelby was going to like this barefoot nonsense, but I figured I'd done my bit. I left her sashaying towards Tom Wright.

Mrs Shelby kept me in the office for the next couple of hours, trying to sort out an Excel spreadsheet for her. It wasn't my job to help in the office, but it beat the usual morning tasks. After a quick lunch break, it was all feeding and wiping and laundry. I saw Lucille Leonard twice in passing, and she smiled and waved. In the late afternoon, I glanced into the dayroom and saw her surrounded by men, her laughter high and light as she tried to teach them card tricks. I wondered if she was going to be trouble.

At finishing time, Stefan was waiting for me in reception. He squeezed my arm. 'We go for a drink?'

It was tempting. We hadn't been for a drink for weeks, but I couldn't. 'Better not.'

'Of course. You must tell me if I can do anything. Any time, I will help.'

Those eyes. That smile again. The tugging and taunting in my belly. At least it confirmed I wasn't dead inside. Not yet. He held the door open for me. I'd almost escaped into the late afternoon sun when I heard Lucille's laughter again. I turned, and she was standing watching us, arms folded, her fingers picking at the bright shawl around her shoulders. The narrowed eyes and frown belied the laughter.

'Always took the best men for yourself, didn't you, Princess?'

2

THERE WAS A bottle of Harris gin in my kitchen cupboard. It had been teasing me for weeks. When I reached the end of my street, I was tempted to go home and sink into oblivion. A nice thought, but it wouldn't happen. I'd not be sleeping in my own bed tonight, and there would be no gin. I kept walking.

Ten minutes later, I eased my key into the lock and opened the door. I climbed the stairs, and the only sound in the flat was the ticking clock in the living room. It drove me mad, that clock, but she wouldn't hear of getting rid of it. It had been a wedding present, fifty-odd years ago. It was going to outlive her, and probably me, she always said.

Sunlight streamed through the bedroom window, holding her in its spotlight, the lined parchment of her face, the thinning hair, the huddled body. The window was open, and two brown leaves danced on the quilt, their jagged edges scratching through the silence. The hand beside her cheek was a scrawny web of veins and tendons, gnarled fingers and spotted translucent skin. The blue strap of her night dress had slipped off her shoulder, exposing the taut stretch of grey skin over the sharpest of bones. Her vulnerability dragged at my heart. It wouldn't be long now. It couldn't be. And all the secrets would die with her.

Her eyes opened. Through a rheumy haze of pain, I saw a brief glimpse of mischief. 'Did you think I was gone?'

A cough that sent spasms through her body stopped the hint

of laughter. I held her until the shuddering breaths subsided, leaving her lips blue and her breathing shallow. I wanted to call the doctor. She wouldn't have it. 'Just get me a pill, Kate. Stop fussing. I'll be fine.'

There was enough good stuff in her bathroom cabinet to keep the drug population of Inverness happy for a few months. I could make my fortune when she was gone, or maybe I'd just get stuck into it myself. I passed the tablets to her with a glass of water. 'Gran, why don't you keep them beside the bed and take them more often? That's what they're for.'

She gulped them down, sank back into the pillows and sighed. 'Told you before. Don't want to end my days in a stupor. Cup of tea would be nice.'

I returned with the tea, and she was still ashen. I hoped the drugs would work soon. She was eating so little, they would surely go straight into her bloodstream.

'Did you see anyone today?' I asked.

She rolled her eyes. 'Place was like Piccadilly Circus. Carers and nurses in and out. Just when I thought I was going to get a minute to myself, Sullivan appeared.'

Ted Sullivan had been her downstairs neighbour for fifty-odd years. He was a right-wing bigot with a very soft spot for Gran, despite her berating him every time they met.

'You want to have heard his nonsense. Brexit means Brexit, don't you know? Glad I'll not be here to tell him I told you so when it all goes wrong.'

'I'm not.'

She nodded. 'I know, love. How was work?'

She sipped at her tea, frowning at Smyth's behaviour, and smiling at the head-dicks and Stefan's expert handling of Madame Shelby. The grandmother's tattoo would have made her laugh if it wasn't for the evil thing growing in her chest. Sadness engulfed me. I'd never heard anyone with a laugh like hers. It had embarrassed me so often, yet I would have given anything to hear it again.

At last, I could see the beginnings of a lazy, drug-induced smile. 'I like the sound of Stefan,' she said. 'Is he handsome?'

Stefan was gorgeous. Tall and dark, with perfect teeth and deep brown eyes. When they looked into mine, I wondered if he saw the truth. I hoped not. 'He's all right.'

'Available?'

'No, he's got a wife and child.'

Her eyes drifted closed. 'But you fancy him.'

Outside, I heard the laughter of children. I remembered the words Gran had said so often when I was wee. *Always best to tell the truth, Kate.*

I hadn't believed her then, and I still didn't. 'I don't fancy him.'

'His wife needn't know, if you're careful.'

I smiled and took the mug from her. If those pills were making my grandmother encourage adultery, maybe I should try a couple. Her next words whipped the smile off my face.

'Your mother was never that fussy. A wedding ring didn't stop her.'

My heart was dancing, wee spikes of nausea rising in my throat. My mother's life, and her death, when I was a child, were surrounded in secrecy. For years, I'd pestered Gran, wanting to know everything. But did I want to know this?

She didn't wait to find out. 'He was married with kids. They say she was having it off with him in Dunain Woods.'

Anger crept through me, making my hands shake. 'Dunain Woods? Was he a patient at The Craig?'

My voice was too loud, and her eyes shot open. She frowned. 'No, he was staff.'

'And he was having sex with a patient? What did you do about it?'

She shrugged. 'Didn't know until years later. A nurse, Liz Barclay, told me. Met her in Beauly one day, myself and Meg. He was long gone by then. They both were. It was too late.'

'What was his name?'

'Can't remember. He wasn't your father.'

I hated to feel anger towards her, but really? 'I'm not stupid, Gran. I was five when she went to The Craig. How could he be my father?'

There was a weak smile on her face as she whispered: 'Sharp by name and sharp by nature.'

My anger slid away. I laughed. 'Didn't buy it, did I?'

I stroked her papery, wrinkled cheek until she slipped into sleep. I heard Maria, the carer, let herself in. In the hallway, I whispered to her, bringing her up to date. She smiled and nodded, then she reached for my hand and squeezed. 'She love you very much, you know?'

I knew. What I didn't know was how I was ever going to live without her.

3

HE FANCIED SHE was sitting beside him on the fallen tree trunk in Dunain Woods. Sunlight was sparkling gold through her hair, and she was smiling that smile. He whispered his apologies, as he did every year, then he strained to hear an answer. There was nothing but the sighing breeze and the singing of forest birds. He looked up at the nearest tree. The sunlight flickered and danced through the branches, just as it had that day, over twenty years ago. The blue tits and coal tits were still flitting and darting and disappearing. Though the noose was long gone, its shadow was always there, imprinted on his brain.

In the end, it wasn't the whispering voices that had stopped him. It was the voice in his own head. If he went through with it, they'd be certain of his guilt. They'd read far more than the truth into his final desperate act. And so, he had breathed into the pain and felt a loosening of its grip. It wasn't gone. It would never go, but maybe he could bear it. His optimism hadn't lasted, but he didn't want to think about what came next. It was long ago. It was past.

He took her journal from his pocket and he read again of her fragile and unfulfilled dreams. The unravelling, and the fearful catalyst that brought her to him. He read of the child, Kate, and he could see her, a tiny scrap clinging to her grandmother's hand, eyes wide with hope. Not for the first time, he wanted to hunt down the man responsible for it all. Killing him would not suffice. He closed his eyes and imagined. And then he opened his eyes and laughed. These were not new thoughts. Every year, he sat in the forest, read the journal and imagined. And every year, he did nothing.

He put the journal back in his pocket, and he walked on. Soon, he reached the walled hospital cemetery with its strange, twisted trees rising from a thick carpet of moss and fallen leaves that covered the last resting place of the unknown nineteenth-century paupers. There were only a couple of gravestones, and he wondered if there had ever been anything to mark the other graves, or had the patients just been discarded in anonymity, with no family or friends to mourn them?

Down the track, and he could see the duck pond. It had been a favourite spot for patients and their visitors, a welcome relief from the stifling darkness of The Craig and its unhinged inhabitants. Children throwing food for the ducks, running up and down the paths, their laughter cascading through the trees. A lovely place, until visiting hours were over.

Bush therapy, the staff had called it, as they'd turned a blind eye to the patients that had nipped along the road to the bushes round the duck pond, usually in pairs, sometimes more. They were consenting adults, mostly. They needed some relief, and it helped cut down on incidents within the hospital. There were rumours it wasn't just patients that had indulged in bush therapy, but the names of any participating staff were kept quieter than the graves behind him.

A woman was standing by the pond, head down, eyes on her phone, thumbs tapping. She didn't see her collie dog sprinting towards her, a long branch in its mouth. She was oblivious until the branch whacked her in the back of the legs and sent her stumbling into the undergrowth. As he helped her up, the dog dropped the branch. He looked closer. It was no branch. It was a bone, a long human thigh bone.

***

THE FEMALE COP brought him a cup of tea. He didn't want to pick it up in case his hands shook. It wasn't the discovery of the bone that made him nervous, just the experience of being in a police station. Not that he'd ever been arrested. Why so scared, then? Perhaps it was the relatively unfettered power of the police, the knowledge that they could lock him away. He smiled. Paranoid, much?

The cop scribbled on her notepad. Her pen didn't work. Muttering, she left the room. He picked up the cup. His hands were steady enough. The tea was lukewarm.

She returned with another pen. 'Where are you going to stay tonight?'

He shrugged. 'I'll find somewhere. Any chance of getting my tent?'

She shook her head. 'Afraid not. So, full name?'

He hesitated. The older he got, the more he resented both the name and the predictable reaction.

'Mr…?'

'Tarantino. Daniel John.' He leaned back in the chair and waited.

She put her pen down and smiled. 'You're kidding me?'

He shook his head. 'I tend not to lie to the police if I can help it.'

She looked a little embarrassed. 'Cool name.'

'My father was Italian. No relation.'

He looked at his watch. Her smile slipped away. Down to business. Date of birth. Address. Occupation. What was he doing here?

He told her he came up every year and camped in the forest. He'd arrived yesterday. Planned to stay for ten days, including a few nights on Skye. He'd set up camp late afternoon. Nothing out of the ordinary until the bone incident. Didn't see any other bones. Didn't investigate where it came from. Just waited with the dog owner until the police arrived. He wished now he'd gone back and packed up his tent while he waited.

She nodded. 'It's unfortunate. Any personal items in the tent? Money? Phone?'

Daniel's hand hovered over the inside top pocket of his jacket. The journal was there. It was safe. 'Just my rucksack, food and clothes. I've got my wallet and phone. Do you know if they found any more bones?'

She shrugged. 'Can't say. Sorry.'

'Could it have come from the cemetery?'

She put her pen down, then she looked behind as if to check no other officer had sneaked in while they were talking. She lowered her voice a little. 'Between you and me, our enquiries are not focusing on the cemetery.'

4

THE SPIRES OF the sprawling Victorian stone buildings rose above the security fencing and scaffolding into the murky morning sky. Set high on a hillside on the outskirts of Inverness, the complex used to be known as Craig Dunain Hospital, and before that, the Northern Counties District Lunatic Asylum. Locally, it was The Craig. You didn't even have to give it a name. *Up the hill* was enough, the euphemism used as an insult, a joke or a threat. Everyone knew what it meant, including my classmates. *Your mother's up the hill and round the bend.*

I'd lived with my grandparents since birth. In my pre-school days, there was a shady figure in the background, a mother with skinny arms that would reach for me from a bed next to mine. I remembered squeezing round that bed in the mornings, tiptoeing from the room. I don't know if I was being considerate or avoiding being caught. The day I started primary school, I came home, and the bed was empty. Next time I saw her, my mother was up the hill. In my memory, The Craig was where she became real to me.

The hospital had closed sixteen years ago. A subsequent arson attack destroyed some buildings, but it hadn't stopped the slow development into a complex of luxury townhouses and apartments that would eventually become Great Glen Hall. I shivered at the thought of living here. No matter how luxurious they made it, they could never change what it had been. I was certain you'd be able to count on one hand the number of locals tempted to buy.

I'd taken occasional trips up the hill ever since I was old enough to come alone. Just once or twice a year. I didn't stay long, and I never told Gran, not even when the fire was in the news, and I had come up to have a look at the damage, hoping to find the place razed to the ground. The visits never gave me peace, and I didn't know why I still bothered, but Gran's words had unsettled me, and I couldn't stay away. I remembered all those childhood visits, my hand held tight in Gran's, sometimes too tight. I'd complain, and she'd apologise, loosening her grip, but still she'd squeeze now and then as we got closer to the entrance, and all those dark windows above and around us, watching. The best days were when Mum was waiting by the door, smiling. I'd run into her arms. She'd hold me so tight, and I'd know, just know, this was the day she was coming home for good. It never was. I'd get bored and wriggle from her arms, run down the corridor past small huddles of patients and visitors. Even from a distance, I could tell when Mum and Gran were bickering. I'd make my way back, seeing the anger on Mum's face, the tears in Gran's eyes, their voices fading to whispers.

It was always my boredom that ended the visits, and that bothered me for years. We should have stayed longer, I'd tell Gran. She'd smile and shake her head. It was no place for a child, and Mum understood that. Taunted by my mother's pale, waif-like face watching us leave, I wasn't sure I believed Gran. Afterwards, I'd dream of Mum. She was made of chocolate, and when I reached for her, she'd melt away.

He was married with kids. They say she was having it off with him in Dunain Woods.

I looked to my right, towards the woods. The layout of the land had changed, with new roads and housing, but I could see the tops of the trees. The woods had once been a place of fun for me, during visits, but subsequent events had rendered them a place of nightmares. Maybe one day –

'They found bones.'

My heart almost bounced out of my mouth. I turned and saw

27

a man in his fifties. He had good teeth. High cheekbones and sallow skin, shabby clothes hanging from his skinny frame. He didn't make eye contact. Just nodded towards the woods.

'Bones. They found bones this morning. Cops been back and fore ever since.'

I shrugged. 'The cemetery?'

He shook his head. 'I sneaked along for a look. It's not the cemetery.'

Fingers hooked into the holes in the security fence, he leaned close. There was a lost look about him as he stared at the buildings. 'Maybe it's someone who died in the cellar.' A shiver ran through him. 'It was so dark down there. So cold. I know people died. I heard their screams.'

I knew then he was an ex-patient, and possibly even a current patient of New Craigs, the psychiatric unit just along the road. I said nothing. I don't think he'd have heard me, anyway.

***

As I'D SUSPECTED, it hadn't taken long for Lucille Leonard to cause chaos. I arrived for my late shift to be told the card tricks had progressed to card games. The residents were used to playing Snap and Go Fish. She'd introduced poker and cleaned most of them out of their pocket money. Three of the men had gone to Mrs Shelby asking for some of their savings, and the daughter of one resident complained that her mother's gold bracelet was missing. Attempts to get the money and bracelet back had led to Lucille barricading herself in her room, threatening suicide. Her husband arrived just before me. Mrs Shelby sent me along to see how he was getting on. I found him crouched at her door, whispering endearments and wincing at the florid responses.

'Mr Leonard?'

He grunted and pushed himself to his feet. He was heavier than he'd been when the wedding photo was taken. He looked trampled upon, his shirt creased and hanging out of his trousers, sweat running down his shiny brow. He wiped it away and rubbed his meaty hand on his leg. There was no doubt he'd punched above his weight when it came to looks, but there was a kindness in his eyes as he tried to smile.

'I'm Kate. Do you want me to try talking to her?'

'Don't think it'll do any good. Not when she gets like this.' He shrugged. 'Worth a try, I suppose.'

I knocked on the door. 'Lucille, it's Kate.'

'Fuck off.'

'We talked yesterday, remember? I picked your dress for you.'

There was silence in the room. At the end of the corridor, I heard whispering. Three elderly ecstatic faces watched us. They hadn't had this much fun in years.

'You going to let me in, Lucille?'

Silence.

'What's your first name?' I asked the husband.

'Mick.'

'Lucille, Mick wants to talk to you.'

There was a sudden burst of activity behind the door. The frantic scraping of chair legs, thumping and banging and swearing. She pulled the door open, her hand shooting out and grabbing Mick by the front of his shirt.

'Get the fuck away from her. Now.' She pulled him into the room. Through the crack in the door, I saw him stumble and fall onto the bed. 'He's mine, Princess. Keep your hands off, right?'

As the door slammed shut, I heard stifled laughter. It was Stefan. 'She not your beastie today?' he whispered. 'She think you try steal her lovely man. But what is this Princess stuff?'

I shrugged. 'Who knows?'

'Must be your beautiful smile and face.'

My heart erupted in a frenzy, my cheeks flushing like beacons. 'Aye, right.'

He shook his head. 'You Scottish people, you always say this *aye right*, as if you trust nothing and no one.'

From the bedroom, I heard the rhythmic sound of the headboard knocking against the wall. My eyes met Stefan's, my cheeks flushing even more. He tried to keep a straight face, but he couldn't.

5

DANIEL'S SURNAME HAD a similar effect on the people on the Isle of Skye. It started when he tried to hire a car. Despite the evidence of his driver's licence, the woman looked at him as if he was trying it on. 'Tarantino?'

He nodded and drummed his fingers on the counter. 'Is there a problem?'

She smirked and shook her head. Kept on smirking while he filled out the paperwork. He told himself not to snatch the keys from her, but he did. Unperturbed, she winked at him and told him to enjoy his stay, Mr Tarantino.

At least at the B&B, the man didn't ask his name. Just told him to fill in a form, before demanding a sum that would have bought him a luxury weekend in London. The man opened the door to show Daniel into his room. Through the large window, he saw the view, and all comparisons with London disappeared. It was late afternoon, and a soft yellow glow was setting across Portree Bay. In the distance, the jagged edges of the Cuillin mountains shimmered. Daniel didn't think he'd ever seen anything more beautiful. He turned to thank the man, but he wasn't there.

On a deserted hillside north of the bay, Daniel sat on a bench and opened the journal. He flicked to the back pages and her sketches. Was he really that young when he'd sat and indulged her? And that smug? He smiled and remembered. He was smug and invincible and certain he had fixed her.

If only she had sketched herself. He had no photos of her, and whenever he tried to remember, her features would shimmer and dissolve. He'd grasp and try to reassemble them, but it was impossible. There were dreams, but they came less and less often, and even then, she was mostly just a shadow. Sometimes, he saw her as she was in her last moments. That wasn't an image he wanted to keep.

He turned the page and looked at the child. Same eyes, same smile. Though her mother's pencil strokes were light on the page, the sketch fading a little more each time he opened the journal, there was a robustness about the child that her mother had lacked.

He didn't turn the page again, for he knew what the next sketch would do to him. In the forest, the other day, he'd fantasised about what he'd like to do to the man that had started all this. But what about the faceless man on the last page? Had he been responsible for the horrific way in which it had ended? Despite the tranquil setting, Daniel felt his heart begin to race. Was it jealousy? Had he wanted her, or had he only wanted to save her? He wasn't sure. He'd never been sure.

He ate in a restaurant overlooking the harbour, then he sneaked into the guest house, hoping to avoid any conversation. No luck. The owner appeared from a room next to Daniel's. He nodded and smirked. 'Nice evening, Mr Tarantino.'

Daniel smiled. 'It certainly is.'

6

ON MY DAY off, I sat beside Gran on her bed and we watched the film, *Nae Pasaran*. For me, the tale of the East Kilbride factory workers who refused to work on Pinochet's aircraft engines during his bloody dictatorship was inspiring and boring in equal measure. It captivated Gran. I watched her instead of the film, and I wondered where she got her strength. They had given her three weeks to live five months ago. She'd refused a place in the hospice, preferring to spend her last days at home in the flat she'd lived in for over fifty years. No special adjustable bed for her. She would make do with the divan she'd shared with her late husband. No need for a fuss, she kept telling us.

My gran, Rebecca Alice Sharp, was the hardest and the softest person I knew. The kindest and most critical. She'd changed over the years after Mum and Granda died. She told me she'd tried so hard to do everything right as a wife and a mother. She thought she'd got the wife bit right, but maybe not the mothering. So, she'd relaxed. Stopped trying so hard to be the perfect person, the perfect role model, and she just became herself. My best friend.

She'd eaten well yesterday for the first time in ages. When I'd told the nurse this morning, she'd smiled a sorry smile and said I shouldn't read too much into it. It was unusual not to need oxygen and a morphine pump at this stage, but it wasn't unheard of. Everyone was different. As for the sudden appetite, terminally ill patients often rallied near the end. I had to be prepared, she'd said. I really wasn't.

'Ellen.' Gran gripped my hand. 'It's nearly finished. Drugs, please.'

Ellen was my mother. I didn't correct Gran, hoping she'd let something slip, preferably something about the question that stalked my dreams – the identity of my unknown father. She hadn't so far.

When the film was done, and the pills were taking effect, she asked me to find *Question Time* on catch-up.

I smiled. 'No. It's not good for you. You get so angry.'

'But these pills are turning me into a softie. I'm losing track of what's going on in the world. I need to keep up with Sullivan and his nonsense.' She stared into space, and then a smile spread across her face. 'He proposed again yesterday. Said he'd look after me, wouldn't leave my side.'

I wanted to go to the creepy old bastard's door and…

She took my hand. 'Don't frown. More chance of me winning the next Loch Ness Marathon than marrying that man, though he's not all bad. Listen, you don't need to stay tonight. Go home to your own bed. Get a good sleep.'

'I'll stay, Gran.'

She shook her head. 'Get yourself out for a while. Some fresh air. I'll be fine. Angela's coming, from the Carers Trust.'

The doorbell rang, and her features relaxed into a smile. 'Too early for Angela. Maybe it's Meg. Help me up, Kate.'

It took so little effort to get her into a sitting position. There was nothing left of her. Just bones and eyes and attitude.

'Comb my hair. Quick. And get my cardigan. Shove that plate and cup in the wardrobe, and shut the drawer.' Her eyes scanned the room. 'Tie the curtains back and straighten the rug.'

I was surprised there was still anyone at the door by the time I'd done her bidding and made it down the stairs. It was her Quaker friend, Meg. She'd brought an album of photographs and a Tupperware container of pancakes.

Gran looked so pleased to see her. 'Kate, put the kettle on before you go out.'

Meg smiled and squeezed my arm. 'I'll do it, love. You get off.'

At the bottom of the stairs, I glanced in the mirror. My hair was a mess, my face pale, dark circles under my eyes. I hadn't worn make-up or jewellery for weeks. It was all too frivolous and unnecessary. The seeping ache of imminent loss had cut my life back to the bare essentials.

***

My toes stirred the tiny diamonds that sparkled on the river. The sun and the water were warm, and a breeze whispered through the trees in the Ness Islands. It was heaven. Occasionally a passing dog found my hidden spot, joining me for a moment, then disappearing. A heron landed close by, oblivious to the secret watcher. It didn't stay long before taking off across the river, long legs trailing behind.

I only meant to go for a short walk, read a bit and listen to music. Until Stefan sent a text from the Gellions Bar. I swithered. I could be there in ten minutes. Quick drink and back to Gran's. She'd hardly have missed me.

The oldest pub in Inverness, the Gellions was Stefan's favourite, with a fabulous selection of cask beers. He'd been working his way through them for the last couple of months. When I arrived, he was in deep discussion with a barman who had the knowledge of a sommelier, if there was such a thing in the world of beer. Samples were provided, and Stefan settled on something with notes of gooseberry and grapefruit. No matter how good his English teacher was, I'd have bet Stefan hadn't a clue what either of those things was, but I said nothing.

We took our drinks through to the back section of the bar. There was no one else there. He waited for me to sit, and then he hesitated. He did this every time. Looked at the seat beside me, and the seat opposite. He swithered, then he sat beside me, as always. I wished I knew what he was thinking. Was sitting opposite more appropriate for a date and sitting next to each other something friends might do? I didn't mind where he sat. Nice though it was to look at him, there was something cosy about being side by side. Sometimes his leg would brush against mine, but he never let it linger. I wondered if the touch left a memory in his body to be treasured later, the way it did in mine.

He filled me in on the latest from the madhouse. Lucille had taken to her bed again. He wasn't allowed to go near her.

'Why not?'

He shrugged. 'Mrs Shelby, she think this Lucille will try touching me.'

I smirked. She was no fool, Mrs Shelby. 'What else?'

Turned out there had been a miracle and a disaster. After months in his squeaking old wheelchair, Smyth had walked. Finished his lunch, wiped his mouth with his napkin, and stood. Pushed back the chair and walked from the table. Stefan had caught Mrs Shelby as her legs buckled, and he'd deposited her in Smyth's wheelchair.

'Go after him,' she'd shouted, so Stefan had pushed her along the corridor, following Smyth. The miracle didn't last long. Soon, his legs were wobbling, and he was clutching at the dildo rail on the wall.

I laughed. 'The dildo rail?'

Stefan shrugged. 'That what Mrs Shelby say.'

'It's a dado rail.'

'Dildo? Dado? Who cares? Smyth, he push open Mrs Bell's door. When we reach, he is sitting on her, like she is a soft cushion. Poor little Mrs Bell. She is ruined. Cannot speak, cannot breathe. Her lips, they are blue. When we get him off her, she throw up, and there is blood.'

I shrugged. 'There was blood yesterday, so probably not all his fault, but poor Mrs Bell.'

'This is not all. Her son arrive just as we pull Smyth off. Angry man. He keep shouting he will sue. Mrs Shelby, she is in… how she say? In quite a fankle.'

Our laughter was a salve for my troubled mind. I forgot about Gran and all the unanswered questions. Stefan chose a different beer for his second pint. It had a deep and toasty flavour, apparently, but it didn't live up to the first pint. Too soon, he looked at his watch.

'Time to go?'

He nodded. 'Martyna say I drink too much.'

I'd never met Martyna. I'd asked him what she was like. He'd hesitated for a little too long, I thought. She was strong, he eventually said. Brave. She was a good mother to the boy. It was always 'the boy'. I don't think I'd ever heard his name.

He took his phone from his pocket and unwound his earphones.

'What are you listening to?'

'Amy Winehouse. I like this voice.'

'Me too.' I waved him off, then I called him back. 'Look up dildo in your dictionary when you get home.'

He nodded and took his notebook from his pocket. Scribbled and left.

I stuck in my earphones. Gin and tonic. Florence and the Machine. Bernard MacLaverty. Didn't get much better. Engrossed in the wonderful prose of *Grace Notes*, I didn't notice him until he sat opposite me. His scent, so different from Stefan's, brought unwanted memories of lazy Sunday mornings in bed, stretching into the afternoon. Whispered plans and promises. Lies.

I looked up, and he was a mess. He'd lost weight and his hair was all over the place, a frown distorting features I had once thought so attractive. He said something, but I couldn't hear him over the music. 'Do one, Paul.'

His lying mouth kept moving. I looked at my book and I didn't raise my head until I was certain he'd gone.

7

THE CLOCK IN the living room had stopped ticking. There was no rasping, no coughing, no impatient moaning from her bedroom as she tried to shuffle her fragile bones into a sitting position. Just a strange scent in the air, like nail varnish remover. I opened the bedroom door and Maria was sitting by the bed. Her hands were clasped in prayer, her eyes closed, as she whispered in her own language. I coughed, and she opened her eyes. She tried to smile, but unshed tears glimmered, threatening to spill over.

'She's not...?'

Maria shook her head. 'No yet. She wait for you. I have call the doctor.' She rose and bent over Gran, kissing her on the cheek. 'Precious lady, I will miss you. I leave you togethers.'

Togethers. Eyes closed, hands entwined, Gran's acetone breath on my face. My desperate whispers. All the things I should have said during the years of frustration when I didn't realise I had all I needed and so much more.

The sound of her rasping breath scratched through my whispering. Her eyes were closed, her blue-tinged lips smiling. 'You're back.'

'I shouldn't have left you, Gran. I'm sorry.'

'Nonsense. Nice walk?'

'Yes.' I didn't tell her I'd been sitting in the pub laughing and reading, when I should have listened to the nurse and stayed here.

'Been in the loveliest place.'

'Where?'

'Don't know. Warm and peaceful. People there, waiting for me.'

I swallowed the little gasp in my throat. 'The doctor's coming.'

The slightest shake of her head. 'No need. Your father…'

She took a breath and I could hear it wheezing and shuddering around the disease in her chest. I knew I should stop her from trying to talk, but it might be the last chance to get some answers.

'Sorry. Her secret… she didn't tell me.'

'Don't worry, Gran. It's okay.'

It wasn't. It really wasn't. And not just that I didn't know who my father was. When Gran was gone, I'd never again say those words to anyone. *Tell me about her.*

A smile flickered around Gran's mouth. She lifted her hands as if to greet someone. 'It's Granda. And… and…' She gasped, her smile growing. 'Ellen. My wee girl.'

My heart lurched into my throat and I wanted to shout at my dead mother that we didn't need her here. We didn't want her. Not now.

Gran sighed. 'And Mam and Dad. Everyone.'

Everyone but me.

And just as if she knew the envy and loneliness that taunted me, she turned and smiled. 'Darling Kate. My sunshine.' Her voice was just a scratchy whisper. 'Don't tell them.'

'Tell them what, Gran?'

'Never loved anyone as much as I love you.'

I held her hand as her life slowly slipped away. Her limbs became cold, the skin mottled, yet still she breathed in short, shallow gasps, and I found my breathing synchronising with hers. I wasn't one for self-pity, but my world was going to be such a lonely place without her. I wished I could go too.

The doctor came and checked her over. He said little. Just a sad smile and a pat on my shoulder. He had someone else to see, he said. He'd come back. I told him to let himself out and leave the door open. Minutes later, someone knocked on the downstairs door. I ignored it. Soft footsteps climbed the stairs, and the door was pushed open.

'Forgive me, Kate,' Ted Sullivan said, his eyes shining with tears. 'I saw the doctor. He wouldn't tell me anything, but I knew. I… I couldn't stay downstairs.'

He sat on the other side of the bed, taking her right hand in his. We didn't speak. About two hours after her last words, she took a final gurgling breath, and she was still.

***

IN THE PALE morning light, I sat curled in the chair in her living room. Grief was like glass in my lungs. Each breath hurt and I savoured it, never wanting to forget. The flat was quiet and cold, as if they'd taken more than just her body away last night. It was as if her very essence had followed them as they'd manoeuvred her remains round the tight bend of the stairs.

The top drawer of the sideboard was slightly open. I uncurled my aching bones from the chair and looked inside. It was almost bare. Gran had taken to packing up and chucking out straight after her diagnosis. Just her birth and marriage certificates, her NHS medical card and an envelope with my name on it. Inside, there was a brochure for personalised eco cardboard coffins, with a receipt stapled to it. She'd only gone and ordered her own coffin a month ago.

There was also a little handwritten note in a spidery, pain-filled scrawl that meant it was recent.

Kate,

I'm sorry, my darling. I wish I didn't have to leave you. I wish I could have given you the answers you wanted. But you need to stop looking back. Leave that job and go to university. Don't waste any more time.

I've told you so often how much your mother loved you, but I don't

*know if you believed me. That day, the day she should have come home,
I understand why you felt betrayed, but it wasn't her fault. She was
ready to be a mum again, and she loved you more than anything.*

*As did I. Your strength, your courage, your spirit. You were the
greatest inspiration in my life.*

Gran xxxx

*P.S. Make an appointment with Mr Low, the solicitor, right away.
I hope it's not too much of a shock…*

P.P.S. You'll love the coffin ☺

A shock? Maybe she'd left everything to charity. Having spent her
life campaigning and looking after others, it wouldn't surprise me,
but she'd always spoken as if the flat would be mine. That was
the only reason she'd bought it from the council. Her hatred of
Thatcher and everything she stood for had stopped her for years.
No way was she going to betray her class and deplete the social
housing stock. Her neighbours didn't have her principles. When
most of them had betrayed their class, and I'd moved out and
taken my name off the tenancy, Gran gave in.

As for university, I might have known she'd get it in one last
time when I couldn't answer back. Everyone had expected me to
go when I left school. English was my best subject. Perhaps I'd
become a teacher, Gran had said, with more excitement than I
felt. She'd wanted my mum to go to university, apparently, but she
wasn't interested. Not until it was too late. I started to complete the
form, and then I woke one morning and felt the weight of Gran's
expectations forcing me down a road I didn't think I wanted to go.
When I put it off, she was devastated. I'd do it one day, I'd told her.

Instead, I took an office job with the council. It was never
going to set the heather on fire, but I had decent pay, a pension,
flexi-time, good holidays, sound colleagues, and the office was
within walking distance of home. I'd been promoted twice. Sorted.
Until I messed it all up.

I didn't mess up so badly that I couldn't have got another office job or moved to a different section within the council, but my head was all over the place, my confidence gone, and maybe I just didn't like myself enough to try too hard to get back on track.

Gran had brought up university again. Reminded me I'd always said I was only putting it off, not giving up on the idea. I might have considered it until the day I sat with her in the doctor's surgery when he gave her the results of the tests she hadn't even told me she was having. Lung cancer? Was it not just asthma? She'd never smoked, hardly drank anything. He'd said something about passive smoke, pollution, genetics. Gran had shrugged and smiled, as if he'd just given her the weather forecast.

Never one to give up trying, she said I could still apply to university. If the doctor was right, she'd be gone by the time term started. The bluntness of her words had angered me; that and the fact that she was dying and leaving me alone. I wasn't going to university, I told her. I'd been offered a job in a care home, and I was just waiting for the disclosure to come through. Gran did not take the news well. She couldn't speak. One of her friends had died in a local care home the previous year, and Gran had been so angry at the lack of care she'd received. The home had since been closed down after a damning report. If I wanted to care for people, there were other ways to do it, she'd said, reeling off a list of volunteering opportunities. I didn't have time for volunteering, I told her. I needed a job, and I needed it now. My mind was made up.

I read the note again. *Your strength, your courage, your spirit. You were the greatest inspiration in my life.* How I wished I could see myself as she had done.

8

JAMIE OGILVIE HAD such an insignificant life. It hadn't always been that way. There had been family. A wife. A house. Two children. Recently, after a bender, he found he couldn't remember their names. Took him three days. He wrote them down then. Luke and Maria. No chance of remembering their faces, or their voices, or even how old they were now. Adults, living it up down under with kids of their own, no doubt. Little tanned Aussie kids.

There had been former workmates. He used to bump into them in the pub. It'd start off okay. A couple of jars, a laugh. They'd seem happy enough to be with him. But then that niggle would start poking at him, like a wee hammer behind his ear. Tap, tap, tapping. He'd still laugh and chat. They would too. But the hammer would keep going.

A few more drinks and he'd see himself through their eyes. They knew. The wee cruelties, the nasty side to him. The rumour of that other thing. Might not say anything, but they knew. As soon as he left, they'd be talking about him, ripping him to bits. One night, the beat of the hammer taunted him so hard, he followed one of them out of the pub and down an alley. Jumped him from behind and battered him senseless. Spent the next few days trying to remember why. He was certain the guy had said nothing out of order, nothing about the past. He'd dreamt of the attack. In his dream, the guy had turned and seen him coming down the alley. He'd smiled and opened his arms in invitation.

Funny thing was, it was his own face that looked back at him as he threw the first punch.

He hardly went out now. Bought his food and drink online, and hoped he wouldn't know the delivery person. To avoid conversation, he never looked them in the eye, though the odd thrawn bugger tried hard. Watched all the shite of the day on TV. Put his rubbish out in the dead of night. He could go days without speaking to anyone except the old dear.

She was standing at the living room door now, her wrinkled hands twisting her wee flowery pinny. She came into the room and perched on the edge of the chair.

'What's up, old dear? You look peaky.'

She reached her hands out towards the fancy electric fire. It wasn't even giving off any heat. Just a fake flame that flickered and danced. He could lose himself for hours watching it.

'Worried about you,' she said.

'Why?'

She shrugged. 'Where do you think you'll go if you die tonight?'

He laughed and lifted his can, tipping it towards her. 'No doubt about that, old dear.' He raised the can and swallowed. 'I'll not be needing the fire where I'm going.'

'It's not too late.'

'It was too late twenty-five years ago. You should know that.'

She shrugged. 'I never blamed you. Not really.' She tapped her head. 'Something wrong in there.'

He laughed. 'If only I'd known a good psychiatrist.' He pushed himself to his feet. 'Don't worry. I'm not planning on going anywhere tonight but my bed. Sandwich?'

She shook her head. 'No, son. I'm fine. Not one for eating at this time of night. You shouldn't either. You're piling on the beef.'

From the kitchen, Jamie shouted through. 'Aye, old dear. Just think how I'll crackle and pop when those flames get me.' His laughter was so loud, he didn't hear her reply. By the time he went back through, she was gone.

***

JAMIE'S FLAILING HAND knocked over a glass of water and sent the alarm clock skiting across the floor. Its shrill din echoed in his head, chasing away the fragments of a dream he didn't want to remember. Didn't want to get up either, but the alarm clock was dinging away on the other side of the room. He'd have Mr Moaning-face at his door again, reminding him that some people had to work night shift, and a degree of neighbourly consideration wouldn't go amiss. He hadn't bothered replying last time. He'd just shut the door on his neighbour, but he had tried to be quiet, to prevent more visits.

He silenced the alarm clock, then he mopped up the puddle on the bedside table, shaking water off the book he'd been trying to read. He used to love reading in his bed, but not so much lately. His eyes were sore and gritty, and the words seemed to blur and melt together. Hopefully get that sorted today.

He got off the bus at the Post Office. Inverness town centre was quiet, just the way he liked it. The workers had gone to work, and the shoppers weren't yet out in force. Or maybe the shoppers had given up on the town centre. Charity shops, tartan tat, phone shops. That was it. Oh, and a couple of prominent fire-damaged buildings surrounded by perpetual scaffolding. The place was a joke.

He'd get this appointment over with, pick up some shopping in the Coop and get off home. Put his feet up and watch some sport. That was the plan until the words on the billboard outside the newsagents crashed into his head.

Human remains found in Dunain Woods.

The words rendered him a mumbling idiot at his appointment, scarcely able to respond to questions about how long his eyes had been affected and whether he was on any medication and blah blah blah. He left with drops for dry eyes. There had been more said about diet and blinking and supplements, but the words evaded him.

Outside, the town seemed to have erupted into a frenzy of busyness. Jamie couldn't move. Back inside and he asked the receptionist to phone him a taxi. In the car, he stayed low, his eyes fixed on the driver's bald head, his nails scratching at the thin scar that ran across the back of his hand.

He asked the driver to go round by the Co-op. Eyes down, only glancing up when he had to, Jamie grabbed the essentials. Should have kept his eyes down while he waited in the queue at the kiosk. He didn't. Looking up, he saw the newspaper stand, and he didn't seem able to stop his shaking hand from reaching for a copy of the local paper.

9

THE BONES FROM Dunain Woods were read at the Scottish Police Authority laboratory in Aberdeen. The skeleton was intact, so they were able to set the bones out in their anatomical position. The only bone that had suffered post-mortem damage was the femur found by the dog. It showed thin deep scratches attributable to carnivore scavenging, and wider grooves likely to have come from the teeth of rodents. For some strange and fortuitous reason, no further bones had been scavenged from the last resting place of the skeleton.

The remains of pink flowery nylon fabric in the grave hinted at a female occupant. Not conclusive by any means, but the reading of the bones upheld that theory. The small skull with rounding of the frontal bone and chin; the slighter mastoid process and jaws; the absence of a brow ridge. The flaring of the hip bones; a circular pelvic inlet; a large pelvic outlet.

As for the age of the female, they deduced that she was elderly when she died. The bony spikes on the edges of the spinal vertebrae, and other signs of bone wear supported that theory. All her teeth had been extracted. No dentures were found with the skeleton.

There had been a fracture of the right forearm. A robust callus on both bones indicated the fracture had happened quite some time before death. Possibly even in childhood.

The amount of time between death and discovery was going to be harder to determine. The fragments of fabric suggested a timescale of at least twenty years, or someone with a liking for vintage clothing. The botany and entomology reports would help, in due course.

The long bones suggested a short person, though further calculations involving cranial, vertebral and ankle bone heights would be carried out.

So, despite a considerable amount of painstaking work, the reading of the bones was not yet complete.

However, there was one incontrovertible little clue in the initial report. The tiny U-shaped hyoid bone that lies between the chin and the thyroid cartilage, anchoring the tongue, had been fractured. Sometimes attributable to gunshot injury or a car accident, there were no other signs to support either of those theories. The almost certain cause was strangulation. Most likely suicide by hanging, or a murderous attack.

10

THE RIVER NESS runs through the heart of Inverness, its banks punctuated by a succession of church spires and steeples, hotels and guesthouses. I followed the river from the Archive Centre, where I'd registered Gran's death, past the Ness Islands, Eden Court Theatre, and the Cathedral to the town. I'd always lived on the west side of the river. The best side, I'd tell my friend, Eilidh. She'd been brought up on the other side, and we'd met when we worked in a local restaurant as teenagers. We didn't let our rivalry over which side was best get in the way of our friendship, though we both knew who was right.

I reached the main bridge. On the other side of the river, on a steep hillside, Inverness Castle towered over the town. I needed to cross to that side, the dark side, with its shopping centre and fashion chains. I wanted something to wear to the funeral. But I couldn't face it. Too many people. Too many shops. And yet, I didn't want to go back to my flat. I'd spent so little time there recently, it no longer felt like home. And Gran's flat was too quiet and sad.

A seventeenth-century Highland clairvoyant, the Brahan Seer, had prophesied that a litany of disasters would occur when a certain number of bridges were built over the River Ness. The fifth bridge was built just before the start of World War I, the ninth not long before the Piper Alpha tragedy. The details of both events seemed to fit with the seer's prophecies. There was another prophecy attached to a ninth bridge – the Highlands would be overrun by ministers without grace and women without shame.

That settled it for me. I crossed the road to the Glenalbyn, an old-fashioned pub on the riverside. I sat at the bar and ordered a large gin and tonic. The barman tried to chat, as if it was just another ordinary day. He had a lovely smile, but I had nothing to say. Didn't he know? I felt as if I had an enormous sign attached to me, proclaiming my loss.

A hand caressed my shoulder, and I wanted to tell whoever it was to go away. I was glad I hadn't. It was Stefan. The shadow of tears in his eyes almost made me cry. He enfolded me in his arms. I wished I could stay there forever, but it was over too soon.

'Mrs Shelby, she tell me,' he said, as he settled on a stool. 'I call you, but you don't answer. I go to the Gellions, to Lauders, to the Phoenix.' He smiled. 'I even go to Spoons.'

That made me laugh. Wetherspoons had been high on our list of preferred pubs before the Brexit vote. An excellent choice of gins, a good enough choice of beers, though not quite up to the standard of the Gellions, and a decent menu, and all cheaper than anywhere else. But we'd agreed, no matter how hard up we were, we couldn't support the Brexiteer owner of the chain.

'Then I see you through the window,' he said. 'I'm sorry, my friend.'

I nodded. 'What are you having?'

A couple of drinks, some fish and chips, Stefan's gentle chat, and I felt almost human. Being with him made me feel safe. Maybe Gran was right, maybe... Don't be stupid, I told myself. He was spoken for. I'd tried that before. It didn't work out well. As if he could read my errant thoughts, he said he had to go. Martyna was on night shift. I told him I didn't know when I'd be back at work.

He frowned. 'What I do without you?'

'Get yourself out of there. Go to college. Anything but mopping up shit. You're worth so much more.'

He shrugged. 'College, with this Brexit? I feel worth nothing. I should go home.'

I apologised for Brexit and the government and the ineffectual opposition.

He frowned. 'Kate, why you drink alone? You don't have friends?'

I laughed. 'I do. That's why my phone was off. They haven't stopped calling all day. I just wanted a bit of peace.'

It was true. Though I'd lost some friends at work when I messed up, all the old ones were still there. I had seen little of them lately. Something had happened on the day of Gran's diagnosis. A drawing in, a keeping out. I'd even given up my ticket for Belladrum Music Festival in July, first time I'd missed it in years. As soon as my friends had heard about Gran, they'd called.

'Don't worry about me,' I said. 'Go.'

He was putting his jacket on when I saw a *Still Game* DVD sticking out of his pocket. I laughed. 'Where did you get that?'

'Donald, the van driver. My teacher, she say I must watch more films, read some books. This is the way to learn. Soon Mr Smyth and the other head-dicks, sorry, dickheads, will think I am a Scottish man. I watch it later.'

'I don't think it's quite what your teacher had in mind. You're going to need the sub-titles.'

'No. I do not. I will learn.'

I nodded and waved him off.

My legs were a little shaky by closing time. The barman walked me home. We kissed at my door. I told him he couldn't come in; I was in mourning. He smiled and said I was beautiful, and I thanked him for the lie.

I woke in the night, my clothes and the light still on, the room swaying around me. I longed to hear Gran shuffle and cough in the next room. Fool. I wasn't even in her flat. Still, the silence taunted me. Nausea forced me from my bed. I threw up, undressed, lay down, and watched until the pale light of dawn crept in round my curtains.

11

FOR TWO DAYS, Jamie Ogilvie hardly left his bed. He wasn't alone. Whenever he was about to slip into sleep, he felt Ellen's slim body spooning his from behind. He could smell her. A mix of soap and grass and desire. The first time he felt her there, he'd smiled and turned, but she was gone. After that, he just lay and let her curl against him. Sometimes he spoke. Whispered reminiscences. She never answered, but he heard that laugh and her little sighs. He wondered what had brought her back after all this time. Was it the story in the paper?

On the third day, he awoke to a different smell in the air. It was stale, like rotten leaves and dead wood. It was the old dear. He felt her weight settle on the edge of the bed, and Ellen was gone. The old dear's scratchy voice reached into his head, scouring and scraping.

'My goodness. Oh, my goodness. Smells like a badger's backside in here. What is wrong with you?'

You're not so fragrant yourself, he wanted to say, but he kept quiet, in the hope she'd go. Not a chance.

'She's been here, hasn't she?' Rancour curdled her voice. 'That piece of work. Piece of shit.'

'That's not very Christian, old dear. Aren't you supposed to love thy neighbour and all that?'

'Hmm.'

She was quiet then. He waited until he was sure she'd gone.

Time to get up, have a shower. There'd be no more sleep, no more cuddling in, no more –

'How could you?' The rage in her voice shook the room. 'That tart! Wasn't just you, humping her in the woods. I followed her, time and again. Saw her with God knows how many men.'

He pulled the quilt over his head, but she pulled it away. 'You're a disgrace. Always were. One smile from that tart, and your vows and your children, they meant nothing to you.'

She was right, but it didn't make it any easier to hear.

'You're an animal. You're –'

He threw the quilt off, his hands reaching for her throat. She laughed as she slipped away from him.

It was a chore to shower and dress. He had no appetite, but he forced down a slice of toast. What he needed was a stiff drink, but he'd wait until the late afternoon. Had to have some self-control. He paced the flat, switching the TV on and off, standing on the balcony staring at the river, trying not to think about unwelcome things and lost people. He struggled over a sandwich at lunchtime. Ate about half of it, then he watched the clock. Made it to half-three. Still early, but he couldn't wait any longer.

There was nothing wrong with his drinking ability. Slipped down as easy as ever, calming the wee spikes of terror that kept rising from his gut. A few drams and he could pick up the local paper without his hands shaking. The story hadn't changed since the last time he'd looked. Wasn't even much of a story. A couple of paragraphs on the front page. Probably old bones from the cemetery, someone buried long before he was born.

He opened the paper for the first time. Nothing but shoplifting, police assault, battered girlfriends, drugs. He recognised some surnames. Probably knew their parents or grandparents back in the day. Further on, there was an article about a battle of the bands at the Ironworks. He used to love live music, but that was so long ago. Maybe he should go. Sneak in when the lights were low. Stay at the back. He peered at the page, trying to see the date of the event, but his eyes were dry and gritty, the words blurring on the page. Maybe time to try those eye drops.

What a faff. He thought he heard the old dear giggling behind him as he squinted into the bathroom mirror and felt the liquid running down his cheek, but she wasn't there. At last, he got some in.

The event was a week on Friday. His heart raced, and he knew there was little chance he'd go. He flicked the pages over, getting towards the end of the paper. His eyes hovered over the death notices, hoping there was someone he knew. He could do with cheering up.

And there it was. Rebecca Alice Sharp, Ellen's mother, was gone. It didn't cheer him up any, but he knew then why Ellen had come back. She wanted him to have what was rightfully his. It was time.

12

MY GRANDFATHER, JONATHON Sharp, was a Quaker. Raised in Brighton, he moved to Inverness to work in the Rose Street Foundry. Gran was born just around the corner in Victoria Square, now the multi-storey car park. Her family had moved to the new council estate in Dalneigh by the time Granda made his appearance. They met in a corner shop on Academy Street, where she was working. She thought him pompous with his odd accent and his quiff. And even if she had liked him, he was posh, and right out of her league. He disagreed. At last, she gave in. Their first date was at the Empire Theatre. Gran couldn't remember the name of the film they saw. Probably saw little of it, I'd said. She'd smiled. Maybe that was it, though he was a gentleman, mind. Always a gentleman.

Gran had forsaken the church of her parents as soon as she was old enough. It wasn't that she didn't believe in God. She just couldn't bear to see the Sunday pomposity of some of the so-called elect. There were no secrets in Inverness, and she knew what went on in their lives the other six days of the week.

And so, when Granda introduced her to the strange new Quaker doctrine where women had always been equal to men, where she wasn't told what to believe, and all she had to do was see 'that of God' in everyone, while campaigning vociferously for social justice and peace, she was smitten.

When I was younger, I sometimes went to meetings for worship with her. I knew the drill. An hour of silence, occasionally broken by words of inspiration or guidance from anyone that felt moved to speak, and sometimes by utter drivel. Gran never spoke out. Not once. I asked her what went on in her head during the meeting. She shrugged. It varied; a bit like the spoken testimonies. Sometimes the silent waiting and stillness brought deep spiritual communion with God, with herself, with the others. It brought insight and guidance, answers even. And sometimes she spent the hour obsessing over every itch and ache in her body, every snub or insult of the last forty years.

On the day we gave thanks for the grace of God in the life of Rebecca Alice Sharp, Meg read out the words I'd written about Gran. I didn't dare do it myself. It was hard enough to keep my composure listening to Meg, with her gentle voice and her own stories of their friendship and Gran's devotion to her daughter, Ellen, and to me.

After that, I expected silence, but people bobbed up and down with tales of Gran's random kindnesses, bolshiness, subterfuge and direct military action. The time she orchestrated a boycott of the local butcher when he'd sacked his message boy because he was ten minutes late back after lunch. He'd been helping an old man that had collapsed in the street. Her campaign saw the boy reinstated with a pay rise. How she used to sneak into the La Scala cinema on a Saturday morning without paying, and then she'd give the money to one of the down-and-outs that hung around the town. How she'd saved a wee girl from drowning at the Glebe Street Baths. And been sacked from her first job in a local bakery for sneaking pies out to Forty Pockets, a local worthy.

Ted Sullivan spoke with eloquence of her compassion, her resilience and her perseverance. She'd persevered mercilessly until he'd agreed to volunteer for a local charity. The experience had changed his life. As had she. I almost warmed to him.

We laughed so much, I kept expecting her cardboard coffin to shake. Talk about Gran having the last laugh. The thing was completely covered with a collage of her consecutive and beloved Siamese cats, Binky, Barnaby and Boss. I'd hated those cats. Sleek, spoilt, superior; each one had given me the creeps, the way they sat on a satin cushion with their eyes closed, like little mini gods, waiting for her to hand-feed them with warm fish or chicken. I was so glad the last one had gone before her.

My friends were there. Susan was a physiotherapist, the most driven person I knew. There was a man with her. I did a double-take. Peter Lilley? He was in school with us and Susan had hated him. They'd snogged at a party and she'd found out later it was a bet between the boys. He'd won. Kissed fifteen girls in one night. I never did tell her I was one of them too. They looked close. Interesting.

Amy the hairdresser came, with her perfect hair, nails and make-up. I always felt like a scruff beside her. I wished I'd made an effort. Even just an appointment with her to get my roots done. But my appearance had been the last thing on my mind. I'd do it soon. I noticed a diamond sparkling on her ring finger. So, Gary's persistence had finally won her over. Unless she had someone new. I should know this. I'd find out later.

I hadn't seen Eilidh since her divorce. She seemed happy, but she'd always been good at masking. Even her best friend, Louise, hadn't guessed at the years of domestic abuse Eilidh had endured. Louise, a primary school teacher and the most sensible of my friends, was now quizzing Peter Lilley, telling him she was certain they'd met before. I hoped they hadn't kissed too.

I almost cried when I saw Lisa, a married mother of three and my oldest friend. We'd started school together. When she said her son was fourteen, I realised I hadn't seen him since he was about eight. I hadn't even met her youngest. They'd moved to Caithness years earlier, but it wasn't so far away that I couldn't have made an effort to keep in touch more often. I swore I'd make time to catch up with them all when this was over. There were others. Old schoolmates and neighbours that I'd lost touch with. It seemed Gran had made a lasting impression on so many people.

I wondered what my friends made of the handsome man who stayed close to my side throughout. I introduced Stefan, but I didn't say who he was. I wouldn't have known where to start. I wondered if they saw his hand reach for mine as the coffin descended into the dark gaping hole. I wanted to hold tight and never let go. Until I felt the cold, harsh touch of his wedding ring.

13

THERE WAS A lost look about Kate Sharp. Despite all the people around her, she was lonely, head bowed and shoulders slumped as they lowered the strange-looking coffin into the open grave. When she looked up, Jamie gasped. That face. It was Ellen. A few years older, but the same eyes, same colouring, same nervous little smile. He ducked down, his shaking hands reaching for the nearest gravestone. On his knees, damp seeping through his jeans, he scraped lichen off Gerald Smith's gravestone. No one cared enough about Gerald to keep the grave tidy or leave flowers. Jamie used to leave flowers on Ellen's grave, before he turned into a sad hermit, scared of his own shadow. Her grave had always been immaculate and bright with colour. Sometimes, as he made his cautious approach, he'd see one or both of her parents there, bending and tidying. And then, within a couple of years, it was just the mother, tending the joint grave of her daughter and her husband. She'd spend a long time there, and sometimes he'd have to leave without laying his flowers. He'd put them on a random grave, someone that looked neglected, like Gerald Smith.

They were moving away from the grave now. Heading his way in splintered groups. Kate was talking to an old man. Jamie couldn't make out their words, but the familiar tone and rhythm of her voice forced out an aching groan. And his heart felt like a train, rumbling and racing through his chest. By the time they passed close to him, he couldn't hear a word.

He was so glad to get home. From under his bed, he pulled out a shoe box, coughing as dust motes rose and danced in the beam of light from the window. It was here. It must be. He scattered photos around him. His frowning father, the vicious bastard that had made him everything he was. His supercilious sisters. The brother that had always hated him. If he'd had an open fire, he'd have burned the photos long ago. Just a few left. His best friend at school, long dead. Two girls that he'd trained with. Both gorgeous. Why had he never made a move? Probably because he was a wimp in those days. Couldn't believe anyone would reciprocate. His confidence came later, with the qualifications and the power.

It was the last photo, and it lay face down. His heart soared into his throat as his fumbling fingers tried to grasp the flimsy print. He closed his eyes and turned it over. Perhaps he wouldn't look. Perhaps he'd just put it in the box and pile the others in. Shove it back where it was and forget again.

But he couldn't.

The photo showed Ellen barefoot in the woods, leaning against a tree. The sun was shining, and he could see her long legs through the thin dress that fell around her. Those eyes. That smile. His heart.

He put the photo in the drawer by his bed, and he started planning.

14

It was such a long day. After the cemetery, we had soup and sandwiches at the community centre. Susan and Peter asked if I wanted to meet them later for a meal. Eilidh and Louise wanted me to go for a drink. I couldn't face it. Stefan and I went back to my flat. He chose the music while I opened a bottle of wine. The mellow voice of Townes Van Zandt was welcome, though I knew there was a lyric or two that might get me if I wasn't careful.

'Can I ask a thing, Kate?'

I guessed what he was going to say. No one could have stood at that open grave without reading the inscription on the stone and wondering about the other occupants, or one in particular.

'Why you don't speak of your mother?'

I shrugged, and then I did. As I told my tale, the colour drained from his face. 'They taunt you with this "up the hill", your school-friends? This is horrible.'

I shrugged. 'They were just kids. And my life was different. No one else had a mother in a mental hospital. No one else lived with their grandparents. At that age, I don't think it's deliberate cruelty. They just don't think, don't understand.'

'But this can give you scar forever.'

I nodded. 'It can, unless you beat the crap out of them until they shut up.'

'Beat the… the crap?' He thought about it, then he laughed. 'I get it. I like this.'

He didn't ask what happened to her, and I was glad. It had never been easy for me to talk to anyone but Gran about her. She'd told me so often that Mum had been a great mother until she got sick. It wasn't her fault. It wasn't mine. It wasn't anyone's. And my mum had tried hard to get better for me. I believed all that. It was the next bit I had difficulty with. No matter how often Gran told me it was an accident that took Mum at the end, I wasn't entirely sure she believed it herself. I knew the details, but they left room for doubt. And that fed a bitterness within me that sometimes soured my miniscule store of memories.

Stefan asked me for more tales of Gran. The music faded out, and I could have talked all night, but it seemed no time at all before he was looking at his watch.

'Time to go?'

He nodded and stood. 'I'm sorry.'

'Don't be. It was so good of you to come today.' I put my glass down and pushed myself from the chair. 'Thank you.'

He smiled. 'You move into your grandmother's flat?'

I nodded. 'In a couple of weeks.' I hesitated. 'I might sell it. Buy somewhere else. I'm... maybe I'll go to university.'

It was as if someone had charged Stefan's body with a thousand amps. His smile could have lit up the town. 'Kate, Kate, Kate.' He held my hands. 'You must. Yes, you must. You know what you study?'

I shrugged. 'Maybe literature.'

'This is books, I think? Good books?'

I nodded, and he hugged me tight. When we separated, I saw a dark shadow on his temple, just at the edge of his hairline. How had I not noticed it before? 'Your head – what happened?'

He waved one hand, his eyes avoiding mine. 'Is nothing. Just the boy, he... what you say? He wallop me with a... a digger. I must go. I see you soon. I help you clear flat and move. You get some good sleep tonight.'

There was little sleep to be had. It wasn't just my grief. It was the shock Gran had mentioned in her letter. I'd almost told Stefan, but I still couldn't believe it. Gran had always been careful, and there had been an insurance pay-out when Granda died suddenly at his work just two years after my mother. Gran had invested this, and eventually used it to buy the flat, but I thought there was probably some left over. A few thousand, maybe. If it wasn't going to charity, I'd wondered if it would be enough to pay off the debts that weighed me down. It made me angry to think of Gran's money paying debts that weren't mine. Not morally mine, anyway.

I hadn't told Gran how I was struggling; that the money I'd saved while I'd worked for the council, the money I'd hoped to put towards a deposit on a property, was almost gone now. Reluctant to expose myself for the fool I'd been, I didn't want her trying to help me out.

Mr Low, the solicitor, told me that Gran had left the balance of her bank account to various charities, and the flat to me. I couldn't ask for more than that. I'd thanked him and got up. But that wasn't all, he'd said. There was another sum of money, held in shares.

When he told me how much it was, I'd gasped. Where did it come from? Why did Gran stay in an ex-council flat in Dalneigh, with clapped-out furniture, when she could have lived anywhere? Why hadn't she said anything?

Turned out my grandfather had inherited the money when his father died and they sold the family home in Brighton. He and Gran hadn't touched it. They'd invested it for me.

I lay in the dark and considered the possibilities again. I wouldn't get the money for another few months, so I wasn't about to make any drastic changes. There was probably still time to apply for university this year, but I didn't think I was ready. Should I give up work, maybe travel? There were so many places I wanted to go. Gran and I had been to Barcelona when I was fifteen and we'd always said we'd go back. I wanted to go to New York, Las Vegas, Nashville. To the Niagara Falls and the Rocky Mountains. To Berlin and Prague and Austria. Poland, even.

And there it was. The thing that was probably going to keep me right here in Inverness. Something that money couldn't buy.

15

THE SKY WAS darkening and the birds were silent. The only sound in the forest was the crunch of feet and paws on the thick bed of leaves and needles, muted occasionally by blankets of the softest moss. The dogs and their handlers had worked an area around the site of the remains, then they'd moved further into the woods. They'd found nothing. They were ready to pack it in until the sudden frantic barking of the young spaniel split the air.

She was a funny-looking wee thing. Black and white, with short legs and a tan ring round one eye. It was her first outing after completing her training. Though she was keen, no one expected much from her. Now, she was dancing, yapping and scraping around a fallen, lichen-coated tree in a small clearing. The tree looked to have been down for years, its trunk embedded in the ground, brittle branches twisting this way and that. A command from her trainer and the spaniel dropped to the ground. She was silent then, tail wagging, waiting for the hand contact, the praise, the dog biscuit. Back to the van then, before the hard work began.

The second skeleton was considerably larger than the first. It lay on its side in a grave that was shallower than the first one and covered by the fallen tree trunk. There were shoes this time, and they looked to belong to a male.

When they'd done all the work on-site, the remains would be bagged and transported to Aberdeen for another detailed forensic examination. Crucial though the eventual laboratory report would be, an immediate glance at this skeleton provided the local police with significant clues.

Blunt force trauma, as the name suggests, involves a blunt instrument used with great force. Here, blunt force trauma had been applied to the skull in three places, fracturing the left brow ridge and eye socket, and causing stellate fractures of the parietal and occipital bones. Might not have been the only injuries this person received; might not even have been fatal injuries, but they certainly suggested foul play.

16

To my surprise, I was glad to be back at work. I'd had enough of my own company. Except for Smyth, I liked old people. Probably because I was raised by my grandparents. Despite Mrs Shelby's complaining, it was hard not to spend time talking to the residents, especially the ones who didn't get visitors. Mrs Paterson, a wee woman from Buckie, a former English teacher, was delighted to see me back. I'd been reading to her during my lunch break. We were halfway through *Wuthering Heights*. It was her favourite, and one of mine. Smyth had the flu, and he'd been banished to his room under strict quarantine. Fantastic. As for Lucille Leonard, she'd taken to her bed again, after an altercation over a half bottle of vodka brought in by her husband. Mrs Shelby told me not to go near her, and that suited me fine.

Stefan, too, seemed happy to have me back. When we were alone, I asked him if he'd discovered what a dildo was. It was cute the way a wee flush crept up his neck as he nodded, then laughed.

'How's *Still Game*?'

He frowned. 'Is a bit difficult. The sub-titles are in the funny language too. I think Donald is, how you say, at it.' He fished his notebook out of his pocket. 'Tell me, what is this tadger thing?'

I tried not to laugh and ended up snorting. 'Look it up when you get home.'

I wanted to tell him about Gran's money. I had told no one, and it was constantly poking at me. But a nurse came for him. She needed a hand with big Jimmy Reid. He was refusing his tablets again.

I might have told Stefan when we stood outside at the end of our shift, but he said he was in a hurry. He had to pick the boy up from his grandmother. But first, he had a quick funny story to tell me about his friend Adrian, who worked on a local farm. It involved a goose and a postie.

I was distracted by a woman approaching from behind him. It was her walk that alerted me. Purposeful. Direct. She had short dark hair, a full figure. Well-built, Gran would have said. Stefan was flapping his arms and shouting something in a high voice. I wondered if the postie was female, though I was certain he'd said it was a man. The woman stopped. Our eyes met. Hers were intelligent, insistent, piercing. Stefan's arms fell to his sides, his voice tailing away as he realised I wasn't listening. He looked over his shoulder. 'Martyna?'

I'd imagined his wife as small, blonde and pretty, a perfect contrast to his height and colouring. Someone for him to protect. Because he was a protector. I saw it in the way he dealt with the residents in the care home, even Smyth. To me, Smyth was just a horrible bigot. To Stefan, he was a lonely old man who needed to be cared for.

Martyna was nothing like I'd imagined, and she certainly didn't look like she needed any protection. She wasn't conventionally attractive, but there was something about her. They made a striking couple with their height and colouring. They fitted together. I imagined 'the boy'. He'd be tall and dark too. A little wild, maybe, if he took after his mother, for there was something more in the eyes that now stared at me. I couldn't put a finger on what it was, but it made me a little uncomfortable. Maybe it was just the feeling that she'd caught me with her man.

She said something in Polish and Stefan introduced us. She smiled. 'Is lovely to meet you, Kate. Stefan tell me much. We go for a drink.'

Stefan shook his head. 'The boy –'

Martyna waved her hand. 'He is fine with my mother. Come.'

17

On Bridge Street, Daniel Tarantino swerved to avoid a drunk exiting the Gellions Bar. He collided with a pushchair. As the drunk mumbled an apology and lurched up the street, Daniel apologised to the young father. The child slept on. The smell of beer and the warm laughter oozing from the pub drew Daniel in.

He'd returned from Skye a couple of days ago and had booked into a guesthouse on Kenneth Street. Got his tent and belongings back this morning, and considered pitching up somewhere for his last night, but the weather didn't look too promising, and he was enjoying the cooked breakfasts and the comfy bed. He'd had a good walk today, up to Essich Farm. The rain had held off, and he'd enjoyed the views across the town and over to the Black Isle. He'd succumbed to his aching feet at Lochardil and caught a bus back to the town.

Inverness had changed little since he was last here. Had changed little since he was first here, though he'd heard it was one of Europe's fastest-growing cities. Didn't feel much like a city. And the Gellions didn't seem to have changed one bit. He perched on a stool at the corner of the bar. The first half of the pint went down fast. He looked at his watch and it was too early to eat. He'd make the pint last, then maybe one more. At the sound of raucous laughter, he looked up. There were three people sitting at the table beside the steps down to the back section of the bar. The laughter came from a dark-haired woman sitting facing Daniel. The other two had their backs to him, but their posture did not suggest a sharing of her good humour. The man seemed a little hunched, staring into his pint. The fair-haired woman beside him was leaning back in her chair, giving off an air of boredom. The laughing woman drained her pint glass and thumped it down on the table. She said something to the others. Something forceful. The man hunched even lower. The other woman stood and gathered up their glasses.

Daniel lifted a copy of the *Inverness Courier* from the bar. It was days old. The bones were front-page news. He hadn't asked anything of the cop who gave him back his tent earlier. It wasn't the same officer as before, and Daniel saw no point in inviting a rebuff. He read that the police were treating the death as suspicious, though the remains had not yet been identified.

He was aware of the fair-haired woman ordering drinks, the man coming up and giving her money to pay for them, and then taking the drinks back to the table. It wasn't until he sat down again that Daniel looked directly at the woman. A wave of panic almost knocked him off the stool. His eyes widened and his jaw dropped open. He had not expected this. But why not? Inverness was not a big place. And yet, he'd never considered the possibility. In his head, he had preserved her as a few pencil strokes on a page. Even though he'd thought of her just the other day, on a Skye hillside, he hadn't wondered where she was now or how she looked as an adult. Turned out, she looked just like her mother.

His reaction had not gone unnoticed. How could it? She smiled and asked if he was all right. Daniel nodded, hardly trusting himself to speak. She came round the bar to where he was sitting, and she put her drink down. 'I'm Kate.'

He knew that. His smile felt like a grimace, his teeth dry and the corners of his mouth aching.

'You looked a bit shocked there.' She glanced in the mirror behind the bar. 'Oh, my God... no wonder. I've aged ten years since coming in here, and my roots are a disgrace. Shouldn't be allowed out in public.'

He shook his head. 'Sorry, I was miles away. It… it wasn't you.'

'That's good. Hope you don't mind me talking to you. I'm tipsy and I need to escape.' She glanced over her shoulder. 'Ever feel like you've landed in an alternate universe? Maybe even Hell?'

Daniel laughed. 'Only every day.' He held out his hand. 'I'm Daniel.'

She had a firm grip. 'Hi, Daniel. You on holiday?'

'Yes. Heading home tomorrow.' His eyes strayed to the newspaper, and words jumped from his mouth. His tent, the bones, the police. Her smile faded. Of course, it did. Fool. He moved on to his holiday on Skye. Expensive holiday, it had turned out. He'd had to buy new clothes and toiletries, and the cost of accommodation was not cheap. Still, it was amazing. He told her of the Fairy Pools and the Quirang. The Old Man of Storr and the Cuillin.

Her smile returned. 'We always wanted to go to Skye, me and my… my gran.' The light in her eyes dimmed. 'Won't happen now. She died last week.'

'I'm sorry.'

She shrugged. 'Shit happens. So, where's your home?'

'Hertfordshire. Stevenage.'

'What brings you up here?'

He wondered how she would react if he told her the truth. Or even a little of the truth. He gave her a smidgen. 'I used to live here years ago. I come back every summer.'

'A pilgrimage?'

'Something like that.'

There was an empty stool beside him. She pulled it back from the bar. 'Do you mind?'

He could have said he wanted to be alone. He could have said he was leaving. He did neither. Just shook his head. 'Not at all.'

18

I was ENJOYING Daniel's company when Devil Woman gripped my arm. She delivered her words with all the charm of the Gestapo. 'Who. Is. Your. Friend?'

I prised her fingers off me. 'This is Daniel. Daniel, Martyna.'

Daniel accepted her outstretched hand, and he looked as if he regretted it. When she released his crushed fingers, she launched into a Polish song. Reminded me of the Eurovision Song Contest, and Saturday evenings with Gran in front of the TV, scarcely understanding a word. Not easy competing with the jukebox, but Martyna was undaunted.

I hadn't wanted to go for a drink with them. I was tired after my first day back, and I knew I wouldn't be at ease. She'd insisted. It took little time with them to dispel the notion that they fitted together. She hadn't stopped talking since we left the care home. She constantly interrupted Stefan, until he gave up, withdrawing into a shell of something that looked like resentment, a look I'd never seen on his face. She was throwing the drink back. Stefan couldn't keep up with her. I did. I had to, for my sanity.

Daniel had a slight smile on his face as he watched Martyna. I was glad he was smiling now. The look on his face when our eyes met. It was as if he'd seen a ghost. Intrigued and desperate to escape, I couldn't not speak to him then.

Martyna finished, bowed, and beckoned Stefan across. 'We go now, Kate,' she said. 'We leave you two together. Alone.'

'Nice to meet you, Martyna,' I lied.

'And you, my wee Kate.' She pinched my cheek. 'We will be good friends. I know this. Say goodbye, Stefan.'

He pushed past her. 'I say hello first.' He held out his hand to Daniel. 'I am Stefan, Kate's friend. Is nice to meet you. Look after her.'

He smiled at me. There was sadness in his eyes, and it made my heart sore. 'I see you soon, Kate.'

At the door, after she'd pushed Stefan out, Martyna turned and made a crude forearm jerk.

I shook my head, and Daniel laughed. 'Can I be blunt?'

'Please.'

'She hates you.'

I shrugged. 'The feeling's mutual.'

He frowned. 'Be careful.'

I wondered what he meant, but I didn't ask.

'I'm going for something to eat,' he said. 'Would you like to join me?'

I didn't even think about it. 'Definitely.'

We were getting ready to leave when the door swung open. I groaned. As if things could get any worse.

Paul Gibson frowned as his eyes swivelled between us. He looked even seedier than he had the last time we met in the Gellions, the day Gran died. His blond hair looked greasy and unkempt, and his clothes were scruffy. Was this really the man I'd given up so much for?

'Kate…'

'Go away.'

'But, Kate, she's thrown me out…'

There was a little beer left in Daniel's glass.

'You finished with this?'

He nodded, and I poured the beer over Paul's head. It was sweet the way Daniel moved between us as if to protect me. I wished he'd been there to protect me the first time I met Paul Gibson.

'Sorry about that, Daniel. Will we go?'

As the door was swinging closed behind us, I heard a plaintive cry. 'But, Kate… he's far too old for you…'

19

DANIEL FROM STEVENAGE *was* too old for me, handsome though he was, with his dark hair greying at the sides, his brown eyes, wide smile and toned muscular frame. I'd never fancied older men, not least because of the unknown father situation. I liked him, though. He was good company, a decent guy. I'd swithered over where to go when we left the pub. I'd spent too much in the Gellions, and it was a couple of weeks until pay day. It was definitely a Spoons time of month, but even without the Brexit dilemma, I wouldn't have suggested it. I knew very little about Daniel, and though we hadn't met in the most salubrious of surroundings, I was fairly sure sticky carpets and tables, a three-mile hike to the toilets, and the threat of a jakey stealing poppadoms from your plate wouldn't be his thing. Not that there was any shortage of good eating places in Inverness. I just wanted to be sure it was the right place for Daniel, and somewhere I could afford.

I suggested the Mustard Seed, a converted church just a short walk away, on the riverside. Not quite Spoons' prices, but reasonable enough, and the food was always good. Turned out it was Daniel's favourite. It was unusual to get a seat without a reservation, but we were in luck. Our table was on the upstairs terrace, overlooking the water.

Daniel raised his wine glass and clinked it against mine. 'Cheers. I didn't think the Gellions could get any more interesting after Martyna, but I must ask: who was the guy you drowned?'

Over his shoulder, I saw twilight falling, its muted light sparkling on the river as it rolled past. The sky was streaked with shades of red and pink. As I put my glass down, I realised I hadn't spoken to anyone about Paul since everything had fallen apart. Gran hadn't liked him. She didn't say so, but I knew. I'd wanted so much for them to get on well. There was a time when I thought she was jealous. Angry, even, that I had left her alone. Stupid, stupid me. She'd never have held me back from the right person. A sudden rush of loss brought the threat of tears. I closed my eyes and felt Daniel's hand on mine. His touch was gentle and fleeting.

I opened my eyes and wiped away a tear. 'I'm not crying over Paul Gibson. He's no one. Just a waste of precious time I should have spent with Gran. I keep thinking I'm coping with her death, and then suddenly I'm floored.'

He nodded. 'That's how it goes with grief.'

The waitress brought our food. I waited until she'd gone. 'I try not to have regrets, but where he's concerned, I fail miserably.'

Afterwards, I would wonder why I told this stranger all about it. Maybe it was easier that way. I hadn't told Gran or my friends the whole sordid tale of how I'd fallen for a work colleague's partner, watched in guilty silence while she almost had a breakdown over him and his secret new girlfriend, moved in with him far too soon, realised it was a huge mistake, and got my comeuppance before I even had the satisfaction of telling him it was over.

'I didn't set out to steal him,' I said. 'I can't deny I liked him from the first time we met. He was attractive, funny, interesting. I envied my colleague, Stacey. To be honest, the way she spoke about him sometimes, she didn't sound that happy. Still, I didn't have any plans to hook up with him. That was all down to him. Everywhere I turned, he was there. At the gym, walking home after work, having a walk at the canal. He even turned up twice at the end of the workday, saying he was meeting Stacey, when he must have known she had a day off. Suggested we go for a drink. Said he'd texted her, and she'd meet us in the pub. Then he said he'd got a text and she couldn't come. Seemed feasible to me.

'And all the compliments and the flirting, sharing his work problems, telling me about his father's death when he was fifteen, and how it had affected him. I didn't think I was naïve, but he was such a player. He had me reeled in before I knew what was going on.' I took a long gulp of my wine. 'When Stacey and her cronies found out, the shit really hit the fan. I was the talk of the steamie.'

Daniel had been quiet while I spoke. Now he shook his head. 'The what?'

I smiled. 'Steamies were public washhouses in the fifties and sixties, where the women met to do their washing. You can imagine the gossip. Only, at my work, it wasn't just the women. There were a couple of guys who excelled at bitchery. I didn't think it could get any worse until we moved in together.' I shook my head. 'I won't even go there, but it wasn't fun.' I shrugged. 'Nothing I didn't deserve, though.'

Daniel frowned. 'Were you and Stacey friends?'

I shook my head. 'We got on okay, but we had little in common.'

'And he had been living with her?'

I nodded. 'A couple of years.'

'I don't think you should beat yourself up so much. Sounds like he was the cheat, not you.'

I shrugged. 'Suppose, but it's not right, is it? Not when you know someone is spoken for. It was great between us at first. Paul was spontaneous. Surprise weekend breaks. Midnight fishing and hiking trips. Me thinking we were going for a walk along the canal, but it turned out he'd hired a pleasure cruiser for the day. He hadn't a clue what he was doing, but it was great fun. One Sunday morning, I had period pains, and I snapped at him to leave me alone. He drove to Perthshire to get me truffles from the Highland Chocolatier.'

Daniel smiled. 'Who wouldn't fall for all that?'

'I suppose, but I should have seen through it. The signs were there. Just took me a while to notice that he was weak and needy, a malcontent. Nothing was ever right with his work, his friends, his family. I realised the impulsive behaviour was a distraction because he didn't know how to be still. It was as if he was scared of stopping, in case he was confronted by his real self.'

'A profound observation.'

I laughed. 'Missed my vocation in life. Before long, everything he did annoyed me. It was gnawing at me day and night. The sickening realisation that I'd made a terrible mistake. And there was no one I could talk to about it. Gran didn't like him. She thought we'd moved in together too soon. I didn't want to prove her right. So, I just buried it for a while. Then, before I even had the satisfaction of telling him it was over, he left me, to go back to her. Oh, the celebrations at work. You'd think she'd won the lottery. I couldn't stay.'

'I'm sorry, Kate.'

'That's not the worst of it. I let him talk me into getting a credit card for him. Couldn't get one himself. Said it was just a misunderstanding. He left me in serious debt, on top of rent I couldn't afford, and monthly payments for all the furniture we'd bought.'

Daniel shook his head. 'What a creep.'

'The good news is, he looks like a wreck now, and it seems she's chucked him out.'

He smiled. 'Dessert?'

I shook my head. 'Couldn't take another thing, thanks.'

When the waitress brought the bill, Daniel grabbed it before I could reach it. I frowned. 'Let's go halfers.'

He shook his head. 'You can get it next time.'

'When? Next year?'

'Next year.'

20

OVERHANG, KATE?
> *Aye*
> *Bad?*
> *7ish. You?*
> *8. We drink more when we leave you*
> *Puking?*
> *Maybes soon*
> *Is Mrs S about?*
> *No. I go sleep in linen cupboard. What you do?*
> *Clearing out Gran's flat*
> *No! I help*
> *There's lots to do – you can help when you're free*
> *Ok. Be careful. No heavy stuff. This man will do it*
> *Thank you* ☺

I didn't tell Stefan I'd found another man, and I wasn't feeling too happy about it. I'd barely slept. A combination of the impending gloom that always came with my hangovers, and annoyance with myself. I didn't usually approach strange men, go for a meal with them, tell them all about my disastrous love life, and then arrange to meet up the next day to clear my grandmother's flat. Leaving aside the fact that Daniel from Stevenage could be a rapist or a mad axe murderer, I wasn't sure I wanted anyone there, not even Stefan. It was going to feel as if I was wiping away Mum, Gran,

78

Granda, and all the memories. But I had a rented flat full of my own furniture, and it had to go somewhere.

I hadn't been looking for his help when I'd told Daniel what I was going to be doing the next day. Turned out he wasn't leaving until the sleeper train in the evening. He offered to hire a van to take stuff to the dump and the charity shop. What a score. I couldn't drive, and he seemed keen. In my befuddled gin and wine-soaked cloud, I could think of no good reason to turn him down.

I forced myself out of bed. Couldn't stomach anything but a glass of water. Showering was the last thing I felt like doing, but if Daniel and I were going to be getting up close and personal, whatever his intentions, I didn't want to smell bad.

He was in the van outside Gran's flat when I arrived. He got out, bearing two Costa coffees and a couple of bacon rolls. I could definitely go a coffee now. Not so much a bacon roll. I wouldn't take anything from him, though, until he told me how much I owed him for the van.

'Kate, you don't have to.'

'I do. No argument. You paid for the meal last night. You're not paying for this.'

'It wasn't much.'

'How much?'

He sighed and told me. It wasn't that much. Not for a woman of my means. I took the coffee and let him have both rolls.

***

HOW MY GRANDPARENTS ever got the teak sideboard into the flat was a mystery. There was no way it was going out in one piece. No matter which way we turned it, a leg would foil us, jamming against the banister or the doorway or the skirting board.

'I have an idea.' I squeezed round the sideboard and went down the stairs. In the shed that still smelled of Granda, twenty-one years after his death, I found a saw.

Daniel took a little persuading. Was I sure I didn't want to keep it? I was certain. I'd had a pang at the start, and then I'd felt as if Gran was prodding at me to get going, get rid of all the old-fashioned, beat-up furniture, and make the place my own. I handed the saw up to him and he set to. Legs off, it slid out like a dream. We came back in, and I noticed a scrunched piece of paper on the stairs. It must have been stuck somewhere inside the sideboard. I turned it over, and I felt my legs wobble. I sank down onto the step, smoothed it out and stared at the pencil-drawn sketch of me and Gran. We were laughing, our heads close together. It was dated January 1993. I was six then.

'Are you all right?'

I looked up and nodded. I wiped a tear from my cheek, then I passed the sketch to him. 'Me and Gran.'

The page shook in his hand. He steadied it with his other hand. He was silent for so long. At last, he looked at me. His smile seemed a little forced. 'She looks lovely.'

I nodded. 'She was.'

'Who… who drew this?'

No way was I going there, so I just shrugged. He handed the picture to me. I put it in a box of papers in the spare room, and we carried on. I'd deal with the memories later.

A couple of hours, and we had all the big furniture out. Daniel had insisted on helping me remove the living room and bedroom carpets. I'd said I could do it myself, but he wasn't having it. Just as well. It would have killed me on my own.

We rested on the bottom step of the stairs, and a shadow fell across us from the open door. I'd expected him sooner. 'Mr Sullivan. You must have been out.'

He frowned and nodded. 'I was, Kate. Quite a shock to see a van here and the door open. I thought it might be burglars.' He stared at Daniel and waited.

'This is my friend Daniel – he's helping me to move some things.'

They shook hands.

'Can't be too careful,' Sullivan said. 'There was a suspicious-looking character hanging about as I came round the corner. Staring at the property, he was. I didn't like the cut of his jib. Not one bit. Big fellow. Scruffy. Soon saw him off. I'll be keeping an eye out for him.'

'Thanks, Mr Sullivan; we can all sleep easy in our beds with you around.'

'Your grandmother… she always said that.' He shook his head. 'Miss her more than I can say.'

I swallowed. 'Me too, Mr Sullivan. Me too.'

In the van, there was a newspaper on the dashboard. *More Inverness bones: both deaths suspicious.*

'Yikes.' I glanced at Daniel. 'Two bodies? Does that not freak you out? You sleeping there and all.'

He grimaced. 'A bit. But I've been coming up for over twenty years, and I've experienced nothing untoward. It's just bones. There are lots in the cemetery, and they've never bothered me.'

I shivered. 'Presumably they weren't murdered.'

***

BACK AT THE flat, I offered to make us some lunch before we took the last of the bags to the charity shop. We were in the kitchen when the doorbell rang. It was two uniformed police officers, a young female and an older male.

'Is Dr Tarantino with you?' the male asked.

I smiled. 'No.'

The female officer spoke. 'Daniel Tarantino.'

'Tarantino? That's his surname?'

She looked a little peeved. 'That's his surname.'

'And he's a doctor?'

She nodded and stared. I shouted up the stairs. 'Dr Tarantino, police here to see you.'

21

THE WOODEN SPOON dropped to the worktop, splattering soup across the top of the cooker. Daniel rushed to the living room. His jacket was folded on the windowsill. He tugged at the zip of the inside pocket, but it wouldn't open. Maybe he'd leave the jacket, get it later. But maybe he wouldn't have time, if the police… The zip cranked open.

'Daniel?' Kate called from downstairs.

'I'm coming.'

He pulled the journal out of his pocket and looked around. The room was empty. So was Kate's grandmother's bedroom, except for the stuff they still had to take to the charity shop. He remembered all the boxes they'd piled at the side of the other bedroom when they'd lifted the carpet. They weren't for the charity shop, not yet, Kate had said. He eased the door open and lifted the flaps of the box nearest the door, just as she shouted again. The sketch she had found on the stairs was at the top. He shoved the journal underneath it.

Downstairs, Kate was looking bemused, and the police officers were looking impatient. 'Dr Tarantino, we'd like you to come into the station,' the older officer said.

Daniel smiled. 'Of course. Anything to help. Will it take long?'

The officer shrugged. 'Who knows?'

'It's just I hired a van to help Kate take things to the charity shop. We're not quite finished. I have to return it soon. And I'm catching a train home this evening…'

The officer looked at his watch. 'An hour do you for the van?'

Beside him, the female officer raised her eyebrows.

Daniel nodded.

'See you at two o'clock. Please don't be late.'

There was a burnt smell in the kitchen, and the soup was stuck to the bottom of the pan. Daniel frowned. 'Sorry, Kate. I was looking forward to that. Did you make it?'

She nodded and smiled. 'Not your fault, Dr Tarantino.'

He grimaced. 'I have thought of changing my name.'

'No way. It's well cool. What are you a doctor of?'

He felt a flush creep up his neck. 'Medicine. I'm a psychiatrist.'

***

IN THE STATION, the young female officer Daniel had seen the first time round looked disappointed. 'You weren't entirely honest with me when we spoke, were you?'

'No? I thought I was.'

'Didn't tell me of your own connection to Craig Dunain. Your time spent there.'

Daniel shrugged. 'We didn't discuss Craig Dunain. I didn't see the relevance of my past to the bones that were found. Is there a connection?'

She raised her eyebrows. 'You tell us.'

'There's nothing I can tell you.'

'Tell us about your annual visit to the area. Why do you come?'

Where to start? Daniel shrugged. 'It's hard to explain. It was a formative experience for me. Not an easy one at the end, but it had a huge influence on my life. There were a lot of positives, despite everything.'

The older cop had been silent until then. He sighed and sat up straighter. His voice was shot through with a hint of boredom. 'Does the name Mary MacLeod mean anything to you?'

There was a sick feeling in the pit of Daniel's stomach. He nodded. 'I knew Mary.'

22

WHEN THE DOORBELL rang, I thought it might be Stefan on his way home from work. I'd hoped not to see him yet. I felt uncomfortable about the previous day and Martyna. And I didn't want to have to lie to him. I should have told him about Daniel when we texted. It wasn't Stefan. It was the young female police officer that had called earlier. 'Kate Sharp?'

I nodded. Behind her, I saw a creeping shadow, followed by Ted Sullivan's head and shoulders. 'Everything all right, Kate?'

'It's fine, Mr Sullivan. Just... just something to do with my work.'

He frowned. 'You know your grandmother never liked you working there. Officer, I'd like a word with you afterwards, if I may. Want to report a suspicious fellow loitering earlier. I'm at number three.'

The officer nodded. She smiled at me. 'Can I come in?'

I brought a couple of plastic crates through from the spare room and we sat. She didn't want coffee. She got straight to the point. 'How well do you know Daniel Tarantino?'

The disapproval on her face when she heard I hardly knew him at all, that we'd met in a bar, eaten a meal together, and I'd allowed him to help empty my late grandmother's home.

'He try anything on?'

'It wasn't like that. He shook my hand when we parted outside his guest house last night.' I shrugged. 'He seems like a decent guy.'

'Did he say anything about the bones that were found at Dunain Woods?'

I nodded. 'Told me he was camping, which he does every year. Something about a dog and a bone. I presumed that's why you were here earlier.' I frowned. 'But how did you know where to find him?'

She ignored my question. 'Do you think he was following you before you introduced yourself?'

That was a creepy idea. 'Do you think he was?'

'Does the name Mary MacLeod mean anything to you?'

I shook my head. She looked a little shame-faced, and I knew she was going to tell me something I didn't want to hear. 'Kate, I know about your mother, about Craig Dunain and what happened to her. I'm guessing Tarantino didn't tell you he knew her?'

Shit. 'No.'

'You didn't know he was a psychiatrist?'

I shrugged. 'Didn't ask.'

'Really?'

Her supercilious disbelief got to me. 'He likes pizza, but cheese gives him heartburn. He longed for Springsteen's last album and was disappointed. He grows three different types of broccoli in his garden. Last autumn, he did a road trip from Montreal to Quebec. He kayaked with beluga whales. Next year, he hopes to walk the Pacific Crest Trail. How he earns the money to fund his lifestyle wasn't something that particularly interested me. I didn't feel the need to define him in that way.'

'Whatever.' She was looking at me as if I was the most pretentious git she'd ever met. She stood and tucked her notebook back into her pocket. 'See if you remember anything more important than his dietary intolerances or what he grows in his garden, please call us.'

At the bottom of the stairs, she turned. 'What exactly do you do for a living, Ms Sharp, if you don't mind me defining you 'in that way'?'

'I work in a care home.'

Her smile was triumphant. I nearly let her go, but I had to ask. 'Did Daniel work in Craig Dunain when my mother was there?'

She hesitated, then she nodded. 'Aye, he did.'

23

Jamie Ogilvie sang 'Born to Run' at the top of his voice for the fifth time. Belting it out, he was, ignoring the thumps and shouts from the night-shift neighbour. He had a good voice. Could have made a living from it. He wished he hadn't smashed his guitar that time, in a fit of rage at the world and everything it had thrown at him. He lurched from his chair and headed for the kitchen for another can, still singing.

He pulled the top off the can, then he slid open his balcony door and stepped outside. It was the one good thing in his life, this flat. Although the harbour could be noisy when the timber ships were unloading, he liked being close to the river, being able to take the air without fear of meeting anyone, and without the hassle of a garden. Wasn't the best area in town, but it was a fine flat.

As he watched two canoeists heading for the mouth of the river, he wondered again what Daniel Tarantino was doing in Inverness. Hopefully nothing too enjoyable right now, if the police had acted on Jamie's anonymous tip. He hadn't expected anything from his trip to the Dalneigh flat. Didn't think Kate would be there, and he certainly didn't expect to see Tarantino helping her clear it out. Finding those two together had chased away any lingering sympathy he'd had for Kate. He remembered her as a child, a little runt of a thing, hanging on her grandmother's arm, or peeping round a chair, watching him. He'd smiled at her once and she'd stuck out her tongue. Wee shite.

She didn't look any friendlier now. Arrogant, she was. And flirty, just like her mother. Gazing into Tarantino's eyes as if he was the Messiah, all signs of her grief gone.

He slid the door shut. The old dear was in the living room. He raised his can. 'How the heck are you doing?'

'I'm very well, Jamie. You?'

'Tickety-boo. You don't look so good. You've got that pinched look about you. I can smell the disapproval. Don't like me drinking, do you?'

She shrugged. 'Doesn't matter to me. It's your life. Not that you'll be around for long with your diet, and that rancid fat hanging around your middle.'

He laughed. 'Watched a documentary the other night about a man that weighed over sixty stone. Think I've got a bit to go. You'd nurse me, though, wouldn't you, old dear, if I couldn't move for the fat?'

'That'd be right.'

'You would. I know you've got a soft spot for me. Always had. You'd a soft spot for DJ Tarantino too.'

Big mistake. He wanted to smack the vicious smirk off her face before she opened her mouth. She laughed. 'Wasn't the only one, was I?' She started writhing in the chair. 'Oh DJ, you're so cool. Oh, DJ, you're so handsome. Oh, DJ, do you want to come a walk in the woods with me?'

As he watched, her face seemed to change, to morph into Ellen's. He plunged his hand down the side of the chair, scrambling for the remote control. Telly on. Music channel turned up, until she'd gone, and the neighbour's thumping was drowned out. And all the time, scratching at that thin scar on the back of his hand.

24

MARY MACLEOD HAD been one of his patients, Daniel told the officers, and she'd left Craig Dunain suddenly, not long before everything fell apart. He asked if the bones were hers, but they would tell him nothing. Just question after question about Mary, Ellen, Kate. Did he usually go around picking up young women in bars? He rarely went to bars, he told them. It was a spur-of-the-moment thing. And he hadn't made a move towards Kate. She spoke to him. Yes, he'd recognised her, and no, he hadn't told her he knew her mother, but he had hoped to do that today. He still might, if they let him go soon. Yes, he liked Kate very much, but not in that way.

The officer smirked. 'Did you like her mother in that way?'

'She was my patient.'

He laughed. 'So? We know about the investigation.'

Daniel's stomach lurched. He struggled to keep his voice steady. 'They cleared me of any impropriety.' He looked at his watch. 'Is this going to take much longer?'

The officer slammed his pen on the table. 'It'll take as long as it takes, Dr Tarantino. Maybe if you were to give us something helpful, it would hurry things along. So, no one was worried when Mary MacLeod left? No one cared enough to make a fuss about it? Why was that?'

He shrugged. 'She was a voluntary patient. Free to leave when she wished. I seem to remember she went to stay with a relative somewhere. I can't recall the details.'

'Any other patients go missing around that time?'

Daniel shook his head. 'Not that I remember.'

'Tell us about your own little episode.'

He sighed, then he told them again.

At last, half an hour before the sleeper was due to depart, they let him go. He ran from one station to the other. Though he usually slept well on the sleeper, he knew that wouldn't be the case tonight.

25

I sat on the bare floorboards in the corner of Gran's bedroom, remembering the look of shock on Daniel's face when he saw me in the pub. He hadn't been following me, I was certain. Was he shocked because I looked like my mother? He'd reacted oddly too when he saw the sketch. Presumably, he knew Mum had drawn it. I was so glad I hadn't spoken about her. Not one word. I hadn't been sure how to say goodbye to this man that I hardly knew, yet liked very much. At last, he'd leaned across from the driver's seat to hug me. It was uncomfortable, with the gear stick and our awkwardness between us. And yet, it felt reassuring. I'd have put money on him being a good guy.

My phone beeped. It was Stefan.

Kate, how you get on? No lifting big stuff remember.

I didn't answer. I stared into space and wondered just how close Daniel Tarantino and my mother had been. I considered going down to the train station and demanding answers. But maybe he wouldn't be there. Maybe he'd been detained in connection with the bones. In a fit of childish pique, I kind of hoped so, yet I doubted it. Whatever secrets Daniel Tarantino was hiding, I couldn't see him being involved in suspicious deaths. But was he the one having it off with my mother in the woods? Or had they met earlier? Was he my father?

I pushed myself to my feet. Time to go back to my own flat. I took the sketch with me. I lifted it from the box and saw a slim journal beneath it with the words *Do Not Open* written across the front cover in my mother's handwriting. Weird. I had looked in all the boxes recently. How could I have missed that?

***

BACK HOME, I made my dinner, washed up and pottered around. Anything to avoid the journal sitting on the coffee table, eyeballing me. At last, I sat and lifted it. I turned it over in my hands. I'd wanted answers for so long, but now I was scared.

It started on 1st January 1985. My mother was fifteen. She and her friend, Hazel, had sneaked a bottle of Advocaat from Hazel's parents' drinks cabinet. Mum had puked on Hazel's bed. I googled Advocaat on my phone. Eggs, sugar and brandy, with a custard-like consistency. Yugh.

In early March 1985, on Mum's sixteenth birthday, they were in Brighton for her grandmother's funeral. There were tiny sketches of both piers and the sea-front, people on deckchairs, seagulls perched on beach signs. She wrote of sharing secrets with her cousin and saying goodbye to the grandmother she wished she'd seen more of. How cool it would be if they could live in Brighton. Inverness was rubbish in comparison.

I smiled as I remembered a summer day in Brighton. Just Gran and I. We were on our holidays. We stood on the pier searching for a glimmer of France, the desolate beauty of the burned-out West Pier shimmering in the distance. Warrior seagulls pinched our chips, and there was endless pinging and jingling of fruit machines. Our whispered laughter as we lay in the twin beds of the guest house later, the same seagulls screeching outside.

30th March; just one line: *Hazel did it (JE)!*

Hazel did it again on 14th and 23rd April, 16th and 30th May. If 'it' was what I thought it was, Hazel was a bit of a goer, the initials in brackets different each time.

The next entry was 28th June 1985. The date was written in

blue ink, followed by an enormous sad face. Oddly, the writing below was in black ink, and it differed from the previous and the next entry. It was tidier, more mature. No exclamation marks, no initials, no abbreviations. The last of the words were squeezed onto the second of two pages. I guessed she'd inserted the date and the sad face in 1985 and left the pages blank. The words in black had been written later. I read the entry, and I felt my world begin to unravel.

28ᵀᴴ JUNE 1985

☹

The room is so dark. Something feels weird. I wriggle around and realise I'm wearing a nightie. I never wear a nightie. I hate the way they ride up around your waist during the night. The mattress is hard and a little lumpy. The quilt's too heavy. It's not my bed. I can smell Styx perfume. I remember Hazel spraying it behind her ears and between her breasts earlier, before offering it to me. Disgusting stuff. She'd chucked the bottle onto one of the twin beds in her room.

I struggle onto my side. That's where I am. Hazel's room, in the spare bed. Her parents are away on holiday, and we'd had a party for her birthday. There's someone sitting on the other bed, watching me. Someone big. I find the switch for the lamp and flick it on. If I wasn't feeling so sick, I'd laugh. It's the giant teddy her brother won for her at the shows. It's sitting below a Bob Dylan poster. They both look dopy.

My knees are sore. I touch them and wince. They feel grazed. And my head aches, as if someone is inside, hitting me between the eyes. The light doesn't help, so I put it off.

The house is silent. Where is Hazel? And how did I get here? I try to piece the night together. I remember the sun streaming in the open window, Hazel and I putting on make-up. Bursts of laughter and the smell of burgers cooking on the barbecue outside. Blondie singing 'Sunday Girl', and me laughing 'cos it was Friday. Not that funny,

I know, but the vodka was seeping into my blood and my head and everything seemed funny and happy and light.

And then in the garden, so much laughter and dancing. Too little food and far too much vodka. Those eyes watching me. He didn't dance. Just watched and smoked, leaning against the fence. He was someone's cousin, Hazel said.

It blurs then. I remember the night getting darker and colder. Inside, in the kitchen, there was kissing. Fumbling. Nausea. Hazel laughing and pulling me away from Someone's Cousin. Dancing in the living room, but my legs weren't really working.

And then it's just black. It feels as if I've lost hours. Was he there in the lost time? Did he leave? Did I pass out? Shit. Where is Hazel? I groan and turn onto my side, my back to the door. I pull the curtains apart a little and see the start of daylight.

The door opens. I turn and it's not Hazel. It's Someone's Cousin with his piercing eyes and high cheekbones, curly black hair and drooping moustache.

He sits on the bed and peels back the quilt. His hand eases up the hem of the nightie. I shake my head. 'No.'

He shrugs and lies down beside me. He's going to do it anyway, he whispers.

Later and forever, it's my complicity that haunts me. No moving. No crying. Not another word said. Not to him, not to Hazel, when she later emerges from her parents' bedroom and whispers her goodbyes to Len Arnold. Not to anyone else. Ever.

It's the start of the unravelling. It's the losing of myself. It is the end.

I dropped the journal to the floor, all my stupid hopes and dreams disappearing. I was born exactly nine months after that June night in 1985, and my father wasn't a psychiatrist in Stevenage with a cool surname. He was something else entirely.

26

AT THEIR BRIEFING in Burnett Road police station in Inverness, the investigating team considered what they had so far on their female skeleton. The starting point was the anonymous caller suggesting the bones were those of Mary MacLeod. He had been very specific. She'd gone missing from Craig Dunain in May 1993. From the islands, she'd been a patient of Dr Daniel Tarantino, and they hadn't got on well. Something to do with rumours about his relationship with a patient, Ellen Sharp. There had been an investigation. Tarantino was involved with Ellen Sharp's daughter now. They'd find him with her at an address in Dalneigh.

They had found Tarantino with Kate Sharp. He had denied that he and Mary hadn't got on well. She was a bit of a trouble-maker, he'd said, insisting that she hadn't caused trouble for him, but she wasn't popular with the other staff or patients. Stirring, gossiping, judging, pilfering; that kind of thing. Nothing serious. Just low-level pettiness. It wasn't uncommon in The Craig, he'd said, or in any other psychiatric hospital.

The records from Craig Dunain Hospital painted a sketchy picture. A wee woman from the Isle of Lewis. No family. Admitted in 1971, at fifty, with a diagnosis of major depressive disorder. It was a local GP that had referred her. His name was recorded as her next of kin. Teeth all removed in one go in 1973. Years of treatment that eventually led to stability, with intermittent dips in her mood, usually around Christmas and other holidays, and any time discharge was suggested.

In the weeks leading up to her disappearance, she'd been unsettled. Twice, it was recorded, she'd spoken of leaving to live with a cousin in Dundee. The last record was on 23rd May 1993. Tablets given. Breakfast eaten. Mood good. Went to church. And never came back. She'd left a letter saying she'd gone to Dundee, and there had been a phone call from Mary the following day to say she'd arrived safely.

There was something odd about the two mentions of the cousin in Dundee. It looked as if they might have been added to the records later. Same handwriting as the original entries on both days, but the ink was thicker, suggesting a different pen. It looked like it was the same pen that recorded the letter left by Mary MacLeod, and the phone call. No sign of the letter now.

There had been no reason to hold Tarantino. No evidence to link him to anyone's death. Not yet. They agreed that the next step was to have the hand-writing in the records examined forensically and locate the former staff and patients; see what they had to say about Mary MacLeod.

As for the second skeleton, it was a man. Younger than the female. His teeth were intact, which would help with identification. And officers were able to lift three clear finger marks from a large silver St Christopher pendant with a broken chain, found in the grave.

27

JAMIE OGILVIE'S DAYS spent sitting in his armchair in his boxers seemed like a lifetime ago. He was busy now. On a mission. He even went to the Battle of the Bands. Stood close to the bar and watched the young ones making arses of themselves. The state of them. Girls wearing little more than underwear. Boys out of their heads. A couple of scuffles broke out close to where he was standing. Was that what passed for a fight these days? He'd watched two lads square up to each other, throw a few punches that landed nowhere, and he'd taken a laughing fit. The music was great. Fair cheered him up.

The old dear didn't like him going out. No, indeed. Said he was far too old for that nonsense. He'd be a laughing stock. But he wasn't. There were older ones there. Not as old as the old dear, right enough, but older than him.

There was one person he'd hoped might be there, but no luck. No sign of her at the grandmother's flat either, not since the day he'd seen her with Tarantino. Still, he kept watch. The flat hadn't been emptied or put up for sale, so he was certain she'd be back. The old man in the flat below had spotted him. Eyes of a hawk, and a tongue like a razor. Marched up to him and demanded to know why he was hanging about. Though Jamie's hands shook with rage, he hadn't answered. He'd just shrugged and walked away.

He bought a high-vis waistcoat and a clipboard. He found a shop in town that sold wigs. It was a pop-up shop, according to the assistant. A what? A short-term sales space, didn't he know? The in-thing. Taking over the retail world; rethinking traditional shop spaces. High flexibility; low investment. How he'd laughed.

The old dear had laughed too when she saw him in the retro wig. Told him he looked like a paedo. At least he hadn't bought the 'tache to go with it, he'd said. He didn't tell her about the grey comb-over. It was more expensive, better quality. He put it on in Tesco's toilet.

There wasn't a lot of excitement to be had in staking out a flat in Dalneigh, but it gave him a purpose. It was dry today, so he wandered up and down the road, doodling on his clipboard. There was a clearing with a few sheds opposite the block of flats, and another to the side. Handy to hide there when the neighbour appeared.

He knew by now that the neighbour went out every weekday morning at ten o'clock on the dot. Returned at lunchtime three days out of five. The other two days, it was late afternoon before he got home.

One of these days, she'd come back. He'd find an excuse to speak to her, get to know her. He'd tell her… tell her everything. And maybe she'd be able to help him out with that missing item.

There was a shop on the corner. Just the thing when he got the urge for a packet of crisps or a can of Coke. Not so handy if you were trying to avoid the news headlines, though. But what could he do? Another body, the billboard said. Both deaths suspicious.

Outside, he leaned against a fence and tried to keep his thoughts from spinning into darkness. Maybe best to forget his stupid idea of getting to know Kate. Forget that thing he wanted from her. Go home and drink himself into oblivion.

He looked up and cursed as he saw the door of the flat closing.

28

IT WAS SO strange to climb the stairs in Gran's flat, knowing she wasn't there. I could count on one hand the number of times that had happened in my life. She was always there, always waiting, kettle on, smiling. Even when I crept in after a drunken night out, she'd call from her room, ask me if I'd had a good time. Now, it didn't even feel like her flat. I hadn't been round for a few days, not since Daniel and the finding of the journal. I'd only come today because a joiner was laying laminate flooring. The place smelled musty, and my spirits plummeted. I hadn't thought it was possible to feel any worse. Did I really want to move in? Not that I had much choice. My landlord had already let my flat to an eager young couple. They'd been round to measure up for curtains and blinds. I hoped they'd have more romantic luck there than I'd had.

I'd brought the journal back with me. For such a wee book, the weight of its contents was a constant threat to my sanity. I shoved it back into the box in the spare room, wondering if I would ever dare read another word. All those years of wanting to know who my father was. All the imagining. Never imagined an answer like that.

I opened all the windows and gave myself a talking-to. This place was home. It always had been. It'd be different when the new flooring was laid, and I'd moved in my own things. I'd hired a man with a van for the move and chosen the one-man option. He'd been round and given me a quote. There had been no doubt in my mind at the time that Stefan would help, but that was before I'd met Devil Woman. What if he brought her along? The last thing I wanted was her knowing where I lived. I hadn't seen Stefan since the night in the Gellions. We'd had consecutive days off, so we hadn't worked together. Today would be the first day.

While the joiner got started in the living room, I called van man from the kitchen. He said it was too late to find another man. I'd help, I told him. There was nothing too heavy. Not really.

'Don't want to be sexist, love, but you're not exactly built like Helle Trevino, are you?'

'Who?'

'Female bodybuilder.'

I rolled my eyes. 'Leave it with me.'

I noticed a splash of soup crusted on the hob. I'd missed it when I'd cleaned up after Daniel. Meeting him felt like a dream now. It had all been so surreal: the easy way between us, and the stupid hope that he was more than just a random guy I met in the Gellions. I looked at my watch. Time to head to the madhouse.

***

STEFAN HAD A black eye the size of a fist. He smiled and gave me a warm hug. 'Kate, it's so good to see you.' When he pulled away, he pointed to his eye. 'I have accident.'

'Smyth got you at last?'

He laughed. 'No, the boy. We bend over to stroke the grandmother's dog, and the boy, he lift his head back so fast and he bangs me.'

Very accident-prone, that boy.

'Listen,' he said. 'I have bad news. It's Mrs Bell. She die on Tuesday.'

In my fragile state, the news hit me hard. It always cast a gloom over the place when someone passed on. But not for long. The speed with which the room would be cleared and reallocated was a frightening reminder that this was a business and not a wee family, as it sometimes seemed.

He squeezed my arm. 'She is very peaceful at the end.' He smiled. 'I don't forget your move on Monday. That is the first day of my holidays. I don't do anything else but paint all week. We have good fun with the move.'

Fun was the last thing I expected.

***

FOLLOWING A STREAKING incident that had shocked two of the living dead out of their stupor, Lucille had taken to creeping around the care home wrapped in a purple blanket. When I spoke to her in the corridor, she didn't lift her head. Her hair was greasy and uncombed, and she smelled bad. I asked a downcast Mrs Shelby if I should try to get her to have a shower.

She shrugged. 'We've tried. It's hopeless. She didn't even recognise her husband last night. He said it's not unusual. Apparently, she ricochets between apathy and agitation, depression and mania.' She frowned. 'At least apathy is easier to handle than the earlier behaviour, but I don't think we can keep her here. She's so disruptive, and she needs specialist care. Even Tom Wright came and told me this is not the place for her. It's her third care home. She'd have to leave the area to find one that specialises in her type of case, but her husband doesn't want that.'

'Will I try?'

'Okay, but don't spend too long with her. Plenty other work to be done.'

I found Lucille curled in a corner beneath the window in the dayroom. She was singing to herself. I couldn't make out the words, but she could certainly hold a tune. She let me help her to her feet and then to her room. In the shower, I saw there was nothing to her. Like Gran, she was all parched skin and sharp bones. I remembered Mrs Shelby mentioning that chronic malnourishment was a factor in Korsakoff's.

Lucille sat huddled in a towel on the chair while I combed the tugs from her wet hair. Though I tried to be gentle, it must have hurt, but she didn't flinch or make a sound. When I said I'd get a hairdryer, she shook her head. 'Leave it.'

I chose a fuchsia dress with long sleeves. She let me slip it over her head without a word. She even let me put on her sandals, and we walked to the dayroom. It took a while on her skinny, shaky legs. It was as if she'd aged thirty years or more since her first visit to the dayroom. I sat her in a chair beside the window. The tortoiseshell cat from the neighbouring house was perched on the windowsill. Their eyes met and held, a flicker of a smile hovering on Lucille's lips.

'I better get on,' I said. 'I'll come back and see you in a while.'

Her eyes didn't leave the cat, as she whispered: 'Thank you, Princess. You're good to me. I know I wasn't always kind. I'm sorry.'

29

ONE LOOK AT the weariness etched into Kate Sharp's face, and Jamie knew he couldn't abandon his plans. When she'd left the grandmother's flat, he'd followed her. She was hurrying somewhere, and he was soon out of breath. He couldn't stop, though. She walked just like her mother. Same narrow hips and long legs. In his mind, he was back in the forest, and Ellen was walking in front of him, his hands aching to touch her.

Kate had stopped at traffic lights, and he stood behind her, so close, he could smell her shampoo. There was a book peeping out of the top of her shoulder bag, but he couldn't see the title. Damn. He'd love to know what she was reading, so he could read it too, now that he'd sorted out his eyes. She plunged her hand into her bag and brought out her phone. The book shifted and he could see part of the cover. *Potato Peel Pie Society*? Weird. Maybe he'd give that one a miss.

She rang someone called Susan. Her voice reminded him of whispered calls with Ellen. There hadn't been many, but each one was etched in his memory. She thanked Susan for coming to the funeral, then she shrugged. Just have to get over it, get on with it. There was a bit of teasing about someone called Peter. Kate couldn't wait to hear the details. And a bit of banter about Stefan. He was just a friend, honest, Kate insisted. Better go. She was on her way to work. They'd have to meet soon.

A care home? That had brought Jamie up short. He'd thought

she was maybe a social worker or a legal aid lawyer. Something self-righteous. Had to be, with that air of confidence that her mother had lacked. Of course, she could still be a social worker or a lawyer. Plenty of reasons for either to go to a care home. But he thought not. Something in the way her feet had dragged as she'd approached the entrance. A slight resignation and unwillingness that suggested a job she disliked. She was almost at the door when someone had shouted her name.

It was a tall man in his early thirties, and Jamie thought he'd seen him at the graveside. The man bounded towards her, grabbed her and held her just a little too long. Cheered her up a bit. Their loud chattering faded as the door swung closed.

At home, Jamie asked the old dear if she remembered the wee one. Her face lit up with a rare smile. She nodded. 'Aye, I do. Poor wee mite, clinging to her grandmother's hand.'

'She's gone, the grandmother.'

The old dear nodded. 'She'll be all on her own now.'

He thought about that when the old dear had gone. She'd need friends now, Kate. Someone to tell her about her mother, tell her the truth. He wondered what Tarantino had filled her head with. He'd soon put her right.

30

DANIEL WAS EXHAUSTED after two lengthy mental health tribunals. The first patient whispered in his ear throughout the hearing, pleading with him to stop inserting thoughts into her head, words into her mouth. It was his fault she kept saying stupid things, apparently. If he'd only stop it, they wouldn't lock her up again. He wished it was that easy to manipulate his patients. He didn't go back for their decision on her detention. He had other patients to see, and he'd certainly be seeing her again very soon.

A jumped-up solicitor who thought he was Rumpole of the Bailey represented the patient at the second tribunal. The patients deserved a robust challenge to the threat of detention, and a bit of cross-examination kept the professionals on their toes. But two hours of it? The specialist member fell asleep at one point. He woke with a start when the patient erupted and shouted at his solicitor to shut the fuck up. Perhaps the patient was saner than Daniel had realised.

He left work early, tired and hungry. At home, he ate in the conservatory, overlooking his enclosed garden. It was a while before he realised he was being watched. He smiled at the little sparrow heads that peeped out of gaps in the hedge. It had been an early start, and he'd forgotten to feed them. Their intense stares made him rush the last of his chilli.

When he'd filled up the feeders and put seed on the bird table, he started weeding the flower beds. About time. He hadn't done any gardening since he got home. Had done little but work and think of Kate. In his head, he had composed letters to her, but none of them made it to paper. He just didn't know how or where to begin his explanation and his apology. And he didn't know what to apologise more for – his recent deceit or his historical failures. Did she know now about his involvement with her mother? She'd hate him for saying nothing. He wondered if she'd found the journal. It was a cowardly thing to do to leave it in a box like that, but he'd feared the police would take it. Not that there was anything to incriminate him or anyone else in it. He just didn't want it in their hands. It was too precious. And Ellen had told him she wanted Kate to know the truth about her father when she was older. Harsh way to let her know, but maybe it was for the best.

He kept going back to that moment in the Gellions when their eyes had met. He could have, should have, left. Even after she'd come across and spoken, he could have made his excuses and left. He didn't have to ask her to go for a meal, offer to help her the next day.

Oh, but he did. From that first look, he could have done nothing else. It was like meeting the Ellen he'd hoped to resurrect all those years ago. Sorted, confident, feisty; the girl Ellen might have been, if not for Someone's Cousin.

The trowel abandoned, he went inside. He wandered for a bit, picked up a book, put it down. Switched the telly on, then off. He surfed the internet. And then he went to the drawer of the bureau and took out a small card and envelope.

31

THE FLOWERS WERE stunning. Lisianthus, alstroemeria, freesias and roses, in muted shades of lilac, purple and pink. All my favourites. How could Stefan know? And why give them to me now, in the old place, and not later, when we'd moved everything into Gran's flat? He was smiling, the enormous bouquet in his hands. I was so glad he spoke before I thanked him and made a fool of myself.

'Someone likes you, Kate.'

I hardly needed to look at the card then to know who the flowers were from.

Kate. I'm so sorry. I've been a fool. I love you. Please have me back. Paul xxx

I considered texting him to say okay, and why didn't he move all his stuff back in tomorrow evening, but it seemed a little unfair on the new tenants. I filled the wee middle sink with water and shoved the flowers in.

I wasn't having much fun with the move. Though van man and Stefan did all the heavy lifting, I had been up and down the stairs a thousand times with boxes and plants and stuff. Why did I have so many books? It was ridiculous, but I couldn't bear to part with them. There was something about a new book. All those pages full of promise. I always read a good book at least twice, but even the bad ones captivated me. Maybe if I tried again, I'd find something I'd missed.

It didn't help to know we'd have to do it all again at the other end, twice. When we arrived at Gran's with the first load, I jumped out of the van, went to open the door, and realised I'd forgotten the key.

'It's fine,' I told Stefan. 'There's a spare buried in the garden. Been there for at least twenty years. You keep him occupied, so he doesn't see where it is.'

Stefan nodded. 'He has a shitty look.'

'Shitty?'

'This is what you say when you don't have trust for someone?'

I laughed. 'Shifty. Aye, he does a bit.'

Back to the old place for a second load. While Stefan and van man did the heavy stuff, I did the last of the cleaning. I was thinking of Mum and the journal, wishing there was someone I could talk to about her. I considered Meg, Gran's friend. She'd known Mum all her life, but she was such a gentle soul. Too gentle for the questions I wanted to ask. The skirting boards done, I pulled out the drawer by the sink to check I hadn't left anything. Just the phone book. I remembered Gran's words.

Liz Barclay told me. She was a nurse there. Met her in Beauly one day.

I flicked through the phonebook until I found the 'B's. There was an E. Barclay in Beauly. I keyed the number into my phone. I wasn't sure I'd ever do anything about it.

When we were leaving, Stefan told me not to forget the flowers.

'I'm leaving them for the new owners.'

He looked at me as if I was quite mad.

***

I CAME BACK from paying van man, and Stefan was standing in the middle of Gran's living room, frowning. 'Kate? How you clear this place? Where everything has gone?'

I swithered again, on the brink of telling him a host of lies. But I couldn't. I asked him to sit. He looked worried.

'Remember Daniel from the Gellions?'

the internet, though he was paying for it as part of his package. Maybe time for a trip to the phone shop. That he could consider such a thing without his heart bouncing him out the door made him smile. And what do you know? When he looked up, the wee tart thought he was smiling at her.

Despite his disdain, her eyes stirred something deep inside, fascinating and terrifying him. Those kinds of urges were long gone, weren't they? She was around the age his own daughter would be now. It was obscene. And it was delicious.

Beyond Kate, he saw the dark-haired woman stumble from her stool and lurch towards the toilets. His eyes followed her, and so did Kate's. Her smile gone, she put the empty wine bottle on the bar and headed back towards her companion. He frowned at her words. They both looked towards the toilets, then they grabbed their jackets and headed for the door.

When the dark-haired woman emerged from the toilets, Jamie was waiting, ready to buy her another drink. Ready to offer a listening ear. Ready to find out what exactly was going on.

His frown deepened. 'I never forget Daniel.' A tinge of crimson rose up from his neck. 'Martyna... she... I was shamed.' He shook his head and tried to smile. 'What about this Daniel? He help you? You good friends now? He send you the flowers?'

'Yes, he helped me. We're not friends. And the flowers were from my ex.'

'Oh. He don't want to be your ex now?'

'Looks like it, but I still want him to be my ex.'

'So, Daniel – you don't like him? I think he was good man. I know this. He wasn't shifty.'

I nodded. 'He seemed nice.' It was my turn to blush. 'But it wasn't like that. I didn't... nothing happened.'

An awkward silence hung between us. At last, Stefan broke it. 'He's a bit too old?'

I laughed. 'A bit.'

'You can still be friends. Like us.'

'I don't think so.' I told him about the bones and the police, and that Daniel had been a doctor at Craig Dunain when my mother was there, and he hadn't told me. Stefan frowned. 'What you think he's up to?'

I shrugged. 'Dunno. If I had a phone number, I'd call and ask him. I suppose I could find his work number online, but I don't know if there's any point.'

Stefan nodded. 'Is difficult.' He squeezed my hand. 'We move things. We set up TV. Then we eat and drink.'

It looked good when everything was in place. When we were ready to go, I opened the little tin mint box with the rusted lid, and put the spare key back. I remembered how Granda always had mints in his pocket. Outside, I buried it in the loose stones by the drainpipe. I wondered if my mother ever had to dig it up after a drunken night out. I'd had to do it at least twice as a youngster, and once after a night out with Paul.

The evening sun was shining. 'No Gellions,' Stefan said. 'We go somewhere else today.'

32

Jamie Ogilvie hadn't been along the canal in years. Not since the kids were wee. The girl was still in the pushchair then, the boy kicking a ball along the path. A pang squeezed his guts. They should have been good days, but he was too busy shouting at the boy for getting close to the water and cursing the girl for falling asleep too late in the day. And all the while, thinking only of Ellen.

Now, in the early evening sun, he followed Ellen's daughter along the canal path. She was doing a lot of laughing. Flirt. And the guy was lapping it up. It was the one from the care home. There was no touching, but anyone could tell they had the hots for each other. He was foreign. Eastern European, by the sound of it. A little closer and he could see the guy's left hand swinging by his side. Yes. There was a ring. He didn't know whether to be happy or sad that Kate had inherited so much from her mother. Tart.

He'd got lucky this afternoon. He'd stayed on the main road that intersected with Kate's street, leaning against a fence, studying a newspaper. It wasn't a local paper. Last thing he wanted was more news of the Dunain Woods bones. Another van had come. This time, they were putting stuff into the flat. Was she going to live there, or was she getting it ready to let out? Nice furniture. Tasteful. Not stuff you'd leave for tenants. Time would tell.

The evening sun was warm. There was a gap in the bushes by the side of the towpath. Kate stopped and looked to her left, to the cemetery where she'd just buried her grandmother. She said

something and the guy put his arm round her. She leaned her head on his shoulder for a moment.

On the other side of the canal, there was laughter from some children watching their two dogs swimming. Jamie didn't mean to let his eyes stray beyond them, upwards and over the tops of the trees, but he couldn't stop himself. In the distance, The Craig was grey against the green of the surrounding trees, its edges hazy, almost shimmering, as if it wasn't real. A ghost of a hospital that held all his secrets. If it could talk… He tore his gaze away. No time for that nonsense. Kate and her man had moved on, and he had a job to do.

At Tomnahurich Bridge, they turned to the right, cross the bridge, and into the driveway of the Beefeater. Jamie loo around, then he pulled off his wig and stuck it in his jacket po

***

God, she was a tart. Feeding him her chips. Giving him as they linked arms to drink a shot. Another one, and said something loud in his own language. She gazed eyes locked, and Jamie held his breath, waiting for to make a move. They didn't. Just laughed, and sh another glass of wine.

From where they were sitting, neither could se Jamie could. He saw the tall, dark-haired wor before she crossed to the bar and ordered he careful where she sat. Not in their line of sig could watch them in the mirror that ran alc She had an Eastern European accent, a we raging. Who knew this subterfuge malark

He watched Kate pick up the wine be empty. Her companion nodded, ar the bar. Jamie made a play of fiddl Hadn't a clue what he was doing.

33

THERE WAS A magic tree below the canal path, with low sprawling limbs stretching and tangling this way and that. It was magic for many reasons. As children, my friends and I spent hours clambering over it. We fell off hundreds of times without ever hurting ourselves. We'd drape blankets over its branches, making dens and tents. One day it would be a pirates' ship, the next a haunted house. As a teenager, on separate occasions, I had my first kiss, my first drink, and my first cigarette, sitting on it. I repeated the kissing and drinking from time to time. Not the cigarette. One of my classmates claimed its magic had got her pregnant at fifteen. She thought she'd only had a drunken fumble under its branches until a doctor told her otherwise.

Any other time, I'd have told Stefan he was sitting with his back against the mast of *Queen Anne's Revenge*, the slave ship seized by the notorious Blackbeard. I'd have told him all the stories, and he'd have loved it. Not tonight. He'd been silent all the way along the path, turning every so often to look behind. It seemed like a lifetime ago that we'd laughed and joked our way towards the pub.

When he spoke, his voice was hushed. 'Kate, what do I do?'

'What do you mean?'

'I tell her I'm helping Adrian put up a fence. She is not happy since the Gellions. She will… she will…'

And then I knew. His injuries. It wasn't the boy. I remembered other cuts and scratches and bruises, blamed on the boy or the grandmother's cat or a DIY disaster. I once lent him a Tracy Chapman CD, and he returned a brand new one. Said he'd sat on mine. More likely ground under Martyna's cloven hoof.

Back at the flat, I opened a bottle of wine. Stefan sat on the sofa and I sat on an armchair. There was no music, and an awkward silence between us. It was a first. At last, Stefan put his glass on the small table that sat between us. 'Kate... I have not been good to Martyna. I have... I have never love her.'

My heart somersaulted. It shouldn't be a surprise. They didn't fit. They couldn't. But they were married. He must have had feelings for her at one time, surely. What did this mean? I spoke without thinking. 'Your head, the black eye – it wasn't your son. It was Martyna.'

He sank back into the sofa, eyes wide, a flush creeping up his face. 'Kate, I never never hit her.' He picked up his glass and his hand was shaking. 'She is... different and difficult. She is... I think she is not well. Always money, money, money. And now Kate, Kate, Kate. This is all she talks about.' He looked at his watch, then he drained the glass. 'I should go.'

I didn't want him to go back to that monster. 'Is there anyone you can stay with?'

He shrugged. 'There are many friends from home, but everyone, they know everyone, and soon they will even know in Poland.'

I nodded. 'Sounds like Inverness. You're very welcome to sleep on my sofa.'

'What?' His eyes widened in mock astonishment. 'Your so lovely purple sofa? I think you don't even like people to sit on it.'

I laughed. He was right, but I'd make an exception for him.

'Thank you.' He shook his head. 'But I must go home.'

'At least help me finish this.' I poured the last of the wine into our glasses.

He tried to smile as he changed the subject. 'You decide about studying?'

I shook my head. 'I hate decisions.'

114

He nodded. 'I never decide anything. I just let Martyna do it.'

'How long have you been married?'

It seemed such an innocuous question, but it made his hand lurch. The wine almost sloshed out of the glass and over my sofa. Almost, thank God. He put the glass down on the table.

'Stefan…'

He looked up at me, his face distraught. 'We are not married, Kate. And the boy, he is not mine. I only ever marry my Anya.'

***

STEFAN'S HEART-RENDING STORY was interspersed with bits of Polish as he tried to sort it into something coherent for me. He and Anya had been childhood friends and teenage sweethearts. His hand shaking, he showed me her picture on his phone. She had short curly blonde hair and a beautiful smile. She was the one I'd imagined. They fitted together.

They'd married young and planned to travel. Anya chose Inverness. She was a nurse, and she hoped to improve her English and sit exams so she could nurse here. Four months before they planned to leave, she fell pregnant. It didn't change their plans. And then she found a lump on her breast. At eight weeks pregnant, she was diagnosed with breast cancer.

Stefan stared into the distance for so long, it seemed he'd forgotten I was there. I didn't move. I didn't say anything.

'They say get rid of it, our baby.' His voice was brittle. 'Have treatment, make this cancer thing small, so they can cut it out. But, Kate, she won't do it.'

I brushed tears from my cheeks.

'I try to tell her, please, please, do what they say. And I think she hates me then because I want to kill our baby. She show me on her phone what it is like. Just a little spot, but it is growing every day.' He shrugged. 'She can't do it. She won't. She only lives for three more months.'

I wanted to cry. I wanted to hold him. But already, he was talking of Martyna. He continued to stare into space, but there was no emotion in his voice now, just determination. Martyna was Anya's cousin. A single parent, she was good to him. They grew close. He liked her son and her mother. They were a good family.

'I knew, Kate, that I still have to go away. Inverness sounds like a good place for me. Martyna wants so much to come with me. Her and her boy and her mother. Without ever stopping, she goes on and on and on.' He shrugged. 'I'm still sad and scared I will be lonely, so I say yes to everything, even that we say we are married, for she tell me that will make life more easy here. Kate, I am weak and stupid man. I was not good to her. She is angry with me now. She knows I don't feel this way about her. I have made her a bad person. She was good person before.' He stood. 'I must go.'

At the bottom of the stairs, he took my hands. 'Kate, you are the best friend to me ever. You make me so glad I have come to Inverness. I wish… I wish…'

I wished too, and it didn't involve him sleeping on my sofa. Over his left shoulder, I could see our reflection in the mirror. We fitted.

He smiled a sad smile. 'I must make things right with Martyna.'

I doused the flickering sparks of hope, and I nodded.

'I see you at work next week, Kate. You take care.'

34

WHAT A NIGHT! Jamie hadn't known he still had it in him. Three times, they did it. Three times? Of course, fantasising about the devil incarnate herself, wee Kate Sharp, had helped. He'd almost shouted her name at one point. Thank feck he'd had the wherewithal to bite his tongue until it bled. Phew. Martyna would have killed him if she'd known what he was thinking. Almost killed him anyway.

She was a strange one. Spilled as soon as he'd bought her a drink. Told him all about her cheating husband and his mistress. Kept calling Kate something that sounded like '*djivka*'. It wasn't a compliment, whatever it meant. As the drinks went down, her temper grew. Between rants, she'd stared at her phone, tapping and scrolling and sighing. Jamie had got bored. Said he was leaving. Told her to look after herself. She had almost a full pint, and she gulped it back in one go.

'I come with you. I show Stefan.'

Show Stefan? She'd certainly shown Jamie. And now he was firmly back in the saddle.

Turned out she and her man lived down the Ferry, not that far from Jamie. She'd sloped off before dawn. Just as well, really. There was no way he'd have risen to the occasion again in the morning. His body felt like a wrung-out dishcloth. And yet, when he remembered the earlier part of the evening, the walk along the canal, watching Kate's hips and hearing her laughter, he wondered if maybe…

'Pervert.'

Aw, naw. He pulled the cover over his head.

The old dear pulled it off. 'Think I couldn't hear you and her at it half the night? Tart. Where did you pick her up?'

'None of your business.'

'You're revolting.'

'Fuck off, why don't you?'

She did.

35

OUT IN THE corridor, I heard Tom Wright tell Mrs Shelby she was the most beautiful woman he'd ever seen, and if it wasn't for his dear wife, he'd ask for her hand. Mrs Shelby didn't break it to him that his dear wife had died ten years ago. 'She's a lucky woman, your Catherine. Now, let's get you back to your room for your afternoon nap.'

'Oh, Mrs Shelby, you're a one. Any excuse to get into my room. Best leave me at the doorway, so we don't get overwhelmed and act in an unseemly manner.'

She laughed. 'Aye, that would probably be for the best.'

Though it would have been fun if Stefan was with me in the laundry room, listening and laughing, I was glad he was on holiday. My head was all over the place. Whenever I thought of Martyna abusing him, I wanted to beat her up. That would be right. She could annihilate me with one withering look. I couldn't help blaming myself for their troubles. If I'd kept my distance, maybe things would be fine between them. I was a fool. Only yesterday, when van man left us, I'd entertained a fantasy of how it would feel if Stefan and I were moving in together. At the pub, I'd flirted shamelessly. If Martyna hadn't appeared, who knew what might have happened? But I knew. Stefan wouldn't have done anything. He was no Paul Gibson. He was good. Far too good for me. It was of minor consolation to me that my choice in attached men had improved.

Though I hadn't admitted it straight away, I was smitten from day one, and it wasn't just Stefan's looks. When I started at the care home, I was in shock, grieving after Gran's diagnosis, fragile and scunnered after my fall from grace. I didn't want the job. I didn't want to work at all. I just wanted to curl up and cry. I don't know if Stefan saw or felt my wounds. I certainly didn't speak of them. Knowingly or not, his friendship gave me the nourishment I needed. He was never pushy. Just warm and kind and good fun. So easy to be with. He was clever. He'd been a civil servant in Poland, in human resources, but he never acted as if the job in the care home was beneath him. And he was strong enough not to let the bigots get him down. Someone hassled him in Spoons on a work night out, accusing him and his pals of taking jobs from locals. While I fumed in the corner, he bought the man a drink, and sat down with him. It probably didn't change the head-dick's opinion, but they parted on good terms. He'd seen heart-breaking racism at home, he told me, fuelled by Poland's ruling right-wing party, and things were only going to get worse. Inverness was a breeze.

It was after I told him of Gran's illness that we started spending more time together just the two of us. I realised now why he was so understanding, though his experience of the devastation caused by cancer had been much worse than mine. Typical of him, he hadn't felt the need to talk about his experience, as so many others did. He hadn't even told me about his own grandmother. He was just there, listening, whenever I needed him. I wondered if that would still be the case.

On my way to the office to give Mrs Shelby a note of the laundry supplies we needed, I passed Lucille and her husband in the corridor. I'd only seen a glimpse of her earlier, watching television in the dayroom, and she'd looked okay. I smiled at them both. Mick smiled and nodded his head. Lucille erupted.

'What the fuck are you looking at her for?' She whacked him over the head, then she lunged at me. I backed away until I was against the wall. Her face was right in mine, her breath hot and foul. 'Bitch. Don't think you can attack me again. Bang my head off the floor. You're mental.'

Mick's eyes were wide as he pulled her by the arm. All the way down the corridor, she kept turning back and muttering.

My news wiped the smile off Mrs Shelby's face. She seemed to age in front of my eyes. What would the press say? The Care Inspectorate? The police? It was disastrous, a catastrophe. It was the end.

'I didn't hit her.'

'I know you didn't.' She sounded impatient. 'But that isn't going to stop the circus. I knew the minute I saw her she'd be trouble. And now, I'll only make things worse if I tell her husband she can't stay. I think it best if you just go home now. Take tomorrow off. You'll be paid. I'll try to smooth things over. I'll phone you tomorrow and let you know if it's safe to come back.'

I should have been pleased to get away early and have an extra day off, but, as I stood outside the door, I felt like a leper, banished on the word of a nutcase. I wanted to go back in and stake my claim to my job. A movement below the lush red fountain of hydrangea blooms by the door distracted me. The neighbour's cat was stretched on her side, spine contorted into a bow, claws splayed, mouth wide. She rolled onto her back, twisting this way and that in the soil, then she lay still and looked up at me. The stripy softness of her underbelly was tempting, but I'd been caught out before by her soft purring and her sharp teeth. She wouldn't trick me again. She and Lucille were two of a kind.

I took out my phone and called the nurse from The Craig. She answered almost immediately. 'Hello.'

Oh, feck. 'Hello. Is that Liz Barclay?'

'Yes, dear.'

'Did you... did you used to work at Craig Dunain?'

'I did.'

'My name is... it's Linda Morrison.' Why did I say that? 'I...

I'm doing a project for college about The Craig. I wondered if I could come and speak to you. I could be with you by four.'

'That would be fine, dear. Have you got my address?'

***

I'D ALWAYS LIKED Beauly. We used to take a run out on a Sunday, Paul and I. It was only ten miles from Inverness, with a regular train service, plenty of good eating and drinking places, a supermarket and a fine range of small shops. I never told him I fantasised about us living there in a house of our own, our children playing in the garden and going to the village school.

There was an air of calm in the complex of tiny sheltered houses. Clean windows, and little neat gardens, grass well cut and bushes trimmed. As I knocked on the door, I had no idea what I was going to say.

Liz Barclay was small, with thinning hair and a smile that reached deep inside me, turning some of the darkness to light. 'Hello, my dear. You must be Linda.'

'Hello.' From inside, I could hear a game show jingle. It reminded me of Gran and her religious adherence to Countdown. Drove me nuts, the Countdown timer. I'd shut myself in my room, headphones on until it was done. 'Sorry, I'm interrupting your programme.'

She shrugged, that smile still beaming. 'Heap of rubbish.' She pulled the door further open and stood aside. 'Come in.'

While my eyes roamed around the room, taking in the ubiquitous glass-fronted cabinet full of ornaments and faded photographs, she made us tea. She brought it through on a tray with a plate of crackers and cheese. 'Sorry I don't have any cake. My neighbour's taking me shopping tomorrow.'

I took the tray from her and put it on a side table, then I poured us each a cup. She sat beside me on the sofa. And all the time, she smiled.

We sipped our tea in silence. She'd put the TV off as soon as I came in. At last, I heard her sigh. She put her cup and saucer on the wee table beside her. 'Listen, dear, I know who you are.'

I almost choked on my cracker. The saucer was shaking in my hand, the cup rattling.

'Why don't you just put that down?'

I did as she asked. I swallowed the dry crumbs and turned towards her. 'I'm sorry.'

She reached up and brushed my hair back from my face. 'You're so like your mother.'

36

JAMIE WAS READY to head out for a spot of surveillance when someone knocked at his door. He didn't feel the usual rage at the numpty that had left the downstairs door open. He didn't even check the peep hole before opening the door. How times had changed. It was Martyna. He'd have taken her in, but he could hear the old dear muttering in the background. He grabbed his jacket from the peg. 'Just leaving for town. Come on, you can walk me down the road.'

Martyna rolled her eyes and sighed. Narky bitch. It was little wonder her man was tempted to go elsewhere. Out in the street, she started her rant. Kate... blah... Stefan... blah... *djivka*... blah, blah, blah. He switched off and only switched back on again when she nudged him. 'You listen to me. I need help.'

No arguing with that. 'Aye?'

'I want to hurt her like she hurt me.'

Jamie stopped and turned towards her. The look on her face. Pure evil, and he'd seen enough of it to know. He held up his hands. 'Leave me out of that.'

She laughed and punched his arm. 'I joke.'

Aye, right.

'You want a drink?'

He looked at his watch. A bit early, but what the hell? 'Where's your man? You said he's on holiday this week.'

She smirked and took out her phone. Scrolled and tapped,

just as she had done the previous night. 'Hah. He tell the truth for once. He is fishing. I hope he fall in. He so very sorry today for his forgetting to tell me he met Kate for a drink last night.'

So, no mention of helping Kate with her move? Jamie was saying nothing about that. 'How do you know he's telling the truth? He could say he was anywhere.'

She laughed. 'Yes, he could, and he does. But now I know for sure.' She held up her phone. 'This does not lie.' On the screen, there was a map and a pulsing blue dot. 'I put app on his phone. I tell him he need it so he doesn't lose it. He thank me. Fool.' She tapped some more. 'Hah, now I get alarm when he leave.'

'So that's how you knew where he was last night?'

She nodded. 'And every night now.' She took Jamie's arm. 'Come, I am thirsty.'

***

JAMIE DIDN'T WANT to hurt Kate. All right, he'd taken a bit of a dislike to her for her over-confidence and her sluttish behaviour, but what he really wanted was to get to know her, and find out if she had what he was after. She intrigued him and reminded him. She did other things to him too, but he didn't want to think of that. It wasn't right. Not while he was sober, anyway. A few drinks, and he suspected he might be persuaded otherwise. But not to hurt her.

Alcohol had removed Martyna's inhibitions too. Between graphic descriptions of what she wanted to do to Kate, she'd grip Jamie's leg and whisper things she'd like to do to him. Though her touch and her words were not unwelcome, it was all a little disconcerting, especially when he caught sight of them in the mirror behind the bar. What the hell did she see in a big lump like him? She might be a nutter, but she was young and attractive enough. It made no sense. Unless the old dear was right. She always said evil attracted evil. Hindley and Brady. Fred and Rose West. Could Martyna see in him what he really was?

Her phone pinged. She looked at the screen. 'He home now. Better stay there and get on with the painting. No sneaking off to someone's place in Dalneigh like yesterday. I will find out who it was. Maybe where the *djivka* lives.'

'What is that you keep calling her?'

She wrote it on a bar mat. *Dziewka*. 'It is a person that gets paid for their sex.'

'A prostitute?'

'*Prostytutka*. Oh my God, exactly.' And she was off again.

She went to the toilet and Jamie considered leaving. She was costing him a fortune. She kept going on about how much money he must have, living in that flat. He wasn't hard up, but he certainly wasn't for sharing it with her. Even her lewd promises were beginning to bore him. He hesitated too long. She was on her way back, and she had someone with her.

He was a scrawny wee thing with the face of a weasel. Restless, beady eyes stared from under the rim of a grubby baseball cap. He was chewing gum, his little pointy chin wagging up and down. Dodgy as anything. Jamie patted his back pocket. His wallet was still there. With this kind of guy, you'd be checking every couple of minutes.

'This is Victor, my neighbour.' She poked the weasel on the shoulder. 'Victor, this is Jamie. You say hello.'

Victor nodded his head. 'Hello.'

'Victor.' Jamie nodded back. 'How you doing?'

Martyna laughed. 'He can't tell you that. He only know hello.'

Just as well, really, 'cos Jamie wasn't remotely interested in how Victor was doing.

Victor muttered something in Polish.

'He ask if you will buy him a drink,' Martyna said.

Fuck's sake. 'One drink, then we go.'

Martyna nodded. 'He have vodka and Coke.'

There was much whispering and nodding of heads while Jamie waited to be served. Again, he considered leaving, but his jacket was on the seat and he couldn't face making a scene. He was paying for the drinks when a hand gripped his arse and squeezed. With a vulgar laugh, Martyna lifted her drink and Victor's from the bar.

Victor's vodka disappeared in seconds. He hung about a bit, obviously waiting to see if he'd get another. No chance.

37

THERE WAS A photograph of a young Liz Barclay in her nurse's uniform on top of the glass cabinet. Same smile. Pristine white apron, collar, cuffs and hat. She saw me looking at it and she smiled.

'Long time ago, that was. Long before I met your mother. I remember Ellen very well. You too, just a wee tot, and so inquisitive. You used to hide behind the chairs in the lounge area and the entrance corridor, watching, listening, giggling.' She sighed and stared into the distance. 'It was so tragic. She was doing well. I'm convinced she'd have managed fine at home, that she wouldn't have been back in.' She shrugged. 'What do I know? It's a terrible disease. One of the worst.'

'Did it have a name, her disease?'

Her eyes widened. 'They never told you?'

I shook my head. She hesitated.

'I won't tell anyone what you say, I promise.'

'Ach, it's not that. Though I shouldn't breach my duty of confidentiality, who's going to be bothered about that at my age and after all this time? And you are the next of kin. It's just... what good does it do to go over these things?'

'It would help me. I know so little.'

She nodded and took a deep breath. 'It was schizophrenia.'

I felt a rush of nausea. 'Is it hereditary?' Surely that must be the only reason Gran hadn't told me. Whenever I'd asked, she'd just said Mum was mentally ill. I presumed they hadn't diagnosed a particular condition. I should have demanded to know.

Liz nodded. 'There can be a genetic element. I've a feeling there was a family history, but it wasn't a close relative.' She shook her head. 'I shouldn't have told you. You're just going to worry about it, aren't you?' She squeezed my hand. 'I'm sure you're fine. You're stronger and older than she was when she first got ill. I think there would have been signs by now.'

I shrugged. 'Lack of ambition and appalling choice in men?'

She laughed. 'When The Craig first opened, they'd have locked you up for less, according to the records in the Archive Centre.'

'Could a stressful experience – a sexual assault as a teenager – have contributed to my mother's illness?'

Liz stared at me without answering, and I wondered if she knew about Someone's Cousin. 'Probably,' she said, at last.

'Will you tell me about her?'

Liz nodded. 'She was very pretty, like you. And clever. Such a talented artist. Always sketching in a notebook. She must have filled several of them. She used to spend hours in Dunain Woods, walking and sketching. Sometimes she scribbled in a journal too, but that wasn't for sharing with anyone. She was so vulnerable when she first came in. Scared and deluded. She... Ach, I don't want to speak out of turn...'

'Please do.' I was almost on the edge of the sofa. I shuffled backwards. 'Anything you can tell me would be welcome.'

'She believed your grandparents were conspiring against her to take you away.'

I shook my head. 'They wouldn't have done that.'

'They certainly seemed like good people, desperate to help her. If I remember rightly, when she got better, her relationship with them improved.'

I was glad to hear that. 'I'm amazed you remember so much about her. You must have had lots of patients over the years.'

Liz smiled. 'I did, and some I remember better than others.

Your mum and I got on well. But how did you get my name?'

I hesitated, not wanting to sour my visit. It had been lovely to hear someone speak so positively of my mother, and to get the information Gran should have given me long ago.

'Go on,' she said. 'I would understand if she'd written or said something negative about me. I didn't always get it right.'

'It was something my grandmother said. You told her, a few years after my mother died, that she had been having sex with a married staff member in Dunain Woods.'

It felt as if the temperature dropped a few degrees. Liz's face paled, and I saw a sheen of sweat on her brow. She wiped at it with a shaking, liver-spotted hand.

'There was a rumour,' she said, at last. 'An old woman… Mary someone…'

I remembered the name the policewoman had mentioned. 'Mary MacLeod?'

She nodded. 'Yes, that's right. But you couldn't trust what the patients said. Always telling tales on one another and trying to get each other into trouble. I don't know if there was any truth in it. Ellen was certainly up and down and all over the place and, like I said, she spent a lot of time in the woods, but whether she was alone, I don't know. I… I reported it after she passed. There was some kind of investigation, but I don't think they found anything. It was all very hush-hush. He left then. I don't know where he went.'

Liz was quiet for a while. When she spoke again, her voice was low. 'I was off that last day. I wish I'd been there. Maybe she wouldn't have gone to the woods. Maybe we'd have chatted and passed the time until her parents came to pick her up.' She shrugged. 'Ach, who knows? The nurses were always busy. Not much time for chatting.'

'Do you think my mum was well enough to go home?'

Liz nodded. 'Definitely. She was doing great. She was discharged once before, and then she came back in a terrible state. They said she'd thrown herself in front of a car.'

I groaned. There was a vague memory of Mum being home, and then just gone again, but no details. 'I… I didn't know that.'

'I'm sorry, dear. She wasn't hurt. She'd reduced her medication, and she was having some problems. Your grandmother thought she'd gone out to meet a man that night. Maybe it was that guy, the one Mary mentioned. Who knows?'

'And he was staff?'

She nodded. 'It wasn't something that happened often. Not like in the early days.' She shook her head. 'I could tell you stories from when I was a student that would make your hair curl. Some of the staff were dafter than the patients. But by the time your mother was in hospital, that kind of thing was very much frowned upon. If he'd been caught, it would have ended his career.'

'Was his name Daniel Tarantino?'

The indignation on Liz's face was almost comical. She gasped. 'Dr Tarantino? Absolutely not. He was a gentleman. The best.' She shook her head. 'I've often wondered what happened to him. He was so young then.'

'He's a psychiatrist in Stevenage.' I told her how we'd met.

She smiled. 'Everyone loved him, except the other psychiatrists. They thought he was too friendly with the patients, too caring. He stood when a patient came into the room. Spent too long with them, and he sometimes lent them textbooks to read about their condition. God forbid the patients should actually know something about their own ill-health.' She frowned. 'You know, there *was* something about your mother and him. I can't…' She shook her head. 'I can't remember, but I'm certain he wouldn't have acted without integrity. I'm delighted to hear he didn't give up his career, after what happened to him. It was a shame.'

I wanted to ask what happened to Daniel, and I wanted to ask if she believed it was an accident that took my mother in the end. But she was looking tired, and I had a more important question. 'Can you remember who he was, this man?'

Liz tapped the fingers of her left hand on the arm of the sofa. It seemed an age before she spoke. 'He was big. Huge. Can't for the life of me remember his name, but he was a nurse. A smile that would light up a room. But I never liked him. There was a meanness about him.'

Reluctantly, I said it was time I was going. She smiled. 'Please come again. I've enjoyed talking to you.'

She'd offered a lifeline I wanted to hold on to. 'I'll do that.'

We were standing at the living room door when her phone rang. It was on a table beside the sofa. 'Just a minute,' she said. She frowned as she listened. 'Yes, yes, I knew Mary MacLeod. Yes, her too.' She hesitated. 'I don't remember him. You could try Margaret Cameron. She's younger than I am. She's kept in touch with others. Hold on and I'll get her number.' She had an address book beside the phone, and she read out a phone number. She looked at the clock. 'Okay. I'll see you soon.' She listened and her face paled. She sank onto the sofa, her fingers tightening on the phone, as she glanced up at me. 'Yes... yes... I remember him. No, I don't know where he lives. Margaret Cameron might know.'

She put the phone down, worry etched on her lined face. 'Police. They're coming to speak to me about Mary MacLeod. Something to do with those remains found in Dunain Woods.' She took a deep breath. 'The nurse we spoke about. They've just reminded me of his name. It was Jamie Ogilvie.'

***

I RESTED MY head against the cold glass of the train window. I felt as if I'd been run over by something heavy. It had squeezed everything out of me, leaving a dull emptiness. My work worries were gone. They meant nothing compared to what my mother had endured. Two men had abused her. I wanted to find them. I wanted to look them in the eye and tell them I knew what they'd done.

38

I WAS GLAD I'd programmed the heating to come on. The flat was warm and there was no smell of damp. It felt like home. I made dinner and took it through to the living room. I watched TV, then I washed up and made a cup of tea. Back in the living room, my hand hovered over the remote control. It would be so easy to switch on and switch off. Lie on the sofa until it was time for bed. Or maybe I should try to find out the likelihood of my having inherited more from my mother than just her looks and an interest in men that were already spoken for.

There was so much information online. It seemed schizophrenia was a complicated interaction of genetic and environmental factors. One website claimed having one schizophrenic parent meant a 10 per cent risk for the offspring. Both parents and the risk jumped to over 40 per cent. I sure hoped my father was just a bog-standard pervert, and not an insane one.

I wondered about the family link Liz Barclay had mentioned. The closest relatives after my mother's parents were her grandparents, then aunts and uncles. If one of those categories had the illness, the chance of my mother succumbing on genetic grounds was still less than 5 per cent. I sent off a quick text to my mother's cousin, Anita, in Brighton, asking if she knew if there was schizophrenia in the family. We rarely contacted each other, but she'd been in touch when Gran died. It only took minutes for her to answer. Her father, my mother's uncle, was diagnosed with schizophrenia in his early twenties. He stabilised on medication and lived a normal life until he died of cancer in his fifties.

Another webpage and I discovered that stress could be a factor in the onset and course of schizophrenia. Was it all down to Someone's Cousin? Had he disturbed a sleeping beast that might have lain dormant without his attack?

Though I was exhausted, I knew I wouldn't sleep. It wasn't only the 10 per cent risk that troubled me. I couldn't get my mind off the sketchbooks Liz Barclay had mentioned. I'd searched for them earlier, and I couldn't find any.

It was dark outside. As ever, looking at the sparkling stars made a lump rise in my throat. Closing my eyes, I remembered the words my mother had whispered so often, and then I shoved them back in their hiding place.

I manoeuvred Granda's old wooden ladder out of the shed and through the front door as quietly as I could. I was glad the ladder wasn't metal as it clashed repeatedly with the banister. Last thing I wanted was an investigation by Ted Sullivan.

There wasn't as much in the attic as I'd expected. Gran's Christmas tree and the box of decorations were closest to the hatch, no doubt so she could reach them each year without the big ladder. I stepped onto the floored area. There were a few old suitcases, some rolled-up carpet, and a pile of boxes, some of them labelled in Granda's neat handwriting. *Toys. Photos. Receipts. Work. Brighton. LPs.* There was an old turntable and speakers. As I shone the torch into the corner, I gasped, then I smiled. My old doll's house. Well, Mum's doll's house first, then mine. Granda had made all the furniture, Gran all the furnishings. It had been covered in plastic sheeting to protect it from dust.

I checked the suitcases. Nothing but luggage straps. I opened the unlabelled boxes. One had technical journals and Granda's textbooks. Another had cookery books. Mixed books in a third. I almost stopped then, but I opened a fourth, and there they were, notebooks and sketchbooks, several of them. I put them over by the hatch. I was ready to go back down when I did one final sweep with the torch.

Beyond the boarded area, towards the back wall, I could see something yellow. It looked like fabric. Was it clothing? I stepped carefully across the beams, with their insulating wool in between. I lifted the object. It was a rucksack.

I tipped the contents out on the floor of the spare room. Another couple of sketchbooks. Pencils and charcoal. A heap of cassette tapes and a Walkman. A book about Norse mythology and Sylvia Plath's *The Bell Jar*. I wondered if she'd read it. I'd tried, and hadn't got very far. A little too close for comfort, I expect. There was a photo of Mum inside the front cover of the book. She was standing in the woods, against a tree. She looked so happy. I had a special box in the drawer by my bed, where I kept her photos, along with the letters and cards she'd sent me from The Craig. There were school photos, a couple of holiday snaps, and a handful of pictures of Mum holding me as a baby. She looked so young; just a child herself. But it wasn't enough. I'd wanted to see her at all ages, enjoying herself, posing with her friends, dressed up for going out. I'd asked Gran why there were so few photos. She'd shrugged and said people didn't take photos so much then. No mobile phones or digital cameras. They didn't even have a family camera until Mum was in her teens, and then she didn't want her photo taken.

'Why not, Gran?'

'She thought she was ugly. Too skinny. All those freckles.'

'I think she was beautiful.'

'Me too. Just like you.'

In my bed, I turned the pages of the largest sketchbook. Young people, old people, others with vacant faces who probably didn't even know they were being sketched. A series of pictures of a young woman dressed in black, with short hair and round glasses. She looked interesting, clever. At the top of the page, surrounded by a border of hearts and stars, were the words: *'Lady Sif'*.

There were several sketches of a younger Liz Barclay in uniform. More nurses and some doctors. And then I came to a young Daniel. So handsome. No doubt many of his patients had fallen for him over the years. I wondered how Mum had felt about him. Despite her protestations, Liz Barclay had said there was something in her memory about Daniel and my mother.

In another sketchbook, on a double page, a series of sketches of a nurse. He was broad and muscular, his bulk making the wooden chair on which he sat look tiny. On the left-hand page, he looked pensive, moody, quite ordinary. When I looked at the right-hand page, I did a double-take, my eyes flicking back to the first sketches, and I wondered if it was the same man. It had to be – the bulk, the hair, the eyes. And yet, when he smiled, the difference was incredible. His smile was mesmerising and I couldn't stop looking at him. I remembered Liz Barclay's words: *He was big. Huge. A smile that would light up a room.*

I turned to the last few pages and my heart leapt. Sketches of me on my own, me with Gran, me with Granda. All three of us together. I wondered why Gran hadn't told me, hadn't shown me. It made no sense. Unless they just couldn't bear to look at them, didn't want to remember.

I propped up the photo of Mum on my bedside table, and I tried to sleep. It was hopeless. For the first time in years, I wanted her. I needed her. I lay there and imagined I could feel her skinny arms around me, her voice whispering all the broken promises, all the lies. She'd get better. She'd come home. She'd love me forever. She'd never leave me.

But now, I felt no anger towards her, only sadness and regret. I still didn't know if her death was an accident, but even if it was suicide, how could I blame her? I couldn't imagine what life must have been like for her, a mother of a young child, incarcerated with such a devastating illness. I prayed I would never know.

Part II

39

AROUND THE AGE of fifteen, Ellen Sharp began to hope she'd been adopted. She longed for a mother who wore short dresses and lunched with friends, and a father in the Rotary Club. She wished she had parents that went to dances and parties, and spent Sundays with hangovers. She wanted her father to have a Triumph Spitfire, and her mother a Ford Cortina estate, with room for two family dogs. She wanted to go on regular shopping trips with her mother, family meals in restaurants, and holidays in Blackpool. She imagined living in a Victorian stone villa with high ceilings and patio doors to the garden. And a brother to look after her, to drive her and her friends to parties and not tell her parents if she drank too much. Basically, she wanted the life of her friend Hazel.

Instead, she had Quaker parents who aspired to a life of simplicity and social responsibility, moderation and abstinence, honesty and integrity. Happy with their poky council flat and their beat-up old two-door Morris Marina, strictly for weekend outings and special occasions, their idea of a social gathering was to host a small discussion group at the flat to explore and share their spiritual experience.

When Ellen begged for a pet, they found a slightly moth-eaten second-hand Siamese cat that hadn't settled in a family with young children. Binky immediately established himself as her mother's cat, rarely acknowledging Ellen, and never responding to her attempts at affection. When the family finally got a camera, her mother spent hours photographing the damn cat.

Ellen knew she was a disappointment to her parents. The demanding and complaining, failing to work hard at school, the barely concealed mockery of their insignificant lives. She wasn't completely deprived. She could go to discos and dances, but her father always had to come and pick her up. They didn't stop her from going on school or Guide trips, but decisions were always preceded by a serious family discussion about whether they could afford it, and what they might all have to forego in its place. She was allowed fashionable clothes, but they were usually birthday or Christmas presents, rarely just a treat. She could stay over with friends at weekends, but there had to be a 'wee chat' before she left, when one or both of them would tell her they trusted her to be sensible and careful, to act with integrity and self-worth, and, above all, to have a good time.

Ellen mostly heeded their words. At fourteen, in the bushes at the edge of the park, she had her first taste of cider. She didn't like it, and she hated what it did to her friends, especially Hazel. All that stupid giggling and staggering about.

At fifteen, Hazel graduated to vodka. Still the same silly behaviour. But now the evening was spent trying to keep the local boys from taking advantage of Hazel and holding back her friend's hair while she threw up.

The boys all vied for Hazel's attention. She had boobs. Ellen didn't mind. She wasn't ready for a boyfriend, and certainly not one that hung about in the park drinking, scrapping and throwing up. They'd never fancy her anyway, with her flat chest, skinny legs and freckles.

When Ellen was almost sixteen, on New Year's Eve, Hazel persuaded her to try Advocaat. She liked the feeling, all light and funny, until she threw up on Hazel's bed. She'd take a little vodka and Coke after that. Not much. Never enough for it to affect her behaviour, or make her parents suspicious. They weren't entirely against alcohol. They thought it had its place for special occasions, but she never saw either of them under the influence.

And so, at Hazel's sixteenth birthday party, in June 1985, Ellen expected to have a couple of vodkas, look after Hazel, and, hopefully, keep her away from lecherous Len Arnold. He was in his early twenties and married, and he'd taken to hanging about outside the school in a blue van, offering Hazel a lift home. She lived five minutes from the school, but still she took him up on his offer, though Ellen was sure the journey involved a detour to a quiet place, a quick session in the back of the van, and a drop-off nowhere near her home.

Ellen worried about her friend and her growing reputation for being easy. Inverness was too small to avoid gossip, but Hazel didn't seem to care. She didn't care about much but drink and boys. To her parents' dismay, she'd decided against taking a job in her father's insurance company when they'd soon leave school. Instead, she and Ellen had got jobs in a local supermarket where Hazel fancied the butcher. He was married too.

Earlier in the year, ten days before Ellen's sixteenth birthday, her grandmother had died. Ellen spent her birthday with her parents in Brighton. Sick of her friends asking her what she was going to do to celebrate her birthday, she was relieved to get away. It was cool in Brighton. The shops were amazing, and they'd had a family meal in a restaurant overlooking the sea front.

Perhaps that was why Hazel was determined, at her birthday party, to get Ellen drunk. It was a lovely summer evening, their last day of school. Hazel's parents were away, and everyone else was drinking. And so, Ellen went along with it. It was fun at first. Her shyness gone, she felt invincible. Dancing no longer felt awkward, and she made people laugh.

Her last clear memory was standing at the patio doors, looking out as the sun set into the trees. The colours of the sky were amazing, the clouds shifting and forming spectacular shapes and patterns. The world was beautiful and life full of promise. No more school. A new job, money, opportunities. She remembered smiling as she felt confident fingers caress the back of her neck and trickle downwards.

40

WITHIN MONTHS, ELLEN'S parents had to deal with the discovery that their teenage daughter had not been sensible and careful, or acted with integrity and self-worth. They would never discover that having a good time hadn't come into the equation either. At least, not after the initial euphoria of drunkenness.

They put the moodiness in the early stages down to her new job. The tiredness and sickness must be a stomach bug. Later, her increased appetite and sore back must be because of the physical nature of her work, carrying boxes and bending and lifting. But why had she started to wear such unflattering, baggy clothes?

It wasn't fear that made Ellen drag it out. It was the delicious secrecy. That tiny heart beating inside her. The faintest fluttering movements at first, and then the frantic dancing that no one else could see or feel. It belonged to her entirely. A tiny being that had wrapped its little fingers round her heart.

And then there was no hiding it. They had just finished their dinner, and her mother stood to clear up. When Ellen told them, her mother sank into her chair, dropping a plate on top of another. Both plates smashed, the cutlery skiting across the table.

There was no anger. Just tears in her father's eyes, and a blank look on her mother's face, as she asked Ellen to go to her room. Ellen refused. Whatever they had to say, they could say in front of her. There wasn't much said. How far on was she? Had she been to any appointments?

She was seven months pregnant, and no, she hadn't been to any appointments, and she had told no one.

'Not even…?' Her mother stopped. She picked up the broken bits of plate and took them through to the kitchen. She never asked who it was, and Ellen wished, yet again, that she had normal parents that would shout at her, a father that would demand to know who had violated his daughter, and threaten to kill him.

In bed, she heard her parents talking long into the night. The next morning, it was all practical arrangements. She'd have to leave her job. Her mother would make an appointment with the doctor. No doubt they would discuss her options with her.

Her options? Ellen had laughed. There was no option. She was keeping the baby. Both parents' eyes now glistened with tears, and Ellen knew they were tears of relief.

***

ELLEN WANTED NOTHING more than to sit and hold her daughter all day. Watching, stroking, poking the little rolls of baby fat and caressing her tiny fingers and toes. Never in her life had she known or imagined such love. Her world had changed entirely, and she was flooded with tenderness. Instinctively, she knew what each cry meant, though there wasn't much crying. Kate was a contented baby, easily satisfied.

That didn't stop Ellen's mother from interfering, always knowing better. Pushing them to go out. Babies needed fresh air. Ellen needed exercise. Couldn't stay in their room all day. Wasn't healthy. And why was the window closed?

Bloody windows always open. They might as well be outside. At least then there was no one nipping Ellen's head. She'd walk along to the park, proud as anything of her red corduroy pram. She'd sit on a bench, holding and watching. She'd stay out as long as she could, even though it meant more bother when she got home. Where had she been? What was she doing? Who had she seen? Met anyone special?

Anyone special? Her mother was so transparent in her desperation to discover the identity of the mystery impregnator. And yet, she didn't ask. Sometimes Ellen would drop a random name into conversation and watch her mother wind herself up. Was it someone she'd heard of before? Someone from school. A friend's brother. A teacher, even. How Ellen laughed. She'd never had such a secret before.

***

HAZEL PHONED. THEY met in the park. She scarcely glanced into the pram, and that suited Ellen just fine. So many questions. Why had Ellen not told her? Why just give up work like that? Why wouldn't she speak to Hazel on the phone? Who was the father? As Ellen refused to answer, except to say she wasn't going back to work, she could see the rage growing in the friend that had always had the upper hand. Her stupidity surprised Ellen. Wouldn't take much to work it out. But Hazel had never been any good at arithmetic. She hadn't even noticed there was anything wrong with Ellen that early morning the previous June. Ellen had thought she'd have to tell her friend what had happened, before Hazel or her mother discovered it, but when she'd checked the bed, there was nothing there. Shouldn't there be blood? It was only later, reading a library book, she'd discovered not everyone bled the first time.

All Hazel had been interested in that morning was telling Ellen the intimate details of sex with Len Arnold, and it had sounded a lot more fun than sex with Someone's Cousin. When, at last, Ellen got a word in and said she couldn't remember going to bed, Hazel said she'd undressed her and put her to bed, to stop her making a fool of herself. Everyone thought Ellen had gone home.

Not quite everyone.

Ellen smiled as Hazel walked away, knowing their friendship was over. She didn't need friends now.

41

KATE WAS ASLEEP, lying on her back, arms stretched above her head, little opaque eyelids fluttering. Ellen wanted to lift her and hold her, but she'd never get home if she did that every time the notion took her. She tucked in the blanket, smiled, and looked up. He was standing outside the Carlton, smoking a cigarette. His eyes narrowed as if he was trying to place her.

I'm going to do it anyway.

Ellen had put Someone's Cousin in a box deep in her brain, a box that was never meant to be opened, for there was no way to reconcile his actions with the miracle that was her daughter, and she didn't want to have to try. She wondered if she imagined the look of fear on his face before he dropped his cigarette end and concentrated on grinding it into the pavement. She wondered if his eyes followed her and her red corduroy pram as she walked away. She felt invincible. He was nothing, and he would never know how it felt to hold her precious baby. All the way home, she smiled, occasionally breaking into laughter that made people turn and stare. Let them.

Her mother was out, volunteering with some campaign or other. Though it was too early, Ellen bathed Kate. As she scooped the sparkling water over her daughter's perfect skin, she told stories of another father, one that loved them both. He couldn't be with them now, but he'd come some day, and he'd take them away from this little flat and their little world.

The look on her mother's face when she heard Kate had been bathed. Served her right. She was a thief, always stealing precious moments from Ellen.

That night, as Kate snuffled in her cot, the darkness of the room crowded in on Ellen. She tried desperately to nudge the lid back on that box in her head, but now it had been opened, it would not close. And neither could she close her eyes for fear that the door would open, and Someone's Cousin would sneak his hand beneath the sheets. When she could stand the fear no longer, she crept into her parents' room and begged her mother to come and sleep with her.

***

THE FEAR GREW until her mother slept with her every night. Sometimes she would lie awake and listen to the snuffling and shuffling from the cot, and the sound of her mother's soft snoring, and Ellen would smile into the darkness. She was safe. Other times, a heavy dread would descend upon her, making her scream into the pillow, trying to silence the whispering voice that told her she was useless and undeserving, that everyone would be better off without her, that it would be so easy just to end it all before morning. Imagine, the voice would whisper, imagine not having to face the dawn and another day of holding herself together, another day of pretending, another day of seeing his face whenever she closed her eyes.

It was compelling, that voice. It encouraged her to list the ways. She was scared of her own blood, always had been. Perhaps there were tablets in the medicine cabinet in the bathroom. One night, she slipped from her bed and checked. A packet of glycerine suppositories, three and a half paracetamol and a tin of Imperial Leather talc. Her laughter woke her father. Bleary-eyed, he appeared at the bathroom door in his pyjamas.

Ellen had always been closer to her father than her mother.

He was easy to be with. Never raised his voice, never expected her to talk about anything she didn't want to. He was just there, always. But these days, he wore a perpetual look of concern that only shifted when he held Kate. Then his face would relax and crease into a map of smiles, and she knew he was a thief too. Her baby wasn't safe here.

Suicidal thoughts gone, she crept back to bed and plotted their escape. They'd leave and go far away.

For weeks, she planned. She had savings and a cousin in Brighton that would help her find somewhere to stay. Not that she told her cousin she was coming. She didn't trust anyone enough for that kind of collaboration. She'd make her way down and beg her cousin not to tell them where she was.

Three days before Ellen planned to leave, her mother took ill. She had never known her mother to be ill, and she wondered if it was a ploy. Maybe she'd talked in her sleep, or left her journal lying around. She didn't think so. Perhaps her mother just knew, like she knew everything (except Ellen's greatest secret). Or maybe she really was sick.

There was a hint of relief when she postponed her plans. It had troubled her that she'd have to sleep alone wherever she ended up. Though she wasn't daft enough to think Someone's Cousin would follow her and creep into her room, she knew that was exactly what his spectre, released from the box, would do. And so, she put her plans aside, and she nursed her mother over the worst of the nameless lurgy. It was nice to have her mother rely on her for a change, to have their roles reversed. She didn't get much sleep with her mother tossing and turning, coughing and sweating buckets. Still, it was nice.

42

HER HANDS ON the black plastic seat, Ellen pulled the swing back. The chains squeaked and Kate laughed. At three years old, she couldn't get enough of the swings, and they spent hours in the play park. When she let the seat go, Ellen saw the tall skinny man through the gap between the chains. He smiled and nodded at her. Kate swung forward, her little body blocking out the sun for a moment before she swung back down. The man was gone.

Every time they went to the play park, he was there. Sometimes he stood in the middle of the park, his thin body wavering against the sun. Sometimes he sat on a bench at the edge, close to the bank that led to the canal. Once, he moonwalked along the path behind the houses. Though he never came too close, Ellen knew his features. He had greasy dark hair, green eyes with bronze flecks, and a long nose. Little hands. She called him Solomon. Sometimes he followed them back to the flat, staying at a distance, scooting into gardens whenever she turned her head.

In the shop at the end of the street, twice a month for three months, Ellen bought a copy of every Sunday newspaper. She spread them out on her bed, her eyes flicking over the pictures and the headlines, searching for stories of missing or abducted children. That she didn't find any did not put her mind at rest. What else could Solomon be up to?

Life had become complicated over the last three years. There were only certain routes Ellen could take when she left the flat.

Houses that must be avoided, because the patterns in the curtains told a terrifying story. Sections of roads with crazy painted lines she dared not cross. Bushes that hid unnamed dangers and telephone boxes that weren't what they pretended to be. She had stopped answering the phone in the flat because of the static and strange clicking in the background.

Though Solomon's presence worried her, she didn't mention him to her parents. They had taken to looking at her in a puzzled way when she spoke, as if she was using a language they didn't understand. Sometimes she pulled them up on it, and all the other subtle little things they did to undermine her and her parenting. They'd back down then, desperate to avoid confrontation or disharmony in front of Kate. They were sneaky like that; didn't want Kate to see them as they really were.

The night she heard Solomon's wee hands trying to open the bedroom window, his long nails scratching against the glass, Ellen knew she had to get away. The plotting began again, and this time in earnest.

She bought a train ticket to London, and a new hold-all that she stuffed under the bed. She would leave it in the shed the night before, and pick it up in the morning. Two days before they were due to go, her mother commented on her nervous excitement. Ellen said they were going on a trip to Aviemore early on the appointed day, with a friend from the toddler group. 'And I don't need you to sleep with me anymore.'

Her mother asked at bedtime if Ellen was certain. She hesitated, then nodded. She'd be fine.

She was fine, as long as she stayed awake. Whenever she dropped off, Solomon's nails scratched down the windowpane, disturbing Kate until she began to moan and turn in her bed. By the morning, Ellen was exhausted and terrified, consumed with the Dread. She accepted her mother's offer that night. It was only one more night, then a new life. Everything would be fine.

***

IT WAS COLD on the train platform. Her constant pacing back and fore didn't warm Ellen, but at least Kate slept on, wrapped in a blanket. Ellen stopped and stared down the tracks into the shimmering distance. She saw the sketchy outline of a man walking down the middle of the track. His pace was slow and steady. The clouds parted, and a shaft of sunlight illuminated him. Behind him, twin lights appeared, and a voice announced the impending arrival of the train. He didn't turn. Just kept on walking. As the train loomed behind him, Ellen screamed. Her knees buckled, and she fell into darkness.

'Are you all right, dear?'

There was something soft under her head, and a face above her. The smell of coffee and cigarettes. Ellen rolled over and pushed herself to her knees. Kate was still sleeping. 'The man?'

'What man, love? Can you stand?'

She nodded and stood, her head swirling like one of Kate's little plastic windmills.

'When does the train go?'

'Five minutes. Do you think you can get on? Maybe better to stay here and call a doctor.'

No way. They helped Ellen and the pushchair onto the train. Someone put the holdall in the luggage rack. Kate slept on.

This train is bound for Inverness. It will stop at…

As the words faded away, Ellen leaned her head against the window and closed her eyes. She hadn't failed completely. She'd made it to Perth before the Dread forced her from the train and made her buy a ticket back to Inverness. It was a start. Maybe next time…

***

THAT NIGHT, ELLEN went into town on her own. Vodka and

music filled her body, loosening and lightening, until she felt like she was just air. When she stopped dancing and stood at the bar, she ignored the guys that tried to talk to her. She walked home, through a light fall of snow, past three of the houses she usually avoided. The curtains were silent. She danced on the crazy lines on the road, and nothing happened. Solomon was gone. She'd found the answer.

Her mother was snoring, so Ellen slept on the sofa. She dreamed of the man at Perth station. Arms and legs stretched out in a star jump; his body was plastered to the front of the train like something from a child's cartoon. She woke up laughing.

43

ELLEN TRIED TO keep her drinking to the weekends. She'd start at home. A splash of vodka added to a can of Coke, to give her courage before she'd leave to meet one of her imaginary friends. Mostly, they were mothers she claimed to have met in the park with Kate, or girls she'd met on a previous night out.

She'd walk into town, still avoiding the bushes and the telephone boxes, a battle raging in her head over where to go. There were a couple of pubs frequented by old men and other loners, where she could sit at the bar without feeling too conspicuous. There were downsides to that, and not just the threat of a persistent barfly. In a quiet bar, she couldn't avoid the voices.

There were three of them. Two men and a woman. One man was a singer. He wasn't very good. The other man was a whisperer. He was the friendliest, and sometimes he told her she was beautiful and special. She liked him. And the woman was a demon.

They weren't always there. Sometimes they disappeared for weeks. Other times, they taunted her day and night. In a quiet pub one night, the demon told her the barmaid had slipped poison into her double vodka. She resisted the urge to pour the vodka over the barmaid as she grabbed her jacket and left, the drink untouched.

Angry, and determined not to give in, Ellen tried another quiet pub. As soon as she sat on a stool by the bar, a guy sat beside her. He had dark brown eyes, long hair tied back in a ponytail, and a cute smile.

'Do you mind if I sit here?' There were other empty bar stools, several of them. Ellen shrugged.

'Pint of lager, please, and whatever she's having.'

'She?'

He smiled. 'I don't know your name, do I?'

'No, you don't. Large vodka and Coke, please.'

They clinked glasses. He told her his name was Andy. Eyebrows raised, he stared at her and waited.

'Ellen. I'm a single mother.' He looked a little taken aback. She smiled. 'Feel free to sit elsewhere.'

'Why would I?'

They had a few drinks. Afterwards, Ellen couldn't remember what they talked about, but whatever it was, it had silenced the voices. Before she left, he asked for her phone number.

***

ON SUNDAY AFTERNOON, Ellen took Kate to Whin Park to meet Andy. He pushed Kate on the swings and caught her at the bottom of the slide. They walked through the Ness Islands to the town and ate in Pizzaland. It was the perfect day. That night, Ellen whispered to Kate that maybe Andy was the daddy they'd waited for.

He wasn't. Ellen didn't hear from him again. She spent weeks going over everything that had been said between them in their brief acquaintance. In her desperate search for clues, she wrote it down. A chart of her words and his responses. Her mind invented all kinds of scenarios and subterfuge, until she had her mother setting the whole thing up, telling Andy to make a move on her in the pub. His instructions were to reel her in, let her think he liked her, and then dump her. Just for the hell of it.

Or maybe her mother hadn't set it up to begin with. Maybe after Ellen got home that day, after she'd told her mother what a good time they'd had, her mother had tracked Andy down and told him some lies to put him off. That must be it. She was scared if things went well between Ellen and Andy, she'd lose Kate.

Whatever her mother had done, Ellen resolved to be more careful in the future. They were at war and she couldn't let her mother win.

***

THE VODKA DIDN'T always give Ellen the courage to see her plan through. Sometimes, before she reached the town, or even as she stood at the door of the pub, the demon would start goading in her high sparkly voice. It was suspiciously like the voice of a PE teacher Ellen had hated in school, a small pretty woman that had surrounded herself with the beautiful bullies and the sporty swots, a woman that had ignored Ellen because she wasn't beautiful and she couldn't run to save herself. The demon told Ellen she was ugly, she was fat, she smelled bad. Kate was going to die while she was out drinking. She'd head home, feigning a headache or stomach ache. Early bed and more vodka.

On nights when the voices were resting, she'd feel the excitement growing as she neared the town. It was going to be a good night. And it often was. She perfected the art of fading into the crowd by never standing too long in one place and flitting about as if she was looking for her friends or returning from the toilet. She'd do that in a couple of pubs before it was time to head to a disco. All she wanted to do was dance.

Though it was easier to be alone, and not have to read every signal and glance for its true meaning, sometimes she gave in, if the guy was cute and persistent. Whatever had gone wrong with Andy, she couldn't forget that just talking with him had silenced the voices.

She went out with some of them again, though she never let them collect her from the house. She never told them about Kate, and she always changed their names when she told her parents. Every few weeks, she'd get that talk from her mother, the one about being careful. She'd play dumb and make her mother spell it out. Was she on the pill? She'd smile and refuse to answer.

Ellen wasn't on the pill, because she didn't need to be. She had no desire to take things further than kissing and the odd fumble in the back of a car or a doorway. With no friends, there was no one to ask, so she didn't know if it was normal not to feel more. Was her lack of desire the fault of Someone's Cousin, or had she just not met the right person?

Ellen loved the confidence she got from drinking. It was the only time she liked herself, but she soon discovered there was a tipping point beyond which it wasn't safe to go. A bad hangover, and the Dread would be unbearable, her head a mad scramble of voices shouting, singing and screaming. To maintain her fraying sanity, she kept a careful count, never going over her own limit.

She lost count, though, of the number of nights her mother bathed Kate and put her to bed. And the number of mornings when she felt a small hand caress hers, and then the light touch of Kate's lips on her cheek. The bedroom door would open and close, and then she'd hear the muffled chat and laughter between her daughter and her mother.

Her mother took Kate to nursery. Give her mother her due, which Ellen rarely did, she waited for Ellen to do it first. She knew she should, but there were too many terrors involved. And so, she stayed in bed and waited for Kate to come running in, jump on the bed, snuggle under the covers, and tell her everything she'd been up to. The child amazed Ellen. She was bright and funny and brave. She was nothing like her.

44

IT WAS CHRISTMAS Eve, but there was no joy in the Dalneigh flat. Two helicopters were hovering overhead, Ellen whispered from under the bed. It was the Russians. They'd been stealing her thoughts for days and now they'd come for her. Her mother enticed her out as her father watched from the door. She led Ellen to the window and opened the curtains. 'See,' she said. 'There's nothing there. Just stars.'

'Nothing there?' Ellen's voice rose to a shriek, and Kate moaned and stirred in her bed. 'You can't see either of them?' She broke away from her mother and scurried back to her hiding place.

The sedative the doctor injected kept Ellen asleep for most of the next morning. At regular intervals, Kate would leave her pile of presents and go through to the bedroom. 'Mummy's still sleeping. Oh, dear.'

Though Ellen remembered little about the episode, and nothing of the helicopters, a terrifying darkness stayed with her. It was worse than the Dread. Perhaps it was the effort of trying to rise from the sedation, so she could enjoy Christmas Day with her daughter. It had felt like a heavy blanket on top of her. Her parents told her little. She'd been unwell. The doctor had given her an injection. She'd get an appointment soon.

She didn't ask what kind of appointment. When the letter came, she almost required sedation again. A psychiatrist at The Craig? There was nothing wrong with her, she told her mother.

Just a bit tired and stressed. It wasn't easy living with your parents when you had a child. All she needed was a place of her own. She wasn't going to any appointments. They were the ones that needed a psychiatrist. They were sick, trying to steal her child.

On the morning of the appointment, her mother persuaded Ellen she had to go. If she didn't, the doctor would come back, and they might decide to detain her.

On the bus, she wrapped her long scarf around her face and pulled her woollen hat as far down as it would go. Slumped in the seat, only her eyes were visible. She wished she'd worn dark glasses, though they might have looked a little odd in January.

Lost people with sad eyes and open mouths wandered the grounds of The Craig. Ellen kept her head down until she was inside, in the creepy, dark silence.

She spun a fine story for the psychiatrist. The stress of single parenthood and having to live with a difficult mother. Constant arguments. Drinking a little too much over a sustained period. The Valium she'd found in the bathroom cabinet and the Christmas brandy. Not a good mix.

He stayed quiet until she was done, then he fed back everything the GP had noted from her parents. 'Cowering under a bed. Russian helicopters stealing her thoughts. Followed by persons unknown. Telephone is being tapped. Won't use a telephone box in case it transports her to another world. Being mistreated by the family. Suspects them of wanting to harm her and her child.'

She nodded. 'I am being mistreated. My parents are not good people. I don't remember any helicopters.'

'Who was prescribed Valium?'

'Valium?'

He took off his glasses and stared at her. 'You said you took Valium with brandy before the helicopter episode.'

Ellen shrugged. 'I don't know whose it was. It was just there, in the cabinet.'

There were lots more questions and, by the time he'd finished,

Ellen was exhausted.

He put his pen down and folded his arms. 'I'll see you again in three months. These are significant concerns, but I don't think there's any point in considering treatment just yet.'

Result.

'Stay off the booze and Valium, eh?'

Ellen decided not to go straight home. Let her sneaky mother think they'd incarcerated her. In the pub, she ordered a large brandy. She grimaced as it burned her gullet.

'You could try some lemonade,' the barmaid said.

'Any Valium?'

The barmaid did a double-take. 'Pardon.'

Ellen laughed. 'Only joking. Lemonade will do.'

Not bad. Still, she switched to vodka when the brandy was done.

***

THE DISGUST ON her mother's face. Staying out for hours, coming home stinking of booze, and had she even gone to the appointment?

Ellen nodded. 'I did. Turns out there's nothing wrong with me. You'll have to try harder next time if you want to get rid of me.'

Her mother left the room, but not before Ellen saw a tear run down her cheek. The old Ellen would have gone after her and apologised. That Ellen was gone.

***

THREE MONTHS LATER, Ellen saw the psychiatrist again. She didn't tell him Solomon had returned, and he was lodging with Mr Sullivan in the flat downstairs. She didn't tell him the man that worked in the corner shop had captured her mother's cat and implanted it with a tracking device. As far as she knew, the psychiatrist was in on the conspiracy.

45

ON A WARM August morning, Ellen awoke to see Kate standing by the bedside in her school uniform. She was little and beautiful, and so proud of herself and her shiny shoes. Ellen wiped away a tear, then she leaned over the side of the bed and held her daughter tight. Kate wriggled away. 'Silly Mummy. Bye.'

'There's still time for you to take her.' Ellen's mother was at the door.

Ellen shook her head.

It was hard to make out the demon's words, muttered over the sound of the shower, but Ellen got her drift. The muttering became louder as she dressed and put on her makeup. She told the demon she agreed with her entirely, and there was no need to shout.

There was a bottle of vodka under the bed. She put it in her rucksack and left the house. In the corner shop, she bought two packets of paracetamol.

By the time she'd walked the long canal towpath to Dochgarroch, swigging as she walked, she was guttered. There had been no counting of units. No need this last time. She'd had a pleasant conversation with the whispering man as she walked. He agreed with the demon. There was nothing else she could do, though he told her not to be so hard on herself. She had tried. She really had.

It was busy at the locks. Motor cruisers, barges and canoes lined up, waiting for the lock gates to open. Ellen sat on the canal bank and watched the whole people with their real lives, laughing and chatting.

Her head swimming, she lay on her side on the grass and took one packet of paracetamol from her backpack. She counted as she popped the pills out of their little pockets. She laid them out in rows on the flat surface of one of her cassette tape boxes. Maybe not enough. She took a strip from the second box and added them.

Through her headphones, Hothouse Flowers were singing "It'll Be Easier in the Morning". It'd be easier, all right. Easier for everyone. When the singing man in her head joined in, butchering Liam's soulful voice, she shouted at him to shut the fuck up. It worked, although it made people turn and look at her.

Next on the compilation tape she'd recorded from the radio, finger poised over the pause button to avoid any DJ interference, was Big Country's "Chance". She listened to half of it, smiling as she realised she no longer felt so lo-oh-ow. She fast-forwarded to the next one, the last one on that side of the tape. It was "Vincent", Don McLean's tribute to Van Gogh. Coincidentally fitting as the last song she'd ever listen to. She'd been good at art. Her teacher had encouraged her to apply to art school. She wasn't interested in continuing her education then, or in leaving Inverness. The teacher had grimaced when Ellen told her she'd got a job in a supermarket. Snob. Maybe one day, the teacher had said. And maybe that would have happened, were it not for Someone's Cousin and Kate.

Her eyes on the row of pills, she wondered again how her beautiful child could have resulted from the wickedness of Someone's Cousin.

The demon laughed.

***

THE WHISPERED WORDS echoed deep inside her, beyond the pain in her head and her stomach and her throat. They told her she was special and strong and loved. She remembered when she used to trust those words and the person who was stroking her hand. Something rose from her stomach, chasing the words away, gurgling upwards and splashing out. She was surrounded by a blur of people calling her name, telling her to wake up and calm down, wiping her face and raising the head of her bed, until she was sitting up. Her eyes were fuzzy and sore, but beyond the flurry of people, she saw her mother's face. Pale and sad and old. Her mother's lips moved, mouthing Ellen's name.

'Kate?' Ellen whispered.

Her mother smiled. 'Kate's fine.'

And then someone ushered, or maybe even pushed, her mother towards the door.

'No.' Ellen tried to get off the bed. 'Mum.'

'I said, calm down.' The nurse had stained teeth and BO. Her fingers were like talons pinning Ellen against the bed.

'Mum!'

At the door, her mother shook off the nurse that was ushering her out. 'I'm not going anywhere.'

Through the pain, Ellen felt a rush of love and shame.

***

THE DOCTOR'S WORDS were harsh. Ellen expected they'd have been worse had her mother not been sitting beside the bed, looking like a wee bulldog chewing a wasp.

'Paracetamol and alcohol.' He had a posh voice and a sneering tone. 'What were you thinking?'

Ellen shrugged. 'I wanted to die.' Her voice was croaky, her throat still raw from the tube they'd shoved into her stomach.

'By performing on a busy canal bank before falling into the water?'

Performing? She searched her memory. The canal bank, the people, her Walkman, the tablets. Lying down, listening to "Vincent". There had been no performing. 'That's not... that didn't happen.'

'Oh, it did.' He glanced at his notes. 'Dancing, badly. Singing, loudly. Bowing to the watchers, ripping off your headphones, and tumbling head over heels into the canal.'

She shook her head.

'Several witnesses, and, lucky for you, two off-duty doctors. Had they not pulled you from the canal, noticed the empty paracetamol packets, and called an ambulance immediately, we wouldn't be having this conversation.'

'And I'm supposed to be grateful? I don't want to live.'

'Ellen.' Her mother squeezed her hand. 'Don't say that.'

The doctor shook his head. 'You were drunk. You were stupid. And you were lucky. But don't fool yourself into thinking everything is all right. The damage from an overdose of paracetamol can take days, weeks and even years to manifest itself. Pain just here?' He placed his hand on his right side, pushing up beneath his rib cage.

Ellen nodded.

'A dull ache?'

She shook her head. 'It's quite sharp, and it's pulsing round into my back.'

He smiled. 'Good, good. That's your liver, all right. If you're a woman of faith, I'd suggest a few prayers tonight, and maybe, just maybe, you'll get away with no permanent damage. The psychiatrist will see you tomorrow.'

When she was alone, Ellen took her rucksack from the locker. It had been brought in with her, and someone had kindly picked her Walkman and headphones off the canal bank and put them inside. The compilation tape was in the Walkman, but it wasn't the quiet side that had last played. She looked at the handwritten list of songs on the fast side. Nausea churned in her stomach as she remembered the demon telling her to turn the tape over and dance in her bare feet on the grass. And more. She should sing along to the last one, the demon had said. She had a good voice.

It was a blatant lie. Ellen had a terrible voice. The thought of drunken singing along to any song in public was bad enough, but to this one? She'd recorded it from the radio the previous week and hadn't got round to deleting it yet. It was Right Said Fred's "I'm Too Sexy".

46

THE LAST TIME Ellen had been in Raigmore Hospital with her mother by her side, wearing her best coat, she was in a ward with three other mothers. Kate was hours old, swaddled in a white honeycomb blanket and wearing a knitted skull cap. Without asking, her mother had lifted Kate from the cot and held her far too tight. That look on her face. It was possessive and predatory, and it had terrified Ellen.

The memory terrified her now. It was just the two of them this time, in a single room. All the love and gratitude Ellen had felt the previous day had evaporated as soon as her mother arrived alone. 'Why didn't you bring Kate?'

Her mother shook her head. 'I met the psychiatrist first. Anyway, it's no place for her, seeing you like this.'

The demon poked at Ellen. *Told you. Can't trust them.*

'You're just trying to keep her from me.' Ellen's voice rose. 'You've always wanted her to yourself. You're evil.'

She is.

Before her mother could answer, the psychiatrist arrived.

As the walls closed in around Ellen, the psychiatrist's words sounded muffled and weird in her head, her brain scrabbling to understand. 'Craig Dunain? Admission to Craig Dunain? Are you for real? Mum, tell him.'

'It's for the best, Ellen.' The words sounded as if they'd been squeezed around a rock in her mother's throat.

'How can it be for the best? What about Kate?'

Her mother swallowed and clutched her handbag. She looked defeated, worn out. 'Kate is fine. She'll always be fine. We need to get you well.'

'I am well. My stomach's better and the liver tests came back all right.' She gestured to the drip in her arm. 'Just another day of this and they said I can go home.'

'And then what?'

'I'll be fine. I won't drink. I won't go out. I'll… I'll take Kate to school. I'll be good.' Her voice wavered as she heard the glittering laughter of the demon. 'I promise, Mum. I'll be good.'

Her mother frowned and took Ellen's hand. 'Darling, you need help. We can't cope with you. Not any longer. It's not fair on Kate.'

'Ellen.' The psychiatrist leaned towards her. 'Tell me about the man hit by the train, and why you think the government kept it quiet. The long, thin man that follows you; the dangers in the bushes at the play park.' He glanced at his notes. 'The bugs that are eating your brain. Tell me about the voices. The singer, the whisperer, the demon.'

You told them? Why would you do that? Now you're really going to pay.

Ellen clutched her head. 'I didn't, I didn't.'

And she hadn't. She'd stopped telling her parents these things long ago. There was no point when they didn't believe her. Her mother's eyes were on the window.

'Mum?'

Her mother wouldn't look at her. How did they know all that stuff? The demon screamed the answer.

You wrote it down, you stupid, stupid girl.

She groaned. 'My journal.'

Neither of them answered.

'Where is it?'

Nothing.

Ellen pushed her mother's hand away, and she grasped the

intravenous line. She wound it round her hand. 'Give me my journal.' She tugged a little, and felt a sharp pain in the back of her hand as the cannula moved. 'If you don't, I'm pulling this out and I'm leaving.'

Her mother looked up at the psychiatrist. He sighed and took the journal from his pocket. He put it on the bed beside Ellen.

'So, you're going to section me based on silly things I've written in my journal? My private journal no one was supposed to read.'

He shook his head. 'I was rather hoping you'd agree to a voluntary placement, without compulsive measures.'

For a moment, she thought she had a choice. She was wrong. If she didn't agree to a voluntary placement, he said, he'd enforce it. And if she tried to leave The Craig without the agreement of the staff, she'd be sectioned.

'So, either way, I'm going to The Craig?'

'That's about it, but if you come in voluntarily, no one can say you've been sectioned.'

It was only then Ellen noticed the small suitcase on the floor beside the bed. Yesterday, her mother had brought in enough for a couple of days. Why bring more? And then she knew. Her mother had planned this long ago, and Ellen had made it easier for her with her stupid suicide attempt.

Her mother reached for her hand. In her eyes, Ellen could see shame, and beyond that, a hint of victory. She pulled her hand away. 'You've wanted to get rid of me since Kate was born. Don't touch me. Don't visit. Dad can bring Kate. I never want to see you again.'

47

CRAIG DUNAIN WAS a place of fear and sadness. High ceilings, massive windows, dusty, faded furniture, the smell of antiseptic and boiled cabbage. Long echoing corridors, with doors and alcoves to hide so many dangers. The demon told Ellen there was a threat round every corner. A machete-wielding patient, a syringe-wielding nurse, a scalpel-wielding doctor. That she didn't encounter these threats meant nothing. Next time…

The first patient she met, a statuesque woman with protruding front teeth, asked her if she had a cigarette. Ellen would soon learn that cigarettes were the most valuable currency in The Craig, and not a day would go by without the same question being asked of her several times. Disappointed at the answer, the woman told Ellen she was a mind reader, and Ellen's thoughts were evil. The woman was right. Ellen couldn't stop thinking of ways that she could have, should have, killed her mother before it came to this.

A student nurse showed Ellen where she was going to sleep. She'd hoped for a room with two or three others, rather than a single room. She hadn't expected a sixteen-bed dormitory. 'In here?' Her voice sounded weak and whiny.

The student nurse nodded. 'It'll be fine. It's not full right now. About ten patients.'

The beds were close together, separated by metal bedside cabinets. Curtains could be pulled around the bed, but they were only for use by the staff, the student nurse told her, unless you were getting dressed and undressed.

'You're here.' She led Ellen to the top of the room, the closest bed to the nurse's station. 'They always put the new ones here, for observation.'

Ellen certainly wasn't the one most in need of observation, if the moaning and crying throughout the night was anything to go by. And then there were the constant trips to the bathroom, and the whispering of the nurses, encouraging, cajoling, and then threatening.

Just as Ellen thought she might drop off, the demon started. She told Ellen in whispers broken by sinister laughter that she would never get out of here. Not alive, anyway. Kate had already been trafficked out of the Highlands. Ellen would never see her again. When the demon began to describe in minute detail what was going to happen to Kate, she screamed for the nurse.

***

ELLEN WAS A guinea pig. It was a new drug, and they needed young women to test it. It was developed by the Russians, and they'd recruited Ellen's mother to help find the right subjects. It was best if the women had already given birth, in case fertility was affected. They chose nervous types, like Ellen. Women who needed their mothers to sleep with them. Women who had been abused. Women who were too close to their fathers. Women who loved their children too much.

The psychiatrist was a smug man. He had greasy-looking hair, a bulbous nose and restless piggy eyes. He kept licking his lips, like a lizard, and the action made Ellen nauseous. 'But you're not on medication, Ellen, except for the light sedative you required last night. You're being assessed, that's all. We don't even know yet if you will require medication.'

Ellen laughed. 'Nice try. It's in the water. I can taste it.'

'So that means everyone in this place who drinks the water,

including me, is being medicated?'

Ellen shrugged. 'I'm sure there's a way to make sure only the patients drink it.'

He didn't deny it. Just smiled. 'You have a daughter?'

She nodded and felt the lump rising in her throat. It was there all the time.

'Tell me about Kate.'

Ellen frowned. 'You can't recruit her. She's too young for these drugs. They would kill her.'

He nodded. 'Tell me how you feel about her.'

Ellen closed her eyes and rocked in her chair. 'She is light and love. She's my... my saviour. She is the most perfect being ever. That's why they want to steal her.' Her eyes shot open. 'The demon... last night... she said Kate's already gone. They've taken her. Phone the police —'

He held up his hand. 'I've spoken to your mother this morning. She said to tell you your daughter is fine. Your parents are coming in to see me shortly.' He leaned towards her. 'Ellen, you said your mother was recruiting women that had been abused. Do you come into that category?'

Abort. Abort. Abort.

Ellen shook her head. 'I never said that. You know nothing about me. I don't want to talk anymore.'

***

THE SUN WAS streaming through the big dormitory windows. It was quiet during the day, so different from the torture of the previous night.

'What are you doing in here?'

The voice made Ellen jump. She was about to answer the demon when a nurse appeared in front of her. She had curled grey hair, pinched lips and a sharp chin.

'I asked you a question. We don't encourage patients in the

170

dormitory during the day. Something goes missing, they'll all blame you.' She frowned. 'So, what is it?'

Ellen swallowed the threat of tears. 'I just wanted to get something from my locker.'

'Hurry up.'

The nurse stood and watched while Ellen took her Walkman and a couple of cassettes from the locker. 'I suggest you go to the dayroom,' she said. 'That's what it's for.'

The dayroom was long with a high coved ceiling, furnished with clusters of sofas, chairs and tables. There was a television at one end, a piano at the other. Ellen sat in the corner, as far from the other three occupants as she could get. They were playing cards amid much shrieking and accusations of cheating. She drew up her legs and wrapped her arms around her knees. She put on her headphones, switched on her Walkman and drowned out their noise.

In the warmth of the sun, Ellen couldn't keep her eyes open. A sharp tug at her arm brought her round. It was the mean nurse. 'Wake up. You've got a visitor.'

In the entrance hall, her father held her so tight, and for so long, she wondered if he was crying and trying to hide it. She was. Crying, but not hiding it. At last, she pulled away. Her father wasn't crying. He just looked sad. He wiped the tears from her cheeks and they sat. He passed her a carrier bag with everything she'd asked for when she'd phoned the previous evening, and two magazines, a packet of Kit Kats, grapes and a bottle of juice.

'Thanks, Dad. Did Mum not come to see the doctor?'

Her father nodded. 'I took her home and came back.'

'So, she didn't even stay to see me?'

He frowned. 'She had to be home for Kate, and you said –'

Ellen nodded, tears welling in her eyes again. 'What did the doctor say?'

'He just wanted a bit of background. He said it's going to take time to get to the bottom of it. It's early days. Listen, love, he was asking about the family history. There's something I told him, and

I should have told you before, but I didn't think it was important.'

A brief fantasy cascaded through Ellen's head. She was adopted, just as she'd suspected all those years ago.

'It was my brother, Adam. He spent time in a psychiatric hospital when he was in his late teens.'

'Adam died.'

Her father nodded. 'He did, but that was later.'

'Was it suicide?'

'No, love. He got over that – he was doing well mentally. It was cancer of the stomach that took him in the end. Didn't respond to treatment. But the thing before that – it might be the same thing.'

'Do you think I'm mad?'

Her father took her hand. 'No. I think you're not well.'

'Dad, I need to know… are you part of this? Did you know what was going on?'

He looked so lost. 'Part of what, love?'

'The plan. Mum's plan.'

'Ellen, there is no plan. Mum loves you. We just want you to get well.'

She stared into his eyes, and she couldn't see any of her mother's scheming. She remembered Sunday trips in the car with him. Just the two of them. He'd let her sit in the front and open the window as far as it would go. She'd feel the wind on her face, and she'd laugh out loud. She'd come home with her tummy full of ice cream and crisps, and her hair all tangled in knots, like a bird's nest. Her teeth would water as her mother tugged and muttered and frowned. The first time they went to the car wash, the big rollers grinding against the windscreen and bumping over the roof terrified her. She'd thought they were going to be squashed. He'd held her tight and whispered that he'd never let anything hurt her.

'Will you bring Kate at the weekend?'

His eyes widened. 'Bring her here? Is that really what you want?'

He's in on it.

Ellen nodded. The demon was right.

172

48

IN A HORRIBLE little room, where rows of ancient books buckled and shifted, bending into patterns of secret code that she couldn't decipher, two horrible little men sat and watched Ellen. She didn't tell them about the books and the secret code. They wouldn't have listened. She was surprised both their egos could fit in the room. The new one, Dr Ross, hadn't even looked at her when the lip-licking lizard introduced them. Angry with her father and the mean nurse, who was now sitting behind her, sniffing, Ellen didn't bother to answer any of the questions she'd answered the previous day. There were new questions, obviously a result of the meeting with her parents. Would she say she was socially isolated, sleeping too much, lacking motivation?

She shook her head. 'I'd be quite happy if everyone would just leave me alone.'

The Lizard frowned. 'So happy that you tried to kill yourself?'

Ellen shrugged. 'I was tired, and I knew my parents were winning. They planned it all.'

He licked his lips and nodded. 'It's an elaborate plan, isn't it? They somehow knew you would try to commit suicide, though you'd never mentioned it, and you hadn't tried before. In effect, they made you do it, so you would be taken to hospital, and from there to here? All so they could keep your daughter, who lives with them anyway?'

Tell him to fuck off. Arrogant bastard.

Ellen didn't. Neither did she tell him that, when he put it like that, it did sound kind of daft.

'Had you written of your suicidal intentions in your journal?'

Ellen shook her head. She hadn't had suicidal intentions until the morning she saw Kate ready for school.

'It would be very helpful for us to see this journal.'

Nice try. 'I destroyed it.'

He looked disappointed. 'Dr Ross, your thoughts?'

They exchanged their thoughts without a glance at Ellen. Probably no underlying physical illness. Probably not a mood disorder. Delusions. Paranoia. Mix of negative and positive symptoms. A genetic component, but a very low risk from an uncle. Lots of nodding of heads and general agreement. Dr Ross had some questions for the Lizard. Was there a history of drugs? Promiscuity?

The Lizard shrugged. 'Not that we know of. She has had a child. Hasn't said who the father is. She…'

'Excuse me.'

They both looked startled. The Lizard frowned. 'Yes, Ellen?'

'I am still here.' She leaned across the desk, pointing at the Lizard and looking at Dr Ross. 'How is he supposed to know if I have a history of promiscuity?'

Dr Ross looked a little troubled.

He's a coward, this one

'Eh, your parents might have told him. Indeed, you could have told him yourself yesterday.'

'I could, but I didn't and I haven't. I've had sex once.'

'And you got pregnant?' Dr Ross smirked. 'Unlucky.'

Bastard.

They both jumped when Ellen yelled: 'I was not unlucky! Kate is the best thing that ever happened to me.'

'Behave yourself. Just settle down.' The mean nurse's tone was harsh, and so was the hand that gripped Ellen's shoulder and pulled her back in the chair.

'Did you have a boyfriend?' The Lizard was leaning towards her. 'Was this sex consensual?'

Ellen laughed and rolled her eyes. 'So, wise ones, what's wrong with me?'

Dr Ross shrugged. 'The symptoms of different conditions often overlap. It can be very difficult to reach a definitive diagnosis.'

The Lizard closed his pad. 'We're going to leave it there for today. We'll discuss your case and come up with a plan. It's likely to involve medication and therapy. You'll have to stay in for a while to stabilise.'

'You realise you're giving them exactly what they want?'

'What is the alternative, Ellen? You go home and carry on as before? You try to kill yourself again, only this time you do it in a quiet place where no one will find you? How is that helping Kate?'

Ellen had no answer. She was listening to the demon explaining the code of the books.

They're all in on it; you're useless; they're going to kill you, slowly; there's no point resisting.

***

THE PREVIOUS EVENING, Ellen had asked for a sandwich, rather than go to the dining room. Today, lunch had been a hideous affair, with stodgy macaroni, cold chips and an elderly patient beside her, dribbling lumpy cheese sauce down her chin and all over her front. At dinner-time, a smiling nursing assistant ushered Ellen from the dayroom and she didn't have the heart to refuse.

The food was passable. Cottage pie and vegetables. And the company was amusing. A tall woman with long grey hair and a baggy beige cotton dress introduced herself, speaking in clipped tones. 'I am the Blessed Virgin Mary. You may call me Mother Mary. I won't be here long. I shall shortly be assumed body and soul into heavenly glory. Help yourself to one of the Holy Bibles in my cabinet when I'm gone, but don't dare touch my pan drops.'

There was a giggle from the girl on Ellen's other side. Dressed all in black, she looked to be around Ellen's age. She was cute, with an elfin face, short spiky dark hair and enormous glasses with black frames. She was in the same dormitory as Ellen, and she'd made such a fuss when the light went off. How would her visitor find her in the dark? She had a small torch, and whenever the nurse wasn't looking, she'd flick it on and off and make patterns on the wall.

'Lady Sif.' She stuck out her hand, the long sleeve of her top rising a little. Ellen saw a criss-cross of lines and scars on the inside of her wrist. 'You can call me Sif. Despite appearances, I'm not really here. I live in Asgard with the Norse gods. Thor is my lover. He visits me on the ward. He has a penis the size of a tree trunk.'

The Virgin Mary erupted. 'Thou shalt have no other gods before me. Lust is born of Satan and the flesh. The lust of the flesh comes not from the Father, but from the world. Walk by the spirit –'

Sif leaned across Ellen. 'Be quiet, you dried-up old prune. Immaculate conception is so overrated.' She smiled at Ellen. 'Why are you here?'

Why indeed? Whatever was wrong with Ellen, at least she knew who and where she was. She shrugged. 'Conspiracy.'

Sif smiled, but it wasn't a mocking smile. 'Another one? Let me know if you want to join me in Asgard. We have room for a recruit. I can help you across the rainbow bridge.' She lowered her voice. 'It's not really the size of a tree trunk. It's comfortably adequate.' She drummed her cutlery on the table, earning herself a glare from the Virgin Mary. 'There's a concert tonight. Oh, the excitement. Beats arguing over the TV or playing Monopoly.'

That must have been what the mean nurse was talking about. As they'd walked back to the ward, she'd given Ellen a lecture on watching her step and not behaving like a little princess, whatever that meant. Keeping her head down, getting rid of the attitude, respecting the professionals. Ellen had considered telling the nurse that respect had to be earned, but there was no point, so she switched off. The nurse had ended with something about being ready at seven for seven-thirty, and Ellen hadn't a clue what she was on about.

49

THE RECREATION HALL was very grand, its panelled walls lined with decorated moulded columns. Ellen stopped to admire the plaster flower decorations on a column, and Sif hauled her away. 'No time for that. Come on. We need to get good seats.'

She shoved Ellen into a seat at the end of the third row from the front. 'Don't say I'm not good to you, giving you the end seat and saving you from the slobbering attentions of one of your fellow inmates.'

Ellen looked round. There were a lot of slobberers and starers, moaners and groaners. There was much wringing of hands and rocking of bodies, and the occasional random stamping of feet. One man kept hitting himself on the side of the head. They weren't even that old, the worst of them. Some were in wheelchairs, others slumped in chairs.

And among them, here and there, sometimes singly and sometimes in groups, there were many that looked just like Ellen or her parents or her grandparents. People she'd expect to see working in the shop or the council office or the doctor's surgery. Maybe even doctors and dentists among them.

Sif tapped Ellen's leg, 'Eyes front. Nurse Ratched doesn't like us staring.'

'Who?'

Sif nodded across the room to where the mean nurse was standing at the door.

'Is that her name?'

Sif's laughter turned all the heads in front. 'If you haven't seen *One Flew Over the Cuckoo's Nest*, or read the book, probably best to leave it for now. I should point out that the real Nurse Mildred Ratched had an attractive face and big boobs, attributes that are lacking in this miserable imposter, but otherwise there are many similarities. I wouldn't advise calling her that to her face. *Psycho bitch* will do.' She took a breath. 'Hope we don't get General George behind us. His running commentary ruined the last concert. And he kept kicking the back of my chair.' She glanced round. 'Phew, it's the depressives. What a score.'

A man sat beside Sif. 'Hey, Neil,' she said. 'How you doing? This is Ellen. Ellen, Neil.'

Neil had a firm grip and a warm smile. Lovely teeth and high cheekbones. He looked sane, if scruffy, in worn jogging trousers that were too short for him, and a faded t-shirt that was far too big. He put one foot up on the knee of his other leg and there were no laces in his trainers.

Though he and Sif whispered, Ellen picked up snippets. *Back in yesterday. Multi-storey car park. Voices.* She glanced at Neil and saw a shiver run through his lean body. 'They were like knives, those voices' he said. 'Cutting and goading. Worst ever.'

Sif patted his arm. 'You'll get there.'

Ellen realised then that her voices had been quiet since she'd left the doctors' room. Maybe the medication in the water was working.

The concert started with an elderly man singing in Gaelic. He had a wonderful voice. At the chorus, several patients joined in.

'Gaelic mafia,' Sif muttered. 'They're a cult. Whispering and gossiping and no one else can understand a word.'

Next was a young man on accordion. His fast tunes were accompanied by the loud creaking of wheelchairs, as their occupants rocked back and fore. A woman with no teeth played the spoons. She was good, running the spoons over her palm and up her arm, then across both knees. At the end, she took a bow, then she lifted her skirt over her head. She was wearing beige pop socks and baggy knickers that almost reached her scraggy knees. To the sound of jeers and wolf whistles, she was bustled off the stage by two male nurses.

Sif laughed. 'Go, Aggie. She's one of the demented.'

There was a succession of mediocre singers, some truly terrible jokes, and a man with an out of tune guitar. Sif knew each patient and which category they fell into. Manics, depressives, demented, personality disordered, alkies, psychos, schizos, undiagnosed, and pretenders. Ellen wondered in which category she and Sif belonged.

A woman played the recorder and the squeaky sound reminded Ellen of her childhood attempts at the instrument, and her mother's unrelenting encouragement. The memory floored her, and soon she was lost in a muddle of confusion, where her mother was her champion one day, and her tormentor the next.

She was vaguely aware of the audience chanting. She didn't catch what they were saying. She didn't even notice the man on the stage until he started singing "Caledonia". The wheelchairs stopped creaking, the coughing and the groaning ceased, and all eyes were on him.

He was enormous. Not fat, just big. Mid-thirties, he had messy dark brown hair that curled a little at his collar. His face was pale, with the slightest shadow of stubble, his features remarkably fine, considering his physique. His eyes were closed, and his voice was like a caress. Soft with yearning, it was breathy and intimate, yet strong and clear. Ellen was captivated.

It ended far too soon. He did a slight bow, and then he opened his eyes and smiled. Ellen felt as if she had been punched in the stomach.

They shouted for more, but the man shook his head. His steps were light as he left the stage. He stood against the wall, towering over Nurse Ratched, and Ellen saw her reach up and pat him on the shoulder.

'So, which camp does he belong to?' Ellen asked, with forced nonchalance.

There was loathing on Sif's face. She turned to Neil. 'What would you say, hun? Sociopaths? Psychopaths?'

Neil frowned. 'The latter, definitely.'

Sif groaned. 'Speaking of psychopaths…'

There was a woman in her late twenties on the stage. She had long dark hair, and she wore a hippy cotton dress with gypsy layers. Her feet were bare.

'Who's she?'

'You've met the Virgin Mary. This one's the whore, Mary Magdalene.'

Neil laughed.

'There's another Mary to be avoided,' Sif whispered, as the hippy began to sing. 'Mary MacLeod. She's been sick with flu this week, but you'll meet her before long. She's a gatherer of hospital secrets. Not a keeper of secrets, though. Beware.'

It couldn't have been easy, following on from the guy before, but the hippy had a good voice. She sang "Belfast Child". As she left the stage, to much applause, someone shouted: 'Show us your knickers!'

Sif rolled her eyes. 'Doubt there's a conscious fella in here that hasn't seen her knickers. Eh, Neil?'

His eyes met Ellen's, and he blushed.

'Poor Ellen,' Sif said. 'She's got to sleep beside her.'

'The next bed?' Ellen frowned. 'It was empty last night.'

Sif smiled. 'The whore had a "sick" night, so she got a private room. She'll be back tonight.'

***

IN THE DORMITORY, there was no sign of the hippy and Ellen hoped she'd relapsed after her performance and gone back to her private room. On the verge of falling asleep, her earplugs firmly inserted, hoping they would block out the ward noise and the voices, if they came back, Ellen felt something soft stroke her face. With a yell, she sat up. The hippy was sitting on the side of the next bed. She was smiling and mouthing something. Ellen pulled out an ear plug. She could hear swearing and muttering from the others, and frantic footsteps as a nurse bustled towards the bed. Beside Ellen, the woman lay down and whispered: 'Night night, Princess.'

No, there was nothing wrong, Ellen told the nurse. Just a bad dream. No, she didn't need something to help her sleep. She'd be fine.

Ellen turned her back on the hippy. It was ages before she slept, and then she dreamed of Nurse Ratched and the hippy laughing at her.

50

Dunain Woods was alive with the ringing of birdsong and shimmering light that flickered through the tall trees, sparkling on the water. They walked in silence past the duck pond and the small graves of the ward pets. When they came to a walled enclosure, where the moss-coated branches of trees linked and bent over each other, forming swooping tunnels and odd shapes, Ellen wanted to stop.

Sif pulled her arm. 'Come on, we don't have long.'

'But what's in there?'

'Just old bones.'

'A cemetery?' She looked back. The ground was carpeted with fallen leaves. There were only a couple of gravestones. 'Who's it for?'

'Paupers. People with no family. It's not in use now. Come on.'

Behind them, the student nurse sighed. 'Girls, we're not going far. Ten more minutes.'

Sif quickened her pace, pulling Ellen with her.

In a small clearing, Sif stopped and closed her eyes. Lifting her face to the sun, she turned three times. Smiling, she opened her eyes, then she knelt. There was a withered tree growing at an angle from a low rock-face, and she held a slim branch in her hand. 'A sacred rowan like this was the salvation of my love, Thor. When the giants tried to drown him, he clung to a rowan, and it saved him.'

The tree didn't look capable of saving a midgie from drowning, but Ellen didn't say so.

'Soon there will be berries. We'll come again then.' Sif broke a slim branch from the tree and split it in two. She passed a piece to Ellen. 'Carry that with you. It'll protect you from the Dunain ghosts and witches.'

'Enough of your nonsense.' The student nurse shook her head. 'Come on.'

The soft ground crunched under their feet as they walked back. Almost at the duck pond, Sif said: 'Tell me about the conspiracy.'

Ellen hesitated. Was there any point?

'It's all right. You don't have to. I just want you to know, I'm not in on it, that's all.'

And so, Ellen told her, keeping her voice low. When she was done, Sif nodded. 'I hear you.'

***

AT LUNCH, SIF pointed out Mary MacLeod, the gatherer of secrets. Ellen immediately disliked the old woman in her pink nylon dress. She was creeping from table to table with a fawning smile and clasped hands, as she tried to wheedle information from people. She was a lifer, Sif said. She'd been in for longer than anyone could remember, and there was nothing wrong with her now, other than nosiness, pettiness and trouble-making. One of the Gaelic mafia, too.

That part didn't bother Ellen. She couldn't understand why anyone felt threatened by island patients conversing in their own language. Let the others learn the language if they were that bothered. There was just something about Mary MacLeod. Something creepy and wrong.

***

THE PSYCHOLOGIST WAS an elderly lady with a piercing posh voice, and she kept pouncing on words and phrases and questioning Ellen until she didn't want to say a thing. Did Solomon follow her every day? If not, why not? Where was he when he wasn't there? The other people at the train station, were they all in on the conspiracy to keep the incident out of the press? Was it feasible that they were all in on it? Could anyone else hear the voices? She wasn't aggressive, and she didn't ridicule Ellen. It was just her challenging questions. Ellen didn't know what to believe anymore.

The psychologist looked at her file. 'Your mother said you were a delight before this began.'

Ellen blinked away the threat of tears.

'Never any trouble. Well, a little moody in your early teens, but who isn't? All seemed well when baby was born, though you were very possessive. She was three months old when you first asked your mother to sleep with you. What was the reason for that, Ellen? Did something happen?'

Ellen shook her head.

'All downhill from there.' The psychologist took off her glasses. 'You know, I had a psychotic episode after I gave birth. Saw all sorts of things. Bats and frogs and locusts. Convinced myself the nurses were trying to kill my baby. Lasted for two days and never came back.' She shook her head. 'Your presentation is different. Started too late for postpartum psychosis. I agree with Dr Ross. Medication. A referral to occupational therapy, some group therapy. I think we'll get you sorted out.'

'What's wrong with me? Does it have a name?'

'Too soon to name it, my dear, but we'll get there.'

'What if there really is a conspiracy?'

The woman laughed.

51

IN THE FADED splendour of the dayroom, where a posse of women whispered and giggled in one corner, and a pair argued over a game of draughts in another corner, Sif sat alone, her feet up on the piano. 'How was the village idiot?'

Ellen shrugged. 'Which one?'

Sif laughed. 'Fair enough. The field is quite wide. The one in the white coat. Did she tell you about the bats and frogs and locusts?'

Ellen nodded.

'She's battier than any patient you'll ever meet in here. So, what's next?'

'Medication, group therapy, occupational therapy. I think that was it.' Ellen frowned. 'Are you on medication? Apart from the water?'

Sif looked a little confused. She nodded. 'Officially, yes.'

'What does that mean?'

She shrugged. 'I'll tell you sometime.'

There was a yell from the corner. Ellen turned to see the chequered board fly up in the air, draughts shooting out in all directions and falling to the floor.

Sif grabbed her hand. 'Run, before they riot.'

***

RIOTING SEEMED TO be the order of the day. First, there was food.

As long as Ellen didn't see the white sauce of the fish pie sneaking out the corner of anyone's mouth, she'd be fine. Across from her, Sif and Neil were talking politics. Well, Sif was talking politics at Neil, her voice loud, as if she was trying to keep him awake. He didn't look good. Hadn't eaten a thing, probably because his hands shook whenever he lifted his cutlery.

Ellen switched off. Her mother's constant ranting against the Tories had exhausted her. It wasn't that she didn't agree. She just enjoyed winding her mother up. At the last election, old enough to be a mother, but still too young to vote, she'd lied and said she'd vote Tory if she could. The look on her mother's face. It was priceless. Ellen hid her disappointment when Thatcher won again.

'So, Princess, what's your story?'

It was the hippy. She was sitting in the chair next to Ellen. At the other side of the table, a scowl distorted Sif's face. Neil blushed again.

'I'm Lucille,' the hippy said. 'Sorry about last night. Couldn't resist it. You looked so peaceful.'

She had a mocking smile and front teeth that slightly overlapped each other. The intensity of her gaze was disconcerting, a scary gleam in her bright green eyes. Ellen wondered if she was related to Solomon. He had green eyes too. Or maybe he was a shape-shifter. Just because she hadn't seen him for a while, didn't mean he wasn't here, in one form or another. 'I'm Ellen.'

'Nice to meet you. So why are you here, Princess Ellen?'

Before she could reply, Sif interrupted, her voice loud and angry. 'Why are you calling her that?'

'Lighten up, Syphilis.' Lucille leaned across the table. 'You do know that's what's wrong with you, don't you? That's what turned you mad. Price of being Thor's whore.'

'I'm a whore?' Sif laughed. 'You've shagged every conscious guy in here, and half the retards. Who was it the night before last? Patient or staff?' She sighed and rolled her eyes. 'Ah, I forgot. Even the most desperate of staff wouldn't touch you with a barge pole, no matter how hard you try. So, if that's not what gets you privileges, what is? Keeping the staff's dirty little secrets? Dobbing people in? Winding patients up to order when they need a scapegoat?'

Lucille's voice shook. 'Shut your mouth, bitch.'

Sif shook her head. 'Make me.'

'Sif…' Neil placed a shaking hand on her arm.

Lucille laughed. 'You too, fuckwit? Why are you indulging her? A Norse goddess? Read the books. You'll find them in her cabinet. Lady Sif has long golden hair. She's a symbol of fertility, a Mother Earth figure, not a skinny, androgynous, self-mutilating goth freak. Have you looked in a mirror lately, Joe 90?'

Sif launched herself across the table. By the time the nurses reached them, Lucille had long angry scratches down one side of her face, and Sif's hand was entangled in her hair. At a nearby table, Ellen saw a man pick up his trifle and throw it at the woman opposite. The woman screamed, and the dining room erupted. As a fight broke out at almost every table, Ellen wondered if there was any rhyme or reason to the individual melees. Were old festering scores being settled? Or was it just a form of entertainment? The staff didn't look amused. Ellen laughed when a trifle hit Nurse Ratched on the chin.

At the next table, there was a new sound. A man, and he was barking like a dog. He got down on all fours and bit the ankle of the man beside him. The bitten man jumped onto the table, and the 'dog' jumped after him, snarling and snapping.

Ellen slid to the floor and sheltered under the table.

***

THEY PULLED THE curtains round Sif's bed. There were three nurses, two of them men. Sif cried and begged and promised she'd behave, she'd sleep, she'd even apologise to that fucking… to Lucille. Anything but drugs. They weren't having it. Ellen shivered as the pleading turned to screaming obscenities. She fumbled in the drawer of her cabinet for her earplugs. Before she could insert them, she heard a whisper: 'Hey, Princess.'

She stared at Lucille with loathing. Lucille smiled. 'You get it now? I'm in charge here. That's what happens to anyone who crosses me. This is the deal – you pay me forty fags a week, I'll protect you, and I'll decide who you can be friends with, and it ain't that freak.'

Ellen's heart pounded as she lay with her back to Lucille. She didn't bother putting in the earplugs. She knew there would be no sleep for her. The stress had awoken the brain bugs. They'd crawled out of her head and they were nibbling their way down her arms. Soon her whole body would be covered in them. The singing voice had started. She tried not to listen, but it was hopeless. Not that the words meant anything. It was just rambling, echoing nonsense.

It wasn't long before she felt a sharp tug as Lucille pulled her hair. It took her mind off the bugs for a moment. 'Wakey, wakey, Princess.'

It happened twice again during the night when Lucille got up to go to the bathroom. Ellen kept thinking of her fork at dinnertime, imagining how, with enough force, Lucille's eyeball would have exploded and splattered across the room. How the singer laughed.

52

Ellen wanted to know what the pill was and whether there would be side effects. She was already being medicated; she told the nurse. It was in the water. The nurse looked at her watch. 'Listen, dear, I don't have time for this. You take it now and I promise I'll come and find you after I've done my round. We'll talk about it then.'

Ellen took the tablet, then she crept into the dormitory to see Sif. There was no sign of Nurse Ratched. The curtains were still round Sif's bed. Ellen peeped through them. Sif was lying awake, staring into the distance. She looked desperate.

'Hey, are you okay?'

It was an age before Sif answered. At last, she shook her head. 'No, I'm not.'

She sounded dopey. Looked it too. 'Is there anything I can do?'

'Can you make me drug-free again?'

Drug-free? Was that what she meant when she'd said she was officially on medication? Was she being given it but not taking it? It was none of Ellen's business, so she didn't ask.

Sif nodded at the plastic cup on her cabinet. 'You could get me some water, please.'

'Water? Are you sure?'

Sif almost smiled. 'It's not medicated, Ellen. Honest.'

Her hand shook as she drank. She passed the cup back to Ellen. 'Have you started medication?'

Ellen nodded. 'This morning.'

Sif tried to smile. 'God help you.'

'Are you getting up?'

She shrugged. 'Why bother?'

Ellen hesitated. She knew she should stand up for herself, but she'd never been any good at that. And maybe it would help if Sif had a mission. 'I could do with your help.'

When Sif heard what Lucille had said, she threw back her blankets and tried to sit up. Something knocked her back down. Dizziness, Ellen suspected.

Sif closed her eyes. 'Don't worry. She works in the laundry. Hardly see her during the day. Just at night. Sneaking around, annoying people, stealing.'

'Why don't we just tell the nurses what she's up to?'

She smiled. 'They know. Symbiosis. Lots of back-scratching going on.' She opened her eyes. 'Listen, I gotta sleep, but I'll be okay later. I'm here for you.'

**

IT SHOULD HAVE been impossible to nap in the dayroom, with Mary MacLeod telling ghost stories at the top of her voice. The white lady and her clammy touch, a certain sign of impending death. The hanged man that walked the geriatric men's ward, dragging a torn sheet behind him. The phantom toilet flusher in the hospital ward. Ellen swithered about going back to the dormitory for her earplugs or her Walkman. If anywhere was going to be haunted, it was this place, and there was enough crap in her head already. She sat as far away from the others as she could get, and she slept.

The nurse woke her just before lunch. She was older than the other nurses, and though she'd been impatient earlier, she was smiling now. 'Didn't sleep well last night?'

Ellen yawned and shook her head.

'Sleep is one of the best therapies you can get.'

She considered telling the nurse why she hadn't slept. Not the brain bugs and the voices. She wouldn't mention those. Probably no point in mentioning Lucille either. Sounded like she was well in with the staff.

'You were asking about the tablets and side effects.'

Ellen wasn't sure she wanted to know, but she nodded.

'It's an anti-psychotic. You'll probably get a bit of dizziness, drowsiness, blurred vision, dry mouth. Those are the most common side-effects. They rarely last too long.' She took Ellen's hand. 'I know it's difficult being in here.' She nodded across to the corner where the Virgin Mary was praying, loudly, and another patient was answering with obscenities. 'Doesn't help when you're surrounded by that kind of nonsense. Have you met The Minister yet?'

Ellen shook her head.

'He'll try to marry you off to anyone standing nearby, so beware. We've had a few who thought it was binding, some of them already married and terrified of what their spouse was going to say. One woman phoned the police to hand herself in for bigamy. Others have nipped off to the bushes pronto, to consummate their union.'

That made Ellen laugh.

'And then there's The Doctor. He's gone home, but if he comes back in, I think you'll probably be able to tell him from the real thing. Some can't. Oh, dear, the hysterics we've had to cope with after his doom-laden prognoses.' She squeezed Ellen's hand. 'So, we just want you to get better and get home as soon as possible.'

Ellen smiled. 'Thank you.' She looked at the badge on the nurse's chest. 'Nurse Barclay.'

'Liz,' the nurse said. 'At least when the charge nurse isn't around.'

53

No ONE ELSE watching the *Neighbours* omnibus could hear the voice from the TV. If they could, they wouldn't look so happy. The voice told Ellen she didn't have long before the medication would kill her. Better get her affairs in order. Make provision for Kate. Did she want buried or cremated? Funeral songs? The demon joined in then. No need for a funeral. No friends. No one cared. Ellen wanted to rock and moan and shout at the voices to shut up and leave her alone, but she didn't want to draw attention to herself. When a nurse came to tell her she had visitors, she stood and felt dizziness ringing in her ears. Despite it, she ran from the dayroom.

The sun was shining through the windows beyond the double doors at the bottom of the pink corridor. Two black figures stood inside the doors, their shapes wavering against the glare of the sun. Were they even really there? Ellen was scared to move, in case they disappeared. And then the smaller figure broke away and ran towards her, yelling and laughing.

Kate's embrace took Ellen's breath and almost knocked her off her feet. She steadied herself, lifted her daughter, and felt a pair of wee legs wrapping around her waist, skinny arms around her neck. Ellen didn't loosen her grip until Kate whispered: 'Mummy, you're squishing me now.'

Kate sat on her mother's knee, but not for long. When she went off to explore, Ellen looked at her mother and saw the tension and wariness in her. Though the demon told her she should be angry with her mother for visiting against her wishes, the whisperer reminded her of long-forgotten childhood falls and sicknesses and upsets that only her mother could put right. She took her mother's outstretched hand and held it tight.

In the café, the women behind the counter made a fuss of Kate, giving her a lolly and some juice. Ellen and her mother had tea and cake, and Ellen described Sif and the concert and told her mother of Liz Barclay's kind words. They walked back to the entrance, arriving at the same time as her father, then they sat on a bench in the grounds until Kate became restless and Ellen's head felt heavy.

'You'd best go now,' she said. 'I think Kate needs to get home.'

'But when are you coming home, Mummy?'

Ellen smiled. 'Soon, I promise. Look for me in the stars. I'll be watching you.'

***

ELLEN SNEAKED INTO the ward. There was no one around, and Sif's bed was empty. She wanted to get her Walkman, hoping some music would lift the Dread that had descended as she'd watched them drive away, that little hand waving from the back seat, and the demon whispering that she'd been a fool to trust her parents, that she'd never see Kate again.

Ellen's locker was a mess, and the Walkman was gone. She hid in the toilet, her back to the door. She didn't want to cry because her head was already sore and heavy, but she couldn't stop the tears. She should have asked them to take her home, instead of leaving her in this place with mad people and thieves. A sudden bang on the door made Ellen jump.

'Princess, what the fuck are you doing in there? I need a shit.'

Ellen had never been a fighter. It was partly fear of getting hurt, but mostly the Quaker teaching of her parents. When she opened the door and saw the arrogant sneer on Lucille's face, already scarred with Sif's scratches, a cold, sharp rush of anger engulfed her. She grabbed Lucille by the throat and pushed her backwards. Lucille stumbled and fell. On top of her, Ellen punched her twice in the face, then she grabbed her hair, pulled her head up and slammed it down on the hard floor.

'Fight, fight, fight!'

The living dead, the ones who slithered along the corridor walls, never raising their eyes, had come to life. Ellen and Lucille were surrounded by dribbling stinking shapes and mad laughter. Toothless grinning faces loomed over them, as Lucille's flailing hands reached for her face. Ellen shuffled forwards, her knees pinning Lucille's shoulders to the floor. She hadn't a clue what to do next. The fight had left her, but the self-preservation instinct was strong.

She looked up, and Mary MacLeod was pushing herself between two watchers, grinning as she wrung her hands, her false teeth clacking.

Ellen scowled. 'What are you looking at?'

Before Mary could answer, a hand grabbed the back of Ellen's collar and pulled her to her feet. On the floor, Lucille was groaning and crying, rolling about like a wounded footballer. 'Looney! Fucking bitch. She nearly killed me.'

Ellen's feet hardly touched the ground as two male nurses hauled her along the corridor. She couldn't see their faces. Just their feet. One of them opened a door, and the other threw her in. She sprawled on the floor as they locked the door behind her.

The room was small and dark, and it smelled of shit. The floor was soft. She heard a noise outside and a window of light appeared on the door. Two eyes peeped in, and, in the minimal light, she could see that the entire room was soft. It was a padded cell. And then it was dark again. She didn't want to move, not with that smell. Anything could be lurking in a corner. So, she stayed where she was, cross-legged in the middle of the room, as the brain bugs rushed from her head, down her arms and her body and her legs. She had to stop them or she would end up a screaming wreck, bouncing off the padded walls. They'd never let her out.

The whisperer whispered. *Think of something good; think of something nice; think of Kate.*

She closed her eyes, and she was back in the labour room. She could hear the muffled cries of her newborn daughter as they cleaned her up. She felt again the vast surge of love as Kate was placed in her arms for the first time. The bugs slid off her skin. Overwhelmed by tiredness, she felt the surrounding area, then she lay down and slept.

A soft touch on her arm awoke her. It had been such a deep sleep, she didn't want to open her eyes, didn't want to see who it was. There was a slight smell of aftershave and fresh air. 'Hey.'

A male voice. She opened her eyes. He was sitting cross-legged on the floor beside her, the light from the corridor flooding the room. Despite his size, she didn't feel threatened. She felt safe. She couldn't have said why. She knew nothing about him, other than he was a wonderful singer. Close up, he wasn't as handsome as he had looked on the stage. He had quite an ordinary face. Nothing wrong with it, but nothing special.

'It's you.'

'Aye, it is.' He smiled and the transformation of the face she had thought ordinary, and its effect upon her, stunned her into silence. It was as if the universe lit up, shooting a bolt of electricity through her heart.

54

LATER, AND OFTEN, Ellen would remember that moment, analyse it, try to make sense of the feelings that flooded through her. It wasn't unlike that first moment of seeing and holding Kate, and yet, it was so very different. She would ask herself, many, many times, if it was fate or just her disordered mind, seeking an anchor, that told her he might yet be her saviour.

'But... you're a nurse. You're not a psychopath.'

His laughter was warm and deep. 'I'm not sure being a nurse and a psychopath are necessarily mutually exclusive, but yes, I am a nurse. Did you think I was a patient?'

'They said you were a psychopath.'

And there it was again – an ordinary face, tinged with a hint of something unpleasant. 'Who said that?'

Ellen had never been a good liar, but at that moment, she surprised herself. 'Lucille.'

'Did she, indeed?' There was an edge to his words.

'Please don't tell her. She'll kill me.'

He raised his eyebrows, and she realised the absurdity of what she'd said. As if Lucille wasn't going to kill her for what she'd just done. Still, she didn't want him to know she was a liar, and she didn't want to get Sif and Neil into trouble. 'Please. No point in making it worse.'

He held up his hands. 'Okay, I promise I won't tell her, but...' The edge was still there, and Ellen hoped Lucille was going to suffer.

He sighed. 'So, what are we going to do about you and Lucille?'

Ellen shrugged. 'What can I do? She stole my Walkman. She's not letting me sleep. She says I have to pay her fags for protection, and she'll decide who I can be friends with. She's a bully, and I snapped.'

He nodded. 'Thing is, there's a pecking order in here. The longer-standing patients, the ones capable of working or helping out, have earned privileges. They see the ward as their patch, and they're suspicious of newcomers disrupting things. It might not be fair, but it's always been that way. Helps to keep the place in order.'

'I haven't disrupted anything. She just doesn't like that I'm friendly with Sif.'

'Sif?'

Ellen shrugged. 'I don't know her proper name, but they hate each other.'

He nodded. 'Ah, the fight at dinnertime last night?'

'Aye. So, I just have to put up with it?'

He put his head to the side and studied Ellen. She wondered what he saw, and what he was thinking. It was an age before he spoke. 'I'm not normally on this ward. Just filling in for someone today, so there's a limit to what I can do. If you promise you won't attack her again, I'll try to make things better.'

'I promise I won't make the first move, but I can't promise I won't defend myself if she starts.'

'Fair enough. Can't ask for more than that.'

He smiled, and Ellen's heart almost exploded.

***

IT HADN'T TAKEN long for news of the attack on Lucille to reach Sif several times. In the dining room, she congratulated Ellen. 'You didn't need my help after all. She'll not be showing her face in here tonight. She'll be skulking in a hole somewhere. Silly bitch. I don't know why she's got away with so much. She and Mildred Ratched are like that.' She crossed her fingers. 'I have considered

she might be the illegitimate lovechild of Ratched and the Lizard.'
She shuddered, making Ellen laugh.

'The nurse,' Ellen said. 'The one that stopped it. He came to talk to me afterwards. He was nice.'

'Yeah?' Sif smiled. 'A nice nurse? Who was it?'

Ellen lowered her voice. 'The one who sang at the concert. You and Neil said he was a psychopath, but he seems nice.'

Sif put her cutlery down. She stared at Ellen with a look that was hard to read. It made her feel uncomfortable.

'Ellen,' she said, at last, 'most of the staff in here are good people. Why else would they do this? They might have their off days or even weeks when they're less compassionate than they could be, but that's life. No one gets it right all the time. We forget their world doesn't actually revolve around us. This is just their job. They have lives and families and worries that have nothing to do with us, and sometimes that affects how they are. Mostly, they're a good bunch. And then, there are a handful of bad bastards.' She nodded towards Nurse Ratched. 'That's one. Jamie O is another.'

'Jamie O?'

'The cute soft pet name for Nurse James Francis Ogilvie. Most charming of charmers. Smile that lights up a room. A voice like treacle. Champion talker-downer.'

'Champion what?'

'He's a master at de-escalating a crisis. The best in the hospital, but only when the face fits. And yours obviously did. Just a great big cuddly bear. But bears have teeth and claws and you should never, never turn your back on one.'

They were both quiet for a long time. At last, Sif spoke: 'Thing is, Ellen, there's always a price for getting into bed with Satan. You're likely to awaken in Hell.'

***

THE LOOK ON Nurse Ratched's face. Pinched and peeved, as if

she'd just been forced to swallow a bunch of nettles. Ellen looked away. All she wanted was to get her aching head down and sleep, with no voices or bugs or hair tugging. But there were no sheets on her bed. She opened her locker, and it was empty. She groaned. What had Lucille done now?

'You. Sharp.'

Ellen turned towards the nurse.

'That's not your bed. You're in the end one.'

It sounded as if the words pained her, and Ellen remembered Sif telling her that everyone wanted the last bed, furthest from the nursing station, with only one neighbour. The downside was a longer walk to the bathroom at the top of the ward, but it meant no other piddlers passing your bed in the night and bumping into it.

Ellen's locker was tidy. She pulled out her empty rucksack and stuck her hand inside. She eased her fingers under the stiff fabric at the bottom. Her journal was safe. Everything was in the locker, except her Walkman. Oh well. She'd ask her parents if they could get her another. She had enough money for that. At least she'd escaped Lucille.

'Clever little stunt, Princess.'

At Lucille's whisper, Ellen jumped. She saw the beginnings of a bruise on Lucille's forehead, and a slightly cowed look about her, the usual swagger gone.

'Hey.' From the other end of the ward, Nurse Ratched was summoning Lucille with a jerk of her head. She looked a little scared. Whatever was going on, neither of them seemed too happy.

'You might be safe for now, but there'll be a reckoning,' Lucille said. 'Don't you forget that.'

Ellen's limbs felt stiff as she pulled back the sheets and got into bed. Reminded her of the time she and Hazel ran up Tomnahurich Hill twice for a bet. She dreaded the morning and another dose of the poison that was wrecking her head and now her body. As she laid her head down on the pillow, she felt a hard lump underneath it. Sliding her hand in, she found her Walkman. It smelled of his aftershave.

55

Dust motes shimmered and danced in the light that spilled through the dayroom window. Ellen was captivated. Outside, the leaves shifted in the breeze. Though it was early February, it was a summer memory that came to her. Sitting in the park with Kate in her arms, face lifted to the sun, the waving branches of the trees making shadowy swirls across the grass. Closing her eyes, she could remember every scent. The softness of baby powder, the delicious tang of cut grass, a distant barbecue in someone's garden.

Before, such a memory would have reduced her to desperate tears. Now, according to Dr Ross, she was showing signs of flat affect, with reduced expression and emotion. It was disappointing, he said, because the side effects of her current medication were far fewer than the others they'd tried. Rather than change the medication, he had added an anti-depressant a week earlier.

She was on her third anti-psychotic in six months. The first had left her so dizzy, she couldn't walk without falling. It was a common side-effect, and it would go, they told her. It didn't. There were other side-effects: stiff muscles, tremors and twitches, difficulty swallowing. They reduced as time went on, but the dizziness got worse. There were benefits of that medication – the voices stopped, and the bugs lay dormant.

On the second medication, she suffered the same transitory side-effects, but no dizziness. This one might work, Dr Ross had said, while crossing his fingers under the desk. Ellen couldn't see him do that, but she knew, because the voices were back, and the demon told her. At that stage, they were just whispers, and she didn't tell Dr Ross. Within a fortnight, they were screaming at her as if to punish her for banishing them. They conversed with each other as if she wasn't even there. They spoke of an elaborate plot within the hospital, involving unnamed staff and patients, to abduct, rape and murder visiting children. For three weeks, Ellen told her parents not to bring Kate to see her. Despite Liz Barclay telling Ellen she and a colleague would sit in the lounge area and watch while Kate was there, Ellen refused. What if Liz Barclay was in on the plot?

The demon had encouraged her to do stupid things, like pouring water over her head at mealtimes or getting up and dancing on the table. One night, after she'd done both during the evening meal, and been hustled from the dining room by a male orderly and Nurse Ratched, Sif had sat on her bed and asked her to stop taking the medication.

'It's messed you up completely, Ellen,' she said. 'Can't you see? You weren't like this when you came in. That's what these poisons do.'

Ellen had shrugged. She no longer knew what was real. She wondered if Sif was a plant, sent by her parents to spy on her. She almost asked, and then she remembered that day in the woods when Sif had assured her she wasn't in on any conspiracy. She'd gripped her friend's hand and promised she would get better.

'Not completely better,' Sif had said. 'I don't think I could cope without you in here.'

And now, although the third medication had erased the voices and allowed a return to normal family visiting, it seemed it wasn't working either. And the anti-depressant was giving her a dry mouth and a racing heart.

'Hey, honey. How you doing?' Sif sat down beside her. She ran her hands through her hair. The sleeves of her t-shirt rode up, and Ellen saw a bandage on each wrist. She looked away. There had been a commotion in the ward bathroom last week, and Sif had disappeared for a couple of nights, presumably to the hospital ward. Ellen didn't know what had happened, and she couldn't find the motivation to ask. Not that she didn't care. She hated the thought of her friend hurting herself, but her head didn't know how to process and react appropriately. How had Dr Ross put it? She was having difficulty translating emotion into a physical reaction. The flat affect was never more obvious than the day a naked Virgin Mary had streaked through the entrance corridor and out across the car park, followed by two yelling orderlies. Ellen hadn't even turned her head.

***

GROUP THERAPY COULD be a riot, a godsend, or a complete bore. Sometimes it was like a cabaret show. Ellen often wondered if the patients were deliberately trying to outdo one another. She always said as little as possible. She'd never been comfortable speaking in a group situation, and even when the voices were at their worst, and the demon was screeching at her to speak out, she wouldn't. On one occasion, she had folded in on herself, rocking and moaning, trying to drown out the demon.

No voices today. Not much enthusiasm either. All Ellen wanted to do was curl up in a corner of the dayroom and watch the dust motes again. Or maybe wander the corridors, in the hope of seeing Jamie Ogilvie. She had seen little of him over the last six months. Just the odd time in the dining hall or the corridors. He'd always smile, sometimes wink, and even at her worst, with voices raging in her head, she'd feel something lift her, even just a little. Maybe that was why she thought of him today. It would be interesting to see if his smile could lift the flat affect.

Duncan, the psychotherapist, didn't look much older than Ellen. He had long hair tied back in a ponytail, the faint remnants of teenage acne, and a CND badge. And he was useless at herding cats. It was hard to take him seriously.

'Ellen, I think we decided last time that you would bring a social skills topic for discussion to today's group.'

'We did?' Ellen had no memory of any such decision. The last group had ended when a new patient shit herself. They could probably have coped with that, if she hadn't plunged her hands into her knickers and started running round the room, brown stuff dripping from her fingers. Ellen and Sif had run for their lives.

'Sorry,' Ellen said. 'I've got a flat affect.'

He nodded. 'Okay. Fair enough. But, people…' He spread his hands and looked round the room. 'This is your chance to improve your interpersonal social skills and decrease your isolation. This place is earmarked for closure. Many of you are going out there, into the community. You need to be ready.'

'I'm ready.' It was the Virgin Mary. She stood and stretched her hand towards the heavens. 'I will fight the good fight with all my might.'

'As if you're going anywhere.'

At the sound of Lucille's voice, all eyes turned to the door. The Virgin Mary screamed and pointed. 'Lucifer – he's sitting on her shoulder!'

A groan ran through the room. Even Duncan slumped a little in his chair, before forcing himself upright and smiling. 'Lucille. Nice to see you. Find yourself a seat.'

Lucille looked around. There was a seat beside Sif and another beside a dribbler that had wandered in just before her. The dribbler wasn't meant to be there. She usually wandered the corridors as if she was searching for her sanity. No one had the heart to put her out. Lucille chose the seat beside the dribbler, probably because it allowed her to sit opposite Sif and smirk.

Duncan looked around. 'Does anyone else have a suitable topic for today?'

Lucille held her hand up. 'Please, sir, I have.'

He laughed. 'No "sirs" necessary in this room. So, what would you like to discuss?'

'Suicide attempts and how disruptive they are for other patients.' She smiled and looked at Sif. 'Especially when they don't succeed.'

Sif shrugged. 'Wasn't a suicide attempt.'

'Self-mutilation by deep cutting, then. The kind that happens whenever it's suggested the patient should go home. Let's talk about the freaks that get off on that kind of shit.'

Duncan coughed. 'What about work? You're all going to have to think about work when you're out in the community.'

'I'm going to work,' the Virgin Mary said. 'My sword is ready. I'm going to hack the unbelievers down. Slice them through their innards. Impale their heads on a spiked fence. Stretch their guts all the way –'

Duncan smiled and nodded. 'Good, good. Now, you're a worker, Lucille. Let's discuss the self-discipline required for work. That could be very helpful to you all. Tell us a bit about your day. Whether you find work rewarding. Whether the benefits outweigh the effort required.'

Sif was leaning back in her chair. 'I'd imagine Lucille finds work very rewarding indeed, given the privileges she earns.'

Lucille gave Sif her middle finger. 'And I would imagine Joe 90 hasn't worked a day in his life.'

Duncan ignored them. 'Ellen, what are your plans for work when you leave here? Do you have a career in mind?'

Ellen wanted to make things easier for him, lighten the atmosphere, but she couldn't. When Sif began to hum Kenny Rogers' song "Lucille", a move guaranteed to send this Lucille over the edge, Ellen got to her feet. 'Sorry. New medication. I can't think. I have to go.'

56

ELLEN PULLED THE winter air deep into her lungs. She should come out more. She'd been allowed out unaccompanied for a few weeks now, as long as she asked first, and stayed around the hospital. She hadn't often taken advantage of it, partly because she felt bad that Sif didn't have the same privilege, but usually because she didn't feel physically up to it. In group therapy, she'd felt a sudden anxiety that made her want to keep moving.

She shoved her hands in her pockets and walked across the car park. A tap on her shoulder made her groan inside. Who was it this time? There were so many possibilities, and few were attractive. Just last week, in the corridor with Sif, she'd felt an arm go round her shoulders. Sif had felt the same. Both thought the other was getting a bit over-familiar. Turning, they saw Jimbo, a tiny homeless man that was admitted every few weeks. He had stumpy black teeth, a wide grin, and nicotine-stained fingers. 'Hee hee hee, girls,' he'd said. 'All the blood comes pouring out. Got a cigarette?'

She turned and felt her stomach flip. Jamie Ogilvie was wearing a brown leather flying jacket, a knitted striped scarf, and jeans. His usually pale face was flushed, as if he'd been walking in the cold. He smiled. 'Hi, Ellen, how are you doing? I haven't seen you for a while. Thought you might have gone home.'

She shrugged. 'I wish. I've got a flat affect.'

'Ah. That's a shame. Did you get home for Christmas?'

'Aye. Just a couple of nights. It was nice, but I… I wasn't feeling good.' She didn't tell him that the voices had taunted her mercilessly. Screaming from the TV and the record player. Waking her in the night. Poking and shouting that everyone hated her, and she'd never be able to come home for good. Kate didn't need her, anyway. See how happy she was with her grandparents, how she always chose one of them over Ellen when she needed help with dressing or opening something or reading. The whisperer had stayed silent.

'I had problems with the medication.'

'Feeling any better than you were when you came in?'

'I don't know, to be honest. Some of the side effects are worse than the symptoms. I haven't tried to kill myself again, so that's probably a good sign.'

He nodded. 'Definitely.' He looked at his watch. 'I don't start for an hour. Do you fancy a walk? It's nice in the woods.'

There was something fizzing inside of Ellen as they walked, her thoughts and her heart racing. It was a new feeling, and she was scared to speak in case the jumbled mess bubbled out of her mouth. She didn't have to speak at first, because he did all the talking. Weather and Christmas and the coming of spring. Easy chat. All she had to do was smile and nod. When they passed the duck pond, Jamie walked ahead, and Ellen could hardly keep up with him. She shoved a piece of chewing gum into her mouth. She wasn't sure if it was the drugs or her nerves that made her tongue stick to the roof of her mouth.

He didn't slow down until they'd reached the cemetery. He apologised then. 'Never know what you might come across at the duck pond.'

Ellen frowned. 'What do you mean?'

He looked uncomfortable, a slight flush on his face. 'Eh… well… it's just… some patients hang about the bushes round the pond. Eh… couples… you know? The staff turn a blind eye. Bush therapy, they call it.'

Though she felt her face flush too, Ellen laughed. 'I've only been here first thing in the morning, with Sif and a student nurse. Probably too early for bush therapy, but now that you mention it, they were always in a hurry passing there too.'

He nodded. 'It's the worst-kept secret in The Craig.'

They settled down to a slow pace, and he talked about music. He was mostly listening to REM, U2 and the Waterboys. Ellen had taped some of their music from the radio, she said, but she hadn't got into any of them.

'You must,' he said. 'Especially the Waterboys' *Fisherman's Blues*. Best album I've heard in years. Kind of traditional mixed with country mixed with rock. I could copy it for you.'

Was he kidding? Didn't look like it. 'Yes, please.'

They reached a clearing with a fallen tree. It had moss-coated twisted brittle branches reaching out in all directions. Jamie looked at his watch. 'Still got a bit of time. Do you want to sit?'

Ellen sat on one end of the trunk. It was solid. Looked as if it had been there for years, as if nothing could move it, and yet, she felt a shudder run through the trunk when he sat on the other end.

'I haven't said thanks for sorting things out,' she said. 'The change of bed, getting my Walkman back. I really appreciated it.'

He waved his hand. 'Don't mention it. Any more problems?'

She shook her head. 'Lucille keeps away from me now. What did you say to her?'

'Nothing much. What music do you like?'

Whether it was the chewing gum, the winter sun, his easy chat, or the magical properties of the tiny piece of Sif's rowan tree she had in her pocket, Ellen had no difficulty speaking to him. They both liked Eurythmics, Human League and Simple Minds. He wasn't so keen on Madonna or Don McLean. Absolutely loved Springsteen, Meatloaf, Eagles and the Doors.

'What about Aztec Camera?' Ellen asked. She'd only recently got into them on Sif's recommendation.

'I saw them at Eden Court a few years ago. Fabulous guitarist,

Roddy Frame. He makes me jealous.'

Ellen smiled. 'You play the guitar too?'

'I try. Don't bring it to the concerts here, though. I'd rather keep it in one piece.'

'You're a brilliant singer.'

He shook his head. 'Nah. Just average.'

'I think the hall full of people shouting for more last August would disagree.'

He laughed. 'You have to admit, the bar was set pretty low. And I don't want to be insulting, but it's not that difficult to excite a hall full of psychiatric patients. You missed the Christmas concert and dance.'

He'd noticed she wasn't there. In a place that size? 'Yeah.' She picked some moss off the tree trunk and rolled it in her fingers. 'Let's just say the voices I was hearing then weren't exactly the quality of Roddy Frame or Jim Morrison. I'd probably have caused more disruption than Aggie with her big knickers.'

'You missed yourself. She pulled them down. A special Christmas treat.'

Their laughter disturbed a wood pigeon. Its squawk echoed through the trees as it fled.

'What did you sing?'

'"Rudolph the –"'

'Uncool. You did not.'

He shrugged. 'Can't be cool all the time. And there aren't that many cool Christmas songs, are there? Someone suggested Lucille and I sing "Fairytale of New York". Can you imagine? I'm sure she'd have loved to call me all those insulting names. The guy definitely comes off worse than the girl in that song, though some of the insults he returns could have been written just for her.'

'Ooh, bitchy.'

'And unprofessional,' he said, with a smile. 'Don't tell anyone.'

'So, what did you sing?'

He mimicked sticking his fingers down his throat. '"O Holy

Night" and "When a Child is Born".'

'They're beautiful, and they'd really suit your voice. I wish I'd been there.'

'Me too.'

***

THE FOLLOWING EVENING when Ellen went to bed, the cassette tape was under her pillow. *Fisherman's Blues* on one side and U2's *Rattle and Hum* on the other. She slid the cassette into her Walkman and listened to the first two Waterboys tracks. She loved the sound, but her eyes were falling closed. Another side-effect of the change to her medication, and one she would have welcomed at any other time. She flipped the cassette over and heard the last two tracks by U2. And then she played the last one again. When she woke in the night and got up to the toilet, the soft sound of "All I Want is You" was singing in her head and her heart.

57

DR ROSS WAS tapping his pen on the edge of the desk as he stared into the distance. The sound was reverberating in Ellen's head like a road drill, shattering her thoughts to smithereens, sending them skiting off in all directions and she couldn't catch them.

'Do you have to do that?'

He looked up, surprised. 'Do what?'

'That noise. It's excruciating.'

'Oh.' He stopped the tapping and went back to his thoughts. No chance of her recovering her thoughts. She wondered if he'd ever apologised for anything. The psychiatrists were gods in here, their word rarely questioned. They were almost as revered as Sif's Thor, though nowhere near as handsome and virile, if her accounts of her imaginary lover were to be believed.

Ellen groaned. She shouldn't have let thoughts of lovers and virility into her head. It was typical. While out in the real world, when she could have had a different guy every weekend, she'd felt no desire. Now, stuck in this place, with a motley bunch of men, too old, demented or neutered by drugs to be of any use to her, her hormones had exploded, leaving her exhilarated and exhausted.

Was it something to do with Jamie Ogilvie? She'd given that a lot of thought as she lay in her bed listening to the cassette over and over, rewinding again and again to hear "All I Want is You". It had started after their walk in the woods, but that was also around the time of the addition of the anti-depressant that had soon lifted the flat affect. As for Jamie, he was as elusive as Ellen's libido had once been. He –

'Ellen, we have a diagnosis.'

Dr Ross's words startled her. Not just the sudden sound, but the importance of them. Her heart began to race.

He put his pen down. 'There are no tests that can give us a definitive answer in this area. As you know, we diagnose by observing the symptoms and the response to treatment over time. I think we can safely say you have schizophrenia, and I would further classify it as the paranoid variety.'

The words slammed into Ellen's brain, crashing and breaking and tearing. She felt a wild howling rise from the pit of her belly, gathering force as it came. She opened her mouth and let it out.

Dr Ross looked at Liz Barclay. 'Nurse?'

Ellen felt Liz's hand on her shoulder, squeezing. 'Ellen, it's okay. The doctor needs to speak.'

The howl became a whispering groan that crawled round the walls of the room, before entering Ellen's head again.

'I appreciate... stigma... concern... serious condition... manage it... medication...'

The volume grew and the doctor's words faded.

A look of irritation, a look at his watch, a look at Liz Barclay. 'I think we'll leave it there for today.'

In the corridor, Ellen leaned against the wall and slipped downwards until she was sitting on the floor, her head in her hands. She heard the manic laughter of a passing old man.

***

WRONG DRESS. WRONG make-up. Old-fashioned shoes. Anger was grinding in Ellen's stomach. Made her want to throw the bag back at her mother. Tell her to fuck off and leave her alone.

'Those are the things you asked for,' her mother said. 'I wrote it all down.'

Ellen rolled her eyes. 'I don't think so. I'm going to look a right state at the dance.' She laughed, but there was no humour in it. 'This is what my life has come to. Nothing to look forward to but a poxy dance in a looney bin.'

'Ellen.' Her mother's voice was weak. 'I'm sorry about the diagnosis, but surely it's a good thing to know what's wrong? Now they'll be able to help you.'

'A good thing? You don't understand. My life is ruined. I won't get a job. I won't get a man. No one is going to want me.'

'Uncle Adam married and had a family after he stabilised on his medication.'

Ellen didn't answer. Liz Barclay had told her she could live an almost normal life, with the right medication and support, by learning how to deal with stress and avoiding alcohol and harmful behaviours. There was no reason she couldn't live an independent life with Kate, and maybe someone else, one day.

Ellen had laughed. 'As if anyone is going to take on a basket case like me.'

'Mummy.' Kate was back from her explorations. She tugged at Ellen's arm. 'Can we go to the duck pond?'

She would have said no, had her mother not complained of a sore hip when she arrived. Ellen tried to smile. 'Okay, darling.'

There was no sign of any bush therapy. Daft though they were, the copulating patients knew to avoid prime visiting time in the early afternoon. Ellen chased Kate up the path and round the outskirts of the cemetery. Her daughter stopped, her hand on the stone wall, her feet jumping on the spot. 'I'm very fast, Mummy, amn't I? I'm the fastest in my class.'

Ellen knelt and enfolded Kate in her arms. 'You are amazingly fast. And beautiful. And clever. And I love you more than anything.'

'Every night, Mummy, I look for you in the stars. When are you coming home?'

Ellen relaxed her grip and held her daughter away from her. 'Soon, darling.'

'Forever?'

'I hope so.'

Her mother was sitting on a bench with her eyes shut, face lifted to the murky sky, and Ellen was torn with guilt. She sat beside her and took her hand. 'I'm sorry, Mum.'

Her mother patted her hand and smiled. 'Cup of tea?'

58

ELLEN FELT AS if the music was inside her, chasing away the fear and the weight of the diagnosis. It was as if every song had been picked just for her. Or maybe that was what she wanted to believe, because Jamie Ogilvie was the DJ.

She closed her eyes and imagined she was somewhere else, where no one knew what she was. It didn't work. Even the vodka didn't help her forget she was in The Craig's recreation hall, surrounded by patients, leaping and clapping and stamping their feet. She was one of them now. No more telling herself it was all a mistake.

Someone touched her shoulder. It was Sif. 'You look gorgeous.'

Neil was with her. They danced next to Ellen, but she moved away. She preferred to dance alone, without the distraction of others, or the risk of someone expecting her to do some naff communal dance like the Slosh.

Not much chance of losing herself to Cher. She lifted her bag and headed for the toilet. In the cubicle, she took a swig from the half bottle Neil had arranged for her. She'd given him money, and he'd given it to someone else. Sif thought it was probably a member of staff, but Neil was giving nothing away. The vodka had magically appeared in a bush behind the café, just before the dance. She'd wanted a bottle, but Neil had asked her how she was going to fit it into her handbag for smuggling into the hall. She'd got the feeling there was more to it, and he was looking out for her. Probably for the best.

It tasted rough without a mixer, but it hit the spot, dulling her pain. She didn't recognise the track that was playing when she went back in, so she stood close to the entrance, her back against the wall, and she watched Jamie. She saw him run his hands through his hair, leaving it sticking out, and she wanted to go up on stage and smooth it down. She wanted him to put on something slow, and they would dance.

'Put your tongue back in. You've no chance.'

It was Lucille. Looked like she'd been on the hooch too. Her eyes were glazed, and she was swaying. Ellen wanted to stamp on her stupid bare feet, crush her toes. But she'd promised Jamie. 'Don't know what you're talking about.'

'Jamie Ogilvie. Prince Uncharming. Might have come to your rescue once, but he would never, never, never screw a dafty. Believe me, lots have tried.'

'Including you?'

'Not that desperate.'

Ellen knew it was a lie. She crossed to the other side of the hall.

'Okay,' Jamie announced. 'Last track before the ceilidh starts again. And it's Black Box, "Ride on Time".'

The music felt like fire flowing through Ellen, cleansing and healing. She was as light as air. Free. Alive. She didn't want it to end.

When it did, she opened her eyes and looked up, and he was watching. Not just watching. He wanted her. She knew it.

***

SIF AND NEIL were giving it laldy in a Strip the Willow, their swirling making Ellen dizzy. The ceilidh music was banging in her head, the stomping vibrations on the wooden floor drilling through her body. Jamie Ogilvie was at the side of the stage with Mildred Ratched and a couple of male nurses. He hadn't looked her way since she'd caught him staring at the end of the disco. At one point, she'd passed close to him. He could have spoken then, but he hadn't. Lucille was probably right.

In the toilet, she drank the last of the vodka, then she sat and waited for the music to slow down. As soon as she emerged, Neil grabbed her. 'Waltz?'

It wasn't exactly romantic, waltzing to a slow accordion tune, but Ellen closed her eyes and breathed in his smell. Their hip bones brushed against each other, and she felt fire stirring inside again. Neil whispered into her hair. He said she was a crazy good dancer.

She laughed. 'Crazy or good?'

'Both.'

He had a cute smile and lovely teeth. Shiny hair and a shadow of stubble.

'Did you really shag Lucille?'

His eyes widened, then he smiled and pulled an imaginary zip across his mouth. 'I don't make the best decisions when I'm not well.'

'Are you well now?'

He nodded. 'Going home next week.'

'I'll miss you. Lots.'

She saw his face flush a little. 'Are you coming on to me, Ellen?'

'Maybe. Would you mind?'

He shook his head, the flush growing.

'What about Sif?' Ellen asked.

'She's my mate, and she wouldn't cheat on Thor.'

'Yeah, but...' Ellen looked around. No sign of Sif. She lowered her voice. 'He's not actually real.'

Neil gasped. 'You're kidding me? Are you going to break it to her, or will I?'

They both laughed. The music stopped. Ellen held onto his hand. 'What now?'

He looked at the door. 'I'll go out first. I'll... I need to get something from the ward. Meet me round the back of the café, at the vodka pickup, in about ten minutes.'

Ellen smiled and nodded. She watched him walk towards the

door. Still smiling, she turned. Jamie Ogilvie was looking at her. His face wasn't ordinary, and it wasn't smiling. It was contorted with something dark and terrifying.

As the band struck up another fast tune, Ellen watched Jamie Ogilvie head for the door. Good riddance.

Sif sidled up to her. 'You and Neil looked close. Anything I should know about?'

Ellen shrugged. 'Not sure yet.'

'Be careful with him. He's fragile.'

He wasn't the only one. There was a shivering in Ellen's body and her head, as if every hope and ever fear and every heartache she'd ever known were all churned up together, mixed with vodka and desire and wild music. It could send her completely over the edge. Neil had said he was going back to the ward for something. She guessed what it was, and she knew she couldn't go through with it. Ten minutes passed. Fifteen. Twenty. She thought of him waiting. She couldn't just leave him there.

When she told Sif she was leaving, her friend smirked. 'Take care. It's a full moon tonight. A whole lot of madness out there. Speaking of which, I'm off to look for Jimmy Mac. He might be a raging lunatic, but he does a fine Canadian Barn Dance.'

The full moon illuminated Ellen's way. It was colder than it had been earlier, a wind whistling through the trees behind the café. There was no one there. She wrapped her arms around herself to stop the shivering. There was a rustle from the bushes.

'Neil?'

Bush therapy or one of the ward cats? She didn't wait to find out. She was almost at the hospital entrance when she heard a voice call her name. Damn. She turned. 'Where were –?'

Jamie Ogilvie looked dishevelled as he stood in the glow of the moon. His shirt was hanging out of his jeans on one side, one sleeve up, one down. There was resentment on his face, a touch of yearning, and a lost quality, like a child that didn't quite know what he wanted. 'Expecting someone else?' The words were tight, as if he had to force them out.

She shook her head.

'Go on, then.' He nodded towards the door, dismissing her.

Halfway up the corridor, Ellen looked back. He was still standing there, watching.

59

THE THOUGHT OF going beyond the cemetery on her own had always terrified Ellen. Too many dangers lurking in the trees. Now, the dangers lurking in her head were far more frightening, and they made her keep walking. She met a woman with an elderly dog trailing behind her, its stick-chasing days long gone. The woman smiled and said hello. Ellen hoped her response didn't look like a grimace, but envy was taunting her as she watched the woman walk on towards the normality of a real life. Was this what her life would always be? Bush therapy with another patient, if he even bothered turning up. Pathetic fantasies about a man that had looked at her last night as if she was shit on his shoe. Sleeping in a sixteen-bed dormitory in a Victorian hospital where she no longer heard the background sounds of weeping, screaming, shouting and groaning. Stepping on cockroaches in the dark. Aching for a daughter who was happier and safer with other people.

The downward spiralling of her thoughts took her off the main path and away from the possibility of contact with the lives of the normal. Away from the hospital and the staff and the patients, to a place where the trees grew close together, surrounded by a carpet of ferns and bluebells, and she had to crouch to avoid low-hanging branches. In a small clearing, she found a hidden place where branches swooped down, meeting a circle of thick bushes to form a moss-carpeted den.

Inside, she spread her jacket on the ground and lay on top of it. The trees stretched upwards forever, the tiniest chinks of blue and white showing between the branches. She imagined a rope and a noose and a long peaceful sleep. Or not so peaceful, if you got it wrong. There was that woman last year in The Craig. Did it inside the hospital, where there was more chance of early discovery. Still alive, with brain damage and paralysis.

In the same way as prisons were teaching grounds for criminals, you couldn't be a patient in The Craig without learning a thing or two about suicide. Guns and trains were the most effective methods, neither of which were readily available to the inmates. Hanging was high on the list, as was falling from a great height. If she could find a way of getting there, Neil's multi-storey car park was a possibility. Or the Kessock Bridge. Water had to be preferable to concrete.

And then there were tablets. Should she be like Sif and pretend to take them until she had enough to do the deed? Trouble was, everyone would soon know all about it if she stopped taking her medication, unlike Sif, who, despite her Norse god fantasy and her cutting, appeared more normal than most of the staff.

Death by cutting your wrists, despite its popular appeal, was at the bottom of the list in terms of effectiveness, as the wounds usually started to close up long before there was enough blood loss for death. It could be done, Sif had told her, with a hot bath, aspirin and a good artery, rather than the surface veins of the wrists. The thought made Ellen shiver.

Planning was hard. Ellen turned onto her side. On the remnant of a tree stump, she saw movement. It was a tiny ladybird, making its busy way somewhere. She watched it raise its spotted shell and unfold its long black gossamer wings. They flapped so fast, it was just a blur, and the ladybird was gone.

Ellen slept.

***

BACK ON THE main track, her hangover gone, the forest looked achingly beautiful. Everything was enhanced: the green of the ferns, the blue of the sky, the yellow of the gorse, the smells, and the sounds of the birds. With a smile, she realised she wasn't ready to check out yet. She remembered a school art trip to Craig Phadraig forest. She'd done a series of sketches of ferns and bluebells, and then a watercolour that had won her a prize. There had been a time when the urge to create art had consumed her entirely. Weekends spent in her bedroom, missing television programmes and telling her mother to tell her friends she'd phone them back. Most of the time, she forgot all about their calls. She'd forget everything, losing herself so completely, that all her worries and stress would disappear.

She'd chucked everything, all her materials and pictures, in a massive clear-out of her bedroom before Kate was born. Now, she wondered why she'd given it up, why she'd thought she couldn't have Kate and continue with her art.

She crossed a muddy area, balancing on a stone and laughing when it threatened to tip her off. Triumphant, her feet still dry, she jumped onto the mossy path. The main track widened and took her down a steep hill, and back round in the direction of the cemetery. One day, she'd go in through the gate. Poke among the leaves for signs of other gravestones. Maybe Sif would come too.

A man was standing by the cemetery wall, in the shadow of a tall tree. He had his back to her, shoulders hunched. It was Jamie Ogilvie.

She took a detour to her left, a path that led upwards for a bit, before levelling out at the back of the duck pond. She skirted round the side, coming out at the car park. She was almost at the hospital when she heard him behind her.

'Ellen.'

His face was pale and drawn. No smile. 'I'm glad I saw you. Just wanted to say I'm sorry about last night.'

Ellen shrugged. 'What for? Cher?'

There was a hint of a smile in his eyes. 'That too. It was a request – couldn't really say no. Eh… it's just I was… I was feeling grumpy when I saw you later, and I'm sorry if I sounded a bit off.'

From the corner of her eye, Ellen saw Mary MacLeod standing near the entrance, watching them.

'No problem.' Ellen smiled. 'Didn't notice.'

'That's good. So, we're okay?'

'Fine.'

He smiled that smile, and she felt it tug at her heart again. She wasn't having it. 'Got to go. See you.'

She could feel his eyes burning into the back of her head as she hurried away. She wanted so much to turn back.

60

THE FEEL OF the clay, the rhythmic turn of the wheel, the quiet concentration, mind and body in perfect synergy. It felt wonderful. The results weren't great. A misshapen pot that Ellen eventually painted with bright spots and filled with sweets for Kate, and a small dish that she gave to Sif. Sarah, the art therapist, asked what she had learnt from the experience.

'I'm never going to make a living from pottery.'

'Bit early to say that,' Sarah said. 'You've hardly started. Anything else?'

Ellen thought about it. 'I liked the way we didn't have to talk to one another unless we wanted to, and when we did, it was easy and relaxed, not hard and scratchy like group therapy.'

Sarah nodded. 'Good observation. Are you coming back for more pottery, or do you want to try the drawing class? We have a model this week.'

'Can I do both?'

'Of course. The male model will be clothed, in case that concerns you.'

Ellen laughed. She hadn't expected otherwise, but it was probably just as well. No knowing what a nude man might do to her raging hormones.

The model was Ron, an orderly from the locked ward. Sarah spoke about observing the model first, trying to understand the balance and weight distribution of the body. She advised against drawing a solid outline and filling it in with shading. Nor should they treat each part of the body as a separate entity. Instead, they should…

As Sarah's words faded out, Ellen studied Ron's face. He was a compact man. Sharp face bones, small nose, thin lips, a trio of tiny faint shaving scars on his chin and deep-set eyes the colour of forest bluebells. After a careful assessment of the proportions and the features, she began.

'Sorry,' she said to Sarah, at the end of the session. 'I didn't get past the face.'

Sarah stared at the picture for a long time before she spoke. 'You might not make a living from pottery, but I wouldn't rule out drawing. You are very talented.'

Ellen squirmed a little. 'It's not that good.'

Sarah raised her eyebrows. 'Believe me, it is. Did you see any of the others?'

Ellen laughed and shook her head. She'd been so focused, she'd seen nothing else.

'How would you feel about some homework? Maybe working on something connected to your condition, something to do with your emotions and how you feel about the condition?'

'I can't do abstract. I tried in school. Not enough imagination. Has to be something or someone real.'

Sarah smiled. 'That's fine. What about someone connected to your condition? Whatever you think. We'll talk about it next time.' She hesitated. 'And, Ellen, challenge yourself.'

Ellen left with a sketchbook, pencils and charcoal. She felt as if she'd been given a gold star.

***

IT WAS SHALLOW, but fun, to draw caricatures of the Lizard, Dr Ross, the psychologist and Nurse Ratched. Ellen didn't even have to look at the subjects to draw them. Their defects were imprinted on her brain. As a counterbalance, she sketched Liz Barclay and Sif, the two bright spots in her stay at The Craig.

Ellen was saying goodbye to her father and Kate one Sunday afternoon two weeks after the dance, when she saw Neil standing in the car park talking to an old man in a car. Sif had eventually discovered from someone else that he'd kicked off after the dance and had to be restrained and sedated. When she asked him, he wouldn't tell Sif what had caused it.

Ellen had time to get away, but she remembered Sarah's words about challenging herself. She waited inside the entrance doors for him. 'Hey. How you doing?'

Though he smiled, Neil looked sad. There was a faint remnant of a bruise around his left eye. 'Hi, Ellen. I'm fine. Just seeing my granddad off… always worry it'll be the last time I see him. Stupid, really. He'll probably see me off in the end.'

'I hope not. Haven't seen you for ages.'

Neil shrugged. 'Not doing so good again. Haven't felt up to going to the dining room. Listen, I'm sorry about that night.' He looked down at his shoes, kicking at some imaginary thing on the carpet.

'Doesn't matter. It was a silly idea. Too much vodka.'

He looked up and stuck out his lower lip like a petulant child. 'Don't say that. It was the highlight of the year for me. It was just… something came up. Something unexpected.'

'Lucille?'

He rolled his eyes. 'Hardly. Did you… were you there long?'

'Nah. Too cold.' She considered telling him she'd changed her mind, but he didn't need to know that.

'Maybe another time.' He smiled. 'Might even meet up in the real world, away from the crap that goes on here.'

Ellen smiled. 'Maybe. Can I draw you?'

She sketched him sitting in a chair looking out the window, a pensive expression on his face. 'That's very good,' he said, when she was done. 'But do I really look that sad?'

He looked sadder than she had portrayed him, but, again, she didn't tell him.

The day before the next art therapy session, Ellen considered her sketchbook. She hadn't exactly challenged herself. Even speaking to Neil had been much easier than she'd feared. She drew a series of sketches of Kate as a baby, based on photographs she had in her locker. Challenging? In a way. She could never look at pictures of her daughter without wanting to touch her, but she was used to that. She closed her eyes, and a face came to her. She hadn't expected it. Hadn't even realised his features were etched somewhere deep inside her, and time had not erased them.

***

SARAH WAS TRYING not to laugh as she looked at the caricatures. It didn't work. 'Don't be showing these to the other patients. We wouldn't want to start something.' She smiled at the pictures of Sif, Neil and Liz Barclay. 'These are quite a contrast. I'm guessing you feel they've been of more therapeutic benefit to you than the others?'

Ellen nodded. 'By a mile.'

'Gorgeous baby. Is she yours?'

'Yeah, that's Kate. She's six now.'

'Definitely worth getting better for. And he is…?'

Ellen's heart beat faster as she looked at the sketches of Someone's Cousin. She forced the unexpected words past a lump in her throat. 'I think he might be the reason I'm here.'

61

MARY MACLEOD DISCOVERED Sif's stash of tablets in an empty coffee jar inside a carrier bag at the back of her locker. What Mary was doing in Sif's locker, when she wasn't even on the same ward, was a mystery. Dementia, some whispered. Just badness, others said. Whatever it was, it meant that Sif had to be restrained and injected twice a day. Ellen tried to be nowhere near the ward when it was due to happen, but sometimes they'd come early. The screaming and wailing were hideous. On the third day, Jamie Ogilvie was one of the three burly male nurses who disappeared behind Sif's curtains. Ellen didn't make eye contact.

He sought her out later that day. She was huddled in a corner of the dayroom with her sketchbook, working on a picture of a smiling Sif, trying to replace the last image in her head.

'Hello.' He sat beside her. She put the sketchbook down on the table and he looked at it. 'Wow, that's amazing.'

'Thanks. How's Sif?'

He nodded. 'She's okay. We had to sedate her.'

'She hates medication.'

He shrugged. 'That's understandable, but it's for her own good.'

'She doesn't think so.' Ellen hugged her knees. 'She prefers her deluded world to one where she's medicated until she feels like a zombie. Where's the harm in it? Surely if she feels more alive and real believing she's Thor's lover, as long as she's not hurting anyone else, it doesn't matter if she takes her medication or not?

Isn't it your job to help her function as best she can, in as happy a way as possible?'

He spread his hands, palms up, his eyes on Ellen's. 'I can't argue with any of that, but it's not only about not hurting others. We have a duty to keep her safe from herself, Ellen, and I don't mean by protecting her from a fantasy affair with a Norse god.' He raised his eyebrows. 'Wouldn't life be simple if we could all get the pleasure she seems to get from an imaginary relationship and not have to put up with the crap that comes from the real thing? You must have seen recently what she's capable of, and the risk to herself.' He smiled, and Ellen felt her heart lurch. 'The staff say she's been much better since you came.'

'What happens when I go home? How can I leave her, knowing she'll be worse?'

He looked a little taken aback. 'You're going home?'

She smiled. 'Tomorrow. Just for the weekend, but Dr Ross said if that goes well, he might recommend a longer stay.'

'That's great news, Ellen.' He sighed and rolled his eyes. 'Bad timing, though. There's a film in the hall on Saturday night.'

'Yeah? What is it?'

'*The Shining*.'

Ellen smiled. 'Aye, right. Mary MacLeod is already terrorising the inmates with her ghost stories and tales of all the murderers in the locked wards. It's only a matter of time, you know, until one of them breaks out and slaughters us all. A trip to room 237 isn't a good idea.'

'Fair enough. It's *E.T.*'

When she laughed, he reached out and touched her forearm. 'It's good to see you smile. Don't worry about your friend. And have a great weekend.'

Ellen couldn't answer. She was trying to ignore the shiver that his touch had sent through her body. It was no use. She could still feel its echo in every cell, even as his footsteps in the corridor faded to nothing.

***

Sif had dark circles under her eyes. When she spoke, her voice shook. 'Bastards are threatening to force-feed me.' She reached for Ellen's hand. 'Feel that.' Her fingers were like a drill, the muscles contracting and relaxing, contracting and relaxing. 'It's poison. Fucking poison.' She groaned and collapsed backwards on her pillows. 'I need to tell you something.'

'Yeah?' Ellen stroked her arm. 'What is it?'

'Jeez, this is so hard, but I have to tell someone.' Sif took a deep breath. 'There is no Thor. No fantasy lover.' She laughed, a dry, hoarse sound that echoed around the dormitory. 'You and Neil, you've been so good. How you kept straight faces, I don't know. It was just a joke, but the Lizard got so excited, I swear he had a hard-on. Leaning towards me, eyes popping out of his head, as he asked: *do you have a carnal relationship with this Thor?* Truth is, I made it all up, just so they'd keep me in.'

'Why would you do that?'

Sif screwed up her eyes and held her breath. 'Because…' Another groan and the words came like a burst of gunfire. 'I'm safer here. There's a psychopath at home, and he made me everything I am. I've never been psychotic. I don't have schizoaffective disorder, no matter what they say. Depression, yes, and it's profound. What child of an abusive monster wouldn't be depressed? Lucille was right. I cut myself whenever they suggest sending me home, trying to cut out the poison he put inside me. It never works, so I just try harder. And now they're giving me this shit, and it can't help me. And I can't tell them because I love him and I hate him and my mother can never know what he's done to me.'

Ellen thought of her father and his safe, gentle love. She tried to persuade Sif to tell the staff.

'They wouldn't believe me. Thing is, my friend, I don't want to live anymore. It's such shit, this world, isn't it?'

'Don't say that. You need to get well, get out of here. We're going to the Railway Club and the Ice Rink.' Sif had told her she wouldn't be seen dead in the places Ellen went. 'I'll wear black lipstick, dye my hair blue. I'll even wear safety pins and chains, and I'll join you in the mosh pit.'

Sif shook her head. 'That's for the sweaty punks. We don't mosh. All you need to do is the Gothic two-step while staring at the floor and showing a general disdain for life.'

'I can do that. Anything.'

Sif smiled. 'Sounds so tempting. I do want to get out of this place. Who wouldn't? Lucille, the Virgin Mary, Mildred Ratched, Jamie O and his mega-watt psychotic smile.' She smiled then. 'The staff are worse than the patients. Who knew?'

Ellen wanted to ask about Sif's hatred of Jamie Ogilvie, but she didn't.

'I'd have to come and live with you,' Sif said. 'I can't go home.'

'No problem. My mother has devoted her life to helping the less fortunate. She'd have you stay in a heartbeat. The flat's tiny, but we'd get by.' Ellen had a sudden thought. 'We can get a place. You, me and Kate. Oh my God, that's such a good idea.'

'It is.' Sif nodded. 'It sounds fab. You've calmed me down now, and I have to sleep when I can. See these tremors? It's like I've swallowed a vibrator. Torture. Listen, there's a bag in my locker. Will you take it? Mary MacLeod was in again today. I don't trust her. Look after it for me. Don't ever give it to anyone.'

Ellen took the bag from the locker.

Sif smiled. 'I love you, Ellen. Not romantically, I promise, whatever Lucille says. I'm not androgynous and I'm not queer. If it wasn't for my bastard father, I'd have fought you for that spot behind the café with Neil.' She shrugged. 'If he didn't turn up for you, he wouldn't have turned up for me. You're special, Ellen. Beautiful, smart and funny and you don't even know it. You've made it so much better for me in here.'

Her words made Ellen blush. 'I love you too. I'll stay until you sleep.'

Ellen hadn't expected to find a friend like Sif, and certainly not in The Craig. Someone that was always there for her. Never pushy. Just there. Making Ellen laugh, calming her down and comforting her, helping her see sense when things overwhelmed her. Sif was bright and funny and compassionate, and without her, Ellen wouldn't have coped. Now, it was her turn to help Sif through this, so they could leave here and do all the things they'd talked and dreamed of.

Ellen sat long after her friend's breathing had settled into sleep, imagining the wonderful possibilities of a life beyond The Craig, a life with Kate and Sif.

When it was time to go, she kissed Sif's cheek. 'I'll see you next week,' she whispered. 'We've got some mad planning to do.'

62

Kate's beautiful face was creasing into little smiles as she dreamed of lions and rhinos, chimps and giraffes, tigers and zebras. They'd been to Blair Drummond Safari Park, and Kate had loved it. She was amazing. Delighted to have her mother home, but not over-clingy or emotional. Just so settled. The old Ellen would have felt threatened, preferring to see her daughter upset, rather than admit that her parents were getting it right. The new Ellen, or maybe safer to say this weekend's Ellen, felt happy and grateful, and so glad to be there. It wasn't sustainable, this false atmosphere with everyone on their best behaviour. She knew that's not how it would be if she was at home all the time. Still, she appreciated her parents for putting so much thought into making the weekend enjoyable.

On Sunday, her parents went to the meeting for worship, and Ellen took Kate to the park. She ran around with her friends, returning every so often for a hug. There was no one hiding in the bushes, and no followers when they walked along the canal bank. Telephone boxes were just telephone boxes, and all the curtains were silent. In the afternoon, they took a drive to Nairn beach.

Snuggled down in her bed that night, Kate asked if Ellen would take her to school in the morning. 'I want my friends to see I actually have a mummy.'

Ellen felt a wave of guilt. 'Does anyone say anything about Gran taking you to school and collecting you?'

Kate shrugged. 'The boys sometimes. I just bash them. Don't tell Gran and Granda, though. They wouldn't like me doing that.'

Ellen laughed. 'I won't. You know I can't collect you from school?'

'Aw.' Kate frowned. 'That's not fair.' She thought for a moment, and the frown was gone. She smiled. 'Never mind. I'll see you in the stars. Put the light off now, please.'

In the living room, Ellen's father had his glasses on, a look of concentration on his face as he watched a documentary about the Sahara Desert, feet up on the battered old pouffe, a mug of tea on the table beside him. Her mother was knitting, her eyes on the TV as her fingers moved, and her head kept a running total of stitches and rows. All so ordinary and so, so special.

Ellen read a magazine, then she went for a bath. Over the sound of running water, she heard the phone ring and the soft mumbling of her mother's voice. She sank into the bubbles, and it was heaven. No patients moaning or crying or banging on the door. No worrying about who had been in the bath before her and had they cleaned it.

When she went to say good night to her parents, she found them sitting in silence in the living room, the light off.

'Who was on the phone?'

Her mother hesitated. 'Just... eh... it was Meg. Some arrangements for a lunch we're doing.'

***

AT THE SCHOOL gate, as children laughed and cried and darted around them, Ellen held Kate tight. 'Look for me in the stars.'

Kate nodded, then she broke away to take the hand of another girl. 'Bye-bye, Mummy. I'll see you soon.' She walked away, and Ellen heard her say: 'See, Lisa, I told you I have a mummy and she's very pretty.'

'She is,' Lisa said, turning to look at Ellen. 'She really is.'

***

MARY MACLEOD WAS sitting on a bench close to the entrance door, wearing her pink nylon dress. Her eyes lit up when she saw Ellen in the car. She waved. Though Ellen wanted to ignore her, she raised a reluctant hand in response. Mary looked as if she might come over to the car. Perhaps Ellen's frown dissuaded her. She shook her head and scurried into the hospital.

Ellen turned to her mother. 'Mum, is there something going on? Dad was so quiet this morning. You both looked as if you hadn't slept. Did I do something wrong?'

Her mother smiled. 'You did nothing wrong. It was a perfect weekend.'

They got out of the car. Ellen opened the boot and took out her bag.

'I can't tell you how good it is to see you like this,' her mother said. There were tears in her eyes and Ellen wondered if that was it. They were just sad she couldn't stay at home.

'Never mind, I might get home for good soon. And I forgot to say, my friend, Sif, wants to come and stay some time.'

Her mother's eyes widened as if Ellen had said something shocking. She closed the boot, and they turned towards the hospital entrance. Liz Barclay was standing there, her shoulders hunched, her eyes red-rimmed, and she was biting at her lower lip. Behind her, a pink hand-wringing shadow hovered.

Ellen looked from Liz to her mother and saw the ghost of a shared secret shimmering between them. She remembered last night's phone call, and she felt herself hovering on the verge of unimaginable loss. She knew then just how fragile her mental state was. If they got back in the car and drove away, she wouldn't have to face up to it.

'Mum? Is it Sif?'

Her mother nodded. 'I'm so sorry, darling. It was wrong of me to lie to you, but I couldn't spoil your last night and this morning with Kate. I... I didn't want to let her down.'

Ellen felt Liz's hand on her shoulder. And then the world went black.

***

THE FUNERAL OF Joan Scott was to be held in private, and Ellen was glad. She had no wish to meet the monstrous father, or the mother who was too weak to be told the truth. She couldn't have heard her friend referred to by that name, and, much as she hated them, she couldn't have looked Sif's family in the eye without telling them she was to blame.

Ellen had spent two days in bed, refusing to eat or speak. She went over and over all that Sif had said and chastised herself for not telling someone. Her own selfishness appalled her. Going off to enjoy her weekend with hardly a thought of her friend.

On the third day, after breakfast, Ellen took Sif's bag from her locker. There wasn't a lot in it. A handkerchief tied around some dried rowan berries. Ellen almost smiled when she remembered the pantomime of gathering and drying them in the autumn, then turning them into a disgusting tea, more bitter than Nurse Ratched. Ellen had drunk it without complaint, so as not to offend Sif. Turned out she didn't believe any of the nonsense herself. There was a book on Norse mythology, and Sylvia Plath's *The Bell Jar*. It was a library book that should have been back three years ago. Ellen slipped her fingers into the empty card pocket at the front. It wasn't empty. She pulled out a slim metal object. It was a wrapped razor blade.

Ellen had heard that morning from Mary MacLeod, who heard it from Lucille, who heard it from Nurse Ratched, that Sif had carried out the perfect cutting suicide. A large dose of aspirin. A hot bath. And a severed brachial artery. She wondered now if Sif had left this blade for her. The thought made her shiver. She shoved it under the stiff base of her rucksack.

There was a cassette tape. It was Aztec Camera's *Stray*. Ellen hadn't yet heard it. Sif had only got it a few days earlier. Ellen turned the cassette over to look at the track list and saw that her friend had circled the name of the last song.

"Song for a Friend" was two minutes long, only four short verses, and it broke Ellen's heart.

***

ELLEN WAS DESPERATE to speak to someone about Sif, to find out if it would have made a difference if she'd reported what her friend had said that day. She swithered between Liz Barclay and Jamie Ogilvie. She'd been aware of them both at her bedside at different times in the first two days. Jamie had whispered her name and stroked her arm, and still she hadn't opened her eyes. Not even his touch had lifted her from the darkness.

She decided on Liz Barclay. She would be easier to talk to. It wasn't to be. Nurse Barclay had gone on sick leave.

There was sorrow in Jamie Ogilvie's blue eyes. It was real. He couldn't be a psychopath, no matter what Sif had said. He sat on the bench and smiled at Ellen. Not the full-on smile. This was a quizzical, lop-sided one. 'I've been worried about you.'

She didn't return his smile. 'Can we talk?'

He glanced at his watch. 'I'm finished in an hour. Do you want to meet in the woods by the cemetery?'

She nodded. 'Do you have a spade?'

His eyes widened. 'Eh... not on me, no.'

'Anything I could dig a small hole with? A trowel or something. Doesn't have to be very deep.'

He shrugged. 'I'll see what I can do. Should I be worried?'

She smiled and shook her head.

63

BENEATH THE ROWAN tree, Ellen dug a hole with the large serving spoon Jamie had smuggled from the kitchen. She placed Sif's dried berries in the hole, with a sketch of her friend, and a letter, then she filled it back in. Jamie helped her to gather stones, and they built a small cairn.

Ellen let her breath out in a long sigh. 'At least I have somewhere to come now. I don't want to visit a gravestone with that other name on it. It would feel like the grave of a stranger.' She looked up at Jamie. 'D'you think I'm mad?'

He shook his head. 'It's important to have somewhere to come and remember.'

'Can I take you somewhere else? It's a good place to talk.'

Ellen led him to her secret den. She'd been back a few times, and she'd found an easier route, with fewer low-hanging branches. Inside, they sat on tree stumps, and she told him Sif's story. He didn't interrupt. Just waited until she finished, then he took a hankie from his pocket and passed it to her.

'Sorry.' She wiped her eyes, blew her nose and clutched the soggy hankie. 'What do you think? Would it have helped if I'd told anyone before I went home? Would they have changed her medication or done anything differently?'

He was quiet for a long time, his elbows resting on his knees. He sighed. 'I don't think so, Ellen, for a few reasons. It wasn't your story to tell, and Sif probably wouldn't have thanked you.

As for her claims about the diagnosis, I don't want to be too blunt, but people with psychotic disorders don't always have the best insight into their own condition. No way was she prescribed an anti-psychotic based on a stupid fantasy. The doctors take their time with the diagnosis. I'm not saying they never get it wrong, but there must have been a significant history and pattern of behaviour before they reached that diagnosis. And let's just say she was right, and there was no psychosis: we both know she was deeply depressed, even if she hid it well. Say you had spoken to someone – the staff wouldn't have changed her medication on your word.' He shrugged. 'They wouldn't have changed it on my word. You might have noticed there's quite a hierarchy in there. The consultants only take notice of the charge nurse, so you'd have had to persuade the charge nurse, who would then have had to locate the particular psychiatrist who might have been off, or busy, or who knows what? Then Sif would have had to be open about everything, and, believe me, if she had already decided what was going to happen, she wouldn't have told them a thing.' He shook his head. 'I don't think any intervention at that late stage would have changed anything.'

His words made sense. 'What about her father? Do you think I should tell anyone?'

He frowned. 'That's a difficult one. He shouldn't be allowed to get away with it, but she said she didn't want her mother to know. And what proof would there be, other than the word of a dead girl? It's a decision for you, Ellen. I can't tell you what to do.'

She shrugged. 'There wouldn't be any proof, I don't suppose. And they're hardly going to listen to me, another psycho.'

'Don't say that.' He smiled. 'I'd hate for this to set you back when you're doing so well. How was your weekend?'

'Great. All the way back here in the car, I was so excited, wanting to tell Sif how well it had gone. I was certain I'd be out soon, and then she'd get out too, and we'd get a place together like we'd talked about.' She felt the tears coming again. 'And then

I arrived and saw Liz Barclay's face and…'

He pulled another hankie from his pocket, but he didn't give it to her. Instead, he moved closer, kneeling on the soft ground in front of her, and he wiped her tears.

'Hey,' he whispered, his hand stroking her hair. 'You're going to be okay.'

She looked up and nodded, then she lifted her hand to cover his. She felt a jolt running through her, like a muted electric shock.

Her words came in a whisper. 'Did you feel that?'

His eyes widened, and he nodded.

When they kissed, Ellen felt as if the universe stirred and moved, planets clashing against each other in a frenzied sparkling dance. There was an explosion, a hundred stars falling around them in a curtain of light. She felt…

She felt him pull away. No…

He sat back on his heels and let his hands slide down her arms. 'I shouldn't have done that. I'm sorry.'

She couldn't speak.

'I've tried so hard to stay away from you,' he said. 'Doesn't mean I don't think about you all the time. But it's unethical. I can't risk your health or my career. They're both too important. And it's not just that. I'm…'

Ellen was on her knees before him. She put a finger on his lips, running her other hand down his cheek.

He groaned and shook his head. 'We can't do this.'

'Are you sure?'

'I'm not sure of anything.'

Ellen smiled and kissed him again.

The forest floor felt like a mattress of silk, the pillow of bluebells forming a halo around her head.

Ellen would never again hear forest birdsong or a breeze sighing through silky beech leaves without remembering the gentleness of his touch, the softness of the skin at the base of his throat, and the smell of his hair. And more. The aching whisper of his words echoed in her heart, chasing away the cold, harsh memory of a twin bed in Hazel's room and a man that only knew how to take.

***

SOMETIMES ELLEN FORGOT about Sif for an entire day. At bedtime, she'd look across the dormitory and a desperate wave of longing would threaten to unravel her progress. How could someone so vibrant just be gone? She'd take out her sketchbook and try to remember every expression, every frown and every smile, scribbling by torchlight under the covers. Other days, the loss was constant from the moment she opened her eyes. There was no other patient she could laugh or cry with. No one to watch out for her or tell her when she needed to get a grip. The world was so dull without Sif. Still, it astounded the professionals that her friend's death hadn't set Ellen back more. They didn't know why that was, and she could tell no one. Her days were busy now. In art therapy, she'd enjoyed more pottery and a lot of drawing. She was hoping to start painting soon. Sometimes Sarah tried to get her to talk about the sketch of Someone's Cousin, but he was back in that box, and she wasn't letting him out.

Group therapy had improved because Lucille had stopped coming. No point, if there was no one to wind up. They discussed useful things like coping strategies and reality checking, the problems of stigma and family conflict. Ellen even looked forward to it. She took cookery lessons and a parenting class. And then there was her own upmarket bush therapy.

She and Jamie would arrive at their secret place from different directions. Sometimes, if she got there first, she'd hear a faint whisper in the rustling leaves telling her he wasn't coming. She'd ignore it, for those voices were long gone. It was just her own insecurity. He was late a couple of times, but he always showed up.

They never had long enough, and sometimes the weather tried to spoil their plans. Though the den was well-hidden, it wasn't waterproof. One rainy day, Jamie produced a thin groundsheet and a massive golf umbrella from his rucksack. 'No one can say I don't know how to spoil a girl.'

His plan worked, and Ellen was kept dry for a time, until a tremendous gust of wind came howling through the forest, catching the umbrella and sending it skiting round the den. Jamie paused and watched it crash and crumple against a bush. 'Do you want to stop?'

Ellen shook her head. They emerged from the den half an hour later looking like drowned rats. The forest smelled so fresh, it was heaven.

64

EVERY PARTING FELT like a knife twisting inside her. She longed to meet him somewhere else – a hotel, or his flat, or anywhere with a bed and a locking door. Not for her, Lucille's sick-room pleasures. He wouldn't agree to any illicit meetings in the hospital. It was too risky. He wasn't unfriendly if they came upon each other, but he was adamant they had to be careful not to alert anyone.

Sometimes when they met in the den, they just talked. Jamie had a store of tales from the old days. Alcoholic staff who sounded more trouble than the worst of the patients, elaborate tricks by patients to smuggle drink into the wards, a nurse that used to sip morphine while she worked. He had tales from the hospital farm that used to give work to the able-bodied men and kept the place supplied with produce. And mortuary tales that made her shiver, though one of them made her laugh.

'It was pitch black, middle of winter, blowing a gale. Thick snow swirling around their heads, as they pushed the corpse down towards the mortuary, in a metal trolley with a hinged lid. The wind was wild. It whipped the trolley out of their hands and it tumbled down the bank. They had some struggle to get it upright again, and back on the path. They reached the mortuary, opened the door and put on the light, then they lifted the hinged lid. The corpse was gone.

'Imagine trying to find a body wrapped in a white shroud in thick snow in the middle of the night. They had to get a team out to search. One of them was running around shouting the name of the dead man into the storm, as if he might suddenly shout, *Over here, guys.* They didn't find him until morning, and he was frozen solid.'

Jamie never told her anything current. Even if there was a scandal or rumours about a patient, he wouldn't discuss them with Ellen, no matter how hard she tried to persuade him. He reassured her Mary MacLeod's locked ward stories were nonsense. There were no murderers on the brink of escape, poised to slaughter the other patients, but that was as far as he went.

He had lots of tales from his student days. The older nurses would humiliate the students by sending them to another ward to ask for something stupid, like a left-handed screwdriver or a fallopian tube. He'd been caught out once, told to ask for a long weight. He got it all right. He'd stood in the corridor for ages, while the nurse allegedly 'searched' for it, before sending him off to another ward, where the same thing happened again. Three wards later, he caught on. He bided his time, then he got his own back on the nurse that had humiliated him. He slipped laxative powder into the nurse's tea. He was off sick for a week. Jamie thought he'd killed him.

***

ON A DAY when sunlight flickered in dancing shadows through the trees, she saw him sitting outside the den, his back to her. She crept closer, but the breaking of a tiny branch underfoot gave her away. She stopped and leaned against a tree trunk. He turned, and his smile rivalled the sun. He lifted a Polaroid camera. 'Don't move.'

She didn't have time to tell him she hated having her photograph taken. He took two photos, and he gave one to her.

'Can I take one of you?' she asked. 'Or we could try to take one of both of us.'

His smile disappeared. 'Can't risk it, Ellen. Not with the likes of Mary MacLeod snooping around.'

'As soon as I go home, I'm getting a photo of you, one way or another. For now, I'll just have to look at my sketches.'

His eyes widened. 'You've sketched me? Is that wise?'

'I've sketched everyone here. No one would think anything of it.'

He looked pensive. 'Are you going home soon?'

'In a couple of weeks. We can still meet up here, can't we?'

He shrugged, a peeved look on his face. 'Suppose so. Won't be long before you meet someone else and don't want to come.'

Ellen laughed. 'No chance of that. I'm going to put my name on the council housing list. Hopefully, I'll get a place soon, and we can meet without beetles and spiders and the threat of pneumonia after heavy rain. Or I could come to your flat.'

He shook his head. 'My flatmates are nurses. It's too risky.'

It seemed everything was too risky. Surely he wasn't bound by ethics forever? There must be cases where recovered patients dated their nurse. She didn't ask him. Didn't really want to hear the answer.

65

EACH EVENING, ELLEN lay in bed, synchronising her breathing to Kate's, and relishing the absence of all the ward sounds she had become so used to. Each morning, despite the medication fog that lasted a couple of hours, she'd take her daughter to school, then she'd walk along the riverside into town. In the window of the Job Centre, there were little white cards of opportunity. She read them, but she didn't go in. Not yet. She'd only been home for two weeks and the plan was to wait a while before any major changes. She went to the council and put her name on the housing list. The fact that she and Kate shared a room gave her a lot of points, the woman said. It might not be too long. She couldn't wait. A place of her own; somewhere Jamie could come. A proper bed. Watching television with him. Spending the night together.

They met twice in the forest after her discharge. She caught the bus up to the hospital. Scarf, hat and sunglasses on, she brought flowers to leave at Sif's cairn. It was the perfect excuse if she met anyone. Both times, he was waiting. No words were said until afterwards when they lay on the mossy ground looking at the chinks of sky through the treetops.

The second time, she could see the worry in his expression as he lay on his back, the sunlight twinkling through the trees. 'What is it?' She stroked his face. 'What's wrong?'

He sighed. 'That… that wasn't good for you, was it? It wasn't like before.'

'It was. I swear it was.' The lie burned her cheeks. She couldn't tell him it actually hadn't been that good the last few times, even before she'd left the hospital. Ellen had put it down to stress, believing everything would be perfect again if they could be alone together somewhere else.

He raised himself on one elbow and looked at her. 'Has anyone spoken to you about the medication affecting your sex life?'

She shook her head. No one knew she had a sex life. Who was going to talk to her about it? She remembered one of Sif's rants about the anti-psychotic drugs causing increased something or other in the blood, leading to a lack of sexual satisfaction.

'Have you… did you ever have problems before me?'

'Before you?' She laughed. 'I didn't have a sex life before you.'

'But Kate…'

'It was once. And don't say *unlucky*, like Dr Ross.'

'I wouldn't dare.'

'I… I wasn't interested before you.' Ellen thought about it. 'Actually, it was after taking the third medication and the anti-depressant that I started to feel like it. Maybe it wasn't you at all.'

He laughed. 'It was me, but it's not unusual for patients with your condition to lack sex drive. The medication often improves that, but eventually, the side-effects of the drugs decrease enjoyment.'

'Shit.' She closed her eyes and frowned.

He kissed her eyelids. 'Don't worry about it. I'll just have to try harder. Listen, would you be able to get away for a night?'

Ellen's eyes shot open. 'Would I ever?! Where? When?'

***

THE DEMON WAS back. Her voice whispered and echoed in time to the motion of the train. Ellen stuck her headphones on and turned the music up loud. When she took off the headphones to hand over her ticket, and then buy a coffee, the demon sneaked in.

He's not coming. He's not coming. He's not coming.
He's ashamed to be seen with you.
You're a fool.

Music louder, a little humming. She stopped when the man in front turned and stared at her.

When she got off the train at Perth, she thought of the day she'd escaped with Kate and then bottled it. She wondered how life might have turned out in Brighton. Would she have a job by now? A partner? Another child? And then she laughed. All that would have happened was a different ward in a different hospital. Kate would have been returned to Inverness or taken into care, and there would have been no Jamie.

In the hotel bar, she ordered a large vodka and Coke. Her hand shook a little as she lifted the glass. She wondered if anyone else was there for a secret liaison. Did they know the rules? She didn't.

He's not coming.

When she told the demon to shut up, the barman gave her a wary look.

The doors slid open. Jamie looked a little vulnerable as his eyes searched the reception area, his face clouded with worry. Perhaps he'd heard the demon too. He checked in, then he went to the opposite end of the bar. He ordered a large whisky and ice. Nothing for her. A brief stab of pain twisted in her gut.

'Can you put it on my bill, please?'

The barman nodded. 'What's your room number?'

'Two-three-two.'

He threw the drink back in one go, then he picked up his bag and walked over to the lift. As the doors opened, he turned and winked at Ellen.

She swithered. Follow him now or have another drink? She chose the latter, though it didn't go down as well as the first. It wasn't the same when she was just having it to make a point. Still, she took her time over it. When she was done, she went to the payphone and called home.

Kate sounded a little distracted, and Ellen felt a twinge of worry. Was the honeymoon period over already? 'I'm actually very busy,' the little girl said. 'Me and Gran are making a cake for you, Mummy. To welcome you home tomorrow. Where are you again?'

'Perth, with my friend.'

Ellen had tried to keep it as honest as she could. It was a friend she'd met in The Craig, she'd told her parents. She just didn't say it was a male friend.

'Okay, Mummy. Gran says you have to be careful because there's a lightning storm coming later. That's why it's all stuffy and hot. Anyway, I have to go or the cake will flop. I love you. See you in the stars.'

In the lift, Ellen's heart raced. She stood at the door of room 232, the demon shouting: *He's ashamed to be seen with you.*

She knocked on the door, and the sound was hollow. Maybe he wasn't even there.

'Tease,' Jamie said, as he took her hand and pulled her into the room.

66

By the time they remembered to eat, it was too late to go out, so they had dinner at the window table, overlooking the river. It was the first time they'd eaten together, and Ellen kept having to remind herself to stop watching him and eat. There was just so much to find out, so many things still to experience together. Anticipation bubbled inside her, fizzing and crackling. A sudden flash of lightning illuminated the sky, and for a moment, she thought she was responsible for it, as if her excitement couldn't be contained. She laughed as a rumbling roll of thunder crashed and echoed and faded, followed by the loud splash and hiss of torrential rain.

He told her of a massive storm he'd watched from a hostel in Sydney, lightning flashing in giant forks and branches across the harbour, the whole city blacked out.

'You've been to Australia?'

'Yeah. Spent a year there after I finished my training.'

'Tell me what else you saw.'

He seemed a little reticent at first, but she persuaded him, and then she listened in awe to his tales of snorkelling on the Great Barrier Reef, with its underwater rainbow of coloured corals, alive with turtles, tropical fish and starfish. His visit to the southeast coast, walking the Great Ocean Road and seeing the amazing limestone sea stacks called the Twelve Apostles, although there were only eight of them. The salt lakes of the outback. Shark Bay. The Sydney Opera House. Ayers Rock.

'Ayers Rock? The dingo baby and the mother who was wrongly jailed?'

He nodded. 'Just a couple of years before I was there.'

'Do you have any photos from your trip?'

'Somewhere – I'll look them out. They're probably not very good.' He frowned. 'You know, the first ten months of that year in Australia – that's the last time I remember being truly happy, until now.' And then he smiled that smile.

She almost asked what went wrong in the last two months of his trip, but she didn't want to chase the happiness from his face.

'And,' he said, still smiling, 'in a club in Melbourne, I saw the second-best dancer I've ever seen.'

'Yeah? Where was the best one?'

'In the recreation hall at Craig Dunain a few months ago.'

It took a moment for it to dawn on her. She shook her head. 'No way.'

He nodded. 'You've no idea how hard it was – how hard I was – watching you dance that night. I wanted us to go to a club tonight, so I could watch you again.'

She looked at the clock. 'We still can.'

He shook his head. 'Don't want to share you with anyone.' He wiped his mouth and put his napkin on the table. 'Maybe next time.' He turned and reached into his bag, where it lay on the floor. 'I've got something for you.'

He slid a flat box across the table. Ellen opened the lid, and she gasped. It was a gold necklace with a heart pendant. There was a trail of sapphires running across the heart.

'Thank you.' She wiped a tear from her eye and reached for his hand. 'No one has ever given me anything so beautiful.'

'Turn it over.'

Engraved on the back of the heart were the words *Yours forever* xxx

When she lay tucked into his body, her back against his chest, his arms wrapped around her, while the rain splashed down, and remnants of thunder grumbled, it was the best, safest feeling Ellen had ever known.

'How was it for you, Miss Sharp?' he whispered.

'Which time?'

'All of them.'

'Perfect.'

And it was. So what if she'd halved her medication after they met in the forest and had taken none for the last three days? It was worth it.

67

A LETTER CAME from the council. Ellen's housing application had been assessed, she was almost at the top of the list, and her doctor had provided the required medical evidence to justify a place in Dalneigh, close to her parents.

They won't let you go.

She'd have told the demon to shut up if her mother wasn't there, frowning.

'It's going to be okay, Mum,' she said. 'You'll be nearby.'

Her mother nodded and tried to smile. 'Are you feeling all right?'

It was hard not to snap. 'I'm fine.'

Ellen knew why her mother asked. There had been a couple of times when she couldn't think straight, another time when she hadn't answered the right question. But she was back on her medication. She'd be fine.

She was only back on her medication for two days when her mother answered the phone and passed it to Ellen. 'It's Joe.

Ellen didn't know anyone called Joe. She didn't expect to hear Jamie's voice. He laughed. 'Hello, Miss Sharp.'

The world brightened. 'Ah, that Joe.'

She sat on the padded seat of the hall telephone table and wished the kitchen door was closed. 'How are you doing?'

'I'm very good. You?'

'Fine, thanks.'

'*Mr G*'s on Saturday. You're going to pretend you don't know me. I'll sit at the bar and watch you dance. Afterwards, you're going to walk up Castle Street to the small car park on the right. There'll be a red van parked there. In the back of the van, you're going to take off your clothes and I'm going to…'

In the kitchen, her mother dropped something metal on the worktop.

'Okay, Joe. That sounds good. See you Saturday.'

Her face flushed, Ellen stood at the kitchen door and fiddled with her necklace. 'Is it all right if I go out on Saturday night?'

Her mother was stirring a pan. She smiled. 'Yes. Who's Joe?'

Ellen didn't hesitate. 'He was a friend of Sif's. He came up to The Craig to visit her, and we went to the café. He's an accountant.'

'Sounds nice.' Her mother lifted the pan off the ring and set it down on a trivet. She peered at Ellen's neck. 'That's pretty. Looks expensive.'

Ellen couldn't bear to take the necklace off, but she'd kept it under her clothes until she could think of an excuse that wasn't too much of a lie. Given the lies she'd just told, a few more wouldn't make any difference.

'Nah,' she said, sticking it back under her t-shirt. 'It was second-hand in a vintage shop in Perth. Looks more expensive than it was.'

***

As THE MUSIC and the vodka flowed through her, Ellen turned and turned on the dance floor. She thought of a picture she'd studied for art in school: Gustave Moreau's *Salome Dancing before Herod*. The thought made her laugh out loud. *Mr G's* was no magnificent ornate palace like the setting in the painting, and she doubted Salome's feet stuck to the floor, though she looked stiff in the picture, holding a lotus flower in one hand, the other extended in a rigid gesture. Ellen was a better dancer. She glanced up at the bar where Jamie sat. He looked mesmerised.

She felt a tap on her shoulder. It was a guy who had hassled her earlier. He looked decent enough. Maybe a year ago…

'Go away,' she said.

'Don't be like that, gorgeous.' He swayed in front of her. She considered asking Jamie for the guy's head on a platter. Laughing, she lifted her bag and went to the bar.

Too much vodka, too little medication, and a dangerous build-up of excitement swirling inside her made her stand right beside him. She could smell him as she ordered and paid for her drink. She turned her back to the bar. She almost choked on a lump of ice when she felt his fingers running up the back of her lace leggings. She glanced sideways at him and he was staring at the dance floor.

She finished her drink and put the glass on the bar.

'Heading off?' the barman asked.

'Yeah. Had enough. Too many creepy barflies.'

She felt a sharp pinch on her arse.

Outside, the moon was high and bright in a cloudless sky, the street heaving with people in various states of inebriation and excitement. Their excitement was nothing compared to hers. Someone tugged at her arm. A departure from the rules? Smiling, she turned. It was the guy from the dance floor.

'Fancy going to a party?'

'No.'

'Come on.'

'Get lost.'

They were standing close to the door. She saw Jamie come out. He was smirking as he walked past her. Her heart was racing, her mouth dry with anticipation.

A shout rang out. 'Jamie O!'

It was one of the bouncers. Ellen saw Jamie frown before he turned.

'I thought it was you,' the bouncer said. 'How you doing, man? Haven't seen you in ages. Not since you moved.'

The party guy tugged at Ellen's arm. 'Are you coming to the

party?'

'No. Go away.'

He shrugged. 'Your loss.'

She watched him wander off down towards the High Street. Jamie was still talking to the bouncer. She turned to go up the street, and the bouncer's next words hit her like a truck. She groaned and felt her bones and her stomach and her heart turn to jelly. She looked back at Jamie. He was ashen. Behind him, the ghost of a figure hovered. He peeped round Jamie. It was Solomon. He winked and smiled.

The bouncer said it again. 'The missus and the bairns… how are they doing?'

68

EACH FORCED INJECTION felt like another violation. Somewhere deep inside, the tiniest spark of defiance would tell Ellen to fight, to be like Sif. But the knowledge that they were going to do it anyway, just like Someone's Cousin, quashed the spark. There wasn't any point in fighting. No point in trying to improve her life. No point in therapy and support. The message was consistent now. No voices telling her she could have a good life, a career, more children. Just one voice now, telling her the truth. There was no point.

So, she gave in and let the staff do what they wanted. She rarely communicated with anyone. When her parents told her their news and how Kate was getting on, she nodded and said nothing, except: 'Don't bring her to see me.'

She ate just enough to stall the threat of force-feeding. She refused to go to group or art therapy, spending her time in the dayroom, sometimes sketching, sometimes listening to music, and often staring at the TV without hearing it.

It was mostly Kate that she drew in her sketchbook, a series of pictures from birth onwards. Where, before, pictures of her child made her ache, now they made her resolute. She was no good for Kate. It was best for her daughter if she stayed out of her life.

She drew a series of pictures of Jamie too, in a desperate attempt to get him out of her head. There was no smile. It was gone from her head and his face. She'd seen him often over the months since she'd been back in, and she had never once acknowledged him.

Not when he came to her bedside in the early days and begged her to talk to him, to let him explain. Not when he supervised the dining hall and stood near her table, watching. Not when she and a student nurse came across him in the car park on one of the rare occasions she'd been persuaded to go outside, and the nurses had stopped to chat. His uniform hung more loosely on him. His face was paler than before. But she sketched him as he had been, as she remembered. Only without the smile.

***

THOUGH LITTLE TOUCHED her, Ellen enjoyed having her hair brushed. Liz Barclay was always gentle, and her chatter was easy, despite the lack of response. One morning, four months after Ellen's readmittance, Liz finished pinning Ellen's hair up and told her she was to be transferred to the new psychiatrist.

'He's very nice,' Liz said. She glanced around, then she lowered her voice. 'Very nice indeed. I think you'll like him.'

Ellen felt the tiniest spark of interest. Not in the 'very nice indeed' doctor himself. Just that it had to be an improvement on the Lizard and Dr Ross. Oh, their disappointment to see her back. It was like being in the head teacher's office. She had been doing so well. What on earth had gone wrong? Why had she stopped taking her medication? Why would she attack a man for no reason? Why would she try to throw herself in front of a car? Who was Joe, the man she was meeting?

She told them nothing. She told no one about that night. How she had run from the club and grabbed the arm of the guy she'd turned down. Told him she wanted to go to the party. Hazy, hazy kissing up against a wall in the town centre. His hands on her body, and then a cold, white rage against him, against Jamie, against Someone's Cousin. Pushing his head back against the wall, punching him and scratching his face.

Solomon was there. He ran along the pavement beside her.

There was a taxi coming, and she threw herself into its path. The screeching of brakes, the screaming of passers-by. Looking up from the ground and seeing the number plate a centimetre from her head, and the faces of two police officers looming over her.

She'd said nothing in the car, nothing in the police station. She didn't react to the news that the guy didn't want to press charges, despite two passing witnesses. Of course, one officer had said, the witnesses hadn't seen what happened before the assault, and if this guy had done something to Ellen, she should tell them.

She told them nothing. Not even her name.

A doctor examined her. Nothing broken, no treatment required, but perhaps a psychiatric assessment?

Back in The Craig before morning, in her torn lace leggings, her new dress filthy and one shoe missing. Back in her old bed. It would be days before she'd discover both Lucille and Neil were gone. The Virgin Mary was in the hospital wing. Her right hand had offended her, and she'd tried to cut it off. And Nurse Ratched had moved to another ward.

***

IF ELLEN HAD been normal and real, the new doctor, who stood up when she came into the room, would have made her stomach flip and her heart beat a little faster. He didn't. Not that she couldn't see he was young and gorgeous, with his dark hair, brown eyes and lazy smile. She just couldn't feel it. He offered her his hand. Even as she put out hers, far too late, she expected him to pull away and pick up a pen or something. He didn't. 'Ellen, I'm delighted to meet you.'

Really?

'I'm Dr Tarantino.' He sat down and leaned towards her, his hands clasped, eyes fixed on hers. 'I've read your notes. Tell me how you're getting on. How are you feeling?'

She shrugged. 'I don't have feelings.'

He frowned. 'That's tough. I know you've spoken before of voices. Are they still there?'

She thought about it. There was no demon, no whisperer, no singer. They'd faded out within days of her readmittance. She hadn't seen Solomon since that night.

He smiled. 'It would be helpful if –'

Ellen held up her hand. 'Don't ask me which ear they speak into. It's insulting.'

He had a friendly laugh. Deep and warm. 'I wasn't going to, but it can be a useful question in the right circumstances.'

'Aye, for chancers.' Jamie had told her they used it to determine if someone was pretending to hear voices. If they said one or other ear, the staff knew they were at it. Psychotic voices were in your head, not whispering in your ear.

He nodded. 'Quite. So, your voices?'

Her silence didn't seem to faze him. He waited.

'There's just one now. It doesn't shout. I don't wake with a start in the night because it's yelled something random at me, something that someone else would find odd, like *bugs are eating your brain* or *Russian spies are following you*. It's different from the old voices. As if it really is just me talking to myself.'

'That's insightful. What makes you think it's you talking?'

'Because I know now that what it says is true.'

'Like?'

'There's no point to anything. Nothing is going to change for me. I'm not capable of being a good mother, and Kate shouldn't see me. Basically, life is shit, and it won't get any better.'

He looked devastated. 'Tell me about the previous voices.'

When she was done, and he'd noted everything, he put his pen down. 'I can see from your file there have been a couple of past attempts to harm yourself. Do you feel that way at the moment?'

Ellen shrugged. 'Not really. Can't face the planning. It's exhausting.'

'Have you planned before?'

'I didn't before either of those attempts, but I thought about it in the forest one day, months ago. Thought about all the ways and did nothing.'

'What stopped you?'

'Dunno. I had a hangover. Felt better when it was gone. Then I started art therapy.'

'But you don't go now?'

Ellen shook her head. 'Too tired.'

He nodded and leaned towards her. He was wearing an open-necked shirt. She could see his tanned skin, and a dark shadow of hair below his collarbone. The memories it brought back made her feel sick.

'I think your symptoms are under control again, but you're profoundly depressed. That's what's causing your lack of motivation, low self-esteem and hopelessness. In fact, it seems to me, you're not just feeling hopeless, you're feeling incredibly sad.'

The tears were so unexpected. Ellen didn't want to let them out, but there was no keeping them in. As they surged up from somewhere deep inside, she feared they might be accompanied by the same wild howling of the day of her diagnosis. They weren't, but if they had been, she had the feeling it wouldn't have fazed Dr Tarantino.

He passed her a box of tissues, then he sat back and waited.

When the tears had subsided, he spoke. 'The first thing we're going to do is increase the dose of your anti-depressant. You're on a very low dose, so there's plenty of scope for an increase. If you give me your word you'll take it, we'll go back to oral medication. I don't think you need the indignity of being injected, do you? And you must see your daughter, Kate, as soon as.'

Ellen nodded.

'I'd recommend starting group and art therapy again. And you need to get outside. Fresh air is a remarkable medicine. How does all that sound?'

It sounded like a lifeline she hadn't expected.

69

UNDER A CANOPY of branches, they sat on the blanket of moss and pine needles, and Kate told Ellen the news of school and the play park, her exploits on the magic tree, and her adventures on Blackbeard's pirate ship. She spoke of the safari park and asked if they could go again the next time her mum was home. It was the first time Ellen had been back in the woods. She'd been for walks with the staff, but never here. Kate had asked to go every time she came to visit. Maybe next time, Ellen would say, knowing there would come a day when she couldn't get away with that any longer. That day was today.

They didn't go anywhere near the secret place, or Sif's cairn, or the fallen tree. The woods were big enough to avoid those places. Still, it was hard not to think of Jamie.

Ellen had met with Dr Tarantino several times now, and the difference between his approach and that of his colleagues was incredible. He actually seemed interested in getting to know her. If he met her in the corridor, he didn't look through her as if she wasn't there. He stopped and made proper conversation. It was quite unheard of. At appointments, he listened and encouraged, and he made sense. She found she actually wanted to tell him things, not like she'd been with the others, where she'd feed them a snippet of something that might be important, then snatch it away and tell them a lie instead.

'Mummy, can we go to the café now? I've had enough woods.'

'Okay, darling. Let's get Gran and Granda.'

Her parents were sitting in the car at the duck pond. Her mother was frowning.

In the café, while her father and Kate were at the counter choosing cakes, Ellen's mother was still frowning.

'Mum, are you all right?'

Her mother smiled and nodded. 'Are you?'

She was. Better than she'd been in ages. 'I'm fine. Why?'

'You just seem a bit preoccupied.'

Ellen smiled. 'You know me too well. Dr Tarantino has asked me to write something. It's… it's quite personal, and I'm nervous.'

The relief on her mother's face. She put her hand on Ellen's and squeezed. 'You'll do him proud, love. You were always good at writing. In primary school, your stories in your jotter made me laugh so much. And your essays in secondary, the ones you let me read, were wonderful.'

'Dr Tarantino asked if I'd consider going to college. Maybe studying art eventually.'

'And will you?'

'I'm thinking about it.'

Her mother's smile lit the room.

***

ALTHOUGH ELLEN HAD left space in her journal for the events of 28th June 1985, she had never expected to fill in the pages. How could she find the words? Not that she didn't remember. Every detail, from the moment she woke up in Hazel's room, was imprinted on her brain. His face, his hands, his smell. She knew now that the effort of trying to keep him in the box had been part of her undoing.

She'd been complaining to Dr Tarantino about the unfairness of the small genetic risk of schizophrenia passing to her from her uncle, and yet not affecting his own daughter. It was unfair, he'd agreed, and then he'd asked about stressful events in her childhood. There had been none, she said. Despite her complaints and wishes that her parents had been different, she now realised how fortunate she'd been. Just because she'd wanted them to be more interesting, it didn't make them poor parents. They'd been wonderful parents.

His dark eyes were fixed on her face. 'A major stressful event in adolescence or early adulthood can awaken a genetic predisposition that might otherwise have lain dormant for a person's entire life.'

In the silence that followed, she was certain he knew. Of course, the Lizard would have recorded her comment about abuse way back at the start. He'd probably highlighted it in her notes as something to be explored again.

Dr Tarantino's smile lightened the tension. 'Think about it,' he'd said. 'If you want to talk about anything next time, or write something down before then, that's fine. Whatever you think best. I'm keen to get you home again, Ellen, as soon as possible, but I think the time spent on this kind of work is invaluable to your understanding of your condition, and staying well after discharge.'

***

IT WASN'T A case of not being able to find the words. They just did not want to come out and be crystallised forever into a story on a page, open to any reader's interpretation. They were her words, safe in that box in her head, even if they strayed from there occasionally. But she wanted to get better, to get home, and she trusted Dr Tarantino to help her do that.

Her permission to go out alone was reinstated, and Ellen wandered around the grounds, avoiding the woods, finding quiet spots here and there when the weather allowed. There was an old man in the hospital who had been there for years, and he made clothes and ropes and harnesses out of grass and wool and leaves. Sometimes Ellen would come across his amazing creations lying in the bushes. She'd sit beside them and make notes on bits of paper, tearing them into tiny scraps afterwards, until she was ready to commit it to her journal.

On the day she was finally ready, she took her journal and her sketchbook to the woods. At Sif's cairn, she sat and spoke to her friend. She didn't tell her about Someone's Cousin. She told her about Jamie Ogilvie, for she had realised there was still a barrier to getting her words out. In remembering and reliving that night in June 1985, it was impossible not to think about her only semi-comparable experience. Had Jamie violated her in the same way as Someone's Cousin?

It was only when the tale had been told to Sif, and Ellen had emptied her mind and eaten her lunch, that the answer came to her. It was an emphatic no. Jamie's love, if that was what it was – she didn't know, because the word had never been said – had not been abusive and invasive, and it had nothing to do with the power balance between them. It had been gentle and good, and even now, knowing the truth about him could not diminish that.

And then the words came. She didn't write of the deed itself. It wasn't necessary.

It's the start of the unravelling. It's the losing of myself. It is the end.

As she wrote the last line, she hoped this could now be a beginning.

70

ELLEN DIDN'T FEEL good the day she went to see Dr Tarantino. Her thoughts were dull and there was an edge of panic in her chest. They spoke about that first. She'd been good until recently, she said. It was hard to take so many steps forward, then suddenly go backwards.

He nodded. 'That's how it goes, Ellen, but it may not be the medication if you've been doing well. Has anything else happened?'

Two things had happened. Writing in the journal had left her feeling exposed and raw. And then, the same day, when she'd bent to straighten Sif's cairn, she'd found a note in a plastic bag, buried in among the stones. Her name wasn't on it, but who else would it be for? It was still in her rucksack, still folded up in its plastic bag.

Ellen didn't answer his question. 'I have to ask you something.'

'Anything.'

'Must you write everything I tell you?'

He put his pen down and leaned towards her. 'No, is the simple answer, but, if you were to tell me something pertinent to your condition, something that anyone coming after me should know about, then it would be difficult for me to justify not recording it.' He shrugged. 'I don't have to spell it out. If you were to say that you believed a traumatic event started this, but you didn't want to tell me what it was, I can write that down. When it happened, how you felt about it. That kind of thing.'

'I don't want to tell you. I want to show you, and I don't want you to write the details anywhere.'

She passed the journal to him, the sketch of Someone's Cousin that she'd torn out of her sketchbook marking the relevant page.

While he read, she watched a bluebottle on the window behind him. She could hear its angry buzzing as it bashed against the glass at the bottom, before settling down and making the long climb to the top. Another angry outburst and it would fall to the bottom and start all over again.

He had the journal in his right hand, his left elbow on the desk, his hand over his brow, so she couldn't see his eyes. It seemed like an age before he put the picture back in place, closed the journal and laid it on the desk. His expression was blank. He didn't look at her as he stood and turned to the window. He slid the bottom half of the window up and ushered the bluebottle down and out. He closed the window, and still he stood there, his hands in his pockets.

'Ellen.' His voice was hushed, and a little hoarse. 'You know what this was?'

'I don't know what you mean.'

He turned, and she tried to read his eyes. Anger. Sadness. Maybe the faint glisten of tears? Surely not. He sat and pulled in his chair, elbows on the desk, his hands clasped together in front of his mouth. She heard him take a deep breath, then he rested his chin on his hands. 'It was rape.'

Ellen swallowed, and it felt like there was glass in her throat. She shook her head. 'Not really. I led him on. Well, I think I did. I was so drunk. And silly. I didn't know what I was doing. I'd never... never done that... got drunk, or the other thing... not before that night.' She lifted her feet onto the chair and hugged her knees. She rocked forward. 'I can't... I don't want to believe Kate came from what you just said.'

He gasped. 'Kate?' His eyes widened. 'I... I'm so sorry, Ellen.'

'Do you... do you think this could be the type of thing we talked about, something that could have sparked it all off?'

He nodded. 'Undoubtedly. However you see it, whatever you call it, and I understand completely your reluctance to name it as

I did, you know he did wrong, and you know it had a devastating effect. You've written that here, powerfully.'

'I saw him,' she said. 'I saw him in town one day when Kate was just a few months old. That was the first night I had to ask my mother to sleep with me. I think that's when it all went wrong.'

Dr Tarantino nodded. 'That would make sense. Ellen, it was incredibly brave of you to write this. No wonder you're not feeling good today. You're going to feel mixed up and probably quite down about it for the next while, but this is a turning point. I'm certain of it. I would like your permission to write in your notes that you've told me there was a traumatic event when you were sixteen that you believe may have been the catalyst. How do you feel about that?'

Ellen shrugged. 'That's fine. I don't want my parents ever to know about it. As for Kate, I think I would like her to know when she's older. I want to be honest with her.'

He nodded. 'No hurry for that. You take care of yourself over the next few days. Please ask to see me if you need to talk before we're due to meet next week. We'll speak then about how you can process this. It could take time.' He hesitated. 'There is one other thing I'd like you to think about.'

Ellen moved her feet to the floor and flexed her shoulder muscles. Everything ached. 'Yeah?'

'I'd like you to think about whether, one day, you might feel up to reporting this to the police.'

Ellen clasped her arms around her chest, holding herself tight, as the cool breeze that blew across the fields below the hospital lifted her hair back from her face. It felt good, as if it might jostle all the bitterness from her like it was jostling the leaves on the bushes. She felt a thin spittle of rain on her cheek, and she hoped it might pour down and wash everything away. It didn't. The wind grew colder and her stomach rumbled.

In her bed, Ellen felt weighed down with weariness. It wasn't a weariness that would let her sleep. Instead, it poked and prodded at her. Had she done the right thing by opening the box and talking about it? Wouldn't it have been safer to have left it all where it was? If it had been a good thing, shouldn't she be feeling better now?

Dr Tarantino's last words taunted her. Reporting it to the police was a terrifying thought. And yet, it might help her move forward. So many mights and maybes – it was hard to know what was best.

And there was something else keeping her awake. The note in her rucksack. She wouldn't be able to sleep until she'd read it.

Under the bedcovers, the light from her torch shone on the faint handwriting. There was no telling when it had been written, but she suspected it was just after she was brought back in. There was nothing to identify the writer or the person to whom it was written. Even the handwriting didn't look like his. Too much of a risk if someone else had found it.

Even if you could bring yourself to speak to me, I couldn't find the words to say how sorry I am. I should have told you. I almost did that first day in our place. After that, I was lost, and it was just too late. I couldn't risk losing you.

There is something else I should have said. Again, I don't have the words to do it justice, but please believe me when I say I love you more than I ever imagined possible. I always will. I miss you so much. Your touch. Your laughter. I feel dead inside.

Perhaps she was a little dead inside too, for the words didn't seem to reach her. She had longed for him to say he loved her. Now, it just made her sad. She couldn't understand where it had all gone. The hope and promise, the glittering tales she'd woven of their future, the feeling of his touch, everything. Was that it? All just fizzled out because of his dishonesty? Or had she hidden it away like Someone's Cousin, in a box so deep in her brain, it couldn't be reached? Maybe one day…

Through a gap in the curtains, she glimpsed the dark sky prickled with a cluster of stars. She thought only of Kate until sleep finally came.

71

DR TARANTINO COULDN'T keep a smirk off his face, though she'd asked him to, several times.

'No one has ever sketched me before,' he said, his lips scarcely moving. 'It's hard to be natural.'

Ellen laughed. 'It's okay, you can relax now. I've got the bones of it. I'll finish it later.'

'Can I see?'

'No.' She put the sketchbook into her bag. 'Not yet. Thank you for that.'

He shrugged. 'My pleasure... I think. So, how are things?'

'Good.' She nodded. 'I've thought about little else but that night since we last met.' She picked up the plastic tumbler of water from his desk. She put it down without having a drink, and she took a deep breath. 'You were right. It was rape. There's no other word for it.'

He nodded. 'That's brave, Ellen. How do you feel?'

'Angry. At myself and him. It wasn't as if I was paralysed with drink. I'd sobered up a lot by then. I could have fought him off. Why did I just let him do it?'

Dr Tarantino laced his fingers together and rested his chin on his hands. 'What do you think?'

'I think... I think it was the words *I'm going to do it anyway.* They seemed sinister, as if he was telling me I had no choice. There was no point in trying to stop him.'

Dr Tarantino nodded.

'But afterwards, I should have recognised it for what it was. Reported it, or even just told someone.'

He smiled. 'I'm going to say something that sounds trite, but I often say it to myself when I'm beating myself up about something in the past that I can't change. Could've. Would've. Should've. Didn't. Can't.'

Ellen smiled. 'I'll try to remember that. But, although I can't go back and change what I did then, I can report it now.'

'Will you?'

She nodded. 'I know they can't prove anything without witnesses, but maybe someone saw him go into the room, or maybe he told someone, or he's done it to someone else. I need to get stronger first. I need to go home. I'll do it then.'

Dr Tarantino frowned. 'Ellen, I've been talking to Dr Ross about that. Although I'm responsible for you, he's my supervisor, so I have to discuss cases with him.'

Ellen gasped. 'You haven't –?'

'No. I haven't told him anything about that, and I won't. It's about you going home. He's concerned because you've never said why you reduced your medication last time. It's not unusual for patients to do that, but it normally happens after a much longer period, when they're certain they're going to be fine without it. With you, I understand it was really early and unexpected.'

Ellen looked over his shoulder, out the window. The leaves of the trees were turning brown. She felt a flush creep up her face.

'Ellen?'

'I… it… it was the side-effects.'

'It's noted that you had very few side-effects by the time you went home.'

Ellen wiped a prickle of sweat from her brow. 'It's not easy for me to say it. I was… I was seeing someone and… well…'

'Your sex life was affected?'

It sounded so matter-of-fact when he said it. Like it was no big deal. Ellen nodded.

'Mmm, that can be difficult.' He thought about it. 'You're likely to be on some form of medication for life, but things move on, they change. There are new anti-psychotics in development, which may not have that as a side effect. And people's life circumstances change and improve. That could include therapies and learning to cope better with stress. What I'm saying is, you may not stay on the medication you're on, or the dose may be reduced. Either of those things could help with that problem.'

'It's not… it doesn't matter for now. I'm not seeing anyone.'

'That's bound to change in time. But any reduction to the medication has to be done under strict supervision. You can't just do it yourself. Okay?'

Ellen nodded.

***

THERE WAS A concert coming up. Ellen didn't want to go, but Mary MacLeod kept harping on about it.

'Another one?' Ellen said. 'It's hardly any time since Christmas.' She'd avoided the Christmas concert by going home before it.

Mary laughed. 'It's three months, Ellen. There's been two concerts since then, and you didn't come to either of them. Go on. Might as well. What else are you going to do?'

She could sit in the dayroom with the living dead, or alone in the ward. Neither was very appealing. Mary was right. 'Suppose so.'

Mary gave a sneaky wee smile. 'Have you heard about Lucille?'

Ellen groaned. 'Is she back in?'

Mary shook her head. 'No. She's only gone and hooked a rich man, Mick Leonard. Local builder. Rumour has it they're talking about getting married. There's hope for us all.'

***

IT WAS ALMOST an exact repeat of the first concert, except Mary

MacLeod and her sidekick, a girl called Sandra who followed her everywhere, were poor substitutes for Sif and Neil. A wave of loss overwhelmed Ellen, and she had to close her eyes to stop the tears from spilling over.

An old man behind her was giving a running commentary on each act, and on the audience. When she turned to look at him, he was speaking into the middle of a toilet roll. 'It's the bonny one with the long legs and the pencils. Giving me the eye. Next, she'll be asking me to come up and see her etchings. Any time, darling. Any time.' He winked.

Mary muttered something in Gaelic. It didn't sound like a compliment. 'General George. Pretends he's not all there, but he is, as long as he stays off the booze. Comes in here to dry out every few months. He's fine now, ready to go home, but he doesn't want to give up the luxury of a warm bed and good food. That's all an act so he can keep his place. He'll be out of here like a shot if Jamie O threatens him with thon electrical torture.'

Dr Ross had mentioned electroconvulsive therapy after her readmission. He'd said if she didn't respond to treatment, ECT would be the next step. Though she knew it had helped others, they'd spoken of lost memory and a foggy haze for weeks afterwards. The thought of it was terrifying. She could well believe that nurses might use it as a threat, though she hated to think of Jamie being that cruel. She shivered and focused on the stage and the clattering sound of Aggie's spoons. Aggie didn't disappoint. At the end, she turned around, bent over and lifted her skirt.

'For goodness' sake,' Mary said. 'Could she not have put on clean drawers?'

The last act was announced, the one Ellen had been dreading. She heard Mary muttering again. 'If Jamie O was made of chocolate, he'd eat himself. Not that there's much of him left to eat these days. Wasting away. Must be the badness eating him from inside.'

She couldn't stop herself. 'Why don't you like him?'

273

Mary shrugged. 'He's wicked. A bully.' She smirked. 'Spent a lot of time at your bedside when you were brought back in, I hear. Looked very worried. And I saw you with him a few times before you went home. Anything to confess?'

Ellen's eyes widened.

Mary laughed and patted her leg. 'I'm joking. I know you wouldn't be that daft. Maybe you're saving yourself for the sexy doctor.'

'I'm saving myself for getting out of this shit hole.'

At the sound of guitar chords, Ellen looked up. He was sitting on a chair holding his guitar. He had no choice over the first song. 'Caledonia!' someone yelled, and half the hall repeated it. Ellen thought his voice was lacklustre. The inmates didn't seem to notice. The third song was something else folky. She heard little of it. Her heart was too sore from the second one.

He'd announced he was going to try something by U2.

'Who the hell's that?' someone had shouted.

'Rubbish!'

'Give us the Alexander Brothers!'

'It's called "All I Want is You".'

For most of the song, his eyes were closed. Despite their protestations at his choice of song, the raw emotion in his voice captivated the audience. On the last line, he looked up and straight into Ellen's eyes.

72

His footsteps echoed down the long corridor as he approached. Ellen looked behind. There was no one else there. As he got closer, she tried to stop her heart from dancing, but it didn't work. The song had wormed its way into her head and her heart, edging the lid off the box, rekindling...

They both stopped. Neither of them smiled. The silence grew between them, but neither seemed to want to walk away.

'I... I've got the afternoon off,' he said, at last.

Good for you, she wanted to say. Enjoy the time with your family.

'Would you... please would you meet me in our place?'

She shook her head. He smiled then, a rueful smile, all the dazzling radiance gone.

'Okay.' He nodded. 'Can't blame you. Take care.'

He walked away.

'I'll meet you at the fallen tree, in an hour.'

***

There was an icy chill in the air and no one else around. When he sat on the tree trunk, his diminished frame scarcely moved it. 'Thank you,' he said. 'I don't deserve the chance to speak to you.'

Ellen didn't disagree.

'Do you remember... that day... the first day, before we...

when I apologised after we kissed and I said it wasn't right?'

She nodded.

'I started to tell you then, but you... you stopped me.'

She'd given that a lot of thought. He was right. Maybe subconsciously, she'd known and didn't want to hear it. And she had definitely been the instigator. There was no doubt about that. But she hadn't then gone on to lie for months.

'You could have said it any number of times after that. When I'd ask what you were doing on your days off, on your holidays, you lied, repeatedly. Told me you shared a flat with other nurses.'

He nodded. 'I know. But telling you would have meant losing you. None of it changes how I feel about you. This has floored me, Ellen. I... sometimes I wonder about my sanity.' He rubbed his hands over his face. 'I don't say that lightly.'

The thought had crossed her mind too as she'd watched him in the dining room, staring into space like one of the lost patients.

'I seem to remember it was your career that you used as an excuse for the secrecy.'

He shook his head. 'That was no excuse. I would be finished if this came out.'

Ellen shrugged. 'So why are we here? You're married with kids. You don't want to wreck your career. All seems very cut and dried to me.'

'God forgive me for saying this, but I would walk away from... from my wife and children in a heartbeat for you.'

Ellen felt a groan rising from her stomach. Despite everyone thinking she was doing so well, and Dr Tarantino talking about sending her home soon, sometimes she felt as if everything was tangled and jangled in her brain. Her condition. The future. Kate. Jamie. Last night after the concert, she'd read his note again, and she'd had to crush the sparks of longing before they ignited into something that might derail her completely.

'Say something, Ellen.'

She shrugged. 'I don't know what to say.'

'I should have left her before now, but I'm weak. Scared I wouldn't cope on my own. I will leave, when I'm feeling stronger, no matter what happens with us. If you… if you still have feelings, we could move away. I could get a job somewhere else, where no one knows about us.'

It would be so easy to agree, or even to carry on as before, but something stopped Ellen. It wasn't just that he was married and she didn't want to be responsible for someone else's pain. It wouldn't be so difficult to put that to the back of her head, ignore it, let him be responsible for the welfare of people she didn't even know, didn't want to know. She couldn't articulate what stopped her from letting him in. 'Can we walk? I'm getting cold.'

They walked the circuit, saying little. She saw him glance down the path towards their secret place. She hurried ahead. At the cemetery, he stopped. He had that lost look about him again, like a neglected child. 'Please tell me if you still have feelings, if there's any hope.'

She pushed herself up so she was sitting on the wall. She looked somewhere over his shoulder into the darkness of the tall, crowded trees. Words and thoughts were jumbled in her head. 'I… I can't go back to how it was.'

'But you still have feelings?'

She nodded.

Jamie smiled, and it was almost the old smile in all its brilliance. 'I don't want to go back to that either. You deserve so much more. I… I'm going to leave my wife. I haven't been happy for a long time. Neither of us is. It was never right. I'm doing it for me, not you. Do you think we could… can we see each other, just as friends, when you go home?'

Ellen nodded. 'I'm hoping to get a place of my own soon. Let's –'

'Aye, aye – what's going on here?'

The voice jolted Ellen. She turned round to see Mary MacLeod and Sandra walking up the path towards them. She jumped down off the wall.

'Looking very cosy indeed, you two.'

'Hardly,' Jamie said, his voice cool. 'Just bumped into each other on a walk.'

Mary winked. 'If you say so.'

As Ellen walked away, she could hear Mary giggling.

Back in the dormitory, Ellen took off her jacket and hung it on the side of her locker. She put her hand into her pocket to take out her journal. It wasn't there.

Pinpricks of rain were falling on the surface of the duck pond. Someone had dropped birdseed on the path, and a frenzy of ducks were pecking and squawking around it. They scattered as Ellen ran past. They sounded as if they were scolding her for her intrusion. She was going to make for the fallen tree. Surely that was where she'd dropped the journal. And then she remembered sitting on the wall. Maybe it had fallen into the leaves in the cemetery. There was no sign of it inside or outside the cemetery wall. She walked away, and then she heard him.

'Is this what you're looking for?'

Jamie came from the trees to the right of the cemetery, walking towards her, the journal in his hand. Without a word, she took it from him.

'You dropped it when you jumped off the wall,' he said, his voice flat. 'I didn't see it until you and they had gone.'

'You read it.'

'Just the entry for 28th June 1985. It dropped open there. I swear, Ellen, I didn't read anything else.' His voice was heavy with emotion. 'I wish you'd told me. You said you only had sex once before me. I had no idea it was like that. That's… it was rape.'

Ellen nodded. From the trees beyond the cemetery, they heard Mary MacLeod's laughter. Jamie grabbed Ellen's arm. 'Come on.' They ran into the trees until they couldn't hear anything except the wood pigeons.

The rain had stopped. Ellen leaned against a tree. Jamie's face was dark with anger and loathing. 'Do you know who he was? His name?'

Ellen shook her head.

'Have you told anyone?'

'I... I wrote it for Dr Tarantino. It was part of my therapy... I –'

'Dr Tarantino?' There were two red spots on Jamie's forehead, his eyes narrowing. 'Why would you tell him and not me?'

'Because he's my doctor, and he's helped me more than anyone. No one else explained the role of trauma in schizophrenia; how it might have been that along with genetics that caused it. He encouraged me to write about it, so we could discuss it. He's even encouraged me to report it to the police. I... I haven't done it yet, but I will when I go home.'

'Sounds like he's doing the work of a therapist and not sticking to his own remit.'

'I couldn't care less about his remit.' Ellen tried to keep the anger from her voice. 'I wouldn't be ready to go home soon if it wasn't for him. I'd still be fucked up from what you and that other bastard did to me.'

His eyes widened. 'You don't think I'm like him?'

She bowed her head, as tears trickled down her cheeks. 'No. I don't think that. I'm sorry.'

Jamie's embrace was strong and safe, and she didn't want it to end.

73

Mary was such an unpleasant wee mix of sneakiness and nosiness. Ellen watched her approach, hands wringing, and that sly, twisted smile on her face. She knew what the old woman was going to say.

'You want to watch yourself in the woods.' Her false teeth clacked. 'Never know what kind of evil is going to come creeping out of those trees, especially around the cemetery.'

Ellen shook her head. 'For God's sake, Mary. He seems perfectly nice to me.'

'Aye, when the face fits. Watch him, that's all I'm saying. Not that he's ever been known as a philanderer in here. Just a nasty piece of work.' She sat next to Ellen. 'It's nice in the woods, though. I like trees. Hardly any where I come from. Maybe you and I could go for a walk one day. Sandra's going home tomorrow. I'm going to miss her. I'm fed up in here.'

Tough shit, Ellen thought, but she said nothing.

***

Dr Tarantino smiled and put his pen down. He stood up to greet her, as he always did.

'Ellen, have a seat, though this won't take long. Lovely to see you. Just wanted to let you know I've spoken to Dr Ross. He thinks we should aim for you going home in a week. You'll have weekly outpatient appointments with me. He thinks that's maybe where we went wrong last time. Should have kept a closer eye. How does that sound?'

'It sounds perfect.'

Liz Barclay hugged Ellen when she told her the news. 'Don't take this personally, Ellen, but I never want to see you again. Well, I'd love to see you again, but not in here. You know what I mean.'

Ellen nodded. 'I won't be back. I promise.'

'That's a girl.' She took a step back, and she frowned. 'Can I ask you something personal?'

Ellen nodded.

Liz hesitated, then she went for it. 'I just wondered, are you… is there someone special?'

Ellen shook her head. 'Just Kate. Why do you ask?'

'I wondered if that was what was behind your relapse last time. Just a feeling I had.'

'There was someone then. There isn't now.'

Liz nodded. There was more going on in her head, Ellen was certain of it. Had Mary said something?

'You take care. Important to get yourself back on track. Plenty time for romance, with the right person.'

***

MARY HAD A smug grin on her face and something secret in her pocket. No, Ellen said, she didn't want to guess what it was. She wasn't interested.

Mary snorted. 'I think you'd be very interested in this. And you wouldn't be the only one, let me tell you. Maybe I should just give it to the charge nurse. I'm sure he'd be very keen to hear what Jamie O has been up to with a patient.'

Dread stole Ellen's breath. 'What?'

'That got your attention.' With her little claw-like hand, Mary took a cassette tape from her pocket. 'Guess where I found this?'

Ellen shrugged and shook her head.

'Under your pillow. And guess who I saw putting it there?' She screwed up her face and mimicked Ellen's words. '*He seems perfectly nice to me.* I bet he does.' She read from the tape, a list of Ellen's favourite love songs, and a few she hadn't heard of. Mary smirked. 'And that's just one side.'

Ellen snatched it from her. 'So what? It's only a tape. I don't know why he would put that there unless it's because he knows I like music.'

'Huh. All the love and stuff on there. You're at it with him.'

'I'm not at it with anyone. I'm going home next week. Why would I do that?'

Mary shrugged. 'Why would he leave this?'

'I'm going to find out.'

'I'll come.'

'No.' Ellen put her hand on Mary's arm. 'It'll be embarrassing enough. I'll come back and tell you what he says.'

She found Jamie busy in a cupboard beside his ward. It only took a moment to tell him what had happened. His eyes widened. 'And she definitely knows it was me?'

Ellen nodded. 'She saw you. I played dumb. This is me coming to demand that you tell me why you were putting a cassette tape under my pillow. So, what will I tell her?'

He smiled and exhaled. 'God knows. Eh... you told me yesterday you like music?'

'Soppy music?'

'It's not meant to be soppy.'

'Okay. Beautiful love songs?'

'Beautiful meaningful love songs.' His smile was gone. 'She could make a lot of trouble for me, Ellen. She's never liked me.'

In the dayroom, Mary slavered like a dog waiting for a treat. 'What happened?' Her false teeth almost fell out, and she had to shove them back in. 'Tell me everything.'

Ellen sat down beside her. 'It's exactly as I said. He thought I might enjoy the music. He was mortified that I'd think there was anything more to it. Said he's married with kids.'

Mary nodded. 'Aye, he is. Effie MacRae's niece used to live next door to him. Says his wife's a torn-faced madam. Australian. He met her over there.'

He'd conveniently missed that bit out when he'd told her about his trip. Ellen remembered his comment about the first ten months there being the last time he was truly happy. Hopefully, he'd met the wife after that.

'And the kids are cheeky brats. A –'

Ellen cut her off. 'I'll never be able to look him in the face again.'

'Not your fault he caused this situation, is it? Ignore him. That's the best way. I hope you gave him the tape back?'

'I did.' She hadn't. It was under the bottom of the rucksack with her journal.

74

IN HER BED the night before she was due to go home, Ellen felt low, assailed by doubts and questions. Maybe she'd never get a job and a place of her own. Kate would probably hate not living with her grandparents. What if the voices began again and she couldn't sleep without her mother?

But mostly it was Jamie. She'd seen him that morning across the dining room. To say he looked unwell was an understatement. He was dishevelled and skinny, his hair unwashed and uniform crushed. He'd given her the strangest look, as if he hated her. She'd tried to find him during the day, but there was no sign of him. She really wanted to see him before she went home.

He should look happy. On Sunday morning, Mary MacLeod went off to church and didn't come back. When they checked her locker, there was a scrawled note saying she'd gone to live with her cousin in Dundee. Mary had phoned later in the day to say she'd arrived safely. According to Liz Barclay, no one even knew she had a cousin in Dundee, but it was in her notes that she'd said twice recently she was thinking of going to live there.

'How can she just leave like that?' Ellen had asked.

Liz had shrugged. 'Voluntary patient. They've been trying to get rid of her for years. I doubt anyone will miss her.'

Earlier that evening, Ellen had filled in the sketchbook with a series of pictures of Jamie smiling. She'd had to do it, to remove from her mind the memory of that look on his face as he'd stared at her across the dining room. Was he feeling insecure because she was going home?

No chance of sleeping yet, so Ellen took her torch and some writing paper from her locker drawer. She listened to his latest tape, and she wrote him a letter.

***

THE MORNING BROUGHT little relief. She hadn't slept well, and there was a grey gloom in the air. It was Liz Barclay's day off, and Ellen was sorry the nurse wasn't there. Her time at The Craig would have been so much harder without Liz.

After breakfast, she asked Dr Tarantino's secretary if he was free. She wouldn't have dreamt of doing that with one of the other doctors. He was free and looking very dapper in a white shirt, navy suit and turquoise tie. Ellen told him so.

'Why, thank you, Ellen. You're looking very nice yourself.' He frowned. 'But are you feeling all right?'

She smiled. 'Just the medication fog. I'll be fine. I came by to show you this.' She opened the journal and passed it to him. 'Not everyone makes it from the sketchbook into my journal. Just the special people.'

He smiled as he looked at the finished sketches of himself. 'Very good, but I think you've enhanced my looks a bit.'

Ellen laughed. 'Not at all. That's you.'

He passed it back to her, and she put it down on the desk. It crossed her mind that she hadn't seen the sketch of Someone's Cousin since the day she dropped the journal in the woods. She imagined his image flying around and landing face down in a muddy puddle. Stamped on and ground into the earth. 'I also wanted to say thank you. I wouldn't have got here without you.'

Dr Tarantino waved his hand. 'Nonsense. It's been all your own work.'

'Mmm.' Ellen raised her eyebrows. 'I think we both know

that's not true.'

'Can I… do you mind if I ask something?'

'Go ahead.'

He didn't look her in the eyes. 'You mentioned a relationship last time you were home. Are you… is it still going on?'

Ellen shook her head. She'd already told him that. 'Better finish packing up.'

He pushed back his chair and stood. 'What time do you go?'

'About one.'

He nodded. 'I'll see you in a week. Take care and keep up the excellent work.'

'Can I give you a hug?'

He blushed. 'Any time.'

His smell and the warmth of his embrace stirred something deep within Ellen. Stirred a little voice too. *This is the kind of man you need.* She told the voice, silently, to shut up.

***

ELLEN OPENED HER rucksack to pack the last of her things. At the bottom, she saw Sif's razor blade. The flimsy wrapping paper had come off, so she folded it in a page from a notebook and slipped it into her pocket. She'd dispose of it at home. Wouldn't want anyone here finding it.

It didn't take long to finish packing. She looked at the clock and thought of phoning and asking her mother to come early, but Jamie was still playing on her mind.

There was no sign of him around the hospital. Maybe a walk would clear her head.

There was a heavy silence in the forest. A gloom that seemed to sweep through the trees, making her shiver. She wondered if there was a storm coming, if the trees were bracing themselves for an onslaught. The whole world seemed different, and it almost turned her away. Almost.

In their secret place, she sat on the soft ground, beneath the canopy of branches, and inhaled. Beyond the smell of pine needles and a slight hint of burning, she could smell him. It wasn't her imagination. He must have been here recently. Maybe he came often. She wished he was here now, and it could be just like the first time. She smiled. So much for her resolve.

She considered leaving the letter here in the den, burying it and telling him on the phone where it was. Or even at Sif's cairn. She was going back that way. But she really didn't want someone else finding it.

There were fragments of scorched paper in a small pit close to the entrance. She lifted a couple of bits and held them up to the light. There was type-written text. *MacLeod... Crofter... District of Stornoway... Extract Entry of Birth*

There were other fragments, but they were too far gone to decipher. She sat back on her heels and wondered. A glint of metal in a pile of leaves behind the pit caught her eye. She brushed off the leaves and saw a folding spade, its blade clogged with earth. There was an area of disturbed soil beside it. She scraped the top off and then she squealed and jumped back. A pair of false teeth grinned up at her. Below them, she could see a patch of pink fabric. As the terrible truth dawned on her, she knew why the forest was so silent. It was frozen with fear.

'Mary,' she whispered. 'Oh Mary.'

Outside, there was a sound of rustling, footsteps approaching. In her mind, she ran through everyone who had a grudge against Mary. Anyone who might have wanted to harm the old woman. There were so many. Patients and staff. Dr Tarantino. He'd angered Mary recently by telling her he would discharge her soon. Please, please, please let it be one of them that has done this awful thing, she prayed. Even Dr Tarantino. Anyone but Jamie.

She held her breath as a shadow darkened the den. She couldn't see his face, but she knew.

'Ellen. I didn't expect to see you here. I thought you'd have left by now.'

She shook her head. 'One o'clock.'

He nodded. 'Will you sit?'

Her legs felt as if they were about to give way, as she sank to the ground. He sat opposite her, cross-legged, and she thought of that day in the padded cell, and his smile, and the feeling that he was going to be her saviour. She could see his face now. It was as if her prayer had been half-answered, for he didn't look like Jamie. Not the Jamie she'd loved and trusted.

'What have you done?' she asked.

He shook his head. 'I don't know what you mean.'

'Those teeth, and Mary's dress.' She nodded towards the remnants of the fire. 'Her birth certificate.'

He shrugged. 'She left them behind. I thought I'd get rid of them.'

There was panic rising in Ellen's chest. It felt like a sharp knife, bursting all the fickle dreams she'd been nurturing ever since she'd written the letter. She felt their fragments floating into the silence between them.

'You don't believe me?'

Ellen didn't answer. She couldn't.

75

Jamie sighed and picked up a dead leaf. She could hear the scratching sound of it rubbing between his fingers. 'I reckon we both have a problem with trust.' His voice was flat. 'I spoke to Mary before she… she left, and she told me she's seen you up to all sorts in the woods with loads of guys. Reckoned Daniel Tarantino was among them.'

Ellen gasped. 'I haven't been in the woods with anyone but you.'

'Why would she say that?'

'Because she's a twisted old bat.'

'Was Neil one of them?'

Ellen shook her head. 'There were no other men.'

'He couldn't have been that keen. Didn't take much to persuade him to leave you alone the night of the dance.'

She remembered Jamie in the moonlight, his clothes dishevelled, and then the fading remnants of Neil's black eye. 'You attacked him?'

He shrugged. 'Persuaded him to attack me, and then I had no option but to defend myself and have him restrained. It never took much with Neil. Short fuse, you see. So easy to manipulate.' He laughed, and it was a dry, humourless sound. 'Still, for all his faults, at least he was being responsible that night. Went back to the ward for his condoms. Did you know he's scared of the dark? And cockroaches. Peed himself once, after I shut him in the cellar.'

This wasn't the man she'd fallen in love with, the man who

289

brought her alive, gave her confidence and hope. He wasn't the man she'd written the letter to. This was the man Sif and Neil and Mary hated.

The look on his face was scaring her now. Anger and bitterness, his eyes screwed up into tiny dark holes. 'I can't believe I've wasted all that time, all that pain, when you were two-timing me. Three- or four-timing, probably. And with that bastard Tarantino. Sleazy, disgusting creep. I've seen him eyeing you up.'

'I haven't been with anyone else.'

He leaned towards her and she shrank back. 'Not even the night we were at *Mr G's*, and that creep was bothering you on the dance floor? You didn't go off with him afterwards?'

Anger exploded in Ellen's head. 'The night I found out you'd been lying to me for months? So what if I kissed him, while you went home to your wife?'

He shook his head. 'I didn't go home to her, Ellen. I waited for you in my mate's van. Fell asleep on the mattress in the back. Hell to pay when I got home the next day, I can tell you.'

Ellen shook her head. 'You thought I would still come?'

He shrugged. 'Who knows? You weren't exactly behaving rationally that night. Dancing like a tart, every guy in the place looking at you.'

There were no words to answer him.

Jamie hit himself on the head with the heel of his hand. 'I still love you, damn it, no matter what you've done. I will always love you.' He laughed. 'I nearly put that one on the tape too.'

He was silent for ages. Ellen's eyes kept straying to Mary MacLeod's teeth, and to the entrance. There was no way of getting past him.

She smiled, and it felt so false. 'The tape was beautiful, thank you. I wrote you a letter after I listened to it.'

He put his head to the side. 'Where is it?'

She slipped her hand into her pocket and rummaged. She found a piece of paper, but it wasn't the letter. She unfolded it, but she didn't take it out. 'Damn, I thought it was here. It must still be inside my journal.'

Though the letter might have bought her time, a part of her was glad he wouldn't see what she had written, for none of it meant anything anymore. She had written it to a different man.

'Ellen, your journal, did you write anything about me in there?'

'You really didn't read it all then?'

He tutted. 'No. What do you take me for?'

'I didn't name you, and there's nothing in it to identify you.'

Wrong answer. Wrong answer. Wrong answer.

The words crashed into her head.

'Where is it?'

'In my bag, in the ward.' A sudden memory came to her. It wasn't in her bag. It was on Dr Tarantino's desk.

He sighed. 'I guess the bottom line is, if we were to make a go of it, would you be prepared to forget what you've just found? Say nothing more about Mary?'

He'll kill you. You'll never see Kate again.

At the sound of her daughter's name, Ellen felt a groan rising in her throat. She had to suppress it. She had to do anything to get out of there alive. She smiled and swallowed the groan. 'Mary who?'

'Good answer.'

His kiss was gentle. Where once, fireworks would have exploded from her stomach, their colours encircling her heart, now there was nothing but terror.

'Turn round.'

'Why?'

He wasn't waiting for her to comply. His hands forced her round, so she was sitting with her back against him. He pulled her in tight, one hand stroking her face. 'This is nice, like that night in the hotel.'

'It was one of the best nights ever.' She tried to turn, to see his face. 'Jamie...'

'Sshh.' His hand moved to her throat. 'Can I trust you, Ellen?'

'Yes, you can.' The words sounded so odd, her voice distorted by fear. 'Please, Jamie. I just want us to be together.'

'And there's been no one else?'

She shook her head.

'I don't believe you. On that, or the thing with Mary. I can't go to prison. It would kill me.'

'Is she… is she here?'

He laughed. 'Of course not. I wouldn't do that. Would have killed me to carry her all this way. She's near the cemetery. I picked a pleasant spot for her. Up in the trees where you and I hid from her that day. Nosy old bat couldn't resist coming to the woods to meet me. I bet she thought I was going to confess. Ask her to be our go-between. Those bloody teeth came flying out and I didn't notice until after she was gone. See when someone's digging a grave on TV with ease, don't believe it. It was a nightmare. Didn't get half as deep as I'd have liked, but it'll have to do. For now.'

The last fragment of the last dream disappeared, and Ellen groaned. As she felt his hands tighten on her throat, she plunged her hand into her pocket, pulled out the razor blade and dragged it across the back of his hand.

'Aarrgghh. You bitch!'

His hands gone from her neck, she jumped to her feet and ran.

76

THE ROAD. SHE had to reach the road. It was closer than the main track. She was certain of it. She'd heard the occasional sound of traffic from the den. The ground was strewn with pine cones, and Ellen's scrabbling feet kicked them in all directions. She didn't know how close he was, because she couldn't hear him for the voices echoing in her head.

Jamie: *Sometimes I wonder about my sanity.*

Lucille: *There'll be a reckoning.*

Sif: *There's always a price for getting into bed with Satan. You're likely to awaken in Hell.*

She didn't look behind. Didn't want to see him, that look on his face that told her everything had been a lie. Ahead, flitting through the trees, she saw a shadow. His shape wasn't clear, but she knew it was Solomon. She followed him down a grassy slope, steadying herself against tree trunks as she went.

She could hear Sif. *I told you. He's a psychopath. You saw it yourself. Over and over. You should have known.*

And she had. She'd seen the way patients flinched at his words, as if they were blows, backing away from him, some with fear in their eyes, some with hatred. And that look he gave, even when his words were not harsh, as if to remind the patients that, although he was being reasonable, there would be consequences if he wasn't obeyed. She'd seen it, and she'd buried it. Was that why she'd been unable to commit to him again?

Above the voices, she heard his feet crashing through the undergrowth. He shouted her name, and it sounded like the howling of a wolf. Above her head, two wood pigeons shrieked and took off.

Her breath was coming in shuddering gasps, the adrenaline of her fear forcing her onwards, her heart racing. There were yawning holes in the roots of some of the ancient trees, and she considered hiding in one of them. But it was too risky. She'd have to keep going. Close to the bottom of the slope, there was a small wire fence. She clambered over it. Ahead of her, there was a track wide enough for a vehicle. She'd never seen it before. Should she follow it to right or left? She didn't know where it might go. Ahead, she heard traffic. She crossed the track.

The forest sloped upwards again, and she scrambled up the slope, grasping at ferns and branches to help her. At the top of the slope, the land levelled, and the trees thinned out.

She could hear him groaning as he tried to climb the slope. Ahead, through a tunnel of shifting trees, she could see the black ribbon of the road. And then she heard his voice. It was just a whisper. *You can't escape me, Ellen. I'm in your head. I'm in your heart. I'm everywhere.*

'You're not!' Her shout echoed through the trees. 'You're nothing to me.'

She ran through the young beech trees, their slender branches coated in silky green leaves, reaching out to catch her. As she neared the edge of the forest, she saw a steep embankment in front of her. She'd have to scramble down it before she could reach the road. There was no sound behind her. She slowed, but she didn't stop.

Her feet slid in the loose shale and leaves. She grabbed hold of a thin branch to stop herself from falling. She held it as long as she could until she was halfway down. She reached the end of the branch and she had to let it go. She heard it spring backwards. Distracted, she didn't see the curved root that rose from the ground in front of her. Her foot caught under it and a sharp pain shot through her leg.

Arms flailing, she tried to grab something, anything, to break her fall. There was nothing. Head over heels, she tumbled down the last of the embankment.

She heard the screech of tyres on the road. Felt the slam of cold, hard metal. Her body was lifted into the air and crashed down onto the tarmac. She heard her name yelled into the day. It wasn't his voice. It was Dr Tarantino's. He was standing over her, the sun bright behind his head.

'Ellen.' He dropped to his knees. 'Ellen.' He took his jacket off and covered her. 'Get an ambulance!'

She heard a car engine racing away.

'I'm cold,' Ellen whispered. 'So cold.'

He stroked her face. 'Stay awake, Ellen. We'll have help soon.' She felt him touch her neck, probing for her pulse. His gentle fingers edged her lower eyelid down.

Behind him, at the top of the embankment, silhouetted against the shimmering green beech trees, watching, she could see the faint outline of Jamie Ogilvie.

'He wants to kill me.'

'No one wants to kill you, Ellen.'

She couldn't keep her eyes open.

'Ellen, please stay with me. Think of Kate.'

She smiled. 'I'm always thinking of Kate.'

There was a burst of light in her head, like a firework exploding in myriad beautiful colours. She felt his arms tighten around her, holding her, holding her back. She wasn't having it. She slipped from his arms and walked towards the light. As the colours surrounded her, she turned and whispered her last words.

Part III

77

I'd fallen asleep sitting up, a sketchbook spread out in my hands. When it fell and hit the floor in the night, I'd awoken with a start. There wasn't much sleep to be had after that. Tossing and turning and questioning. Resenting Gran for not telling me everything. Wishing I'd asked Liz Barclay more. Angry with myself for the bitterness I'd felt towards my mother. And a deep and growing hatred of Someone's Cousin and Jamie Ogilvie.

After breakfast, I sat on the floor in the spare room and looked at the other sketchbooks. There was a series of sketches of me from birth to age six or seven. And the most beautiful delicate ferns and flowers, shimmering cobwebs and trees, insects and birds. There was a den in the woods, sunlight streaming through narrow trees and falling on mossy ground.

In another small sketchbook, there were caricatures of two women and two men, more pictures of Sif and Liz Barclay, and a pleasant-looking man of around Mum's age with good teeth and high cheekbones. I turned the page, and then I turned it back. I knew this man's face. It took me a while to remember. He was the one outside The Craig, the one who had mentioned the cellar. I wished now he had made eye contact, noticed that I looked like my mother, and told me things.

There were more sketches of me as a baby, and on the last page, a man with curly dark hair and a moustache. This sketch differed from the others. It looked tentative, less definite, as if she had done it from memory. The bottom half of the page had been torn out.

I looked at the cassette tapes she'd recorded from the radio. She had good taste. I'd always liked seventies and eighties music. Maybe I'd make playlists from them on Spotify. In a box in the spare room, I found school reports with a similar theme each year: good enough progress; could do better. Achievement certificates from the Brownies and Guides. That made me smile. When I'd told Gran some of my friends were going to Brownies, she'd compared them to a paramilitary organisation, with their rules and regulations, hideous uniform and meaningless vows. When she calmed down, she'd said I could go if I really wanted. I didn't.

There was a scrapbook with coloured pages covered in glued-on creepy winged cherub angels, kittens in baskets, and strange-looking children clasping bouquets of roses. It was quite disturbing.

I hadn't come up with much. If I was to find my father, the starting point would have to be Hazel, and I didn't even know her surname. Provincial though Inverness was, I didn't expect I'd have much luck asking in the pubs if anyone knew Someone's Cousin.

I had to ask myself again, what would be the point? Revenge? Reporting him to the police wasn't likely to get me very far, especially if the only corroboration was the journal of a psychotic patient. But maybe there would be some satisfaction in telling him I knew what he was.

At the bottom of the box was a small yellow autograph book. The entries were dated 1984 and 1985. Must have been from Mum's secondary school days. Her classmates had drawn little pictures and written silly rhymes and sayings and declarations of undying love for my mother and various boys. And there it was, on the last page: *By hook or by crook, I'll be last in this book. Your best friend. Hazel Johnson xxx*

78

AT FOUR IN the morning, Jamie had been ready to kick Martyna out of bed. If he didn't get some sleep, he'd be worth nothing. It wasn't even as if it was all action. There had been quite a bit of that, and enjoyable it was too. But then she just wouldn't stop talking about Kate and Stefan and revenge. At last, he'd persuaded her it wasn't a good idea to stay out all night. What if her man left her? What if it forced him into Kate's arms? That made her check her app again. Seemed he'd been home since early on, only leaving once to go to the shop on Thornbush Road. Unless he'd left his phone at home, Jamie had thought, but he didn't suggest that. Just some gentle coaxing to try and get her to see things from her man's point of view.

'You are right,' she'd said at last. 'I don't want to lose him. I just want to show him he has hurt me.'

Jamie looked at the clock. 'You've probably hurt him too, staying out half the night.'

She nodded. 'Okay, I leave now.'

Like the gentleman he was, he hadn't put on the light until she'd gathered up her clothes and dressed. He was going to ask her if she wanted him to see her home. It wasn't the best of areas for a woman walking on her own at this time in the morning, and he'd regretted not offering last time. And then she'd turned to him, a look of such savagery on her face, it had scared him.

'I will make Kate pay for what she has done.'

Fuck it. She could walk herself home. If anyone was stupid enough to go near her, they'd soon get their comeuppance.

He'd been on the verge of sleep when the old dear perched on the side of the bed. He didn't turn or open his eyes. 'What do you want? I need some sleep.'

The old dear sighed. 'Do you like her?'

'Not really, but a man has needs.'

She put her hand on his shoulder. 'Isn't that what got you into all this trouble in the first place?'

'Probably, but it's been tough on my own. I feel alive again.'

'But that's not down to her, is it? It's the other one, Kate. You changed after you saw her. Why?'

He'd shrugged. 'I guess she reminds me. It was... it was special. Ellen was special. I can't explain it.'

'Do you feel guilty?'

He'd felt his heart race. Perhaps it was just the hangover kicking in. Booze did that to him sometimes, and he'd started far too early today.

She patted his shoulder. 'You need to think about that, son.'

Not then, he didn't. 'Night night, old dear.'

And he wouldn't think about it now either. It was only nine-thirty. Too early to get up. It'd wait. He pulled the cover over his head and closed his eyes.

79

I HEARD MR Sullivan's front door open. I raced down the stairs and caught him at the gate. He did a double-take. 'You're not dressed, Kate. Is everything all right?'

Jeez. It wasn't as if I was out in the street in a sheer negligee at quarter to ten in the morning. I was wearing perfectly respectable pyjamas, covered by a hoody.

'Everything's fine, Mr Sullivan. I just wanted to ask if you knew anyone around here with the surname Johnson. I'm trying to trace a friend of my mother's, Hazel Johnson.'

He frowned. 'Johnson? Not Johnston or Johnstone?' He pronounced the last surname like it was two names. Mr John Stone.

'Johnson.'

'Hmm. Let me think.' And he did, forever. At last, he sighed and nodded his head. 'There was an insurance man used to come round the doors. I'm sure he had a family around your mother's age. They lived on Glenurquhart Road, the big houses across from the council offices. Can't remember which one. Have you tried the phone book?'

'I haven't, but I will. Thank you.'

In the spare room, I picked the rucksack up off the floor. I hadn't checked the front pockets the previous evening. Chewing gum in one, along with a book of matches from a hotel in Perth, and a train ticket dated 27th June 1992. In the other, there was a piece of paper folded into tiny squares. As I unfolded it, I saw faint lines of handwriting. The note was wrapped around a delicate gold heart necklace with sapphires. On the back of the necklace, engraved words: *Yours forever xxx.*

The note wasn't in Mum's writing. Someone else had written it, presumably to my mother. Someone who wanted to apologise for something. Someone who wanted to declare their love. I wondered if it was him, Jamie Ogilvie. I opened the catch on the necklace and put it on.

***

Patrick Johnson had a pleasant face. He was a man I knew I could trust. Not so far as to tell him I might have been conceived in one of the bedrooms of his fine Victorian villa, but enough not to give him a false name or make up some bullshit story for being there. Also, he was holding the collar of a golden retriever with a tail that rotated like a helicopter blade, bashing off the door frame as it strained to get at me and lick me to death. You couldn't not trust a man with a golden retriever.

'Hello. Sorry to bother you. I'm looking for Hazel Johnson.'

He smiled. 'Hazel?'

'Yes.' I hoped she wasn't dead. Not only because she wouldn't be able to help me, but because I couldn't face the inevitable embarrassment and possible upset.

'Give me a minute.' He hauled the dog away from the door and shut it in the nearest room, where it whined and barked.

'I think she likes you,' he said. 'Mind you, she likes everyone. Hazel doesn't live here. Hasn't for a very long time.'

'Is she your sister?'

He nodded, the smile easing off. 'Who's asking?'

'Sorry.' I offered my hand. 'My name's Kate Sharp. My mother, Ellen, was a friend of your sister.'

'Ellen? Oh, my goodness.' He clasped my hand in both of his.

'I remember Ellen. You look so like her.' He frowned. Looked as if he was trying to remember what exactly had happened to my mother. 'I'm sorry you lost her. Can't have been easy.'

I shrugged. 'Long time ago now.'

He stood aside. 'Come in. I'll get Hazel's phone number for you.'

In an enormous kitchen, with family photos everywhere, he searched for his phone. As the dog continued to whine in another room, I looked out the patio doors to the garden and imagined my mother dancing, and Someone's Cousin leaning against the fence watching her. Kissing and fumbling in the kitchen, Hazel pulling her away. I remembered my mother's description of him. *Piercing eyes and high cheekbones, curly black hair and drooping moustache.* I almost gasped. The tentative sketch in the small book. Of course, it even had the letters 'S.C.' below it. That was him.

'Here it is.'

He read the number out and I keyed it into my phone. 'Does she live locally?'

He nodded. 'Raigmore Estate. Give her a ring.'

I think my call woke Hazel. Or maybe she always sounded dopey. 'Kate Sharp? Ellen's girl? Haven't seen you since you were in your pram in the park.'

So, she and my mother hadn't kept in touch.

'Can I come and see you?'

'Now?'

'If that's okay.'

'Suppose so, if you take me as you find me.'

***

I FOUND HER in a midden of a flat. A small, dumpy woman with wild bed head, a map of broken veins on her cheeks, and dark circles under her eyes, she was wearing a short t-shirt and leggings that showed every lump and bump, and there were a lot of them.

I was certain that, had my mother survived, she wouldn't have looked like this.

The flat smelled of mould and beer and sweaty feet. She pushed a couple of pizza boxes off the sofa, so I could sit. The boxes looked cleaner than the sofa. I perched on the edge.

Hazel gave me a sad wee smile. 'You look like her.'

'So they tell me. I don't remember much.'

She nodded. 'Tragic, it was. She was a good sort, Ellen. Quiet. A bit of a mouse, really, but she was a good pal.'

I had already decided I wouldn't be asking Hazel to tell me about my mother. My father, on the other hand…

I'd gone home after speaking to Patrick and I'd torn the sketch out of the book. I took it from my pocket. 'Do you know this man?'

She glanced at it, shrugged and shook her head.

'Take it.' I passed it to her. 'Have a good look.'

She had a good look and passed it back to me. 'Still don't know him. Why do you ask?'

'My gran, she died recently and –'

'Aw, that's sad. Now, *she* was no mouse. I remember when she –'

'Anyway, I was clearing out Gran's flat.' I felt a morsel of shame for my rudeness, but I didn't want to hear anything she had to say about Gran. 'I found a sketchbook. My mother used to draw when she was in The Craig. I thought I recognised the man in the drawing, wondered if he was someone who used to come to the house to see her.'

'Love, like I said, I didn't really see anything of your mother after you were born. I wouldn't know.'

I'd have to go further. 'There was… she wrote in her journal about a party at your house. A barbecue. She… she got quite drunk. Said you were with someone Arnold, maybe?'

She gasped. 'Len Arnold? That's going back a bit.' She laughed, a low, throaty noise. 'Len Arnold. I'd forgotten about him. He was a right chancer. Used to –'

'So, you remember that night?'

'Sort of. There were a lot of parties. Do you know what time of year it was? You said a barbecue?'

'I know the date: twenty-eighth of June 1985. It was your birthday.'

'Ah.' She smiled. 'My sixteenth. I remember. My folks were away. Patrick was out that night, and he came home early, brought some mates with him.'

'Do you remember this guy being there?'

She shook her head. 'Don't remember much, to be honest. Sorry I can't help. Cup of tea?'

I smiled and shook my head. 'That would be lovely, thank you, if I didn't have to go to work.' A lie on both counts.

'Another time.'

I nodded, certain I wouldn't be seeing Hazel again.

I was at the bus stop across from the flats when I heard a shout. I looked up, and she was hanging out the landing window, mad hair framing her worn face. 'Ask Patrick. Could have been one of his friends.'

80

Patrick was in the garden. I was glad I didn't have to go to the door and bother him again. This way, I could pretend I was just walking past on my way home.

He looked up from his weeding. 'Hello again.' He stood, rubbing the small of his back. 'Did you find her?'

I nodded.

'In a state?'

'Not at all.'

'That's good. She has her issues, poor Hazel. Lost her husband and son in a car crash twelve years ago. Hasn't been easy.'

Shamed by every nasty thought I'd had about the state of the flat and the state of Hazel, and my rudeness in hardly letting her speak, I felt the prickle of tears. 'That's so sad.'

He nodded. 'Anyway, I'm glad you found her. It was nice meeting –'

'Do you know this man?'

He looked a little startled as I shoved the sketch at him. He said nothing. Just rubbed his hands on his jeans and took it from me. When he nodded, my heart thumped. 'Looks like a guy I used to know. Cousin of one of my friends. He was older than us.'

My mouth was suddenly so dry, I wouldn't have been surprised if I'd squeaked when I tried to speak. 'Do you know his name?'

He frowned, his eyes still on the sketch, then he nodded. 'Simon Grant.' He passed the sketch back to me, a wary look on his face. 'Can I ask what this is about?'

I folded it up and put it back in my pocket, then I forced a smile. 'Sorry, I should have said. My grandmother died recently and I'm clearing out her flat, looking through my mother's things. She used to draw, and there were lots of sketches of this guy. I just wondered who he was. Hazel thought you might know.' I paused as if I was remembering, rather than inventing. 'Simon? There were birthday cards from a Simon.' I shrugged. 'It's a bit late in the day, but I thought it might help me make sense of all that happened, if I looked up her friends, tried to learn a bit more about her. Silly, really.'

'No.' He shook his head. 'It's not silly at all. But you won't be able to look Simon up.'

'No?' Instead of just feeling like an orphan, I really was one?

'He went missing. Must be over twenty years ago.'

***

My great-grandfather went to school in the building that was now Inverness Library. A single-storey building built in the Greek Revival style, it had an impressive six-pillared portico at the entrance. It was a fine building, spoiled only by its location at the bus station, the source of much of the town centre's air pollution, and haunt of the occasional aggressive beggar. Not that the setting mattered. Inside these doors, a myriad of other centuries and universes and countries awaited.

I was transported back to those Saturdays when Gran would drop me off at the entrance and come back for me an hour or two later. I was never ready for her. It smelled just as it had then, and I remembered the delicious excitement of choosing my books and my corner and starting to read.

I wasn't feeling much excitement after an hour of scanning through old newspapers on microfiche. I'd started in January 1993. It was slow work, scanning each page. At least the *Inverness*

Courier was only published twice weekly. I almost gave up at the end of May. People went missing all the time. Probably didn't even make it to the papers. I'd asked Patrick if there had been an investigation. He didn't know. He'd left Inverness for university by then and he couldn't remember much. Everyone had been certain at the time that Simon had run off with a married woman. He was a bit of a lad.

I decided I'd try June, and then I'd stop. I didn't know why I was doing it, anyway. He'd gone missing. I wouldn't be able to meet him, even if I'd wanted to. No point in reporting him as a rapist. There wasn't any point at all. But I'd always been thrawn, according to Gran. Wouldn't give up, even when it was pointless. And there it was. Friday 24th June 1993.

Concerns about missing Inverness man

Police are appealing for information from the public about the whereabouts of an Inverness man. Simon Grant, 28, has not been seen since leaving the town's Phoenix Bar just before midnight on Saturday 18th June.

Mr Grant, a pipe-fitter, was due to attend a family event the following day, and he was scheduled to go off shore on Monday 20th June. His employer, family members and friends have heard nothing from him.

Mr Grant was last seen wearing a brown blazer-type jacket, a cream shirt and denim jeans. Anyone with any information is asked to contact the police.

There was a photo. It was grainy, but I could see he had changed little since my mother's sketch of him. No matter how I strained, I could see nothing of myself in his face. I printed out the article, then I left. I couldn't face waiting for a bus, so I decided to walk home. I got food in Tesco and picked up a newspaper. Outside, I leaned against the wall and stared at the headline.

Dunain Woods remains identified.

No names were given, but both skeletons had been identified. Further forensic enquiries were being carried out. The female remains were those of an elderly woman last seen in Inverness in May 1993, the same month my mother died. She had been identified from medical records and DNA from a distant relative. I wondered if she was Mary MacLeod.

As my eyes moved down the page, and the words hit me, I gasped. The male remains were those of an Inverness man that disappeared in June 1993, after a night out on the town, aged twenty-eight. He had been identified using dental records and DNA. His next of kin had asked that his identity not be revealed yet.

Were those next of kin mine? I didn't intend finding out. I did wonder, though, at the coincidence of this man who was probably my father being found buried in that place where my mother had spent so much of her time. That place where she died.

81

FECK, IT HAD been a long day, and it was only just past lunchtime. There had been so many long days over the last few years, but Jamie had expected nothing more. That was the downside to his life improving. Increased expectations meant he was no longer willing to tolerate the mediocre routine he'd grown used to. Though he'd slept well enough, he'd woken with the old dear's words in his head.

Do you feel guilty?

He wasn't about to admit it to her, or anyone else, but the crippling guilt never stopped. There was so much to feel guilty for: Ellen, Mary, his children. He'd left his wife just after Ellen died. He should never have married her. Started as a bit of fun when they both worked in a bar in Melbourne, a couple of months before he was due to come home. Turned out not to be that much fun, and he was relieved to say goodbye, never expecting to see her again, and certainly not expecting her to turn up in Inverness three months later, pregnant with his child. His son. Soon, she'd given him a daughter. They were lovely kids, and now he hadn't a clue why he'd let her take them to Australia, or why he didn't keep in touch. Hadn't even kept a photograph. Some father.

Following the investigation into concerns about his relationship with Ellen, though there wasn't a scrap of proof anything ever happened, they'd moved him to a mind-numbing managerial job that he could have done with his eyes closed. Mostly did. The increased salary and pension were bonuses, but it wasn't enough to make up for losing respect and privileges, a job he loved, and the fact that everyone and his dog knew it was a demotion in all but name. And then the years since he'd taken early retirement, festering here, haunted by memories and loss and regret.

He paced the flat, considered going to the pub, saw himself in the mirror and re-considered. The gym might be a better idea. But how could he go to a gym looking like this? He had to start somewhere, but preferably not as the laughing stock of a crowd of toned fitness junkies.

Ten minutes later and he was lying on his back on the living-room carpet, his heart going like a train, sweat pouring off him. Maybe press-ups weren't the best thing to start with. He pushed himself to his feet, gripped the handles of an imaginary skipping rope, and set to. It wasn't long before Mr Moaning-face was thumping on the ceiling. Probably best to stop, even though he could have kept going, if not for the neighbour. Aye, right.

On the arm of the chair, his phone buzzed.

What you up to? I am in Nip Inn. You want a drink? Mx

Heart still racing, cheeks pulsing, sweat running from his armpits, he stared at the phone. Was this what he wanted? Shagging someone else's bird? He laughed. Couldn't care less that she was with someone else. That could be an advantage, in the right circumstances. Trouble was, she was a fruitcake, pure and simple; a nasty piece of work, and he'd known a few in his time. But what else was he going to do with himself?

Okay. I'll Nip Inn. See you soon. Jx

***

THE NIP INN was the closest pub to Jamie's flat, but he'd never darkened its door. It wasn't the hole he'd expected. Just a decent old-fashioned pub, with good light and a tasty barmaid. He hadn't intended to drink, but he found he couldn't bring himself to ask for a mineral water, or whatever wannabe fitness fanatics drank these days. New regime tomorrow. 'Two pints, please.'

Martyna's face was flushed with excitement. She'd been busy this morning, she told him. She'd gone to that street in Dalneigh, where Stefan had been the other night, and she'd found Kate. She'd done well. Unlike Jamie, she'd only had a blue dot on a wee phone screen. And patience. He tried not to laugh at her tale of the stake-out and the downstairs neighbour. She'd scored when the whore came to the gate in her pyjamas, chatting up an old man. The man had spotted Martyna after Kate had gone inside. He'd asked her why she was hanging about. She'd told him it was none of his frigging business. Jamie laughed out loud at that.

She went to the bar and bought whisky. A nice change to see her put her hand in her pocket, but Jamie and whisky had never been a good combination. He liked the taste, but not the effect. Still, it was his last day on the booze. Why not?

'Where's your man today?' he asked.

'At home, where he should be. I give him things to do.'

'Does he know where you are?'

She frowned. 'I am at work.'

She said it with such indignation, Jamie laughed. She was a piece of work, with her silly plans for how she was going to get into Kate's flat. If there was a Polish equivalent of Nancy Drew or Enid Blyton, Martyna had read the books.

'I don't think the drainpipes are strong enough,' Jamie said, still trying to keep a straight face. 'You could just try going to the door.'

She nodded. 'But there is a little hole. She will see me. I don't think she like me; she will not open the door.' She leaned towards him. 'Listen, I have Stefan's phone. I take it when he's not looking.' She pulled a second phone from her pocket and put it on the table beside her own. 'See. The same.' She twisted her face into a grotesque smile and simpered. 'Oh, Stefan, I am silly girl. I forget I have my phone in my pocket and I pick up yours in mistake. Oh, dear.'

Her raucous laughter made everyone in the bar turn and look.

'So, I will text her and tell her I come to see her. She will open the door for Stefan, even if there is no one in the hole. When she open the door, I push in, then you too. We tie her up. I –'

Jamie held up his hand. 'I told you, leave me out of it. You need to think about –'

'I have thinked.' She lifted her glass and threw the whisky back in one go. 'I go for a pee.'

Jamie picked up a newspaper from the next table. They'd identified both sets of bones, but they had given no names. Didn't have to. He got two large whiskies and two pints. Sat back in the seat and thought about Dunain Woods, about Ellen, about DJ Tarantino. He felt his mind spinning into a dark place. So much hurt and anger. There couldn't be any more. Besides, he had things he needed to say to Kate Sharp, and he certainly wasn't saying them in front of Martyna. He'd have to persuade her to drop her stupid idea.

She wasn't interested in talking when she got back. Just texting, texting, texting. Stopping to drink half her pint in one go, then more texting. When she put the phone down, she finished her whisky. 'So, you don't help me?'

He shook his head.

'Okay.' She drained her pint, then she stood. 'I go now.'

Jamie felt the darkness spinning inside his head, dragging him down. He put his hand on her wrist and let his fingers trail along her forearm. 'Why not come back to mine? We can have fun.'

She laughed and pinched his cheek. 'You don't help me, so maybe we don't have fun again.'

Jamie smiled. 'Okay, love. I think I can live with that.'

She almost knocked an old man over in her hurry to get out the door. Jamie stood and put his jacket on. He'd get some booze in the shop. Not whisky. Go home and watch the football. Stop worrying about Kate. She wouldn't be stupid enough to open the door to Martyna. Tomorrow, he'd go up the town and find out about this internet business. He'd get a laptop. Surely there were keep fit classes online. But did you go up the town to get the internet? Maybe you did it by phone. Or maybe you had to be online to get online. Talk about chicken and egg. Whatever, one of the first things he was going to do online, after the fitness classes, was join internet dating. Who needed a mad Polish tart?

The mad Polish tart was standing outside the bookie's, phone to her ear. She didn't turn as Jamie made for the shop. He got a bottle of vodka, some cans, a six-pack of crisps and a couple of bars of chocolate. Might as well make the most of his last night of slothdom.

Outside, a taxi pulled up. As Martyna got in the front, Jamie saw a man in the back seat. It was that wee toerag, Victor. He wasn't letting him anywhere near Kate. No way. He opened the back door, grabbed his arm and tugged.

'Hey.' The taxi driver turned. 'No trouble, okay?'

Jamie smiled. 'It's fine. Victor doesn't mind.'

The weasel was standing on the pavement, looking confused. A twenty-pound note made him smile. He shoved a roll of duct tape at Jamie, muttered something incomprehensible, and he was off.

82

BY THE TIME I reached home, I was exhausted and really low. Why had I bothered spending so much of the day chasing after this man who meant nothing to me? I couldn't even raise the slightest regret that he'd probably been murdered and buried in the woods. What kind of person was I? But then, what kind of person was he? With any luck, Ogilvie was dead and buried too. It was time to leave this behind, get my life back on track. I'd renew my gym membership, start swimming and walking again, meet up with my friends. Book a holiday. I was unlocking the door when Stefan's text arrived. I smiled. Good timing. And then I read it, and I wondered.

Hello my wee Kate. How are you? I come and see you. I leave now. Sxxx

He had never called me 'wee Kate' before, and he never, never put kisses on a text. Maybe he was drunk.

Okay. Door's open.

There was an envelope on the floor inside the door. I didn't recognise the writing. I pulled out a small card with a picture of the most amazing rock formations. I looked on the back. It was The Old Man of Storr on Skye. I knew then.

Kate
I hope you're well. I'd really like to talk to you. I owe you that. Please call.
Daniel

He'd written his number beneath the message. I put the card on the kitchen table, then I put the kettle on. I heard a slight knock at the door, and then Stefan's hesitant footsteps on the stairs. I was kneeling down at the fridge, my back to the door. I could smell whisky. And more.

I turned my head and did a double-take. Not what I was expecting at all. Before I could speak, Martyna launched herself at me, grabbing me by the hair and pulling me to my feet. The milk went skiting across the floor. I yelled, and she clamped her hand over my mouth. Spinning me round, her hand entangled in my hair, she pushed me out of the kitchen and into the living room. From the corner of my eye, I saw another shape on the stairs. Was it Stefan?

Martyna pushed me face down on the sofa. She was muttering in Polish as she pressed on the back of my head. I heard someone else come in. The quick tearing of tape and then she pulled my head up. From where I was lying, all I could see was a length of silver duct tape and big fingers. I was certain they weren't Stefan's.

'Get up, bitch.'

Her hand was still in my hair. I twisted my body round and sat up. The man with the tape was behind the sofa and I couldn't see him. Martyna's face was screwed up and vicious. Half-cut, she was panting. She pulled her hand from my hair, taking a good chunk of it with her, and she wiped at her brow.

My kick caught her in the gut, sending her stumbling backwards. She missed the TV, thank God, and sprawled on the floor. I was only sorry I'd taken my shoes off at the door. I launched myself from the sofa and ran at her. Landed a few good punches on her face and head before I heard laughter and felt firm hands grab me from behind and haul me off her, dragging me backwards.

Martyna sat up. She looked dazed. Obviously hadn't expected wee Kate to fight back.

'Fucking bitch. I show you. Put that stuff on her hands.' My arms were wrenched behind me. I struggled, trying to pull my hands away, but he was too strong for me. I could feel the roll of tape as he manoeuvred it round my wrists, and then the tearing sound. His hands pinned my shoulders against the sofa.

Martyna struggled to her feet. Her lip was bleeding. She wiped it with the back of her hand, smearing blood across her cheek. She was wearing a flimsy orange backpack, like a kid's gym shoe bag. She shrugged it off her shoulders and reached inside.

It looked like a penknife, a little bigger than the ones some kids had carried when I was wee. I wasn't allowed one, though I used to tell Gran they weren't sharp enough to cut anything. This one was. The blade was curved, and it narrowed to a sharp point. As she advanced on me, my anger dissolved. A shaking began, deep inside. I willed it not to show. I would not have this woman know how much I feared her.

She smiled as she sat beside me. 'Wee Kate. Wee prostitute. Why you try to take my man? You can't get one yourself?'

She raised the knife so the point was on my cheek. I felt it scratch my skin. She looked at me as if she expected an answer. Difficult with tape over my mouth. I raised my eyebrows.

'Hah. If you could speak, you would say *we are just friends*? I know is more than that. I hate you. You take him from me. You, with your dead grandmother and your maybe university and all your so good music and books. Miss perfect pretty silly little girl. Why you don't just have Daniel? Why you need my Stefan?'

She saw my handbag on the floor. With a smile, she pulled it towards her. She snatched the folded article I'd printed at the library and tossed it on the sofa without looking at it. My purse next. She was going to be disappointed. With one hand, she turned the purse upside down and a few coins fell on the floor. She pulled out a fiver.

'This is all?'

I nodded.

'So how you going to pay me?'

I shrugged.

'Must pay with pain.'

Shit. I thought about stamping on the floor, but Mr Sullivan wouldn't be home yet.

'What I cut first? Your eyes? Your pretty face?'

Some choice. With an eerie laugh, she pulled her arm back and held the knife high, then she plunged it downwards.

The blade ripped through the arm of the sofa. Grunting, she tugged the knife along the length of the arm, splitting the purple velvet. Bitch. The knife was back at my cheek. Her hand was shaking. 'You, give me drink.'

The hands on my shoulders were gone. I guess he figured I wasn't going anywhere with that blade in my face. I heard him pull the top off a can. He passed it to her, and then he opened another. She scooshed the beer back in a oner and chucked the can over her shoulder.

'Vodka.'

A bottle appeared. She drank it as if it was water, then she passed it back. I heard him take a long drink, then he grunted and belched. Definitely not Stefan.

83

THE SWEATY FINGERS of Martyna's left hand fumbled with my mother's gold necklace, pulling at it until the catch was at the front. She opened it, then she held it up. 'Very nice. I have this.' She put it on the table. 'I don't think I cut you.'

That was good.

'I think I just kill you. First, I let you speak.'

She ripped the tape off my face. It hurt. She pressed the knife harder against my cheek and I felt the skin part.

'So, what you have to say, little bitch? I kill you quick or I kill you slow?'

Preferably neither. 'What about your boy?'

The anger on her face. 'You don't speak of my boy ever.'

'But you'll go to prison.'

'Then my Stefan will take care of him. He is a good man. You have sex with him?'

'No. He is not like that.'

'Are you?'

Good question. Probably best not to be entirely honest. 'No. We are friends.'

'Friends, friends, friends. This is shite. You want him.'

'I really don't.'

'Then he want you and I hate you for that. He tells me lies when he is seeing you.'

There was a glimmer in her eyes that looked like unshed tears.

I went for it. 'He said you are a good person, strong and kind, and a great mother. He said you helped him when Anya died and he couldn't have coped without you. He doesn't want to lose you.'

'Huh. Does he tell you he loves me?'

I didn't hesitate in lying through my teeth. 'Yes. Very much. He will lose you if you do this.'

I could see she was wavering. Silly bitch. She was going down for this, even if she stopped now.

'I can't believe you.' She shook her head. 'He doesn't tell me this. He cannot even kiss me. He say it is too soon, but I don't believe him.' The knife shook against my cheek and I felt the warm trickle of blood. 'I hate you.'

She drew her arm back again. I closed my eyes. Hoped it would be quick.

Nothing happened.

I heard her grunt. Felt her pull against something. I opened my eyes and saw an enormous hand holding her by the wrist.

'What the fuck you doing?'

'That's enough.' The man spoke for the first time. He sounded local. 'You can go now.' He squeezed her wrist. She squealed and dropped the knife. He snatched it up. 'Leave us. We have things to talk about.'

'Talk?' She was rubbing her wrist. 'Why you talk to her?'

'We go back a long way, me and Kate. It's private, so fuck off.'

'You know Kate? You fool me? Fat bastard, I kill you too.'

'Not today, you won't, so do one.'

Martyna shook her head. 'I will get you both.' She reached for the money and the necklace.

'Leave that, and your phone.'

Anger contorting her face, she yelled: 'I don't leave my phone.'

'Lock the door behind you and put the key through the letterbox. When I hear you do that, I'll drop your phone out the window.'

'But you break it.'

'Not if you catch it.'

Her snarl as she backed away reminded me of the dog Mr Sullivan had when I was a child. Horrible thing. Used to snap at my heels until I started carrying a water pistol.

'You will pay, both of you.'

'Aye, right. Piss off.'

She did. I heard the door lock and the key drop on the mat. He opened the window behind me. There was a volley of Polish from outside. He laughed, then he clapped. 'Good catch.'

***

His bulk filled the room, blocking the light from the other window. He had a pale, bloated face and messy dark hair, shot through with streaks of grey. He was breathing heavily as he stared down at me, an eerie gleam in his pale blue eyes. He put the vodka bottle on the table, then he sat beside me, took a hankie from his pocket and raised a giant hand to my face. I flinched as he dabbed at the cut. 'It's not deep. A bit of tape and there'll hardly be a scar.'

'Who are you?'

His smile was radiant. I knew it. But from where?

'We… I… we met… sort of, in the Beefeater the other night.'

I remembered. He was at the bar just before I'd spotted Martyna. And yet, I felt I knew him from somewhere else. A different him.

He kept smiling as he studied me. I felt like a specimen in a cage.

'Please, can you take the tape off my hands?'

'I will.'

But he didn't. He cupped my face in his cold, clammy hands, and I felt sick. His breathing was heavy. My heart raced. I'd heard about things like this. A woman being approached by a man, rescued by another, then raped or worse, by one or both. He must have seen the fear in my eyes.

'I won't hurt you, Kate. I would never hurt you.'

'Then why won't you untie my hands?'

'You're so like your mother.'

Feck's sake. Third time I'd heard that today. I wanted to shout at him that I was nothing like her.

'Even more than I realised before. I miss her so much.'

And then I saw it, behind the bloating and the ageing. He was the man my mother had sketched, the nurse sitting in the chair. He was Jamie Ogilvie.

He took his hands away from my face. The printed newspaper article was on the sofa between us. He was smiling as he picked it up and unfolded it. And then the smile was gone.

The paper shook in his hands as if it was trying to take off on its own. He stared at me, his eyes blazing. 'Do you know who he is, what he was?'

I nodded.

'So why this?' He scrunched it up and threw it across the room. 'Why would you want to find out about him?'

'God knows.' How I wished I could stop the stupid tears that spilled over and trickled down my cheeks. Couldn't exactly wipe them away either.

'Oh, Kate.' He enfolded me in his arms. 'Don't cry. I'm going to look after you. No one is ever going to hurt you again.'

I can't say I felt relieved to hear that. I blinked away the tears. Sniffed and tried to pull away. He wasn't having it. He stroked my hair as if I was a puppy. 'It's all right.'

'What do you want?' The words were muffled against his shoulder.

He let me go. There was a quizzical smile on his face as he wiped my tears away with his thumbs. 'I just want to help you, to get to know you.'

'This makes no sense. You and Martyna?'

He waved his hand. 'Forget about her.'

I laughed. 'After what's just happened? You helped her.'

His smile slipped away. 'I saved you. Anyway, this wouldn't have happened if you'd stayed away from her man. Greeting each other like lovers outside your work; getting him to help you move; flirting your way along the canal bank the other night. And then the performance in the Beefeater. It's a wonder she didn't attack you there. That's where I met her. I've had to listen to her moaning and plotting ever since.' There was a nasty look in his eyes as he leaned towards me. 'And you and Tarantino. Fuck's sake. Tarantino? If you knew what that man did to your mother... He's a charlatan.'

I remembered Mr Sullivan and the large fellow that was hanging about. 'You've been following me, watching me. Why would you do that?'

'Because I could.' He sounded like a child. 'And frankly, Kate, I'm not impressed with what I saw.' Now he sounded like a teacher. Cheeky bastard.

I'd had enough. 'I don't give a flying fuck whether you're impressed. Get out of my flat!'

He laughed. 'Or what?'

'The downstairs neighbour can hear a pin drop.'

He looked at his watch. 'Aye, but he won't be home for another hour or so. Creature of habit, your neighbour.'

'Next door can hear everything too.'

He rolled his eyes. 'Don't make me gag you. I just want to talk. I want to get to know you.' He frowned. 'And I think you have something of mine. Your mother left a journal. Where is it?'

It was in a suitcase in the spare room. I didn't want him to have it. 'I don't know what you're talking about.'

'Fuck's sake.' He pointed at the scrunched-up paper on the floor. 'How did you know about him if you haven't read the journal?'

'Daniel mentioned him. Then I... I spoke to one of Mum's friends. She told me who he was, that he'd gone missing. I went to the library to look it up.'

He didn't look convinced. 'Still don't know why you bothered.

The guy was a loser.' He leaned towards me, his eyes narrowed. 'He didn't remember your mother, not even when I showed him a photograph. Can you believe that? Probably raped so many women, they all blurred into one. Disgusting. You're better off without him. He won't be a father to you now. I can promise you that.'

I didn't ask what he meant, but I could guess. 'You knew him?'

He shrugged. 'I found him. I had a… a sketch. I met him twice in the pub. It was after she'd… she'd gone. It was all his fault. Ellen was going to report him to the police, but she didn't know his name. I loved her, Kate, I'd have done anything for her.'

At best, this man was unstable, and at worst, completely insane. Whatever relationship he'd had with my mother, I could only describe it as abuse. And yet I couldn't stop the words from coming.

'Tell me about her.'

84

THE AFTERNOON SUN sparkled on the discarded can and a drop of beer on the floor beside it. Jamie Ogilvie had his head in his hands, and he was muttering. I heard my mother's name, and I held my breath. At last, he looked up and smiled that smile. It was dazzling.

'She was beautiful. Soft in some ways, but really strong too. Kind. Funny. Smart. I... I... never met anyone like Ellen. Not before or since.' He shrugged. 'Never will.' He smiled. 'Unless you and I could become friends.'

I let that one pass. 'Her school friend said she was a bit of a mouse.'

His eyes narrowed. 'That's rubbish. Okay, she was nervous when she came into The Craig. Who wouldn't be? But never a mouse.' He laughed. 'She attacked another patient, a bully, not long after she came in. That's how she and I got to know each other.'

'You didn't nurse her?'

His eyes narrowed. 'How do you know I was a nurse?'

I shrugged. Didn't want him to know about Liz Barclay or the sketchbook either. 'You must have been a nurse or a patient. I'm giving you the benefit of the doubt.'

'Cheers for that, but I could have been a doctor or a cleaner. No, I didn't nurse her. I was just filling in on her ward the day she attacked Lucille.'

My mouth dropped open. 'Lucille Leonard?'

He shrugged. 'Don't think that was her surname.'

Of course, it wasn't. Not then. 'Did she have long dark hair? Green eyes?'

He nodded. 'A nastier piece of work you never met. Talented singer, though.'

At least that cleared that up. Lucille had obviously mistaken me for my mother. I hoped if I was ever to escape the clutches of this madman, the news would please Mrs Shelby and put any investigation to rest.

'I hardly knew Ellen then,' he said. 'Or for a long time after. I wanted to know her. I wanted more than that, but I tried to keep away. We only really got to know each other when her friend died.'

He told me of Sif and her suicide. Of the cairn they built, and Mum's love of the woods. He said she was a fantastic dancer, and she loved music. 'Most of all, though, Kate, she loved you. Always talking about you. Always waiting for your next visit. Desperate to get home.'

My tears were back. 'She was coming home.'

He nodded. 'She was. I'm sorry, Kate. It was… it was just a tragic accident.' His face paled and his voice weakened. 'She must have been excited. Maybe she was in a hurry. Not looking where she was going.'

He rubbed at something on the back of his right hand. It was a thin scar.

'She came home before that. Do you know why she relapsed?'

He took a long drink of vodka. There was a sheen of sweat on his brow. He wiped it away with the back of his hand and shrugged. 'How would I know?'

He knew all right. He shook his head as if to clear it. 'Thing is, Kate, it's not really the journal I'm looking for. It's a letter from your mother to me. I think it was inside the journal, but maybe not.'

There was no letter with the journal. I shrugged. 'I haven't seen a letter, but I found a note she got from someone. An apology.

Undying love, that kind of thing.'

'Do you have it?'

'It's on the kitchen table.' I'd left it there in the morning after putting on the necklace.

'Can I get it?' He sounded like an eager child.

I shrugged. 'Can I stop you?'

The paper shook in his hand as he read it out. He kept glancing at me as if he was saying the words to me. Creepy. He folded the note. When he looked up, there was something new, something wrong, in his eyes.

'Ellen, I didn't want to hurt you.'

Oh, shit.

He knelt beside me and put his hand on my cheek. 'You just… you hurt me so much, sleeping with Tarantino and all those other guys. Why did you do that?'

Maybe it was best to go along with his madness. 'I… I didn't.'

He grabbed my hair, twisting it in his hand. 'Mary told me. I thought you loved me.' His voice shook with emotion. 'Just me. Not that sleazy doctor. Just me.'

He was leaning closer, his breath scorching my cheek. My heart racing, nausea churning in my gut, I closed my eyes. If he kissed me, I'd throw up.

I heard him groan. 'Kate?' His voice was a whisper. 'Kate?' There was a long pause. 'Yes, Kate. Not Ellen.' His voice was louder now. 'I remember. Ellen's daughter. Where is the journal?'

I opened my eyes. 'I don't know.'

He took Daniel's card from his pocket. He pinned it open with his mobile phone and punched in the number. 'Let's ask Tarantino.'

85

As THE PHONE rang, his feet were tapping on the floor, fingers tapping on his knees, his entire body vibrating with some freaky nervous energy.

'Hello.'

My mouth was so dry, I couldn't speak. Ogilvie kicked my foot and gestured towards the phone.

'Daniel? It's Kate.'

'Kate. Thanks for calling.' He sounded so pleased to hear from me. 'I wasn't sure if you would. How are you?'

'Eh… I'm okay, thanks. You?'

'Good, thanks. I wanted to say sorry for everything. The police. The journal… I shouldn't have just left it in your flat like that without telling you. I wanted you to have it, and I would have told you, if it wasn't for the police.'

So that's where the journal came from. 'I didn't…'

Ogilvie's massive hand thumped the side of my head and almost knocked me off the sofa. I cried out.

'Kate?' Daniel's voice sounded tinny and far away. 'What's going on?'

'I'll tell you what's going on, Tarantino.' Ogilvie's voice was shaking with anger. 'She is a lying bitch, just like her mother.'

'Who is this?'

He laughed. 'You don't remember me? And I looked after you so well during your wee "stay" at The Craig.'

I heard Daniel gasp. 'Ogilvie? What are you doing there? Is Kate all right?'

He laughed. 'Wasn't sure if you'd remember. All those drugs I gave you. My little caring personal touches. Could have affected your memory for life. So, what are you doing now? Nothing too lucrative or important, I hope.'

I could hear Daniel's breathing speed up. 'I'm… I'm a consultant psychiatrist.'

'You what?' Ogilvie picked up the phone and looked as if he wanted to throw it out the window. 'Why would they let you anywhere near a patient after what you did?'

'They cleared me of any impropriety.'

'Cleared? You almost killed yourself in the woods because of your guilt. You had a breakdown.'

'Having a major depressive episode after witnessing the horrific death of a patient was hardly going to stop me from carrying on with my career.'

'Witnessing? It was your fault, you bastard. You were shagging her!'

If Mr Sullivan was home now, he'd certainly have heard that.

'That's not true. I think you were the one having an inappropriate relationship with a patient. And Ellen was hit by a car. How could that be my fault?'

'She wasn't herself. You'd messed with her head. She… she'd thrown herself in front of a car once before. It was… it was deliberate, both times.'

I groaned. Ogilvie stared at me as if he'd forgotten I was there. 'Honestly, Kate, it was his fault. She died in his arms. I saw them from the woods. I watched.'

Daniel stayed silent.

Ogilvie leaned towards me. 'Kate, where is the journal?'

I was determined he wasn't having it. 'I gave it to the police.'

'What the fuck? Why?'

I shrugged. 'They came here asking about Mum. They wanted to know if she left any papers, anything from her time at The Craig.'

His eyes widened. He looked terrified. 'Did you read it?'

'Just the bit about my... my father.'

'You!' He was shouting into the phone. 'Why did you have the journal all this time?'

Daniel sounded weary. 'She left it on my desk that day. I... I looked for her and couldn't find her. It was lunchtime, so I took a walk along the road. She came running out of the trees, down the slope, and... well, you know the rest. She'd told me she didn't want her parents to know about... about Kate's father. I didn't think she'd want anyone to have the journal.'

'She wouldn't have wanted *you* to have it.'

'Probably not, but I didn't know what to do with it.'

'Did she mention me in it?'

Daniel hesitated. 'She... no, not by name. It was clear there was someone she cared for. She drew a sketch on the last page.'

'A sketch of me?'

'I think so, though the features weren't clear. A man lying sleeping, his hand obscuring his face. It was dated June 1992.'

Tears welled up in Ogilvie's eyes as he dropped the phone.

Daniel's voice came from the floor. 'Kate, are you all right? What's going on?'

Ogilvie snatched up the phone. 'I'll tell you what's going on.' He wiped the back of his hand across his nose. 'I loved her, and she broke my heart, sleeping with you and all those others.'

'Nothing happened between us,' Daniel said. 'And I don't believe there was anyone else.'

'Did she speak at the end? Did she say anything?'

'She spoke only of Kate.'

'The letter – she said she wrote to me. It was inside the journal – do you have it?'

Daniel was silent.

'Tarantino!'

'I do.'

Ogilvie's hands were shaking, his voice weak. 'Read it to me.'

86

I LOVE YOU. I should have said it before, but I didn't know if you wanted to hear it. You made my life complete, and I don't ever want to be with anyone else. Just you and Kate, and maybe more children, if you think you would like that. And a dog.

I've agonised over whether to just carry on as before. It would be so easy to go back to meeting up in our special place, where you taught me to love, and where you chased away the spectre of the man I thought had damaged me forever.

The reason I don't want to do that isn't to punish you. To my shame, it isn't even because of your situation. I just don't want to spoil my progress. I want to get home. I want to be the best mother I can be to Kate. I want to get our own place where we can meet without worrying about being caught or seen.

And, in time, I want to hold your hand in the street, in the pub. I want dance with you. I want us to go on holiday as a family. I want us to grow old together. I want everyone to know how much I love you.

The songs on the tape are beautiful, especially 'A Man is in Love'. I want to hear you sing it. And I do agree, and I'm going to give you my all too. Xxxx

The sound of his heart breaking almost made me want to hold him. Just as well my hands were tied behind my back. My heart wasn't exactly in one piece, but I was desperate to hold the shards together. Ogilvie looked up at me, and I could see it in his eyes.

He'd flipped again.

'Ellen,' he whispered. 'I'm sorry. Can you forgive me?'

I nodded.

'I wouldn't have hurt you that day, I swear. I… I was scared you'd tell them what I did to Mary. I panicked. I didn't even try to keep up with you in the woods, not really.' He rubbed at the scar on the back of his hand. 'Too worried about this cut and all the blood. I know you only did it to get away. But I wouldn't have killed you, I promise.'

I could hear a soft voice from the phone, Daniel speaking to someone else. Ogilvie smiled that smile. Beyond the bloating and the ageing and the insanity, I saw the shadow of the man my mother had loved. He picked up the necklace, leaned over and fastened it around my neck. He kissed me on the cheek. 'Yours forever.'

Please, please leave, I begged him silently. Please just go now.

Daniel spoke. 'Ogilvie, I've called the police.'

He shook his head. Thought for a moment, and then he cut the call and switched the phone off. He stared at me, a quizzical look on his face. 'What now, Ellen? What now?'

'I think you should leave before they get here.'

He nodded, and my heart soared.

'We'll go together.'

'What?'

He put his hand in his pocket and took out Martyna's knife. 'We'll put an end to all this. You'll… you'll have to be first, but I promise I'll be right behind you. Wait for me.' He stared for a moment, his head cocked to the side, the blade glinting in his hand. 'Don't be scared, Ellen.'

Scared? I was terrified. Above the rushing sound of blood in my ears, I thought I heard a key turning in the lock downstairs. Ogilvie turned, but not towards the door. He seemed not to have heard the lock or the soft tread of wary footsteps on the stairs, as he stared, eyes wide, towards the dark screen of the television. And then he spoke, and he wasn't speaking to me.

87

THE LETTER MADE Jamie's heart slam against the walls of his chest, like a trapped animal in a cage. Clawing and tearing, until he thought he might just throw himself, screaming, from the window. Perhaps if it was higher up, he'd have done just that. And now the police were coming, and they couldn't take him. There was only one way out. When he told Ellen, when she saw the knife, her eyes filled with fear. He didn't want her to fear him again. A movement startled him. He turned to see the old dear standing in front of the television, as was her way, flowery pinny twisting in her hands.

'What are you doing, son?'

Jamie smiled. 'Don't know why you always call me that.'

She shrugged. 'Just a thing people say. Like you calling me "old dear". They're coming for you, you know?'

He nodded. 'Aye.'

'The other one, the man in the woods. Was that you?'

'Yeah. Degenerate bastard deserved it. Told him I was taking him to a party in the forest. Lots of young girls, wink, wink. He was up for anything, he said. Cried like a baby when he realised.' Jamie shook his head. 'I was a wild beast. That tree trunk might as well have weighed nothing. I'd have torn down the forest if I could. It was all his fault. Someone had to pay.' He laughed. 'Someone's Cousin had to pay.'

The old dear looked at the knife. 'You certain about this?'

'Imagine me in prison?' He shivered. 'No way.'

She smoothed down her flowery pinny. 'You don't need to take the girl with you.'

'Of course, I'm taking Ellen. I can't leave her here.'

'Ellen is dead. You know that. Remember, the woods. The car.'

He shook his head. 'They told lies to get her away from me. She didn't die.'

'Son, she did. That's Kate. Ellen would be older if she'd lived.'

Everything in his head was scrambled. Thoughts and images and sounds. He turned. Ellen was wearing the necklace. Of course, it was her.

'Just you, Jamie. Come with me. Leave the girl. Come on. I'm going now.'

Her image faded.

'Wait,' he yelled. 'Tell me, did you… was it true you saw her in the woods with other men? With Tarantino?'

She was almost gone, but her voice was still strong. 'It was a complete and utter lie, God forgive me. Ellen wasn't like that.'

He groaned and felt his bottom lip quivering. 'I wouldn't have killed you, Mary, if you hadn't said that. I swear I wouldn't. I just got so angry.'

Her laughter echoed around the room. 'Son, you had a folding spade in your rucksack.'

Jamie gripped the knife, the other hand clutching at his head. 'Don't even know what the truth is anymore. Don't know what's real. I wanted to be good. I did. I tried…'

88

AT FIRST, I thought Ogilvie's unseen companion was my mother. Not that I believed she, or anyone else, was actually there. But he did. My heart raced when he spoke of Someone's Cousin and his murder, and then he called the person 'old dear'. I heard the creak of the floorboards on the landing. The possibilities ran through my head. The police? I had heard no cars, and it was too soon after Daniel's call. Paul Gibson knew about the spare key, but, creep though he was, he was hardly going to dig it up and come in uninvited. Mr Sullivan? I didn't doubt for a moment he knew exactly where the key was, even if no one had ever told him. Those eyes saw everything. But if he'd heard the commotion, he'd have barged in by now. And then I remembered the other person who knew.

Stefan peeped round the door. His eyes widened as he saw the knife in Ogilvie's hand. I shook my head in warning, and he pulled back. Ogilvie turned and stared at me, turned back, and spoke to his invisible companion.

He was almost on the edge of the sofa as he asked about Tarantino and the other men. The answer seemed to deflate him. He was clutching at his head, muttering and groaning. He turned and gripped my upper arm, pulling me until I was off the sofa, sitting on the floor between his knees, my back to him. His hand caressed my cheek.

'The knife's sharp, Ellen. It won't hurt. We don't have much time. I'll be right behind you.'

'No.' It was Stefan's voice. He came round and stood in front of us. He had his hands up. 'Don't hurt her. Please.'

I felt a tremor run through Ogilvie's body, as his hand slipped down to my throat. 'It won't hurt. I promise, but who are you?'

'I'm Stefan, Kate's friend.'

'Kate? She's Ellen. My Ellen.'

Stefan crouched down, so he was at eye level with Ogilvie. He smiled, as if it was Smyth in front of him, talking his nonsense. He nodded. 'You don't want to hurt your Ellen.' He reached out his hand. 'Please may I have the knife?'

'You can't.' Ogilvie spoke in the tone of a peeved child. 'I need it. We have to go. Mary's waiting.'

I heard a siren. Stefan's eyes flicked between us. I knew his indecision. I didn't doubt he could overpower Ogilvie, but the knife was hard against my throat.

'What is your name?' Stefan asked.

Ogilvie was silent.

'It's Jamie,' I said.

Ogilvie sighed. 'I always loved to hear you say my name. It made me feel special.'

The siren was closer. I felt Ogilvie shivering.

'Jamie.' Stefan leaned forwards. 'Let me have the knife. Please.'

I yelled when Ogilvie thrust the knife at Stefan. It didn't make contact, but he staggered backwards until he was sitting on the floor, his hands up. 'Okay. It is okay.'

'You can't have her!' Ogilvie shouted. 'She's mine, not yours and not Tarantino's. She's just mine.'

Stefan shook his head. 'She's not yours, Jamie. This is Kate. Ellen died when Kate was a child. You know this.'

Ogilvie groaned. He moved the knife from my throat. 'Turn round.'

'No, Kate.' Stefan edged towards us.

Outside, I heard cars screeching to a halt, doors slamming shut. I swivelled round until I was kneeling in front of Ogilvie.

His forehead was dripping with sweat, his skin pale, eyes full of fear. He brandished the knife in my face, his hand shaking. Tears rolled over his eyelids and down his cheeks. His voice was just a whisper. 'Are you Ellen?'

I shook my head. 'I'm Kate. Ellen died. She fell in front of a car.'

He closed his eyes. I watched his shoulders slump a little. When he opened his eyes, he nodded. 'I chased her,' he whispered. 'It was my fault. My Ellen. I'm so sorry.'

The downstairs door opened. Footsteps pounded up the stairs. 'Police!'

Both hands on the knife, Ogilvie raised it. Stefan grabbed me from behind and pulled me away, holding me tight, his body wrapped around mine. As the sun glinted off the steel blade, my eyes met Ogilvie's. He smiled and plunged the knife into his own stomach.

89

Inverness Courier, 24th February 2017

Sentencing of Inverness Double Murderer

Inverness man James Francis Ogilvie (58), was given two life sentences yesterday at the High Court in Edinburgh for the murders of Mary Agnes MacLeod (73) and Simon Grant (28), both murdered and buried in Dunain Woods in Inverness in 1993. Ogilvie will serve a minimum term of 25 years for each murder, the sentences to run concurrently. The remains of both deceased were discovered in the summer of 2016, and Ogilvie pleaded guilty to both murders later that year. At the time of the murders, Ogilvie was a nurse at Craig Dunain, the former psychiatric hospital for the Highlands and Islands area.

It was painstaking work by the police, including fingerprints left on an object found with one of the remains, and conversations Ogilvie had with key witnesses, that led to his confession. The Court heard Mary MacLeod died by strangulation, and Simon Grant from head injuries. Ogilvie refused to disclose the reasons behind his murderous attacks, but police believe they are linked to the death of a female patient from Craig Dunain who died in May 1993. Her death is now being investigated.

Ogilvie stabbed himself during an incident in August 2016, moments before his capture, but the injuries were not serious. He suffers from a psychotic condition, and a defence of mental disorder was put forward on his behalf, resulting in acquittal in respect of a charge of abducting and assaulting a woman, and threatening the same woman and a man in Inverness in 2016. The Crown dropped further charges of perverting the course of justice by falsifying hospital records in 1993 and making false allegations to the police.

90

WE BOUGHT ICE cream from the stall at the entrance to Brighton Palace Pier, then we made our way down onto the pebbled beach, weaving around and between smiling people, discarded towels and sticky children. It was early May, and Brighton was much warmer than the north of Scotland. We sat in silence until the ice cream was done. I watched two surfers riding the glittering, curling waves.

Daniel turned to me. 'Have you read *Brighton Rock*?'

'It's on my reading list for university. I'll get round to it soon.'

He smiled. 'Such good news. Well done.'

I nodded. It was good news. At last.

'So, how are you doing?'

I blinked away the threat of tears. Though my life had changed so much for the better in recent months, the tears were never far away. I felt as if I was mourning my mother anew. I suppose I was. As a child, I'd got used to her not being there, so nothing much changed when she died. My grandparents were so strong and protective, and though they spoke of her often, I never felt as if I knew her. And there was always that edge, the feeling she'd betrayed me on the last day, when I'd rushed home from school and she wasn't there.

That had all changed. Now, I knew the truth, and I missed her. I picked up a handful of pebbles and let them drop one by one. I shrugged. 'Up and down. I read the journal before I gave it to the police. So much I didn't know about her. Favourite food, her friends, the music. How she felt about me, about Gran and Granda when she was ill and when she was better. About you and Sif and Liz Barclay. And even him. But those voices and Solomon and all the secret signs she saw around her. Believing everyone was conspiring against her. It must have been awful.' I shuddered. 'Such a sad life, and such a waste. I wish I'd read it sooner, but I was certain she'd reveal her true feelings about me, that she'd say she never wanted me. I was scared she'd blame me for everything.'

Daniel put his hand on my arm. 'You brought Ellen great joy. All the time I knew her, she was so focused on you, on getting better and getting home and being a good mum. I don't think she ever had a moment's doubt about you.'

I believed him. I chucked a stone towards the water. 'Did you suspect Ogilvie of being involved in her death?'

Daniel shook his head. 'No one did. I didn't see him in the woods. I was shocked when he said that on the phone. I wasn't even sure there had been anything going on between them. Liz Barclay mentioned the rumour. I asked your mum if there was anyone special and she said there had been, but it was over. I reported it afterwards, but there was no proof. Maybe I should have given them the journal, but there was nothing conclusive in it. That last picture could have been of anyone. The letter could have been to anyone.'

'Do you think he made her happy?'

'I do,' Daniel said. 'And though I know he was capable of cruelty and abuse of power, I don't think he was like that with your mother.'

I'd given it a lot of thought. It was hard to reconcile the Jamie Ogilvie I'd met with the person who wrote the letter to her, and the person she wrote to. Though I would always hate him for chasing my mother to her death, I was glad she'd found some love in her short life.

'Do you mind talking about what happened to you after the accident?' I asked.

Daniel said he'd been suicidal. He'd got a climbing rope from his car and went to the woods. They came after him, and then he broke. Couldn't see any way out of the darkness. He was on a ward in The Craig for a few days. Jamie Ogilvie was there, taunting and whispering. Calling Daniel for everything. Gave him a cocktail of drugs that made him worse. Daniel was in such a state, he couldn't articulate it, far less prove it. Afterwards, he thought he might have imagined it until Ogilvie taunted him with it on the phone. His family had him moved to a private facility in the south, and he never went back to work at The Craig. He had counselling, and he recovered. There was an investigation prompted by Ogilvie's lies about Ellen and Daniel, but there was no evidence of any impropriety.

He took a deep breath and turned to me, his dark eyes shining. 'You probably want to ask the question everyone asked: did I have feelings for her?' He shrugged. 'Truth is, I don't know. I was young and single. Ellen was attractive and interesting. But she was my patient, and I wouldn't have dreamt of acting on any feelings. I hadn't lost a patient before, far less had one die in my arms on a day when she should have gone home. I doubted myself and whether my treatment of her had been wrong. Was she still unwell? Had she done it deliberately?' He shook his head. 'I know now she was ready to go home, and if Ogilvie hadn't been chasing her, she wouldn't have died. But did I have romantic feelings for her? I really don't know.'

'Was there no one else?'

Daniel laughed and said there had been a few too many over the years. He put his hand on my arm. 'I'm sorry, Kate. I wish so much I could have made it all work out.'

I shrugged. 'You did everything you could, and more than any of the other doctors.'

'I should have tried to find you, given you the journal sooner. It wasn't mine to keep. I'm sorry. I think I just wanted to keep a link to Ellen.'

I smiled. 'You can, if you'd like to stay in touch.'

He nodded. 'I'd like that very much.'

'Will you be up in Inverness this year?'

'Yes. In August. I'm glad I'm coming for a holiday and not a trial. It was such a relief when he pleaded guilty, though I wish they hadn't acquitted him of what he did to you.'

I shrugged. 'He was off his head, and I was relieved it didn't go to trial, after the Martina fiasco. She pleaded not guilty right up to the morning of the trial. When she heard Ogilvie was in the cells, apparently doing well on treatment and ready to give evidence against her, she changed her plea. I was dreading seeing him. Anyway, she applied to go back to Poland to serve her sentence. Her mother and son had already left.' I looked out to sea. The surfers were gone. 'I wonder if there'll be any charges from the investigation into Mum's death.'

Daniel shrugged. 'Hard to see how they could prove anything if Ogilvie's not for admitting it.'

'See when you come to Inverness,' I said, 'you don't want to be staying in those woods. I have plenty room for a visitor.'

He smiled. 'It's still a special place for me. I'll probably camp for a few nights, but I'd like to come and stay with you too. Where did you move to?'

'A converted church near Beauly. I'm renting out the flat. Ted Sullivan's managing it for me, God help the poor tenants. We'd love to have you. And Liz Barclay wants to meet you again.'

From behind, I heard the crunch of stones, then I felt arms encircle my shoulders and hold me tight.

After Paul Gibson, I had suspected love was just imagination, a stupid lie we bought into for fear of being alone. Real or not, I was certain it would never be mine. It was different for Stefan. He'd always known love was no lie. He just hadn't believed he deserved to find it and keep it for a second time. With Martyna on remand, we'd stayed good friends. We'd laughed and gone for drinks after work, just as we'd always done, but something had changed. He didn't speak about what had happened, and he never came round to the flat. I wondered if he couldn't face it. Wasn't that easy for me, but I wasn't going to let Ogilvie or Martyna force me out of my home. Luckily, Ogilvie hadn't bled much. Only ruined a couple of good towels. Not a speck of his blood on my purple velvet sofa, which was repaired by a local upholsterer so that even Martyna's attack scarcely left a physical mark.

Susan had stayed with me for two weeks until I was ready to stay alone again. And then life moved on. By the time I returned to work, Lucille was gone, moved to a specialist facility in Glasgow. There was no investigation. Her husband told Mrs Shelby she'd accused every carer she'd ever had of abuse. Mrs Shelby, bless her, contacted Mick later to tell him of Lucille's link to my mother, just in case he had any lingering doubts. I couldn't stop thinking of Lucille and how desperately her life had been affected by her mental health, even after discharge from The Craig. I wondered if it would have been the same for my mother. Though I wanted to believe she'd have lived a healthy, happy life if not for Ogilvie's actions, I really couldn't be sure.

I went back to the gym, and I put my university application in. I had a couple of weekends away with the girls. We went up to Caithness to see Lisa. She came with us to Orkney, where we ate and drank too much, visited every archaeological site we could find, spent a fortune on jewellery, and swam in the freezing sea.

And then, one day, Stefan came to work and told me he was going back to Poland. Nothing was right here, he said, and he would never forgive himself for putting me in danger. But he'd saved my life, I told him. In fact, if it wasn't for his neighbour, Victor, deciding to tell Stefan what was going on, after he'd drank Ogilvie's money, I probably wouldn't be here now. I should thank Victor too. Stefan had rolled his eyes. 'Hah. Victor never did do a good thing in his life. He try to get me to pay him money before he tells me what Martyna and Ogilvie are up to, so I squeeze the truth out of him.' He patted my arm. 'I go tell Mrs Shelby my news.'

I liked to believe that my mum and my grandparents were close by. It comforted me, but I had no illusions about ghosts and signs and voices from beyond the grave. And yet, as I watched Stefan walk away, I could almost feel all three of them shoving me from behind, and Gran muttering in my ear, urging me to get my finger out and tell him.

So I did.

'About time,' Mrs Shelby said when she found us kissing in the corridor. 'But don't make a habit of it in the workplace.'

Now, as the sun shone overhead and the seagulls screeched, I leaned back against Stefan. 'You okay?' he asked. 'You have enough time together? I can go away. I find great record shops.'

I turned. He was wearing dark glasses and smiling. At the sight of him, my stomach flipped, as always.

'It's fine. We've had a good chat. We were thinking of having a walk before dinner.'

He kissed the top of my head. 'Come on. I want to see this house of your grandfather.'

We walked along the promenade without speaking, past the arches and the galleries, the playground and an open-air art exhibition. I thought of Granda. He had been such a still, strong presence in my life, even if only for a short time. I imagined him down here as a boy, him and his brother. I thought of my holiday here with Gran and how we'd laughed. And then I thought of Mum.

Close to the burned-out West Pier, I stopped and turned to Daniel. Though I knew the answer, I had to ask. 'What were her last words?'

He looked out to sea, tears glistening in his eyes, and his words were just a whisper.

My darling Kate, you'll see me in the stars. Always.

Note from the Author

THE FORMER CRAIG Dunain Hospital is still a daunting and commanding presence, situated on an exposed hill on the outskirts of Inverness. Known as the Northern Counties District Lunatic Asylum when it opened in 1864, the hospital took patients from throughout the Highlands and Islands area. The hospital closed in 2000.

An arson attack in 2007 destroyed some of the central buildings, but damage was limited because of the thick stone barrier walls installed during the original construction. At the time of publishing, many of the luxury apartments and townhouses of Great Glen Hall are occupied, but work is ongoing. Despite the construction of a growing number of houses around the former hospital, Dunain Woods, the cemetery and the duck pond are still there.

I had some childhood experience of going 'up the hill' on a Sunday afternoon to visit an elderly relative and long term resident of The Craig. He seemed happy and settled, but there were some poor souls there, and the experience was never without a little excitement.

The early hospital records, which are fascinating and shocking in equal measure, can be viewed at the Highland Archive Centre in Inverness. It was there, on a work trip in 2019, that I felt a story coming on.

If you enjoyed *Unravelling*, you'll enjoy *In the Shadow of the Hill* and *Madness Lies*.

Check out my website at www.helenforbes.co.uk and sign up to my mailing list for news, views and more. Be among the first to hear when my next novel is due out.

And please do leave a review. They are a great help to me and other readers.

Acknowledgements

THANK YOU, AS always, to my readers. Without your support and encouragement, none of this would be possible. Special thanks to my exceptional beta readers, Ishbel, Anne and Connie. Grateful thanks to Clare for her memories of working in The Craig in the late 1980s, and to all who had a story to tell about the hospital.

A huge thank you to my editor, Lynn Curtis, for her wonderful editing skills and helpful suggestions. Many thanks to Ken Dawson at Creative Covers and Kate Coe at Book Polishers for the excellent design and typesetting work, and for their friendly, helpful service.

And to my family and friends, thank you for always believing.

About the Author

HELEN FORBES IS a lawyer and author of the DS Joe Galbraith novels, *In the Shadow of the Hill* and *Madness Lies*. She was born and brought up in the Highlands of Scotland, and lives in Inverness.